D1059275

Titles by Jory Strong

GHOSTLAND
SPIDER-TOUCHED
HEALER'S CHOICE
INKED MAGIC

Anthologies

PRIMAL
(with Lora Leigh, Michelle Rowen, and Ava Gray)

Inked Magic

JORY STRONG

HEAT | NEW YORK

THE BERKLEY PUBLISHING GROUP
Published by the Penguin Group
Penguin Group (USA) Inc.
375 Hudson Street, New York, New York 10014, USA
Penguin Group (Canada), 90 Eglinton Avenue East, Suite 700, Toronto, Ontario M4P 2Y3, Canada
(a division of Pearson Penguin Canada Inc.)
Penguin Books Ltd., 80 Strand, London WC2R 0RL, England
Penguin Group Ireland, 25 St. Stephen's Green, Dublin 2, Ireland (a division of Penguin Books Ltd.)
Penguin Group (Australia), 250 Camberwell Road, Camberwell, Victoria 3124, Australia
(a division of Pearson Australia Group Pty. Ltd.)
Penguin Books India Pvt. Ltd., 11 Community Centre, Panchsheel Park, New Delhi—110 017, India
Penguin Group (NZ), 67 Apollo Drive, Rosedale, Auckland 0632, New Zealand
(a division of Pearson New Zealand Ltd.)
Penguin Books (South Africa) (Pty.) Ltd., 24 Sturdee Avenue, Rosebank, Johannesburg 2196,
South Africa

Penguin Books Ltd., Registered Offices: 80 Strand, London WC2R 0RL, England

This book is an original publication of The Berkley Publishing Group.

PUBLISHING HISTORY
Heat trade paperback edition / February 2012

Library of Congress Cataloging-in-Publication Data

Strong, Jory.
    Inked magic / Jory Strong.—Heat trade pbk. ed.
       p.   cm.
    ISBN 978-0-425-24537-8 (pbk.)
    1. Women tattoo artists—Fiction. 2. Changelings—Fiction. 3. Elves—Fiction. 4. Rape—
Investigation—Fiction. I. Title.
    PS3619.T777I55 2012
    813'.6—dc23
                2011019141

PRINTED IN THE UNITED STATES OF AMERICA

10 9 8 7 6 5 4 3 2 1

ALWAYS LEARNING   PEARSON

ACKNOWLEDGMENTS

Thanks to my parents.

A thousand acknowledgments wouldn't be enough to adequately express how much your support means to me.

One

Fog turned the cemetery into shades of black and gray. It lay on those gathered around the grave, a wet, heavy shroud muting the sounds of grieving as the priest spoke his final words and mourners moved toward the immediate family.

Cathal didn't cross to offer his condolences, though his mother did, resplendent in designer black and tasteful jewelry. He remained in place even as his father and uncle departed without a word.

They glided through the fog like a pair of ravens, black coats shiny with moisture. *Harbingers of death*, he thought, knowing that scattered among the mourners were police as well as FBI and ATF agents.

He lingered, trying to recall the dead girl's face, to dredge up personal memories of Caitlyn, something beyond the smiling photographs present in the funeral home. He failed. All that came to him were thoughts of his cousin, Brianna, and with it, guilt over how seldom their lives intersected.

In the span of a year Brianna had lost her mother and brother. And now this.

Drugs and gang rape and the death of a friend.

Insanity and murder, if not by intention, then by end result.

He should have made more time for her. He should have . . .

With an acknowledgment of failure, he left the gravesite, returning to the long line of automobiles parked against the curb, transport back to everyday life.

Two heavily muscled men emerged from the gloom as his father and uncle neared identical dark-windowed Mercedes. The men opened back doors, then stood, waiting at attention like the soldiers they were.

Words passed between the brothers. Icy intensity rather than heated argument, accompanied by a glance in his direction before his uncle climbed into a car and was driven away.

A sense of foreboding settled around him but he didn't slow his footsteps or refuse when his father indicated with a wave that he was to get into the back of the remaining Mercedes. He surrendered his cell phone, a precaution against being listened in on by the authorities, then got into the car.

The doors closed, walling off sound and the possibility of being overheard. His father's eyes locked on to his. "The animals responsible for this can't go unpunished."

Despite knowing his father's idea of justice involved a shot to the back of the head and an unmarked grave, he said, "I agree."

"Good."

The tension left his father. "Good," he repeated. "A source passed on a name at the funeral. There's an artist who can help us identify the guilty parties. But there's a complication."

The sense of foreboding deepened. "What complication?"

"She might be related to a cop. The guy who passed on the name didn't know whether it was true or not. All he could say for sure was that she's got a freaky way with victims."

"So call in a favor. Have a case file opened. There's enough about what happened to Brianna and Caitlyn to force an investigation. Let the police make arrangements with the artist. Let them handle it officially and prosecute the guilty parties."

His father tilted his head toward the empty parking place in front of the Mercedes. "This is personal business. Something your uncle and I need to take care of ourselves. The sooner the better. If you were around more—and I'm not saying you should be, I understand your reasons and I respect your decision—then you'd know Denis isn't thinking straight. First losing Margo, then Brian. Now this.

"He's hurting. And a man in that much pain is capable of striking out, damn the consequences. That's why I'm asking you to run interference here, to minimize the collateral damage by approaching this woman. Pull the right strings to get her to visit Brianna and come up with pictures of the responsible parties.

"Maybe it'll be simple. Cash for services rendered. Maybe she wants to be a rock star and you can make it happen for her. Maybe she's lonely and you can convince her between the sheets. Show her a little love so she'll *want* to help out here and be willing to keep quiet about it afterward. If you set your mind to it, you can get it done."

"And if I don't? If I can't?"

His father shrugged. "Then my conscience is clear. I've tried to do the right thing, walk the line as much as I can given the situation. But I'm not going to stand between Denis and the animals responsible for drugging and raping his baby girl. I'm not going to turn my back on family. Justice will be served on behalf of those two girls, regardless of whether you involve yourself in this matter or not."

Cathal curled his hand into a fist and fought the urge to answer the verbal jab. He looked beyond his father, at the mourners moving through the fog, leaving Caitlyn to be lowered into her grave.

After a lifetime of keeping his distance, of staying clear of his father and uncle's business, he wondered if he was about to take the first step on a slippery slope that ended in prison or violent death for most of those who took it.

"How much time do I have to convince her?"

"As much as you need as long as you're working it steady. I got Denis to agree to that much. To hold off acting. Brianna . . . Well, you've seen her. She's not going to get any worse in the time it'll take you to come back with an answer."

His last visit to Brianna played out in his mind, bringing rage and despair at how a vibrant, talented girl now had to be kept heavily sedated and constantly watched. "What's the woman's name?"

"Etaín."

"Irish?"

His father shrugged again. "Don't know. All I have is the first name and where she can be found. She's a tattoo artist. Works at a place called Stylin' Ink."

"In San Francisco?"

"Yeah, in the city."

Guilt. Regret. Misgiving. They clawed at him, tearing him up inside and creeping into his guts.

His choice to open a club where people with money traded on their looks and names as they played hard and fast, his involvement with musicians, all of it was an ongoing test of himself—that he could be around vice without becoming what his father and uncle were: criminals.

He saw his mother approaching and knew he had less than a minute before it would be out of his hands. His father glanced over his shoulder and saw the same thing. "You'll do this for the family?"

The question hung between them, tense with time running out. Heavy with choice and consequence. Innocence and guilt, and the ominous weight of lives already shattered and those that might end the same way.

"I'll do it," Cathal said as his mother reached the car. "For Brianna and for Caitlyn." And so he could live with his own conscience when it came to them, and to the artist Etaín.

D esire hummed through Etaín, piercing the layer of purple latex separating her skin from Salina's as if the barrier was nonexistent. It coursed through her, stirring an echoing need, though for a man instead of a woman.

It'd been too long since she'd had sex.

She paused to wipe the excess ink off Salina's back, and to give the hand stretching the skin a break. "You're thinking about doing the nasty."

"And you can tell how? I'm not even looking at you."

"You don't need to be."

She didn't need the visible signs. Salina's emotions spiked through the gloves like a needle plunging in and hitting a vein, dumping something foreign into her bloodstream.

Skin didn't lie, not to her. It was her gift, sometimes her curse, to feel what others felt when she touched them, especially when she worked, and afterward, to catch glimpses of their memories.

Tattooing forged a bond, and to give it up would be to give up living. She'd been doing it since she was thirteen, her first tattoos the stylized eyes on her own palms. They'd haunted her dreams and turned into a compulsion she couldn't escape. It was the same with the elaborate, multicolored vines twisting around her forearms and growing upward from wristbands her mother had inked on her when she was eight.

"One night is all I'm asking for," Salina said. "Come to the club. Hear Lady Steel play and party with us afterward. I'll show you a good time. And it's not like I'm asking you to give up cocks."

Jamaal snorted without looking up from the row of butterflies he was outlining at the base of his client's spine. "Dildos aren't as good as the real thing."

"And you've had both so you know for sure?" Etaín asked.

"I don't swing that way, baby, you know that. Spend a night in my bed and I'll show you what I can do." White teeth flashed against mocha-toned skin. "But I'm warning you, once you've had black, you ain't never going back to those pretty white boys you go around with."

"Yeah, and if I take you up on your offer, I'll be looking over my shoulder for DaWanda."

"There's enough of me to go around, baby. Besides, DaWanda's a church-going woman. She's all about forgiving my sins."

"More like she's desperate," Salina said.

"That was low, and you wearing a shitload of my work. I broke a sweat on your tits and it wasn't because there were mountains to climb and nice big peaks to camp out on and explore."

Etaín laughed, familiar with the scene on Salina's chest. "If you were sweating, it was because you were picturing an X-rated unicorn-and-virgin scenario."

"Probably comparing his cock to the unicorn's horn and seeing he comes up short," Salina said.

"Freud would back you on that."

"You two are some mean bitches, doing me like this. Don't think I'll forget it the next time you come around asking me to put some ink on you."

"As long as you remember payback's hell," Etaín said. "It's going to take another session to finish the work on your upper thigh. One little slip . . ."

"I ain't no fool, soon as I get home I'm going online, see if I can find myself an iron-plated jock. Extra, extra, extra large, so I can keep all my essential equipment safe."

Salina made a choking sound. "Hello. Delusional."

Etaín dipped the needles of the shader into a cap of gray ink. "What do you expect? When's the last time you saw a pack of condoms labeled small?"

Salina snickered. "Or extra small."

"Makes a dildo start looking good in comparison."

"Damn straight."

Etaín paused to study the big-breasted mermaid she was working on before placing her hand on Salina's skin to stretch it. Desire slid into her bloodstream again, a warm pulsing that didn't bother her even if she didn't reciprocate it.

The shop went quiet except for the hum of tattoo machines and the sound of U2. She was putting the final touches on the mermaid's tail when the door jerked open and Derrick stalked in wearing a skintight fuck-me dress and high-heels.

"Don't let me keep you from your business," he said, sniffing for effect. "Life goes on."

The outfit and thick mascara were enough to clue Etaín in, but when he headed directly to the player and changed the tunes to John Mayer she knew he'd been fighting with his boyfriend again.

Jamaal's machine crashed down on his work stand. "No fucking way! I can't work to that. Not today. Not tomorrow. Not ever again after last week."

Two-hundred and fifty plus pounds of muscle headed toward the player with all the determination of an NFL linebacker. Derrick stood taller, thrusting his chin out. "Go ahead. Strike out at me because I'm in touch with my feelings. Everyone else does."

"Knock that shit off, you two," Bryce said, coming around the privacy screen and halting at the sight of Derrick. His eyes widened and his hands went to his hips. "Nice of you to finally show up for work. Now go home and change clothes. Either that or call and re-schedule Orlando."

"Since when do we have a dress code?"

"Since I got finished getting things set up for *your* client, then came out and saw you."

"That's not fair."

"Then sue me. After you get out of drag and stop channeling your inner diva."

Derrick huffed. "Well if that's the way you feel—"

"I do. I'm not having my shop trashed by Orlando when he walks in to get his ass worked on and sees you waiting for him like that."

"You're overreacting."

"I'm the boss. It's my privilege."

"I'll change, but it's under protest."

"That works for me."

"Fine. I'm leaving."

Derrick flounced his way around the counter separating the workstations from the waiting area. He stopped at the door and added, "If I don't make it back in time, you spread Orlando's ass."

"Save the drama queen routine for after hours. You want to act? Dress up like a man and come back pretending you're hetero, at least long enough to finish the work on Orlando."

A violent slam of the door was Derrick's response. Bryce laughed.

"Not very PC," Etaín said.

"I don't give a shit about political correctness." He hit a button on the player, silencing John Mayer and filling the air with Nickelback.

Bryce paused long enough to check the appointment screen on the computer, then cleaned the waiting area and organized the reference materials. By the time he was done, she was putting antibiotic ointment on the areas of the tattoo she'd worked.

He strolled over and stopped next to her. "Nice. What have you got, two, three more sessions to finish it?"

"Four," Salina said. "Maybe five. I don't like being on the receiving end of pain."

"Make sure Etaín takes a picture of this one when she gets finished with it. I definitely want it on the website. Good advertising."

"Putting a picture of Etaín up would be better."

"She's threatened to quit if I do."

"Seriously?"

"Seriously," Etaín said. "And I am standing right here, you two."

Bryce opened one of the packages of nonstick pads on her worktable, exposing the adhesive tabs and handing it to her. She applied it to Salina's back.

"So you think you could fix Derrick up with someone?" Bryce asked.

Jamaal snorted. "Fat fucking chance of that. She can't find someone for her own self. You ever see her out with the same guy twice?"

The quiet businesswoman he was tattooing spoke up, "You ever try to find a good-looking man in San Francisco? One who's not gay, already taken, or a total jerk?"

"Present company excluded?" Bryce asked.

The woman's expression took on the look of a deer in the headlights. "Sure," she said, dropping her head so it rested in the face cradle attached to the massage table.

Etaín hid a smile. Only a serious tattoo aficionado would look at Bryce and think he was gorgeous. His body was a heroin-chic canvas with very few places in need of ink, and plenty that had been pierced.

The ink and metal put a lot of women off. Their loss as far as she was concerned. Both told a story of struggle, survival, and ultimate victory over the demons plaguing him.

He'd been heavy into drugs, dangerous sex, and the fringe lifestyle that went with both, but he'd found his way out of it through his art. The same way she'd avoided going crazy and ending up dead from an overdose or from hooking up with the wrong kind of guy.

Bryce opened a second package and passed it to Etaín. "You know people. What Derrick needs is a take-no-bullshit type, somebody who's going to keep him in line."

"Like maybe someone into whips and chains," Jamaal said.

"A collar and leash work better," Salina volunteered.

Jamaal snorted. "Not touching that one."

Bryce handed a third nonstick pad to Etaín. "What about a cop? You know any gay cops on the prowl for a significant other?"

Etaín met his gaze and raised her eyebrows. "You want me to start hitting up the cops who come around the homeless shelter when I'm there?"

"Sounds like a plan to me."

She shook her head and went back to concentrating on covering the areas of Salina's back that needed it. "Derrick may not be ready to call it quits with the current boyfriend. You know how he is."

Bryce sighed. "Yeah, I know. Too damn sensitive and accommodating for his own good. But think about finding a nice stable guy we can set him up with, okay? His reliability goes to shit when his relationships tank."

"I'll think about it."

He handed her one last pad. "Appreciate it. You heading out? Or hanging to do some art work?"

"I'm gone for a while. I promised Justine I'd swing by the shelter sometime today to go over the final schedule for the fund-raiser. We're in countdown mode now."

"Yeah, thing is coming fast. How many artists you get signed up?"

"Twelve, with another five saying they'll come in if things get crazy. I've already done a bunch of stencils to speed things up. Almost everyone else is bringing some of their own flash, too. Stuff that won't take more than thirty minutes to tattoo."

"I've got a couple of design ideas I'm going to work up and bring with me. I don't want this to get into a pissing contest, so anyone, regardless of whose shop they're from, is free to use them."

"Thanks."

"Plenty of regulars have told me they plan on showing up on Saturday. I'm guessing it's going to be busy. Should be a nice chunk of change for the shelter. "

"It's all good."

Bryce reached out and grabbed the thick wheat-gold braid snaking down her back. "Yeah. It's all good. You and me, we've both done our time on the streets and in shelters."

Etaín shivered, thinking about the wild stretch of her teen years, and her father's way of scaring her straight. It made dying in an alleyway seem good in comparison, though she had to give it to the captain, his method had worked, just not for the reason he thought it had.

"Briefly in my case," she said, shaking off the memory, though the shadow-pain of it lingered from the continued estrangement with the policeman she'd once called Dad.

"That's the best way. Enough to know what it's like and never forget it."

Bryce gave a little tug to her braid. "You've got one more appointment today, a late one. Promise you'll call the shop so one of us can step outside and make sure you get in okay."

"Will do." She didn't need to ask why. A serial rapist had been terrorizing San Francisco and the cities near it for months.

Bryce wandered off as she covered the last part of the mermaid's tail and gave Salina her aftercare instruction, both verbally and in writing. It didn't matter Salina had been through it before, many times. She'd rather err on the side of caution, not just for Salina's benefit, but for her own.

She took pride in the tattoos she created. Each piece reflected on her as an artist.

Fresh tattoos were wounds. They were thousands of punctures to the skin, damage that the body healed, trapping the embedded pigment beneath a see-through layer of thin scar tissue.

Etaín pressed her fingers gently along the edges of the bandages, assuring herself for a final time that they were secure before easing Salina's shirt down.

"Tease," Salina said. "So are you going to come hear Lady Steel play? I'll even promise not to hit on you. Well, not too hard anyway. I can't promise—" Her breath caught. "Shit. Shit. Shit. I can't believe it. That's Cathal Dunne outside the shop. If he comes in, connect with him, Etaín, and I'll owe you for like forever. You don't know how bad we want to land a gig in his club. All he has to do is pick up the phone and the door to fame opens."

Etaín turned to look and felt her own breath catch, but for a totally different reason. Black Irish. Even without hearing his name she would have guessed at his roots. He had the look. Fallen angel and hardened warrior. Piercing blue eyes and a jaw shadowed with stubble.

He wore expensive clothes and carried the kind of confidence that radiated danger. A bad boy dressed in fine threads but unable to hide the truth about himself beneath them.

Heat surged through her just looking at him, settling in her breasts and belly and cunt. It'd been far too long since she'd felt a man's hands and lips on her, a cock deep inside, sliding in and out and delivering pleasure.

She'd applied too much ink, been buffeted by too many emotions not originating with her. Her gift. Her curse. She didn't understand all of it. Only knew how to manage it in a half-assed way that kept her sane and feeling good about herself.

Sex did the trick. Like a pressure valve opening, preventing an explosion and meltdown by giving her body a way to deal with what came with touching people.

Her gaze met his through the shop window and she felt desire whip between them, a visceral command demanding they remove any barrier so they could get up close and very, very personal. She caught herself unconsciously licking her lips, the act so unlike her she nearly turned away from him to resume cleaning the workstation.

A deep, almost foreign hunger gathered inside her even as instinct warned her away from him. He was trouble and she could manage to find enough of that on her own.

Her eyes continued to linger on him, a part of her willing him to come inside. Another part already alarmed at her reaction to him, at the snare of an attraction hard and fast enough to keep her held in place.

Two

Cathal's gut told him he was looking at Etaín and his dick told him he wanted her like he hadn't wanted a woman in a long, long time, maybe ever. He should have swung by Sean McAlister's boat and set the cop-turned-private investigator on to finding the leverage necessary to gain Etaín's cooperation. Because despite his father saying this could be simple, he didn't think it was going to be, though taking her to bed as a way of persuading her had moved to the top of his list. Having her beneath him, his cock buried to the hilt in wet heat, would drown out the voice of conscience. He'd worry about the consequences later.

He opened the door and walked into the shop. There was no point in bullshitting about getting a tattoo. He didn't want one. Never had, never would.

He wondered if she was heavily tattooed beneath the long-sleeved shirt and the jeans that hugged her ass and legs, and whether it would matter when he stripped her out of them, if seeing ink-decorated skin would make him lose interest. By the time he got to the counter he knew the answer was no.

Up close, the full impact sent a lightning bolt straight through his chest and down to his dick. Dark, dark eyes reminded him of a wild, untamed forest and made his heart race in a primal beat having everything to do with conquest and nothing to do with fear.

"Can I help you?"

"I'm Cathal Dunne."

He offered his hand, wanting the touch as much as he needed to get her someplace where he could begin his campaign.

There was a slight hesitation before she reached across the counter, confirming something for him with the first sight of ink. The stylized eye on her palm didn't turn him off. It sent a wave of heat along the surface of his skin as he imagined her hand touching his chest, sliding downward over his belly as if she could see what he needed, what he wanted, and intended to give it to him.

"Etaín," she said and he noted the lack of a last name.

He captured her hand instead of shaking and releasing it. She didn't pull away, didn't try to hide her reaction to the chemistry between them. It was there in her expression, in eyes that seemed even darker than they had moments earlier. In wetted lips parted just enough to invite a kiss and fuel more carnal fantasies.

He fought against inhaling deeply. She smelled good. Like some kind of exotic flower that could only be found by hunting for it.

The feel of her hand in his had him aching to shove it beneath his waistband and press it to his cock. His skin was coated in a light sheen of sweat, as if there'd already been an hour of foreplay.

The desire to skip the preliminaries and get right to the business of fucking nearly overwhelmed him. His body hummed and he could feel a tremor passing from her palm to his, a current of lust looping through both of them.

Etaín suppressed a hard shiver of need. She'd been thinking about sex and here was the offer of it, standing inches away, exuding it.

Lust poured into her, golden fire and the promise of pleasure beyond any she could find elsewhere. His desire pierced the barrier of her skin and scorched through her in a way Salina's hadn't and never would. It merged with her need, like a volatile Molotov cocktail capable of turning resistance and control into rubble, making it a casualty of passion.

She doubted even leather gloves could protect her from his emotions, not this close. Not when the very air seemed to vibrate with possibilities.

Strangers and clients of both sexes hit on her. She was used to it. As if somehow the dreams and the call to ink came with a release of pheromones. But he wasn't like the men she usually slept with, pretty boys who played in bands, long-haired rockers who were wild and free, fun to be with but who didn't make any claims on her after a night of rowdy sex.

It had to be that way. Too much time, too much intensity, too much touch, and her gift changed them, harmed them irrevocably. Stole pieces away from them that couldn't always be replaced.

Her instincts told her to say no to Cathal's invitation. Her body vetoed it with a hard clenching of her channel and the escape of arousal.

His nostrils flared, like a male animal scenting a female in heat, as if on some level he sensed her need for sex. "Do you have a particular piece of art in mind?"

He laughed, a sound guaranteed to turn heads, male and female alike. "No, I'm not interested in getting a tattoo. I came in to meet you and ask you out to dinner."

Behind her Jamaal whistled and said, "A fast mover. I like this man's style, Etaín."

She liked more than that. Even hidden beneath clothing, she could see the perfection of Cathal's unmarked skin in her mind's eye, a canvas wide open for exploration.

Designs formed without her consciously searching for them, the same way those on her own skin had come to her. The same way those she tattooed outside of work did. They had power. That she believed completely.

"Have dinner with me," he said again. "We can go somewhere close, in walking distance. How about Aesirs?"

Jamaal chose that moment to deliver payback. "Go! You need to get laid."

Emboldened, Salina said, "Yeah, go. I'll leave the money for today's session with Bryce."

Cathal smiled, fallen angel looks delivering sinful temptation. "The vote seems to be in my favor."

Bryce added his then, coming around the privacy screen to say, "Go. I'll take care of your machine and finish cleaning up your station. And while you're at Aesirs, scope out the waiters for Derrick. That place is supposed to be loaded with guys hot enough to persuade a straight man to switch teams."

Etaín pulled her hand from Cathal's. The swirling images overlaid along the inside length of his forearms by her imagination disappeared but the loss of contact didn't diminish the heat inside her. If anything, it intensified the craving for the touch of skin to skin.

"I can go now," she said, curious about Aesirs. It was an exclusive restaurant with bouncers to make sure only those expected entered.

Had Cathal suggested it to impress her? Or because going there seemed natural to him and getting seated wasn't a problem, whether he had reservations or not?

She snagged her Harley jacket and came around the counter. His gaze traveled the length of her body, a glance that said he liked what he saw and wanted to see more, a look that stroked her feminine pride without making her feel like a piece of meat.

Derrick, dressed in jeans and tank top, opened the door as they reached it. His eyes went wide and his hand fluttered to his chest.

"Oh delicious, Etaín," he said, still in touch with his inner woman despite the change of clothes and arms fully sleeved in tattoos. "You go, girl."

She cut a glance at Cathal. He seemed totally unfazed, amused if anything. It won him points with her. Huge points. Derrick was one of her closest friends.

They passed through the doorway and out into muted sunshine. She breathed deeply, wanting to draw it inside her the same way she did moonlight at night.

When she was working, as long as there were windows, she could tune out the craving to stand beneath open skies. But the minute she stepped outside it came back with a vengeance, filling her with the need to bury her toes in ocean-wet sand as the surf licked her ankles, to scoop up rich loam in her hands and run barefoot through a dark primordial forest, stopping only to dance around a fire deep in the woods.

She shook her head slightly, clearing her mind of sensations that were familiar yet completely at odds with her reality, like forgotten childhood memories, or, more likely, pretend ones. She was a child of the city. The majority of her brushes with nature had occurred in Golden Gate Park, in museums and aquariums, with forays to the beach, especially in her teen years. Or boating in the bay and delta before her relationship with the captain disintegrated.

She glanced at Cathal. It was easier to think about him than about her family. "Salina recognized you. She said you own a club."

"Saoirse."

She smiled at the utter confidence in his voice. The tone saying, "I'm sure you've heard of it," even if he didn't say the words.

Saoirse. She knew it. A place to see and be seen.

"That explains why you're not worried about walking into Aesirs without dinner reservations."

The scent of his cologne wrapped her in heady lust. The heat between them combined with the sun's rays made her want to shed her clothes and stretch out naked alongside him.

Her fingers flexed, wanting to touch, to explore. A small smile played over her lips as she contemplated which she'd regret more— acting on the desire she felt for Cathal, or fighting it.

He turned his head slightly, enough so their eyes met. "Do I dare ask what you're thinking?"

She laughed. "I imagine there's not much you don't dare."

His smile served as an answer. They drew close enough to Aesirs for the bouncers to move, not to intercept but in preparation for opening the heavy wooden doors.

"I take it you come here often."

"Often enough. I meet my father and uncle here when they want a meal away from home."

She started to ask a follow-up question about them, but the chime of a hundred tiny bells assaulted her, ringing in her ears. "Do you hear that?"

He cocked his head, eyebrows lifting in question. "Hear what?"

She laughed at herself. "Never mind. Overactive imagination. It comes with being an artist."

Yet a few steps later she knew it hadn't been. Her breath caught at seeing the symbols carved into the wooden doors, images that spoke to a core, subconscious part of her, some of the sigils recognizable from her dreams though she had no frame of reference to give them meaning beyond what she herself had assigned them.

Her heart raced, not in anticipation but with deep-seated wariness. The urge to turn back, to suggest they go somewhere else for dinner was strong.

She fought it, refusing to flee from the unknown. She stifled misgivings with curiosity. The symbols carved into the wood held the subtle promise of revealing more about the gifts that defined who she was and how she lived her life.

The doors opened. As they passed through the entranceway, stepping into hushed luxury, the hair on the back of her neck rose. The scent of fire and water filled her nostrils even as it felt as though cold blue flames licked along the intricate vines tattooed on her forearms.

Both smell and fiery sensation lasted only an instant, then were gone. A maître d' stepped forward, staring at her until seeming to suddenly recall his duties. "The usual requirements?" he asked Cathal.

"Yes."

The maître d' turned, leading them deeper into the restaurant. He was tall, hair flowing in a solid black wave and stopping halfway down his back.

Bryce's entreaty to scope out the men for Derrick's sake grounded

Etaín to the world she lived in as opposed to this one. It gave her a place to retreat to until she had time to think about the bells, the symbols, and the weirdness as she'd entered Aesirs.

She looked at the waiters. Not an ugly one among them though their physiques varied. Something for everyone, depending on taste, they glided through the restaurant, living confection that made her mouth water as surely as chocolate did.

"I'm starting to think I made a mistake suggesting we eat here," Cathal murmured.

"Feeling threatened?"

His hand settled lightly on her back, bringing carnal heat and a tightening of her nipples. A stroke to her spine turned her focus solidly back to him.

"Should I be?" he asked, confidence shading nearly into arrogance. A subtext that said, *They can't give you the things I can. They can't do what I can do for you.*

Etaín laughed, making a sweeping glance around the restaurant, eyes lingering on a few of the waiters before giving him an answer. "Probably not," she said, ceding that much to Cathal.

They moved beneath an archway, their destination becoming clear then. Glassed doors, manned like the front ones by men in suits, led to an enclosed terrace. Another layer of privacy.

As she passed through the doorway, bells tinkled again. Not as loudly as when she'd entered the restaurant. This time they blended with the sound of surf, and along her forearms it felt as though the vines were streams, flooded and rushing after a hard rain.

The sound and sensation passed within steps. A low bridge crossed a shallow waterway where koi swam in an endless circle around the dining area.

It was shades of an elaborate Japanese garden, with a decorative brazier at the center of it burning incense as if in offering to an ancestral deity. Elegant. Beautiful. But those descriptions were not what lodged in her mind as she took in the scene.

The water. The sky above and plants in their bed of dirt. The glowing red charcoal and sinuous, thin-smoke scent of rising incense. *Containment*. The word settled inside of her with absolute certainty and brought the same deep-seated wariness that approaching Aesirs had.

She refused to let it take hold and control her. There were far more terrifying things than the unknown. Things she feared. Things she'd seen and experienced.

The tables were small and placed in cozy, private settings, each of them semisurrounded by an arrangement of living plants. All of them occupied except for one.

The maître d' led them to it, pulling out Etaín's chair for her as though she were dressed in fur and jewels instead of jeans and a faded shirt. She draped her jacket over her lap rather than surrender it.

Somewhere along the way they'd picked up a waiter and server, or perhaps both had followed unobtrusively from the start since the maître d' carried no menus. The server balanced a tray on one hand, placed the two glasses of water on the table before departing.

The waiter stepped into the place the server had vacated. He had the same look as the others she'd seen, except up close he seemed so much older. Not in face or form, but in the weight of his gaze as he offered her a menu, the sigils on the red-sun earring he wore adding to her curiosity.

She reached out, but for all his seeming maturity, when her hand was a needle's width from his, he released the menu and it dropped to the table, striking the water glass with enough force to turn it over if Cathal hadn't prevented it.

"My apologies," the waiter said, taking a step backward and passing the remaining menu to Cathal before turning and leaving the terrace.

He didn't hurry and yet there was purpose in his stride. Fluid movement and controlled grace, more the walk of a man who owned the space around him than of one who merely worked in it.

Etaín opened the menu and noted the lack of prices. She laughed and said, "I guess if you have to ask what a selection costs, then they've let you in by mistake."

Cathal's smile sent a rush of heat through her. "Something like that. Order what you want. I'm good for it."

The purr in his voice was like the hot, wet lap of a tongue over sensitive flesh, a promise he was good for a lot of things. "I bet you are," she said, wondering again which she'd regret more, giving in to desire, or resisting it.

E amon stood in his office, captivated by the sight of the changeling visible through the glassed ceiling of the terraced dining area. Her aura was deep gold, more Elven than human though her ears were still rounded.

They'd be sensitive now, an erogenous zone he already longed to tease with lips and tongue and the stroke of his fingertips. She'd stepped through his wards and taken his breath away with the touch of magic to magic, and then he'd seen her.

Mine. It was a decision made in a heartbeat. She would be his wife-consort and magic-bound mate.

It was rare to come across a foundling—and she had to be that to be so openly in his territory, unannounced and without permission. It was rarer still to find a changeling possessed by magic that felt old, so very old. As if she'd been created in Elfhome, the world their ancestors had long ago been banished from.

Shifting his attention to her companion, Eamon frowned as he read the body language between the couple, the subtle signs of sexual interest and the intention to act on it. They hadn't been intimate, *yet*. He read that as well and knew he couldn't afford to wait, to approach her elsewhere.

Cathal's presence was an unwelcome complication. Involvement, especially with a family like the Dunnes, was something any super-natural would try to avoid.

It was hard enough to hide their existence without drawing the attention of law enforcement, and with it all the trappings of secretive agencies and their surveillance paraphernalia. The ability to use glamour to mask longevity had been stripped away by the coming of age of photography and the power of mass media.

The Elven had taken the custom of wearing their hair long as an added precaution to shield the distinctive tips of their ears. Even so, the danger of discovery mounted with technological advances. Cell phones with cameras, the Internet, they made all supernaturals prisoners to the desire to remain hidden from the humans who overpopulated and controlled this world.

There were Elven lords who thought nothing of moving their entire households to a separate holding every twenty years or so, arranging for a recorded death, and eventually cycling back to the first of their lodgings with a different identity, posing as a grandson or granddaughter. There were others who carved out homes in the wilderness. But even that no longer guaranteed privacy, not with satellites and drug runners, the war on terror, and civil strife that spilled over into jungles and villages, bringing United Nations attention because of genocide.

He had no desire to leave San Francisco. It was the jewel in the territory he'd claimed for himself.

Uncharacteristic impatience moved through him as he waited for his second to return and report on the woman below. Rhys opened the door and stepped into the office, joining him at the window. Eamon said, "She's beautiful enough to make a man lose his concentration and embarrass himself by becoming awkward around her. I wouldn't have expected it of you, though, not where a changeling is concerned."

"She's not just changeling and it wasn't her beauty I reacted to. She's *seidic.*"

Soul seer. And more.

The shock of it was like dropping into arctic waters, only to be immediately pulled from them and thrust into a roaring fire. "You're sure?"

"She wears the symbols on her palms."

Eamon saw the warring emotions on his second's face—fear that argued the foundling should be killed versus the knowledge of what making her part of their clan could mean for them, not the least of which was being able to use her gift, her sight and ink, to help their young survive the changeling years.

"I intend to make her my consort-wife. Were you able to gather any information about her?"

"No." A slow flush of embarrassment rose in Rhys's cheeks at having to admit his failure.

Another day Eamon would have lingered and enjoyed the opportunity to tease his second. "Never mind," he said, heading toward the door and by extension, the restaurant, where he rarely made an appearance among patrons who came to see and be seen. "I'll soon know everything there is to know about her. That is, I believe, the purpose of courtship, even among humans."

Three

Cathal wasn't used to silence from a woman he'd shown interest in. Not unless it came as a result of a thorough fucking or a pointed look demanding it.

By now most would have spilled their life stories, their hopes and dreams, plagued him with questions about the musicians he'd discovered and launched into stardom, or hinted at a desire for him to do the same for them, and if not that, for an introduction to the famous.

Etaín's quiet had a different quality to it, neither expectation nor hope, as if she'd already labeled him a potential one-night stand but hadn't yet decided whether or not to act on the attraction.

Did she guess it served as a challenge? He studied her face. Probably not. She seemed as willing to check out the waiters for her friend as to find out what he might have to offer her.

He covered her hand with his, the touch making him imagine shrugging off his shirt and pressing her palm to his chest. When the tip of her tongue darted out to wet her bottom lip, he wanted to suggest they forego dinner altogether.

She smiled as if guessing his thoughts. "If you weren't interested in a tattoo, what brought you to the shop?"

His gut told him that getting to know her well enough to tell her the real reason would take longer than it would be safe to wait. The flyer he'd seen taped to the front door of the shop provided the perfect excuse for introducing himself to her, and for a continued claim to her time.

"I was in the area and you're involved with the fund-raiser for the homeless shelter. I decided to stop in and volunteer to provide music, bands or a DJ, unless you've made other arrangements."

He stroked his thumb over hers and the sensual caress made her nipples tighten against the front of her shirt, spilling fantasies of having his mouth on them into his mind. "I had no idea there'd be a reward for doing a good deed, but meeting you qualifies as one."

"Smooth," she said, her smile making his cock press harder against the front of his pants. "You left it a little late. The fund-raiser is this Saturday."

He shrugged. "I just found out about it, but there's time enough to make arrangements and get the word out. Four full days is plenty, and I've got assistants I can assign to work on it."

"Justine makes the final decisions when it comes to the fund-raiser. I'll have to run it by her but I think she'll be thrilled by your offer."

"And you?"

"Definitely thrilled."

Her nearness, her scent, and the feel of her hand beneath his threatened to cloud his mind. He forced himself to remember a purpose beyond getting her into bed, the need to learn if she was related to a cop.

"Did you grow up in San Francisco?" he asked.

"For the most part."

Her vague answer frustrated him, and not solely on his uncle's account. "Parents? Brothers and sisters? Or are you an only child?"

"Sisters I've never been close to. A brother. I see him sometimes, when it suits him. Their mother isn't my mother. Father . . . If you meet yours here often enough to have a standing reservation, then you're ahead of me there."

She shrugged, turning the conversation by saying, "I'm going to swing by the shelter later this evening. I'll talk to Justine and put my vote in for live music. Any idea who you're volunteering for this?"

"Not yet. There are a number of bands waiting for a slot to open at the club. They'll leap at the chance to do this if I call."

"All on the hope you'll stop by or hear they're really good?"

"Yes."

She studied him for a long moment. "So what does it take for you to pick up the phone and open doors for a band?"

Disappointment stabbed him, a dangerous emotion considering he needed leverage, and delivering musicians into the hands of partners who promoted and managed careers was easy. "Are you asking for yourself? Are you in a band?"

"No. Curious. Salina, who voted in your favor at the shop, is in one."

He smiled, relieved despite his intention not to be. "So I already owe her a favor. Is the band any good?"

"I don't know. She's been after me to come hear them play but I haven't yet."

"What if we make it a date?"

"Just like that? That easy?"

"I think you'll find I'm very easy." He dropped his gaze to where her nipples were visible against her shirt. "Extremely easy in fact."

She laughed. "You're a man. Of course you're easy."

"And you're very cynical."

He turned her hand over to reveal the eye inked into her palm. There was something about the design, about her, that kept him hard and hurting, anxious to have her stroke and kiss his flesh.

His cock didn't protest the idea of seducing Etaín as a way of ultimately gaining her help. If this were a hotel restaurant he doubted he'd bother with going any further than the first available room.

Better that he convince her to do what his family wanted—willingly—so she'd stand a chance of surviving it, than to leave it to his uncle and father. That's what he told himself, but his conscience gnawed at him. And the only way he could suppress it was with images of Brianna, and the casket he'd walked away from before it was lowered into the grave.

"Stylin' Ink wasn't what I expected," he said.

"You expected flash on the walls and bikers hanging out in the waiting room?"

"Something like that. Though this is an expensive district, I probably shouldn't have."

"We're mostly a custom shop. There's some flash in the reference binders, but even the tourists usually want their work personalized. The clientele varies, depending on the artists. Derrick attracts the extremes, gay guys and total homophobes. Jamaal draws a lot of the office-worker crowd. Bryce took over the shop a couple of years ago. His specialty is portraits."

"And you? Do you like drawing portraits?"

"Devotion art almost always. Memorial art, yes, but it's a lot harder sometimes."

"And the difference between the two?"

"Not all artists make one. For me, devotion art is having something like your mother's or girlfriend's face drawn over your heart while she's alive to appreciate the gesture. Memorial portraits depict someone who's dead. If they died a while back, I don't mind it so much. A fresh event is a lot tougher to handle, when getting the ink is a way to process the grief. Emotional pain translated into physical pain."

"Catharsis."

"Yes."

"Do you draw outside of producing skin art?"

"Not often."

Cathal backed off at the tone in her voice, different, firm. As clear an indication not to push further as was the way she'd deflected any probe that might lead to talk about her family.

He traced the eye on her right palm and felt a shiver go through her, one that resonated in him, like an echo and amplification of lust. His thoughts blurred, but whatever he might have said next was interrupted by the arrival of a blond man at their table.

Competition.

The word blazed through him and was confirmed when the stranger merely nodded, making no pretense at what had brought him to the table and where his interest lay. Etaín. And by the expression on her face, she wasn't immune to the blond, or resistant to the attraction.

Like calls to like, Etaín thought, the idea coming from nowhere but settling in with surety as the tattoos along her forearms felt as though they were alive, writhing and rippling and soaking in this man's presence. Not bells this time, but raging fire and stormy seas.

The maître d' and servers were mouthwatering, but this man was stunning. Tiny stones set in intricately marked silver glittered from his ears. Dark blond hair flowed down his back in twisted waves and his eyes were the blue of deep sea.

In every way he was as breathtaking as Cathal, as commanding. Sex incarnate, but perhaps coming with a greater risk.

His attention flicked to her upturned palm and she tensed at seeing something in his expression, recognition maybe, or satisfaction. "I am Eamon. Welcome to my place."

He didn't offer a hand in greeting. Solidifying her suspicions that he knew, that somehow he had strange gifts of his own.

"Etaín," she said, and would have sworn she felt the force of his will pressing to hers, demanding she provide a last name, more in the way of identification. It took a greater effort than it should have to glance away. "This is—"

"Cathal Dunne," Eamon said, turning his head slightly, directing the next words at her companion. "I know of his family."

Dark ripples in a smooth voice. Undercurrents that made her think of jagged reefs beneath the calm ocean surface.

Cathal inclined his head, nothing more.

A silent battle waged between the two men. She felt it against her senses and suppressed the urge to point out they were definitely not junkyard dogs and she was not a bone to be fought over, or to be gnawed on by the victor until his hunger passed.

Eamon turned back to her and his heated look had the same effect on her as Cathal's did, delivering a lightning strike of need. "I'll tell those who work here you're to be admitted any time you desire. Food and drink will be provided at no cost."

His eyes held knowledge of his effect on her. Kissable lips drew her attention so she watched the words leave them. "You'll understand if I hope you arrive unaccompanied so I can join you."

She left the sentiment unanswered. Falling back on a semblance of manners, linked loosely to a social rule about leaving with the one you came with.

A server came through the doors and crossed the bridge, heading toward their table. Eamon said, "Your dinner is about to arrive. I'll leave you to enjoy it."

He left, his presence seeming to stretch across the terrace and claim every inch of it, the unmistakable aura of ownership and power. *And something else*, she thought as the sensation of fire and water along the inked vines on her forearms subsided.

"Well, that was interesting," she said as their plates were placed on the table and the server left.

"For you maybe."

Cathal's voice held dismissal, the absolute confidence of a man who didn't truly worry about a rival when it came to women. She risked feeding his outrageous ego by saying, "Definitely for me. It's not every day two guys who look like poster boys for carnal sin come into my orbit and hit on me."

The smile he gave her curled her toes and very nearly pushed the image of Eamon from her mind. "Carnal sin. My favorite kind. Does that mean you're going to give in to temptation?"

"I'm still undecided."

"Then I'll have to convince you."

Cathal stood and moved to her side. Heat flared in her belly and the scent of him filled her lungs.

He smelled right. There was no other way to describe it.

Her heart skipped and raced. She wet her lips in anticipation and tilted her face up as he lowered his, recognizing this for what it was, even if he didn't. The staking of a public claim despite his outward show of confidence. A reaction to Eamon's arrival at their table.

Her panties dampened further as his mouth neared hers. "Tease," she murmured when he took his time reaching her lips.

He brushed his mouth against hers. "And you're not?"

"I can be. If that's what you like."

He cupped her cheek though he didn't have to worry she would try to evade him. "I'd like anything you'd care to do to me."

"That's a pretty bold statement. I might be into whips and chains."

"Turnabout is fair play."

He covered her mouth with his, licking at the seam of her lips. When she opened for him, he didn't thrust inside but continued to torment her with light touches and tender sucks, the promise of penetration withheld.

Her breasts grew swollen, the nipples tight and aching, crying out for his hand to leave her cheek. Or better yet, for his mouth to move downward.

Desire shivered through her, need too long suppressed. Heat gathered in her labia and she pressed her thighs together to capture it, enjoy it.

If they'd been alone she would have cupped her mound with her hand, touched herself until he forced her hand away and replaced it with his, or rolled on top of her and filled her with his cock.

His tongue finally thrust against hers. Rubbed in a sensual prelude.

A small moan of pleasure escaped but instead of enticing more of the same, it served as the bell announcing the end of the first round and naming him victor. He lifted his mouth from hers, satisfaction and lust in his eyes. "Convinced?"

"That you'd be good in bed? I only had to look at you to know that."

He brushed his thumb over her still-parted lips. "You tempt me to risk a charge of lewd and indecent behavior to get the answer I want, but I'll take the more conservative course. For now. Step foot in my club and all bets are off."

Eamon watched from above, Rhys at his side, as Cathal leaned down, delivering another tormenting kiss.

"I could arrange an accident for him," Rhys said.

The same solution had crossed Eamon's mind though violence was never his first choice when dealing with humans. On the whole, he disliked them, but it seemed dishonorable, given the shortness of their lives, to end them prematurely or cause undeserved hardship.

"Not now," he answered. Perhaps not ever.

He'd been hard from the moment he'd seen her and hadn't imagined his cock could throb more painfully, yet it did. He found it incredibly arousing to watch Cathal touch her, to imagine coming to her bed after the other man had left it and having her spread her legs for him as well.

The reaction surprised him, as did the willingness to even consider sharing his consort-wife with a human. Time would tell, he decided, if the increased desire he felt at seeing them together came from the challenge of taking her away from another, or if there was something about Etaín and Cathal together, a primal connection with roots in the magic filling her and empowering her inherent gift.

Too much was at stake to act in haste, and she was an unknown. "Have someone shadow Etaín. I want to know where she lives and works."

"I've already stationed someone outside, humans, so attention won't be drawn to her. A young couple so they'll more easily find ways to blend."

"Excellent."

"Should I look into her involvement with Niall Dunne's son and learn what I can about her history?"

It was the easy way, but not the most satisfying. "Hold off for now. I'll make contact with her again. Tonight perhaps. Unless she's still with Cathal."

"The clock will start ticking if you're seen too often in public."

"It already ticks. There's no avoiding it. If I'm successful in making her my consort, all of us will need to move and reinvent ourselves elsewhere. She has friends here, and humans she believes are her biological family. They'll age and die unless they pledge themselves and become part of my household."

Rhys captured the red sun of his earring, rubbing his thumb over it as if to ward off bad luck. "How can she be unclaimed? How is it the queen isn't scouring this world for her?"

"We don't know she isn't."

"Our spies—"

"Might no longer belong to us. But more likely, they haven't heard even a whisper about the existence of a *seidic* hidden away and not bound over as the law requires."

"It'd be a coup for the queen if she introduced one to the court. It'd be a way to reward those whose loyalty is unquestioned and strike terror in the heart of anyone who isn't. Binding Etaín to you instead of giving her over will be viewed as a declaration of sovereignty once it becomes known."

"Such a declaration is inevitable. I don't think any other lord would act otherwise, especially after they'd seen her." He hesitated then added, "When she passed through the wards, the magic possessing her felt old, as if it originated in Elfhome."

Rhys's breath caught. "Then why let her continue to roam free?"

"Because I want a willing wife-consort, not an unwilling prisoner."

"You risk much."

"For the chance of gaining more. Tell the couple watching Etaín to report her whereabouts if she parts company with Cathal and settles in a place where I can approach her without making her feel threatened."

"I'll do it now."

Rhys left and Eamon continued to study the couple below as they finished their meal. Curiosity ate at him. Desire. He felt more alive, more excited than he had in centuries.

Ennui was the curse of long life, why intrigues and political maneuvering became a hobby for many, a dangerous amusement in periods when peace existed between their kind and the other supernaturals hidden in this realm.

"Who are you?" he murmured, looking down at the woman who would soon belong to him. "Where did you come from?" *And is it possible you could lead us to one of the gates to Elfhome. Would you want to?*

Would he?

So many unknowns.

Next time, if she arrived with Cathal, he would order them seated somewhere other than the terrace, so he could listen to their conversation. Magic and honor prevented him from doing it now. The first because the area they were in was heavily warded, a place of containment as well as sanctuary, and second, because those humans allowed to sit there during the hours the restaurant was open to them had been guaranteed it was a place of absolute privacy.

Cathal's father and uncle came here frequently. Instinct or paranoia, from their first visit to Aesirs, they'd secured seating on the terrace.

They remained a complication. He had no desire to swell the ranks of those calling him Lord with humans, especially men like Niall and Denis. The sooner he weaned Etaín away from involvement with anyone who had no ties to the Elven world, the better.

Eamon watched as Etaín and Cathal stood, the other man's hand settling on her lower back in a possessive manner.

Her aura darkened as a result of it, rich gold against the shimmering purple of Cathal's. Confirming, in a small way, why he found the thought of sharing her erotic rather than unacceptable. The magic possessing her found something in Cathal it wanted.

She didn't move away as Cathal's body brushed against hers, touched as they halted on the bridge and looked down at the koi. She threw something into the water and Eamon's attention flicked back to the table.

He spotted the small, distinctly patterned bowl, now empty of the pellets it had once contained. Seeing it brought a smile to his face, a surge of pleasure at her whimsy. So few guests asked about feeding the fish.

Pleasure became a spike of lust when Cathal leaned in, whispering something in her ear, using conversation as an excuse to touch his lips to her skin, to place a kiss high on her neck as his hand caressed her spine.

Eamon fought the urge to curl his fingers around his hardened length, his desire deepening in response to the heat flowing back and forth between them.

She pulled away, just far enough to turn toward Cathal and say something, making him smile then lower his gaze to the front of her shirt, and the nipples visible there.

They'll be lovers by morning, Eamon thought, discovering he didn't like the idea of his consort giving herself to Cathal first. Afterward, maybe, if he still found the idea of sharing her with another man arousing and the magic required it.

He decided to summon Rhys and arrange for an interruption directing Cathal's attention elsewhere. But before he could call his second to him, Etaín's hand went to her pocket and emerged with a phone. Her expression and body language changed abruptly. Heated desire and flirtation disappearing so completely Eamon felt certain there would be no need to find a means of separating her from Cathal.

* * *

I've got to take this," Etaín said, dread making her stomach roil in anticipation of the nausea that would soon come. There was only one reason her brother called.

She put the phone to her ear without bothering with a greeting. Parker asked, "Where are you?"

"Aesirs."

The answer derailed him—introducing a pause that if their relationship had been different might have led to a quick question about who she was with or how she came to be there. And then he plowed ahead. "I need your help. I'll pick you up."

"I'd rather take the bike."

Another pause, this one followed by a brisk, "Suit yourself. I'm on my way to SF General now. I'll meet you there."

He ended the connection before she'd pulled the phone away from her ear.

"Trouble?" Cathal asked.

She shrugged, turning away from the tranquility of the koi in their endless circle of water. She'd need someone later tonight, with a vengeance, but she could hardly ask, *Can I come by for sex sometime before dawn?* She said instead, "Thanks for dinner and the offer to help the shelter. I need to head to an appointment."

He leaned in, touching his lips to hers, one hand caressing her side while the other remained a hot brand at the base of her spine. "I want to see you again. I want more time with you."

Etaín let the call, and the reality it represented, fade for just a moment, replaced by coiling heat and the desire to press all of her skin against Cathal's. A dark current ran through him, something beneath his surface, mingling with the lust he didn't bother to hide. When she touched him, she sensed it, and yet she couldn't make herself care. "I'd like to see you, too."

"Tonight?" His hand moved higher, stopping inches away from her breast and making it ache for his touch. "Come to Saoirse?"

"Does your earlier warning still apply? Step foot in your club and all bets are off?"

He kissed his way to her ear. "Wear a short skirt and you won't make it past the first table before you find yourself sitting on the edge of it with me between your thighs."

"Tempting." But as much as she needed this exchange with him, to use later as a reminder life could be good, guilt would come if she lingered, playing when she should be elsewhere. "I need to go."

Cathal stepped away so Etaín was no longer trapped against the decorative railing of the bridge. It was harder than it should have been to allow her to escape.

"I'll walk you back to the shop," he said, and they moved into the main seating area, retracing their earlier steps to the maître d' stand and entrance. He saw no point in pretending he hadn't heard her end of the conversation. "Should I be worried whoever you're going to meet is competition?" *In addition to Eamon?*

"No." There was a brief hesitation. "That was my brother."

He took the hint in her voice and didn't ask her to elaborate, though he wondered if her brother was a cop, and the appointment to draw the face of a criminal. "What kind of bike?"

"A Harley."

"Take me for a ride someday?"

She cut him a look, temptress and tease. "Can you really cede that much control to a woman?"

"For you, yes."

The small, very feminine smile said she was pleased by the answer, and whatever images his question had created in her mind.

As they passed the tattoo shop, Etaín waved at her coworkers on the other side of the glass. The heavily tattooed and pierced man Cathal now knew was Bryce lifted his hand to the side of his face in a "call me" gesture.

"Maybe you should fix your friend Derrick up with Eamon," Cathal said, the thought spoken without conscious intention.

Etaín turned her head to look at him. "Wishful thinking? Or did you pick up on a vibe I didn't, because Eamon definitely didn't register as someone who goes both ways to me."

Jealousy stabbed through Cathal with the recognition he didn't like her thinking about the other man, much less contemplating his sexuality. He let the subject drop.

She indicated a turn and they rounded the corner. A dark blue Harley was parked up ahead.

They reached it sooner than he wanted. He pulled his phone out. "Give me your number."

She did, asking for his in return and keying it in before sliding the phone into her jacket pocket.

Unable to let her go with just a goodbye, he trapped her against the bike, this time holding her flush against the hard evidence of a desire that showed no sign of abating.

She wrapped her arms around his neck. Pressed her breasts to his chest and made a small sound of approval as his mouth lowered.

He couldn't shake the threat Eamon represented. "You don't have to go elsewhere for this. Especially not to Aesirs." *To him.*

"I know," she said, not *I won't*, the answer tease and torment alike, frustration and challenge.

Jealousy seared him again, burning hotter when the touch of his lips to hers sent a jolt straight to his cock. Regardless of the reasons for introducing himself to her, he wanted her more than he could remember wanting any other woman.

A hard thrust and his tongue breached the seam of her lips. She shivered in his arms, tightening her own around his neck and grinding her pelvis to his, making him ache.

Desire coursed through his system like a drug, an addictive high that began and ended with her. In broad daylight there'd be no relief, but that didn't keep him from imagining it, from fantasizing about freeing his cock and forcing her hand to it, her mouth.

His tongue twined with hers. Tangled in sensual embrace as he gave in to temptation, need, tormenting them both by cupping her breast and rubbing his thumb over the taut nipple.

She moaned again, clung. And he liked that he could make her do both. Pressed for more by saying, "Come to the club tonight."

"My brother needs me to do something for him. I doubt I'll be finished before you close."

Tension returned to her body, mental retreat and a silence that said *no trespassing.*

He hated it, and not just because he needed her open and willing to help his family. The impulse to tell her to call him, regardless of the hour, was strong. He suppressed it, refusing to lose control of the situation any more than he already had.

"Maybe tomorrow then," he said, giving her a brief kiss before stepping back, affecting a casualness he didn't feel, not with his body raging, not when there was a possibility his uncle would become impatient and act without regard for the consequences.

"Thanks for dinner and the offer to help with the fund-raiser."

"Let me know what you want, a DJ or live music."

She unlocked her helmet. "Will do."

He told himself to turn and walk away from her. But couldn't. There was something mesmerizing about watching her straddle the bike. Lithe power and feminine lines. Sensual control and inherent wildness. He could easily imagine her above him, guiding his cock to her opening and riding him.

The Harley roared to life. Throbbing thunder and purring beat to accompany the images cascading through his mind.

A glance in his direction, a four-fingered wave and she pulled into the street.

Cathal cursed at having lost his focus. He memorized the license plate number and speed-dialed Sean, glad he paid good money to get a heads-up any time the Feds went fishing on the off chance he'd gotten involved in his father's business.

The private investigator answered and Cathal rattled off the number along with a description of the bike.

"Got it," Sean said. "Now who rides the Harley and what am I supposed to do with this information?"

"The woman's name is Etaín. She works at Stylin' Ink. I want to know everything about her. Where she goes. What she does. Whether she's seeing anyone. Who her family is." He hesitated, finally embellishing on the last because he didn't want to alienate Sean. "She may be related to a cop."

"Am I looking for dirt?"

Cathal felt a twist in his gut. "Leverage."

Silence stretched between. Heavy. Considering.

Sean ended it by asking, "This have something to do with what happened to your cousin Brianna and her friend?"

Cathal's fingers tightened on the phone. Too late he realized he should have waited a day before making the call. At their first meeting Sean had told him he liked to know who he was working for, and since then more than once Cathal had witnessed a hunch of Sean's paying off.

It didn't stop him from bluffing. "Why would you think that?"

A sigh followed. Soft enough not to get the testosterone pumping, but clear enough to convey, *Are you serious? Give me a break here.*

"Two and two usually equals four," Sean said. "And at the risk of putting myself in harm's way to prove it, how's this?

"A kid was buried today. Brianna's friend, and the same one she was with when paramedics were called out to the scene of a drug overdose. I assume the other members of your family were also at the funeral, including your uncle. And now you're trying to send me out on what sounds like personal business involving a woman who may have ties to the authorities, instead of the music business—knowing that despite parting company with the force, when it comes to the

Dunnes, you're the only one I'll work for. How am I doing so far? Am I closing in on four?"

Cathal was tempted to say, *Forget I called.* He could do without Sean's help. But Sean was an ace in the hole, a card he could play if his father and uncle decided to send men to learn more about Etaín. "You're closing in on four."

"Okay. Straight-up, Cathal. No bullshit. No dodging. Truth, but only as much of it as I need to know to decide if I can take this job on. How does this involve Brianna?"

"She was drugged and gang-raped. So was her friend Caitlyn."

"You're positive about this? She wouldn't be the first kid to experiment and get in over her head then claim she was an innocent victim when things went bad."

"I'm positive. Or I wouldn't be making this call."

Sean exhaled loudly, hoping for a different answer and not getting one. Having to wrestle with his conscience just as Cathal had struggled with his. A fight he had a feeling was going to get worse the more time he spent with Etaín.

"You think this woman was somehow involved?"

"No. But I think she might be able to shed some light on the situation. I'd like to keep her as far away from my father and uncle as I can."

Silence. Once again heavy and considering. Then finally, "I'll see what I can find out about her. No promises you'll get the leverage you're looking for."

Cathal mentally shrugged. Anything Sean found was a bonus now that he'd met Etaín. Getting her in bed had become the priority.

"That's fine. You'll bill me regardless."

"Damn right. I'll give you an update later tonight."

"I'll be waiting."

Four

Etaín pulled into the hospital parking lot. Parker was waiting for her, wearing casual clothes to disguise against being made as a Fed. With blond hair touching his shirt collar, he might have pulled it off except for the stranger standing next to him. Everything about him screamed FBI agent, and a cute one at that.

She parked and swung off the bike, freeing the sketch pad and box of pencils bungeed onto the back of the saddle for quick access. She wouldn't need either, but they masked the truth of how she was able to produce images from a victim's memory.

As she walked toward the men, she amused herself by imagining her gaydar would soon start pinging, and in the course of getting to whatever room they were going to, she'd discover her brother's companion had a thing for tattoo artists given to spells of being in drag.

"You won't need the drawing supplies," Parker said by way of greeting, holding out his hand. "I'll carry them for you."

Uneasiness settled in Etaín. Her earlier years with her mother had been a lesson on remaining uninvolved in the lives of other people, of never staying in one place long enough to become comfortable, and therefore careless.

She'd rejected those lessons, but that didn't mean she wanted knowledge of her gift to spread. Even Derrick and Jamaal and Bryce didn't know about this aspect of it.

A cautioning glance at the second agent got her an introduction. "This is Trent. He's with the Bureau. Both of us are on the same case. He knows how you work with victims."

Her unease deepened, edging into familiar anger at Parker. Trent nodded but didn't offer to shake her hand. Didn't say, "Thanks for coming." Instead he said, "She fits the profile."

Parker tensed, then immediately rid himself of it with a roll of his shoulders. "It'll be okay. We'll get in and get out and nobody will be the wiser. Besides, the others have all done shift work. There's no reason to think she'll come to this guy's attention."

"Your call," Trent said. *Your sister.*

She relinquished the pad and pencils, not asking about what kind of predator she fit the victim profile for. That was part of her détente with Parker, and she'd know the answer by morning anyway.

They entered the hospital. Reflexively she shoved her hands into her pockets. Partly in self-defense, partly so the material of her jeans would absorb the sweat from her palms as the impression of narrowing hallways made her feel panicked and claustrophobic.

Voices echoed in her ears, conversations around her competing with the sound of her pounding heart. Parker's fingers encircled her upper arm, steadying her, a comforting presence despite the minefield that was their relationship.

In a private home, she wouldn't have needed it. But in hospitals, always.

They reached the intensive care unit. A nurse looked up, her eyes lingering on Etaín, her curiosity evident.

"Any change?" Parker asked, drawing her attention to him.

Curiosity faded into a pinched, serious expression. "No."

"Has her family arrived?"

The nurse's gaze returned to Etaín. "Not yet. I'm not sure, but I think it could be any time now."

"Thanks," Parker said, taking a step and subtly blocking Etaín from continued scrutiny as he guided her forward. "We won't be long."

The moment it became clear which room they were heading for, Etaín *knew* what case her brother was working on. There could only be one if she fit the victim profile and so did the black woman lying on the bed.

The Harlequin Rapist, that's what the news media had started calling the man terrorizing the Bay Area. He abducted both white and black victims, holding them for days and leaving behind a distinctive set of injuries, though the police wouldn't elaborate on just what they were.

Etaín's stomach cramped at the obvious signs of torture. The woman's fingers had all been broken, as had her wrists and arms. The bones were immobilized but cast-free because the skin was burned, the open wounds forming a random pattern among old tattoos.

As horrible as those injuries were, and that the woman had been repeatedly raped, the damage done to her head was far, far worse. She'd been beaten so severely that her jaw was wired shut and her face swollen. Her skull was misshapen and her eyes moved constantly, rolling flashes of white without connection, seemingly without sight or sentience.

"Is this what he did to the others?" Etaín asked, forcing the words out in a whisper and wondering why her brother had waited so long to ask for her help.

It was Trent who answered, keeping his voice low. "Everything is the same except for the beating. We don't know whether he's escalating, or whether she saw something he was afraid would identify him."

Parker's hand tightened on Etaín's arm in furious determination. "The profiler thinks leaving the victims alive to remember and relive what's been done to them is more satisfying than killing them. If they die, then they win and he loses."

"If they die *while he's got them*," Trent said, qualifying Parker's statement. "He dumped her where she'd be found quickly. The doctors say her brain function is severely impaired."

Etaín didn't ask what the prognosis was. Her presence here was answer enough. They didn't expect the woman to recover enough to tell them anything useful or serve as a witness.

Nothing they might learn from this visit would ever be entered into the records as evidence. That was the cost of her gift. She didn't understand the why or the how, but she did know willfully taking the memories and images seemed to erase them from a victim's mind, or permanently block them.

The men halted in the doorway, obscuring the sight of the hospital bed and patient from the nurses' station.

Etaín kept moving, stopping next to the Harlequin Rapist's victim. Dreading what was to come and gathering herself to get through it.

"What's her name?"

"Tyra Nelson," Parker said.

Etaín wasn't certain she'd be able to help. Always before the victims had been traumatized but *present*, something Tyra gave no sign of being. She looked at Tyra's bare arm and shoulder, trying to find a place where touch would bring the least pain.

There wasn't one. And perhaps in the end, the pain would be necessary for the memories to come.

Skin didn't lie. Not to her.

Etaín touched the eye on the palm of her left hand against a clustered patch of burns on Tyra's shoulder, to raw, oozing wounds. And then the eye on her right palm above Tyra's shattered wrist.

Tyra flinched and whimpered, then lay passive. Leaving Etaín with the sense that what remained of who Tyra had been had retreated further.

"Show me what happened," Etaín whispered. A command. A refrain she repeated, becoming more insistent as the minutes ticked by and the silence grew heavy and oppressive.

She knew her gift was working when the waves of nausea began. Her psyche protesting—fighting against the horror seeping into her subconscious—trying to drive her up and away, as if by purging the contents of her stomach she could expell the images before they took form, becoming a nightmare that would soon seem as if it were her own reality.

The only sign of relief Tyra gave was the calming of her eyes. When brown irises stared out through slit lids, unmoving though still unfocused, Etaín broke the contact, one thought dominating, to get to the bathroom before she threw up.

Parker was already moving forward, hand reaching out, grasping her upper arm as she turned away from the bed. "Next to the nurse's station," he said, anticipating her need, knowing she refused to vomit in front of a victim.

He propelled her toward the doorway and through it, like a missile locked onto a target. Clammy sweat coated her skin. The area around her telescoped in, defined by the sharpness of her focus, the strength of her will.

She reached the toilet and bent over it, vomiting repeatedly. Violent, gut-tearing heaves that caused tears to stream down her face and left her feeling hollowed out and raw.

It took longer for the shakiness to pass. As she left the stall, the nurse who'd answered Parker's questions when they arrived stepped into the bathroom. "Are you okay?"

Embarrassed heat crept into Etaín's cheeks. The earlier sounds of retching and the lingering scent were enough to tell the story, if her overall appearance didn't do it. "I'm fine. Thanks."

She moved to the sink, fighting against making up an excuse. The less said the better. *Always*.

The nurse lingered near the door, curiosity replacing her concern. As Etaín leaned over, rinsing her mouth and face, the woman said, "I've seen you before. At a different hospital."

Etaín took another mouthful of water so it'd seem less rude when she didn't answer. She swished it around, drying her face at the same time, the move allowing her to spit then make a quick escape.

The instant she exited the bathroom she whispered, "Let's get out of here. The nurse recognized me."

"Fuck," Parker said when they were inside the elevator. "What did she say? What did *you* say?"

"I said nothing. She said she'd seen me before at a different hospital."

"Maybe you were visiting a friend?"

Etaín answered with a look.

He exhaled audibly, forcing nonchalance into his posture. "Okay. Nothing we can do now. If Trent and I go back in there and say something to her about keeping your visit under wraps, that'll only make it a bigger deal."

Etaín didn't disagree. The damage was done.

At the hospital entrance Parker placed a hand on her shoulder, halting her and forcing her to turn toward him. "If it'll help, you can stay at my place tonight. Or I can come to yours."

She met his eyes, catching a flickering glimpse of emotion that carried her into a past where love came without conditions, and acceptance was a given. Or she imagined it there. Both possibilities made an ache spread in her chest, like the spider web cracking of shatterproof glass. She wanted to believe things could be different between them. Wanted it badly enough not to trust herself to answer any other way than, "I'm fine. I'll call you if I end up with something on paper."

"Any time, Etaín. Twenty-four, seven. We've got to stop this guy."

"I know." She stepped out from under his hand and took her drawing supplies. After saying goodbye to Trent she set a course for the Harley, her thoughts on how she'd keep herself busy for the rest of the evening. As much as she wanted to help them catch the Harlequin Rapist, she dreaded reaching the point of exhaustion necessary to lie down and go to sleep, because when she did, the nightmares *would* come, Tyra Nelson's memories becoming her own.

Cathal parked his car and got out. Lake Merced stretched in front of him, the sky above it a purple bruise at sunset.

There was no crime scene tape underneath the trees a short distance away, nothing to indicate two girls had been driven there and left to die.

Not for the first time, he wondered what had compelled those responsible to handle the situation this way.

Guilt? Panic?

Fear of consequences?

Or had it simply been a cold-blooded solution?

He walked to the spot, thinking of Etaín. Did the *why* really matter? Was the crime less heinous if drugs or alcohol had led to terrible acts?

Would anything change if the pictures she drew were of boys Caitlyn and Brianna knew? Sons of neighbors or friends or business associates, instead of complete strangers?

Guilt over using Etaín crept in again. He blocked it with thoughts of Brianna.

On his last visit she'd been glassy-eyed from sedation, her wrists bandaged from an attempted suicide. A private nurse hovered nearby, charged with never leaving Brianna alone.

What was justice for a rapist? His father and uncle would answer one crime with another—murder.

Cathal had rejected their way of life, but the possibility he was the same kind of man scared him. He'd known that in agreeing to approach Etaín, he'd taken the first slippery step downward. But now, as then, his thoughts circled back to the inevitable. What choice did he have?

He could tell Etaín to leave San Francisco and go into hiding. He could advise her to hire round-the-clock protection for as long as his father and uncle were alive.

Only death would stop them from doing whatever it took to find and punish those responsible for drugging and raping Brianna and Caitlyn. Prison might shorten their reach and make it more difficult for them to use Etaín, but it wouldn't stop them from reaching.

Or he could tell her the truth—and assuming she was related to a cop and went to the authorities, let the FBI or ATF use her in a sting operation so when his father and uncle went to deliver justice, they'd end up in prison, adding more guilt and loss to Brianna's life while allowing her rapists to go free. But it wasn't just the consequences for Brianna that made him unwilling to be honest with Etaín.

Frustration came with that acknowledgment. Despite rejecting their way of life, telling her risked betraying his father and uncle, his family. And that part of their code went as deep as his love for them did.

Cathal turned away from the lake, making the same decision he had in his father's car. This was the *right* thing, the *only* thing he could do, though he understood why he'd come to this place—to shore-up internal defenses that threatened to go up in flames when he was with Etaín.

He wanted her. And the desire to seduce her, to feel her beneath him, her body joined to his, went well beyond what he felt compelled to do on behalf of his family, or to keep her safe.

People waited in a line outside the shelter, trying to get in and claim a bed before the cold descended and fog worked its way inland. Against a wall, a row of shopping carts held salvaged junk and garbage bags containing castoff clothing.

Glaring floodlights illuminated the harsh face of poverty: Parents with babies in arms and older children at their sides. Veterans and the mentally ill, dumped from institutions after budget cuts. Drunks and addicts whose choices and family histories led to a predictable end.

Etaín drove around back and parked the Harley next to a beat-up Ford. A few steps took her to a back entrance and a knock brought one of the staff members.

"Justine's in the men's dormitory," he said.

She made her way there, traveling down a hallway that had once led to a manufacturing space but was now subdivided into rooms lined with beds, and others with folding tables and chairs.

Justine looked up from talking to a man with stringy brown hair and a meth-addict complexion. Seeing Etaín in the doorway, she finished the conversation and came over. The dense smell of cigar smoke permeated her clothing, sending the message that despite being a petite woman in her sixties, she had balls.

"I need you to do a consult first," she said.

"Cover-up work?"

"No, one of your special tattoos."

Etaín shoved her hands into her pockets and hunched her shoulders, uncomfortable despite having done this kind of work at Justine's request since she was fifteen.

The dreams that had led to the eyes on her palms, the drugs and rebellion, and to finally running away from home had also led her to Justine, who'd been working a teen outreach program back then. If not for Justine, she might never have discovered this aspect of her gift.

Justine had been the one to notice that when she tattooed empowerment symbols onto some of the kids she ran with, the ones who desperately wanted better lives for themselves, then it happened for them. She'd been the one to order reference books and travelers' journals documenting how tattoos held power beyond what most people in the Western world recognized. She'd insisted Etaín read the accounts of how monks used secret ink ingredients and symbols along with chants and rituals to imbue power into the charms they tattooed onto skin as part of their temple duties.

The parallels between what she did as a result of her dreams and what monks did as part of their culture unnerved her still. Celibacy wasn't a remote possibility. Neither was accepting a religious calling.

"You sure this person is ready for the *mojo* tattoo?" she asked, coping by an attempt at humor, though it got her the usual censorious look.

"Teresa is ready. She's trying to stay straight so she can get her child back."

Some of the hunch left Etaín's shoulders. "How old is the kid?"

Justine stopped a few feet away from the room where women without children were housed. "Ten months. He was born addicted and taken by the state."

"He's still in foster care?"

"Yes. Teresa's gone through treatment but she lapsed when she went back to live with the baby's father. Drugs showed up in her urine. He's a user. Her friends are users. You know the story. She tried staying with her mother but there was trouble with her mother's boyfriend.

"Mom chose him, not the first time it has happened if you ask me. Teresa hasn't said as much, but I believe her involvement with drugs started as a way of dealing with a rape when she was preteen. After her mother turned her out, this place became her best chance at staying clean and getting on her feet. I think she can make it, but she could use a little help. Your kind of help. Ready?"

Etaín pulled her hands from her pocket. "Ready."

They entered the room and stopped next to a cot where a girl not much older than nineteen or twenty sat cross-legged.

"Teresa, this is Etaín, the one I told you about."

The girl's eyes met Etaín's, skittering away and then returning, resolute.

Etaín braced herself and offered her hand. After the hospital, she couldn't handle much more direct contact.

The girl took it, the touch pouring fear of failure and loss, along with hope and determination, into Etaín's bloodstream. "Will you do the tattoo?"

Etaín managed to give a squeeze of reassurance before pulling away. "Yes, it might take a few days before I'm ready. What did you have in mind?"

Teresa picked up a small photograph that had been lying on the bed, hidden by her thigh. She held it for Etaín to see. The edges were frayed from being handled. "Lothar. My son. He's the reason for everything I do now."

"I've got a copy of the picture in my office," Justine said.

Etaín nodded but took a moment to study the boy's face. Unlike the work she did in the shop, this had to be done freehand, without a stencil, without a tattoo machine. And like the ink on her own arms and palms, she wouldn't do it until the design with its embedded symbols showed up in her dreams.

"I'll let you know when I'm ready," she told Teresa.

"Gracias."

They left, climbing stairs that were off limits to everyone but staff. In Justine's office Etaín took a chair after carefully folding the promised photograph and putting it in her jacket pocket. They went over the plans for the fund-raiser, wrapping up the old business before she said, "The owner of Saoirse came by the shop today. He's volunteered to provide music for the event, either several bands or a DJ. I'm guessing he'd be willing to kick in some advertising money as long as the club gets mentioned as a sponsor."

Justine pursed her lips. "We've got four days, that's not a lot of time."

"It's time enough. Word will spread, and accepting his offer will mean a bigger crowd."

"You'll serve as liaison?"

Thinking of Cathal, Etaín suppressed a smile to avoid an interrogation. Liaison was already a given. "My choice whether it's live music or a DJ?"

"Yes."

"I'll do it."

"Good. I'll leave it to you then. In the meantime, I need to get back downstairs and see how many beds we've got left."

Etaín called the shop before leaving the shelter. One of the guys who preferred to work evenings and nights answered.

"Is Bryce there?" she asked.

"Yeah, with a client. You need him?"

"No. Just tell him I'm on my way. Be there in about fifteen."

"Okay. He already told us to start paying attention when you were due in, or any of the female clients coming at night. Said to keep our eyes open for anyone who might be hanging around, at least until they catch the rapist."

Etaín shivered, the image of Tyra forming in her mind. For a split second she thought about calling her client and postponing the appointment. But home was a tiny apartment in Oakland and she didn't want to be alone. Sleep would come when it came.

She brushed her thumb over the keys of her phone, thinking about Cathal and wondering if he was at Saoirse. Heat blossomed in her chest, sliding downward as she remembered touch and scent and the hard ridge of his cock pressed against her, his warning about wearing a short skirt to his club.

She had a few of them. Even had the fuck-me heels to go with them though she usually preferred wearing shit-kicker boots.

Definitely a great way to pass the time and get a workout guaranteed to make her go to sleep. If she went to him, the sex would follow, sooner rather than later. And that was part of the problem.

She'd need it later more than sooner. And she didn't know him well enough to wake up in his bed from a nightmare that would send her to the bathroom to purge before she started drawing, obsessively capturing images recorded by another person's eyes.

Of course, it was equally possible all his playing was done at the club, and come closing time, he parted company with whatever woman had captured his attention for the night. The thought sent sandpaper scraping over her skin. She jammed the phone into her jacket and started the Harley, reminding herself getting involved with Cathal beyond recreational sex wasn't possible.

Five

He sat up when he heard the motorcycle. The half-full bag of Fritos fell off his chest, landing near the beer bottle he'd peed in as he waited to see if she'd come back here. He already knew she wasn't at her apartment.

He checked the time, writing it down on a piece of paper with her name at the top. Then he crept toward the front of the cargo van, going just far enough so he had a good view of the tattoo shop.

One of the artists stepped out of the shop and looked around. He flinched back even though he knew there was no way he could be seen. Not in the darkness of the van, and not this far away. He was always careful not to be caught watching at this stage, when he was learning their schedules and figuring out the best place to take them.

Before coming to San Francisco to visit his brother, the thought of everyone knowing about what he did had scared him. He wasn't afraid anymore. He liked hearing people talk about the Harlequin Rapist.

The drone of the motorcycle engine stopped and he licked his lips as she swung off the bike and removed her helmet. She was so beautiful.

When he squinted, it looked like she carried the sun around inside her. He could see a golden glow surrounding her. Day or night, it was always there.

It made him want to reach out and touch her. To make sure she re-

*membered him for the rest of her life and thought about their time together
every time she looked at herself.*

He was almost sure she was going to be his choice. Almost.

*There were a couple of others he was still watching. He needed to get
closer to decide. He needed to see what color her eyes were.*

*They had to be dark. The same way her hair had to be blonde. Real
blonde, not bought from the grocery store.*

*He didn't have to worry about whether or not she'd have tattoos. She
would.*

*It was better if they were on her arms but he didn't care as much about
where they were. He was too smart to be obsessed about that. If too much
was the same, it made it easier to get caught.*

*She went into the shop and he lay back down on the mattress in the
back of the van. He'd wait awhile before he left.*

*Some nights he parked near where she lived. So far she'd always been
alone when she came home.*

*He decided he wouldn't do that tonight. He'd wait and see her again
tomorrow. He'd get closer then, so he'd know for sure if she was going to
be his choice.*

*A giggle escaped as he imagined going into the shop and asking her to
tattoo a small harlequin on his arm.*

A shudder of revulsion followed.

*No. He didn't like them to touch him. If he decided she was next, then
someone else would have to be the one to do the tattoo.*

Etaín shrugged off her jacket and hung it up before retrieving a file
from the cabinet in Bryce's office where the artwork was stored.
She pulled the finished design and supporting photographs of a girl in
her early twenties from the manila folder.

The art she placed facedown on her workstation table, the pictures
faceup. Sadness spread through her chest like a shadow as she studied

the photographs, the emotion a small reflection of the grief that would soon be pouring into her if Kelli showed up for her appointment.

What would it be like to have a child? To lose that child?

Sometimes she wondered if one day she'd want one. If she'd dare have one, knowing the past might repeat itself and she might be forced to leave that child as she had been left.

She'd already learned that loving someone—at least where there was physical intimacy—didn't protect them from her gift. The damage done when she was seventeen, and then again at twenty, to guys she'd thought would be a part of her life forever, still had the power to weigh her down with guilt, though in the end, both of her lovers had overcome it.

Her gaze moved to her own hands. She turned them over to reveal the intricate eyes at the center of her palms.

Her mother had tattoos on the backs of her hands and curling around her wrists. Not the same design, but the eyes were part of them.

She could remember sitting on her mother's lap as they traveled by bus, disappearing from one life and into another as she traced the ink with her fingers, always asking, *What do they mean?* Always getting the same answer. *See but remain unseen.*

Etaín turned away from the memory. There were no answers to be found in it, only pain and longing.

Bryce had done as promised. Her machines were clean and waiting for her, along with fresh needles and latex gloves. She picked up a pad and pencil, drawing without conscious decision only to become uneasy when the image on paper turned into the one she'd seen in her mind's eye on the inside of Cathal's forearms. He was showing up too often in her thoughts and she'd never put her ink on a lover, either before or after the fact.

It's just been too long since I've been with anyone, she told herself, relieved when Kelli's arrival gave her something else to focus on.

Etaín walked around the counter, taking in Kelli's pale features and bruise-shadowed eyes. Even braced for it, her breath caught when she put a comforting hand on Kelli's arm and grief poured into her. "If you're not sure about this—"

"I'm sure. I *need* to do this."

"Okay," Etaín said, letting her hand drop away and leading Kelli to the workstation.

Kelli teared up at seeing the pictures laid out on the table. Etaín picked up the drawing, turning it over.

"Yes," Kelli whispered, her hand shaking as she wiped at escaping tears.

Etaín freed a paper towel from the roll on the lower shelf of her worktable and passed it to Kelli in lieu of a tissue. "I'll make the stencil, then we'll get started."

She did it and returned, the tank top Kelli wore making it possible to do the tattoo without going behind the privacy screen. A quick wash with an antiseptic solution followed by the swipe of a new razor got rid of the hair above Kelli's left breast. Another cleansing wipe, and then Etaín made a pass with stick deodorant before pressing the stencil against skin and smoothing over it to make sure all the lines were transferred.

She removed the paper then took the mirror from its spot next to the paper towels, holding it up for Kelli. "That okay?"

"Yes."

"We'll give it a few minutes to dry while I get the ink ready. Go ahead and lie down. You'll need to stay still. Talking is fine and if you start feeling light-headed or queasy, or just need a break, let me know. There's no time pressure here. This'll take as long as it takes."

Kelli's *okay* was a little shaky but Etaín had worked on higher-strung clients, and Kelli's tattoo was small. She'd get it done in one relatively quick session.

As they waited, she studied the photographs, building her defenses against Kelli's grief by seeing the shades and shadows, visualizing the steps, the combinations of colors and space. It was more instinctive than learned, but even given the strength of her gift, she took pride in actively trying to improve her art with each piece of it.

After she'd placed the ink into caps and gathered all she needed, she put a light coat of Vaseline over the design. "Now the fun begins."

Kelli managed a smile but gripped the edge of the massage table as she braced for the pain. The outline came first and by the time it was done, Kelli's hands lay flat though tears streamed from her eyes, mental anguish melded to physical.

"You okay?" Etaín asked, exchanging the liner for the shader, the concentration on detail helping her to block the worst of Kelli's emotions.

"I'm fine."

She applied a gray wash next, for dimension. Then began working in the color, from dark to light. Adding flesh tones to skin in slow strokes so the portrait came alive, the subtle differences in shade and density creating depth, turning an outline into something evocative, into art that would exist only for a single lifetime.

She held against the heavy emotions dumping into her bloodstream until her throat clogged with them and she was forced into blinking away tears that didn't belong to her. She eased off the foot pedal then and the needles stilled.

A swipe with a paper towel cleared the excess ink from Kelli's skin. "What about a quick break?"

Kelli sat up. "Sorry I'm such a mess."

Between the visit to the hospital and this session, Etaín ached inside her skin and would have shed it like a snake if she could have. She couldn't bring herself to give Kelli a hug, but the smile she offered was genuine. "Don't worry about it. You're doing great."

Kelli's gaze strayed to the reference photographs on the worktable. Her hand lifted, unconsciously reaching to touch the nearly finished tattoo memorializing her daughter.

"Don't," Etaín said, stopping her. "You want a bottle of OJ or a can of Diet Coke?"

"How about the mirror again?"

"Hold off for another fifteen minutes? Thirty tops."

"I can make it." Kelli took a deep, calming breath. "I'm good to go again."

"Let's do it."

Kelli lay back down. Etaín compared the tattoo to the pictures and decided to use a different shader. She picked up the machine and went back to work.

The reality of what Etaín did in the human world slammed into Eamon like a fist to the gut. He'd been alarmed when Rhys brought the news to him, but witnessing it made his chest constrict so it was difficult to breathe.

In Elfhome the *seidic* were said to live apart from others, in small isolated communities requiring will and purity of purpose for a petitioner to reach. And even then, not everyone who approached the *seidic* gained a tattoo.

What he knew of those with Etaín's gift came from rumor and myth and ancient texts, but one thing never changed, the tattoos they created were linked to elemental magic. Nothing good could come of her applying ink to human skin in this way. Worse, a great deal of harm could come, if not to the humans, then to her. She was changeling, more possessed *by* magic than possessing *of* it.

He had to believe some instinct for self-preservation had been at play this long, unconsciously guiding her in the clients she accepted. But it still took discipline not to cross the street and push into the shop, demanding she stop what she was doing.

It required effort on his part not to summon Rhys and arrange for her to be discreetly abducted and delivered to his estate. He wouldn't allow her to continue this once they were bound.

Forcing himself to inhale deeply, he breathed in calm. Nothing had changed with seeing what she did among humans, other than the

rising urgency to have her in his arms and beneath him, forging a
bond first with his body, then later with his heart and magic.

He wanted her as willing wife-consort, not a dangerous, unwilling
prisoner. Meaning that for now, great care must be taken in how he
dealt with her. To that effect he decided to wait until her client left
before approaching her.

As Etaín put the finishing touches on Kelli's tattoo, Bryce emerged
from behind the privacy screen. A thin blonde followed him, her
ears, nose, and lips sporting nearly as many piercings as he had.

She paid and headed for the door. When she reached it, she turned
and said, "See you in a little while?"

"Yeah, sure."

She left and Bryce strolled over. "Iraq?" he asked, putting together
the photo of a girl in uniform and the signs of crying.

Kelli nodded, not giving in to the tears again until she took the
mirror from Etaín and saw the tattoo.

Bryce put an arm around her shoulders.

Etaín sent him a grateful look for stepping in, and started cleaning
up her station, letting Bryce handle the emotional fallout. The day was
catching up to her and the worst of it loomed ahead, in the defense-
lessness of sleep.

Kelli took a final shuddering breath and pulled away from Bryce.
Etaín made quick work of applying bandages and going over the care
instructions. She rang Kelli up and walked her out, waiting in the
doorway until Kelli was in her car before turning back into the shop.

"So, hot date tonight?" she asked Bryce, who for the second time
in one day was taking care of her equipment so she could leave.

"I'm going to get laid. How about you?"

A glance at the clock, a moment of temptation arriving with
thoughts of stopping at Cathal's club before heading home. "I wish."

"Well, the night's not over yet. We've got incoming despite it officially being after hours. You take him, see what he wants, and schedule him. I'm out of here."

Etaín turned and saw Eamon on the other side of the glass.

The night loved him, caressing his features like moonlight on an ocean hiding rip tides. Seeing him brought back the edginess that had been lost under Kelli's emotions. It returned full force with a body-tightening vengeance, came laced with raw desire and the need to blow off steam in a purely sexual way.

Rather than waiting for Eamon to enter, she snagged her jacket and went to him. "This is a surprise," she said, allowing him to maneuver her so they weren't standing in front of the glass, visible to the artists and clients still inside the shop.

"Is it? You had to know I'd come looking for you."

The words flowed through her like the notes of a song. "My own personal stalker?"

"I have questions for you, as you no doubt have them for me."

His fingers circled her wrists, lifting and holding them above her head, pressing them to the wall at her back, the restraint exciting her where it might have led to a hard, fast knee to the groin for another man.

She breathed deeply when he stepped closer, filling her lungs with the sea-breeze scent of him. A moan escaped as his thumbs stroked over the eyes on her palms, sending molten lust straight to her cunt, making her flushed and desperate and wet.

"And then there is this," he murmured against her lips before claiming them, the decadent taste and sweet softness of him pulling her into an undertow of desire.

Where Cathal had demanded, his tongue thrusting, mimicking what he intended to do with his cock, Eamon sipped, turning her need and her eagerness to his advantage.

He took his time, as if it were limitless. One kiss merging into another, his tongue retreating only to return, twining and rubbing with hers, like waves lapping at the land, eroding all resistance until she was the one to close the distance between their lower bodies and grind against the hardened length of his erection.

He took his mouth from hers, but only far enough so their eyes could meet. "Come home with me."

Not a question. Not really. There was no hint of uncertainty as to what he thought her answer would be.

The call of like to like, the mingling of hot lust and dangerous curiosity tried to drown out any reason that would lead to *no*, but failed to. She had to finish what she'd started when she pressed her palms to Tyra Nelson's skin.

"I can't."

Eamon's fingers tightened on her wrists. "Because you intend to go to Cathal? You want him?"

She avoided the first question by answering the second. "You've seen him. What do you think?"

White teeth flashed in the darkness, making her think of a shark in deep waters. "Men don't hold any attraction for me. But I can be flexible in what I allow of a lover. Of you, Etaín. I can even share if I have to, though I'll never believe you prefer him."

Heat pulsed through her with his words, coming with the image of lying naked between the two men. She was used to being hit on, but not like this, where the hints of dominance and threat made her wetter. She was open-minded about sex but had never *craved* what the fantasy he provoked promised, though she did now.

Eamon laughed softly. "Have I shocked you? Or aroused you?"

He leaned in, kissing her again in a sensual exploration, his tongue gliding against hers, each stroke making her cunt clench.

Shifting her wrists so he needed only one hand to keep them held to the wall, he covered her breast and the heat from his palm burned through her shirt and skin, pouring fire into her bloodstream.

She moaned, shamelessly grinding against his cock as he teased a hardened nipple, circling and stroking it with his fingers then clamping onto it to send a jolt of sheer need straight to her clit. She wanted him inside her, wanted to feel the press of his body to hers, skin touching in a hot meld of desire. It'd been so long and everything about him called to her.

A whimpered protest left her lips when he ended the kiss. "This isn't all I want of you," he whispered against her mouth before leaving it, kissing his way to her ear. "This isn't all I have to offer you, but it's a start."

He took her earlobe between his lips and sucked, each pull arrowing molten lust straight to her swollen folds. She tried to free her shackled wrists so she could explore him with her hands and feel his skin beneath her palms but he didn't allow it.

"Come home with me."

"I can't."

His tongue slid into the sensitive canal of her ear, delivering heated desire in a thrust that had her channel clenching, hungry to be filled by him. He squeezed her nipple, delivering pain with the pleasure, a punishment for denying him along with the promise of an exquisite reward for surrendering.

He remained in control, but he wasn't unaffected. His breathing was fast and his cock hard, his eyes a turbulent blue sea.

"Then come back to Aesirs for a drink."

"And a fuck?"

Irritation showed in his face but his voice was smooth confidence. "For starters, Etaín, if that's what you want to call it, but don't think I'll always settle for a meaningless physical act. I'd prefer the comfort of a bed, but as I said earlier, I can be flexible when it comes to you."

Danger rolled off him, an emotional threat, not a physical one. She stiffened in reaction to it, both repelled and attracted, believing he had answers if she was willing to ask the questions.

"I've got to get going," she said, tugging at her captured wrists.

He freed them, accepting her retreat but not without a thinning of his lips. "I'll walk you to your bike."

They walked in silence. When they reached the Harley he took her wrists in his hands again, this time holding them behind her back, using them to imprison her in a way that arched her spine and forced her pelvis against his.

"I can give you some of the answers you're looking for," he said, reinforcing his point by stroking his thumbs over the eyes on her palms. "I can give you so much more."

He leaned in, taking her mouth with his as if trying to storm her defenses. His lips and tongue more demanding than they had been before, more blatantly carnal. Renewing the desire and sending it crashing through her in hot, stormy waves that had arousal flowing from her slit to wet her panties.

When she was trembling with need he released her and stepped away. "Call Aesirs at any time and for any reason. A car will be sent for you. Or come to the door. Day or night, you'll be brought to me."

"That could be awkward if you're with someone."

"I won't be now that I've met you."

The declaration sent emotion skittering through her, too much and too varied to process. In the course of one day, she'd found herself hungering for two different men, caught in twin snares of attraction unlike any she'd experienced before.

She unlocked the helmet then straddled the bike, acutely aware of the way her cunt throbbed where it touched the Harley's saddle. Danger and desire were part of a chorus warring with caution, with the echoes of her mother's warnings against getting involved, and her own experience when it came to letting others close enough to hurt her, or be hurt by her.

"See you around," she said, putting on her helmet and fleeing his presence.

Eamon watched her as she sped away. A car left the curb and followed, the humans assigned the task of shadowing her.

He moved in the direction of Aesirs, aching with need and seething with frustration. And yet the encounter with her had also left him satisfied as well.

She would come to him of her own free will, of that he was certain. And when she did . . .

Desire pulsed through his hardened cock. Lust heightened now that he knew her taste and scent, and the heady feel not just of her body touching his, but the magic filling her. She was a seduction of all his senses, a siren call he doubted he could resist even if he wanted to.

She would belong to him. And undeniably, because she was *seidic*, he would belong to her as well.

Her foundling status gave him the advantage of knowledge. Her being changeling gave him the upper hand when it came to magic.

He intended to use both. Guiding her into her Elven heritage and away from human concerns. All while teaching her that he would also be her Lord, though she would be cherished no less because she yielded to his will.

Six

Seeing her act like a cat in heat had made him angry. It sickened him, the way she'd let herself be touched like a whore.

The beautiful gold surrounding her had darkened then turned ugly with streaks of red and blue when she and the blond-haired man kissed. It had made him queasy, looking at them together.

He wrapped his arms around himself, rocking back and forth to keep from doing what he knew he shouldn't do.

The blond-haired man was going back in the same direction he'd come from. In a minute he would cross the street. If the van hit him, then the man would never be able to touch her again.

"She's not your choice yet," he whispered in the darkness, rocking harder and not stopping until the man was out of sight.

Cathal leaned against the bar, surveying his domain. Despite it being a Monday night, the club was packed. Wealthy tourists occupied as many tables as the regulars, and beautiful, long-legged waitresses hurried to keep up with drink orders.

Onstage five brothers performed, two of them singing a perfect duet, their sound a great blend of folk and rock delivered with passion. The talent and the turnout should have left him satisfied, instead he felt almost as edgy as when he'd arrived at Saoirse.

He didn't need to wonder at the reason. Etaín.

His fingers tightened on the glass in his hand, a defensive move to keep from reaching for his phone. Behind him, the bartender asked, "Get you another drink?"

Cathal glanced down, frowning when he saw only ice cubes. "No."

He refused to anesthetize himself with alcohol, though given the number of times his drink had already been refreshed tonight, he suspected passing out might be what finally stopped his thoughts from repeatedly returning to Etaín. He wanted her and he wasn't used to having a woman say *not tonight*.

Looking away from the stage he scanned the room, seeking a distraction. There were plenty to choose from, some natural feminine forms, and others sculpted in expensive Swiss clinics by doctors who made a fortune creating perfection and hiding the effects of age.

A blonde caught his attention, and held it long enough for her to meet his eyes. Pouty red lips promised oblivion though they didn't inspire him enough to push from the bar and go to her.

When it became obvious he wouldn't, she leaned in, saying something to the women sitting at the table with her before rising and coming to him. "Dance?" she asked, her voice smoky and purposefully alluring.

"Why not."

He placed a hand at the base of her spine and guided her toward an area rapidly filling with couples attracted by the slow ballad.

"I'm Trina," she said, slipping easily into his arms, her lush body pressed to his as if they were already lovers.

"Cathal."

His cock stirred but didn't harden fully until he closed his eyes to savor the music and the sensation, and the woman in his arms became Etaín. Desire returned with throbbing insistency then, a demand to fuck and find release.

She made a purring sound of pleasure at the obvious interest pressed to the juncture of her thighs and belly. But when the song ended and he opened his eyes, she became Trina again, and he knew he wouldn't take this any further despite her sultry smile and sensuous clinging.

His pride and personal code prevented it. He wouldn't take what she offered while pretending she was someone else.

He wanted Etaín. Tomorrow he'd call her. He'd have her.

Etaín rode, sticking to city streets until she crossed the Bay Bridge. Then she headed for the darkness of canyons, places that seemed a world away, roads close, and yet remote enough that people could live a lifetime in Oakland and never be aware of them.

Occasionally she glimpsed headlights behind her. But a car wasn't a match for the bike and soon there was no light but what the moon and stars provided.

Keep going, the phantom voice of her mother whispered. *Leave and re-create yourself somewhere else.*

Too late for that, she silently replied, and why should she listen to the woman who'd abandoned her?

She gunned the Harley. Letting speed and curvy roads force her mind to quiet, to consume her attention until finally fatigue settled around her, threatening to become a shroud unless she slowed down and went home. She made her way to the apartment, parking then climbing the stairs to the studio above the garage.

Enough light streamed in from the streetlamps, passing through open blinds, that she could navigate through the tiny space. She took a shower in the cool anonymity of darkness, soaping her hands and sliding them over skin.

Cathal's image came first, bringing heat along with his erotic threat. Then Eamon's, bringing temptation and the fantasy of having them both.

She touched her nipples, grasped them, remembering the feel of Cathal's hand, the torment of Eamon's. Fatigue retreated as one hand slid downward, between her thighs, rubbing, stroking her clit, dipping into her slit as her fingers became a substitute for Eamon's tongue, for Cathal's cock.

Cathal and Eamon, neither of them dominated when it came to imagining herself beneath them, above them, between them in a tangle of arms and legs.

The hot water struck her skin and streamed downward, licking over her and heightening sensation as her breathing quickened and she found a small measure of relief.

She needed more. The pressure was building inside her from too much ink, too much touching—and yet, conversely, not enough touching.

Leaving the shower, she dried skin that felt too tight, as if it would split away and spill out who she was at her core. *I chose this*, she reminded herself. *I decided to stay in one place.*

Thoughts of Eamon intruded as she dried her hair, tempting her not only with pleasure, but with the possibility of answers. At a cost. Everything always came at a cost. And his?

Resistance rippled through her. Rebellion, as she remembered passing through the doorway of Aesirs into a place where the rich and powerful felt at home. A place the captain and his wife probably frequented.

She turned away from the mirror, blocking thoughts of the man she still thought of as Dad in unguarded moments, with contemplations of Cathal. It didn't bother her he was comfortable at Aesirs. Maybe because his public kisses and possessive touches had proven he was a man who dared to do what he wanted, openly and without worry about censure. Maybe because underneath the potent masculine charm and expensive clothing, there was a raw edge of suppressed emotion.

She pulled on a tank top and boxers then left the bathroom, no longer able to avoid or delay. There were tablets and pencils on a worktable, on the counter separating what served as a kitchen from the rest of the room, on the floor next to the mattress she slept on.

She lay down and finally let her mind go back to the one place in her day she didn't want to revisit, the hospital room and the woman left barely alive by the Harlequin Rapist. There was no point in willing Tyra's memories forward, they would come regardless. And though she wanted to sleep, a part of her fought it in an instinctive reaction to the horror waiting for her there.

It seemed like she lay on the mattress for hours before slowly succumbing, scenes passing through her mind, a montage of images, carnal and poignant and somber. Glimpses into other people's lives that were like looking into a shallow pool, reflections in ink, not stolen existence.

Salina with a girlfriend. Holding a leash attached to a collar.

Kelli saying goodbye to her daughter at an airport. Tears streaming down her face. Fear instead grief. Worry instead of regret.

Cathal in a hospital room with a teenage girl. That same girl lying glassy-eyed in a bedroom with posters on the wall, movie and rock stars. Cathal at a funeral.

Some small part of her sleeping consciousness recognized when the images stopped being random pictures caught in an accidental stream, and became instead memories to be secured behind mental barriers, because they were taken, possessed. They were Tyra Nelson's thoughts and perceptions, her reality.

The faces of rock stars and teen idols slid easily from bedroom walls onto the covers of magazines, a disorganized mess in a convenience store bringing a surge of irritation at having to straighten them for the tenth time since starting work.

She'd be glad to leave this job behind. It was one aggravation after another, and on top of it, now she had to worry about the walk home and the rapist loose in the Bay Area.

Not that there weren't plenty of rapists out there. She knew that firsthand. But this guy was worse than a drunk uncle or the men who didn't think *no* applied to them. This guy was scary psycho and deserved to be put down by a bullet. Death by lethal injection was too good for him.

I need to buy some pepper spray. It was a good thing she already had the knife. It'd saved her a couple of times.

With a sigh she crouched down in front of the magazine rack, her knees cracking and her back aching from being on her feet all day. *Just be glad for the job.* Times are tough. Bad enough there are teachers in line at the food bank. Job didn't pay shit but it was better than being on the streets.

Been there, done that, and managed to get off them. Managed to survive a few months of turning tricks before that crazy john scared her straight with his fists and his gun.

Eight months clean and every day she was getting stronger. Praise the Lord.

Magazines straightened, she stood in time to see the bitch fucking the manager walk in, a smirk on her face as she pulled a bag of chips off the rack and opened it, then snagged a soda, like she owned the place and everything was hers for the taking.

"Time for you to punch out. Overtime eats up the profits."

It's not the only thing doing it. And trust me, I'd like to do some punching.

She held the words back, biting her tongue to keep them inside. Didn't pay to make waves. Didn't pay to let some slut piece of trash get under her skin.

She had her GED now. Come fall she'd start taking classes at the community college. One step at a time and she'd get where she wanted to be.

Her stomach growled but damned if she'd give back a single penny to this place. She punched out, grabbing a jacket and leaving without saying anything.

A taxi went by, not a common sight in this neighborhood. She thought about trying to flag it down or going back in and calling for one, but didn't. The ride home would chew up the money she needed to buy minutes for her cell phone.

If she had a mind to splurge, better to detour a couple blocks and hit the McD's. She decided to go for it, practically inhaling the double cheeseburger in the parking lot and nursing the Coke for as long as she could as she walked, one hand tucked into her pocket, curled around the knife like it was a lucky charm piece.

The streets were deserted. For once she wished the gang bangers were hanging out like usual.

A car backfired and she jumped like it was a gun going off next to her. Fear surged through her. She needed to get home. Better still, the police needed to do their damn job and catch that serial rapist.

She stayed vigilant, aided by enough Coca-Cola in her system to make her bladder feel like a balloon just about ready to pop. If she didn't hurry up and get home, she was going to have a different problem to worry about.

Turning the corner led to another deserted street, quiet except for a few barking dogs and the caterwauling of some old tom. She heard muted music, mostly a beating vibration.

Along the curb, cars were parked practically on top of each other, bumpers nearly kissing. She noticed a van, black, like a hundred others she saw in a day. It looked empty but she wasn't taking any chances.

She didn't need a rapist on the loose to know how easy it was for some pervert to pull you into a van. It didn't even need to be dark for that to happen. Only a couple of weeks ago a ten-year-old girl was snatched on her way home from school.

She gave the van wide berth, congratulating herself on her street smarts; a second later her survival instinct kicked in.

Too late she realized she had swerved close to where a man was waiting. He was on her before she could scream, a gloved hand over her mouth and something pressed to her neck. Taser.

She lost control of her muscles and hot piss flowed down her legs, shaming her despite the terror pounding through her. The helpless feel of it carrying her back to the first time her uncle came around when she was home alone.

A piece of cloth was stuffed into her mouth. It tasted like dish soap. Another was put on top of it, tied off to make a second gag before a bag went over her head.

Her wrists were bound last, behind her back, just as control of her muscles was coming back and she might have been able to pull the knife and fight for her life.

She heard the slide of the van door opening, whisper-soft, like he was trying to hide it. Hope flickered to life. He wouldn't care what she heard if he intended to kill her.

I can survive this. I WILL survive this.

She struggled as he lifted and carried her. It didn't do any good but she wasn't going to give up. She wouldn't ever lie down and be a victim again.

Within steps he'd dumped her into the trunk of a car and slammed it closed. Terror surged into her at having been wrong about thinking the quiet van door meant something.

The engine came to life. In the tight confines of the cramped space, the acrid smell of pee and rubber and carpet sliced through the sack over her head.

She fought to get her hands in front of her. Prayed to the God she'd abandoned in childhood but found again in NA meetings.

Her heart tried to claw its way up her throat. She felt like she was suffocating.

Panic lent urgency to her struggles. She managed to dislodge the hood and rub away the gag. It took longer to dislodge the cloth stuffed into her mouth.

She gulped air, only barely stifling the urge to scream because all it would do was alert her captor. They were traveling fast, like they were on a freeway. No one was going to hear her now.

He hadn't bothered patting her down for weapons. If only she could get to her knife . . .

Her arms and wrists ached as she fought to get her hands in front of her. Sweat soaked the underarms of her shirt and her jeans were clammy and cold against her thighs. Her breathing became a harsh panting the longer she struggled.

Sobs clogged her throat when she felt the car begin to slow. As it crept along she strained to hear any sound other than her heart thundering in her ears, anything that would make her think her screams would be heard.

The car slowed more, then reversed and stopped. She rolled onto her back and drew her legs up against her chest, pain spearing through her shoulders at lying on them with her hands bound behind her.

A sound reached her, like metal doors being shut. Moments later a latch popped and the trunk opened to reveal the ski-masked man.

She kicked, making contact and sending him backward with the force of it, screaming then, praying someone would hear her as he returned to use fists to subdue her.

In his struggles to get her out of the trunk, the sleeve of his jacket pushed upward, revealing white skin above black leather gloves and the bottom inches of a tattoo that went all the way around his arm. Demons, a twisting mass of faces with their mouths open, inhaling souls and terror.

He jerked the sleeve down, calling her *bitch*, his voice holding panic, his fists coming faster. He managed to grab her legs and pull her from the car. Her head struck the bumper and then the concrete floor, sending sharp pain through her skull and then a nauseating throb.

There was a quick glimpse of oil stains and navy blue paint, a mud-smeared New York license plate. She fought when she saw the shipping container, flaked green and rusted.

Splinters from the floor tore at her face as she was dragged inside and onto a bare, heavily stained mattress. The doors slammed shut, trapping her in darkness and steel.

Etaín woke in a panic, the room loud with the sound of harsh breathing, the boxers and tank sweat-soaked and her body shivering violently.

She crawled from the mattress and got shakily to her feet, hugging herself, disoriented, stumbling to the bathroom and retching, though after the visit to the hospital there was little left in her stomach. She splashed hot water onto her face and the tattoos on her forearms warmed, as if absorbing some of the shock and horror, drawing it from her as the vividness of the nightmare memory began to fade.

She forced herself away from the sink, not allowing herself comfort, not then. Usually she started with her pencils, but this time she went to the computer, typing the words as if they were her own. Speaking for Tyra, who might never have any semblance of a life worth living after what had happened to her.

When the account was done she sent it to Parker, pushing the netbook away and reaching for pencils and paper. She matched images to the written account, compulsively drawing, every scene coming to life in a sequence she couldn't deviate from, like frames in a movie, fully captured and in color. Stark and brutal, terrible in the reality they portrayed.

When the last of them was done, she took a shower, tears for Tyra mingling with the water. She hugged herself, this time letting the heat sliding into the intricate, entangled vine tattoos weave a mental barrier.

It was like applying an emotional bandage to a nightmare reality so it was gone, but not eradicated. Separate, like horror-filled pages in a true crime novel she would always choose not to open in fear of reliving it. Compartmentalized behind a closed and locked door without guilt, so she could function, so she could go on to help others.

She left the shower and dressed though she felt far from normal. Her phone rang as she laced her boots. Parker. He must have been waiting next to his computer and held out for as long as he could before calling. She answered the phone, and by doing it, signaled she was finished drawing. He said, "I'm on my way."

"No. I'll come there."

Silence greeted the statement. She didn't explain herself. Didn't tell him she couldn't spend the remaining few hours until dawn alone and didn't want to have to make explanations to a friend.

"You're leaving now?" Parker finally asked.

"Yes."

"I'll call Trent."

The sketches were loose instead of bound. She gathered them, careful to keep them in order though she didn't look at them as she stacked, then rolled and placed the papers in a tube.

Capping the end, she put on her jacket and left, taking a direct route to Parker's place. He and Trent were waiting for her at the end of the narrow driveway. She stopped the Harley and pulled the strap attached to the carrier over her head, passing it to Trent because his hand was there for it first. He turned and jogged toward the front door.

"You want to come in?" Parker asked.

Her skin felt stretched tight, her insides aching, jittery. It was worse now than it had been in the apartment. She took off her helmet, affecting a casualness that didn't exist.

"Sure," she said, following him to the front door.

He opened it, flooding the porch with light and stepping aside to let her enter first. But the instant she was next to him he grabbed her hand, his anger and disappointment pulsing into her. "Christ, Etaín, what'd you take?"

She jerked out of his grasp, his touch and the accusation too much to handle. "What are you talking about?"

"You're standing in bright light and your pupils are fucking saucers so don't bother lying. You get picked up—"

Anger welled up. Hurt. She turned her back and headed for the bike.

"That's right, fucking run away, same as always," he yelled after her.

She felt the sting of tears and quickly suppressed them. She didn't need his shit, didn't need him ripping off the bandages covering the bad memories of her past.

They'd once been as close as if they were best friends, not just brother and sister—until the dreams started, the call to ink she'd once tried to silence with drugs.

She rubbed a hand over her face, hating the way it trembled just a little bit, like she really was strung out, a junkie needing a fix. And maybe she did need one, only it wasn't a high like the one Parker accused her of.

Cathal's face came to mind first, bringing heat to chase away some of the chill. She touched the pocket of her jacket, feeling the cell phone beneath her fingers.

She couldn't bring herself to pull it out and make the call. It was after hours, the club shut down for the night. He'd be in bed now, and maybe not alone.

Images from her dreams slid in. Cathal standing at a graveside. Cathal looking down at a teenage girl with a blank stare.

Etaín shivered. She needed comfort but she wasn't sure she could bear to touch someone, even him.

Memories of Eamon came, of his pinning her hands to the wall, then behind her back. *Aware* of the eyes on her palms but inviting her to come to him day or night anyway, assuring her she wouldn't find him with another woman.

She tugged on the helmet and straddled the bike, refusing to let the warnings of childhood or the danger he might represent stop her. She rode to Aesirs, taking the Harley over the curb and driving straight up the sidewalk to within steps of the front door. She didn't bother locking the helmet to the bike, just took it off and tucked it under her arm, part of her half expecting to be turned away.

She heard the chimes again as she approached, a hundred tiny fairy bells ringing in her ears. Fear tried to take hold and turn her from her course, but she refused to allow that emotion. She needed what she could find with Eamon too much.

The door opened as she lifted her fist to pound on it. A man stood there, as gorgeous as any of the ones she'd seen earlier. "Lord Eamon is at his home. I'll have a car brought around for you."

Lord. It fit Eamon. And maybe it explained the popularity of Aesirs, in part anyway. The masculine eye-candy still got the weight of her vote.

"I don't need a ride. An address will do."

"I'll send for a car anyway. You can follow it, or ride in it, as you choose."

Seven

Eamon stopped in the middle of one of the numerous walking bridges in the mazelike gardens of his estate. He crouched to watch the small leopard sharks swimming in the waterway, hoping the sight of them would grant him respite from the worry Etaín's continued disappearance caused.

She wasn't with Cathal. His home and club had been watched from the moment those following Etaín reported their failure.

The easy way she'd lost them in the canyons troubled him. Stirring misgivings and making him second-guess his decisions concerning her.

It didn't matter she'd lived this long without being discovered by others, or that she was in his city, in his territory. Even as wife-consort, the threat of having her taken and made prisoner by another only lessened somewhat, while the worry and the need for vigilance increased as the focus shifted to keeping her safeguarded against assassination because of what she was—not just *his*, but *seidic*.

He frowned, wondering at what concern had taken her to the hospital, his resolve to extricate her from the grip of the human world strengthened by knowledge of her reason for going to the homeless shelter afterward. Bad enough that she put her ink on clients, but to apply it to all comers at an event to serve the most disenfranchised of human society . . .

Frustration washed through him. Short of imprisoning her himself, he had no way of preventing her from seeing her obligations through. He needed time with her. A chance to set hooks of desire and magic and knowledge. She'd soon stop thinking herself human, stop identifying with them.

He was prepared to take on the responsibility that came with adding a few more of them to his household, but more than a few? His mouth tightened into a grim line. He had no desire to become known as either a Lord overly fond of humans, or one controlled by his *seidic* consort.

With each human introduced to a world where Elves and Dragons and other supernatural beings not only existed, but lived hidden among them, the potential to have it become widely known expanded exponentially. There was much he'd risk for Etaín, but not exposure.

The sea breeze ripple of magic across his skin had him standing and waiting for Rhys to wind his way through the maze. "You've got news of her?" he asked as soon as his second came into view.

"Yes. She's on her way here."

The tension flowed out of Eamon, confidence returning in his choices concerning her. "I will see to her myself when she arrives."

The sedan Etaín followed entered Pacific Heights. It didn't surprise her Eamon lived in an area of embassies and mansions with multi-million-dollar views. But as they approached a walled estate doubt crept in. What was *she* doing there?

She slowed the Harley. Crashing at Derrick's place seeming like a better choice.

The gate slid back before she could act on the thought, revealing Eamon standing in the driveway, sand-gold hair unbound and flowing over a naked, smooth chest. Hands shoved casually into loose black pants ending at bare feet.

Need returned in a hot wave, the subtle vibration of the bike between her legs heightening the desire and turning it into a craving to have Eamon's hand push beneath her waistband and cup her mound.

The sedan continued on but she stopped just inside the gate, racking the kickstand and dismounting several car lengths away from him.

He came to her like fog moving in off the bay, his presence blocking out everything else. Enclosing them. Encapsulating time so nothing existed, nothing mattered except the two of them.

He invaded her personal space, invaded her senses. Determination poured off him. Desire.

Taking the helmet from her unresisting hands, he set it down on the seat then took her wrists as he had before, anchoring them behind her back with one hand and pulling her to him.

She felt the hard ridge of his erection and pressed more tightly to it, grinding against him.

He made a sound of hunger, using the lever of her captured wrists to still her movements so he could control the rub of her engorged clit against his cock.

"I've been this way since you first entered Aesirs," he said.

"Painful. Or so I've been told."

"Very. But now you're here there will be an end to my suffering."

He unzipped her jacket, cupping her breast possessively before capturing her nipple between his fingers and squeezing, making her clit throb. He bit her neck then sucked hard enough she could feel the pull of it between her thighs.

She closed her eyes, giving herself over to pleasure, and as if waiting for just that signal, he stopped, drawing a sound of protest from her, then one of need when he touched his lips to her ear, flicking his tongue into the canal in a heated prelude to filling her channel with his cock.

"Did you come for this?" he asked.

"Yes," she whispered.

Eamon released her wrists but captured her hand in his. Concern spiked through the desire, worry again about how she spent her time among humans.

She was weaker than she'd been when he saw her last though the magic possessing her remained a sensuous weave of water and fire, earth and air and spirit, all in exquisite balance. All so old it was as if she survived only on tendrils slipping from Elfhome and into this world.

Her magic twined with the magic he'd gained control of in order to survive his changeling years. Tugged, as if it would use his strength to fortify her.

He drew her into the maze, stopping next to a small fishpond containing koi and illuminated by lanterns reminiscent of those found in Japanese gardens.

Taking her into his arms, he leaned in, teasing her with the lick of his tongue along the seam of her mouth, with small sucking bites to her lower lip.

She tangled her hands in his hair, clung to him, making a whimpered sound of need that he answered with the full press of his mouth to hers, with the hungry thrust and rub of his tongue against hers.

The leash he'd held himself on broke then as the old magic possessing her pulled at his own in primal demand, mingling in an elemental connection that had no focus other than like seeking like.

With a moan he guided Etaín down to the lush, velvet-soft grass. Covered her body with his.

He wouldn't allow her to make him come, not here. But that didn't mean he couldn't grant her a release. Show her a small measure of what he could do for her.

He entwined his fingers with hers, their palms touching as he held her hands to the soft grass in a submissive's pose, deepening the kiss, grinding his pelvis to hers.

Even separated by clothing, it felt exquisite to have her beneath him. To have her lithe body and supple curves pressed to him.

When small sounds of pleading came from her he lifted his mouth. Intense satisfaction surging through him at what he saw in her face and eyes, desire having a name, a single focus. Him.

"What do you want?" he asked, needing to hear her say the words.

She laughed, thwarting him, the low husky sound of her voice like a fist around his cock. "You have to ask?" she teased, challenging him.

She tempted him to drop some of the glamour he wore like a second skin to hide the iridescent glow of magic and the telltale tips to his ears. "I could make the gardens ring with the sound of my name, spoken by you in pleading tones."

"Do it," she said, her eyes holding carnal knowledge, a dare he couldn't resist answering.

In a quick movement he rose to his knees, straddling her, kissing her again. Changing the focus of his assault by deftly opening her shirt and unclasping her bra, baring her breasts.

The nipples were pebbled by cold air and the heat of lust. They were the dark pink of fine roses and sweet, sweet wine.

He could no more stop himself from touching his lips to them than he could prevent himself from cupping the exquisite mounds they served as peaks to.

She arched her back at his touch, spearing her fingers through his hair as if she'd keep him forever at her breasts.

She needn't have feared he would abandon them quickly, not when she was so very responsive, when the rasp of his tongue and tug of his lips drew cries from her.

His cock screamed at the continued confinement, ached as the tip grew wet with escaped arousal.

He ignored the building urgency, forcing himself to concentrate on demonstrating his power over her in a victory that would ultimately lead to physical satisfaction for the both of them.

Beneath him she writhed, thwarted him by commanding, "More. Harder. Touch me." And he answered the call of lust and magic, the powerful attraction between them, unable to deny her entreaty.

With a final suck to her nipple he released it and kissed upward. His cock throbbing in time to the wild pulse of magic between them that marked each of her heartbeats. He pinned her wrists to the ground again as his fingers freed the button and zipper of her jeans.

"I want you," she said, filling his mind with the roar of fire and causing his testicles to pull tight as her hips lifted off the ground, hurrying the descent of his hand as it pushed beneath the waistband of her panties.

Her shiver of pleasure was mirrored by his shudder of desire at encountering her stiffened clit and slick, swollen folds. "Are you wet for me, or for Cathal?" he asked, trying to find the shape of their future together.

"Maybe for both of you. I fantasized about you both earlier."

He cupped her mound and slid his fingers into her slit. "Did you touch yourself like this when you did it?"

She tightened on his fingers. "Yes. I imagined your tongue. I imagined Cathal's cock."

A second shudder went through him. A moan escaped at envisioning her naked, touching herself, pleasuring herself as she thought about sharing herself with him, and with Cathal.

"Maybe you'll get both," he said, her fantasies and magic creating a desperate ache to be inside her. "But for now, I'm all you need."

He pulled arousal-slick fingers from her channel, reveling in her whimper of protest and the lift of her hips. Needing to make good on his threat, to torment her until the garden rang with the sound of his name.

He grasped her clit, manipulating it. Stroking and tugging and pinching until finally she began repeating his name over and over, begging him to fuck her.

Everything inside him bridled at her use of the word, rebelled at the casual, meaningless implication of it. He covered her mouth with his. She'd soon label what was between them lovemaking, but for now it had to be enough she'd come to him. That he would have her before Cathal did.

Using fingers instead of his cock, he thrust into her channel, the wet heat and tightness surrounding them, making him fight to keep his hips from jerking in time to the press and retreat of each stroke. In desperation he blocked the image of taking her, concentrated instead on the rub of his palm over her stiffened clit.

She came and he took her cry of release, swallowing it down as if in capturing it, he could anchor her soul and her magic to his. Silently promising as he did it that this was only the beginning of what they would one day be to each other.

The edginess that had ridden Etaín for days left in a rush of ec-stasy, a searing release that had her sliding into languidness. He stood, pulling her to her feet and taking a moment to do up the front of her shirt.

The trip to his bedroom was made through a house navigated by moonlight. "Shower with me," he said, the look in his eyes holding the promise of so much more.

"It'll be my third today."

"I think I can make it stand out in your mind from the others."

She stepped away from him, her gaze traveling downward, stop-ping where his cock was clearly visible against the front of his pants. "We'll see."

"A challenge?" The silkiness of his voice sent a shiver of heat through her.

"You could look at it that way."

She bent down and removed her socks and boots. Straightened and shed the jacket and shirt and bra, tossing them onto a nearby chair and leaving her standing in as little clothing as he wore. "Just so we start out even."

"Hardly." His attention was locked on her breasts. "The advantage is yours."

Desire coursed through her, a small thrill of power. Her hands went to the waistband of her jeans. "Are you sure you want a shower?"

She hadn't thought it possible his eyes could darken any further with lust but they did. She undid the top button, the zipper. Revealing blue panties designed to make a man rip them off a woman's body.

In less than a heartbeat he did just that. Jerking jeans and panties to her ankles, shifting the advantage with the press of his mouth to her cunt as his hands caressed her buttocks, holding her in place.

A flick of his tongue over her clit and she shivered at the pleasure his mouth delivered. "Please," she whispered, and he stood, pulling her bare lower body against his clothed one, his hands settling possessively on her naked back.

"You'll please me first."

His voice held a hint of danger that turned her on. Confidence adding to his allure. She liked the edge that came with knowing he wasn't one of her pretty boys.

She ground against his erection, spikes of hot sensation shooting through her at the contact of clit to cock. He lowered his head and thrust his tongue into her mouth, delivering a decadent taste of herself and a hot rush of lust.

Eamon knew he was playing with a dangerous fire. He couldn't take much more of the torment. Already he felt enthralled by her.

"Shower," he said, forcing his mouth from hers though he conceded a measure of defeat by leaving his hand on her as he guided her to the bathroom suite.

He braided his hair, tying it with a cord left on the counter for that purpose. Then reached around and gathered up the silky strands of hers, quickly plaiting it.

The muscles in his stomach went taut with the feel of her fingers curling around the waistband of his pants. He shuddered in pleasure when her thumbs stroked the length of his cloth-covered erection.

Moisture beaded on the tip of his cock head. He knew he needed to be careful about dropping his guard with her. Already she wielded far too much power over him.

"Do it," he ordered. Daring her. Commanding her. Testing them both.

She unbuttoned his pants. Opened them, freeing him, her expression appreciative, her lips parted, a tropical tempest about to descend and he knew he wouldn't survive it.

He stepped out of his pants and opened the shower stall, turning the water on as he guided her to stand beneath the heated spray. Her smile was as devastating as everything else about her, sending molten lust surging through his cock and testicles.

He wrapped his fingers around her braid, unable to stop himself from slamming his mouth down onto hers. Taking. Giving. His hunger intensifying as water struck their bodies in a sultry caress.

"You're like a drug," she whispered against his lips. "I can't get enough of you."

"I don't want you to."

She laughed and his cock jerked against her belly, drawing her attention to it. He could barely breathe as she kissed downward, pausing at his nipples, sucking one while her fingers captured the other. Tugging, squeezing, delivering pain and pleasure that blended into something sublime.

"Etaín," he said, hand tightening on her braid, urging her downward, his buttocks clenching.

She went.

Done with tormenting him.

Done with foreplay.

Or perhaps only intent on discovering the extent of her power over him.

He didn't care as she took him in her mouth, a hand fisted around his cock so she could control the depth despite his thrusts.

White noise filled his head, the raging of a hurricane swirling faster and faster. Gaining strength with each lash of her tongue and pull of her mouth. Building with each of her swallows until it could no longer be sustained, until it dispersed in an explosion of pleasure, a shearing apart that left him fighting for breath, his hands against the shower wall to keep him standing.

She rose from her crouch, wildness glittering in her eyes, and his hands fell away from the wall in favor of pulling her against him, preventing her from speaking by covering her mouth with his.

It was decadent, carnal. Empowering to taste himself on her lips, salt-water and magic.

He stroked her back. Caressing her buttocks and holding her mound against his cock, the water and her presence in his arms reviving him, hardening him again.

He was afraid to allow words. Afraid if he parted from her long enough to leave the shower and make it to the bed, she'd demand he use a condom and deny him the full intimacy of being inside her without protection.

He was impervious to human disease. And she was a changeling, infertile until the magic filled her completely.

Desire pooled in his testicles as she touched him, her hands gliding over his wet skin, the hungry noises she made a hot stroke to his ego, an urging for him to do the very thing he'd fantasized about since first looking down and seeing her on the terrace at Aesirs.

He crowded her against the wall, lifted her. Soul-deep satisfaction filled him when she wrapped her legs around his waist, his kisses and touches destroying her inhibitions and eradicating rational thought.

He found her opening and pressed into her, the heat of her channel and the tight clamping of it on his cock a ravenous welcome that had him thrusting, rushing toward a climax that left them both shaking with fatigue.

Long moments passed before they managed to leave the shower. As he handed her a towel, she said, "I'm on the pill, in case you start to freak out when morning shows up."

He laughed, suspecting she'd always be able to startle one out of him. "And I've got an extremely clean bill of health, in case panic sets in at dawn."

"Then we're good."

Her eyes grew slumberous, fatigue and profound weariness returning to her, as he watched her towel herself dry, making him wonder where she'd been and what she'd been doing since riding away from him at the tattoo shop. Within minutes of lying down on his bed she was asleep.

He settled next to her, fully relaxing for the first time since the bells sounded at Aesirs when she passed through the wards. Even in sleep she looked neither harmless nor defenseless, though there was an open quality to her that accentuated her beauty, drawing him deeper into the maelstrom of emotions her existence and her presence had brought into his life.

He traced a fingertip down the length of her nose, touched it to her lips. He had more questions now than before.

At first glance the colorful vines and hidden sigils inked into her forearms were exactly like those he'd seen in an ancient text that was part of a Dragon's hoard. But looking at them closely, he could see additions, modifications.

Tracing them, he could feel the hum of magic, elemental power mixed in with the ink. He wanted to know how she'd come by the tattoos. Who had made the ink and put the designs on her skin.

She was mystery and puzzle and obsession. She needed him. And he, in turn, needed her, not for himself alone, but for those who called him Lord.

The Elven weren't so much magical beings, as repositories of element-born magic with a will that began exerting itself anywhere between the ages of eleven and thirteen. Its arrival marked the beginning of a changeling process lasting for a dozen years, or twice that number, and ultimately ending in one of two ways, death, or a lifelong balancing act between controlling the magic or being controlled by it.

For many of his kind, the magic came with a voice that whispered its demands. Cajoling and tempting. Ordering and begging, playing on emotions and hormones.

Humans would label it schizophrenia. Elves labeled it a curse brought upon them from being forced to live in this world rather than Elfhome.

In the land of his ancestors Elves lived in harmony with the elements, serving equally as vessel for the magic and wielder of it. The changeling years were merely schooling years, not a struggle for survival as they were in this world.

Ultimately she might be the answer, her ink a way to quiet the voice magic had in this world and the dangerous demands it could make on those it possessed before they managed to control and, therefore, possess it. And if not quiet the voice, then at least the soul sight of her touch would allow him to pass judgment on those whose acts required it.

He freed her braid and spread her hair across the pillow in wet, golden waves. His cock hardened with memories of her in the shower, water cascading over her skin. Her mouth delivering heated bliss and nearly unbearable ecstasy, the sensations heightened as he stood in his element.

Fire, too, was his element. With a whispered summoning of will he brought its warmth, drying her hair before his own. Then he curved an arm around her waist, pulling her back against his chest, his cock throbbing in proximity to her wet, heated sheath.

"You will be mine," he murmured, giving a fleeting thought to Cathal Dunne and wondering if the human would have to be made part of his household as well.

Eight

Watching the news bored him. Even looking at the huge TV screen on the wall, it was hard to pay attention.

He wanted to see if they did a story on the Harlequin Rapist. He wanted to know whether or not the woman was dead. But when the news people sitting behind the long desk opened their mouths, all he heard was "blah, blah, blah, blah, blah." It was irritating, like yellow jackets buzzing around meat.

He dipped his spoon into the bowl, maneuvering it through the milk and separating out the last of the green Fruit Loops by herding them into a little cluster. Just as he scooped them up, the screen flashed to a black woman holding a microphone and standing in front of San Francisco General Hospital.

Right away he knew she'd never be a choice, but he looked down at her arms anyway. They were covered.

He scooted forward then glanced over his shoulder to see if his brother had noticed what was on the news, but no one was there. Kevin must have gone into the bedroom.

The woman said, "This is Latoya Logan. As you can see we're at San Francisco General Hospital where police have confirmed that the Harlequin Rapist's latest victim is in intensive care.

"Police are refusing to give any details as to the nature or severity of her injuries. The hospital staff is also refusing to comment, either on the *victim's condition or the rumor that taskforce members brought in a psychic to help them catch the man who has been terrorizing Bay Area women for months."*

The scene changed to the studio. The woman newscaster said, "Latoya, it was my understanding that an artist was brought in, leading to speculation the latest victim can identify the rapist."

The reporter in front of the hospital appeared in the upper corner of the TV screen. She said, "Right now it's not clear whether the woman they brought in is an artist or a psychic. Off the record, I have been able to confirm that a woman was brought in, and that she is not believed to be officially connected with the taskforce."

"Have they released the latest victim's name?" the male newscaster asked.

"No. I—"

"Hold on, Latoya," he said. "We've got breaking news. A spokesman for the taskforce is about to make a statement."

The scene cut away, going to the room they always showed the taskforce in. Scooting closer, so he was barely on the couch, he concentrated on the faces like he always did, so he'd recognize them in case they somehow started getting close.

The FBI agents were to the far left. The blond one was at the very end. Next to him was the dark-haired one. Usually he didn't remember names, but he remembered theirs because once he'd lived in a home where there were two brothers named Parker and Trent.

Next to the FBI were police officers from different cities. He knew where a couple of the cities were, but not all of them.

A policeman from San Francisco was the only one standing. He motioned for the reporters to be quiet and said, "First of all, the taskforce wants to quell rumors of having called in a psychic. We have not done this, nor will we be doing this. The Harlequin Rapist will be stopped and brought to justice as a result of thousands of dedicated man-hours arising from the cooperative efforts of local, state, and federal law enforcement personnel."

He smiled. They always said that.

He didn't know whether to believe them about the psychic, but he wasn't worried. His brother believed in psychics and supernatural stuff. He didn't.

A reporter yelled, "I heard that an artist related to a high-profile SFPD captain was brought in. Is that true?"

The policeman ignored the reporter. His expression got grimmer.

This is it, he thought, feeling a little burst of excitement.

The policeman didn't disappoint him. He said, "At five minutes after midnight, the latest known victim of the Harlequin Rapist was pro-nounced dead."

The room exploded with the sound of reporters shouting questions but all he heard was, "Blah, blah, blah. Blah, blah, blah."

He turned off the TV and lifted the bowl to his mouth, drinking the rest of the cereal and milk then carrying the bowl to the sink. The blankets and pillow he used for sleeping on the couch were already folded and put away. The only thing he had to do was take a shower so he'd be clean.

People noticed when you stank, especially if they had to spend time close to you. It made you stand out in their memory and then they talked about you after you left. He didn't want either of those things to happen because of his visit to the tattoo shop.

Cathal woke in a tangle of sheets, his hand fisted around an erection, his body humming from erotic dreams starring Etaín. Frustration rode him along with the lust. He couldn't remember the last time he'd settled for his hand instead of a woman's mouth or cunt.

"Fuck."

The word sent a jolt of sheer need through him, followed by a surge of anger at not being able to peel his fingers away from his dick and go take a cold shower.

He slid his hand up and down on his shaft, helpless against carnal fantasies of having Etaín beneath him, thighs spread as he fucked her.

His breathing grew hurried as he imagined what it would be like with her, his heartbeat erratic, the strokes harder, faster, until jets of semen escaped, splashing onto his chest and abdomen in a hot wash of release.

It didn't improve his mood or reduce his frustration.

He got to his feet and went to the shower. He wouldn't let her stay under his skin like this. He'd have her. He'd convince her to help his family. Then he'd be done with her.

Liar.

He hardened again thinking about her, fantasizing about her on her knees in front of him, her mouth pulling on his cock instead of his fist. Sucking him until he found a second release as water sluiced over his skin.

Cursing, he left the shower and toweled dry, every nerve ending oversensitized, abraded.

His cell phone rang as he stepped out of the bathroom.

Crossing to the nightstand he picked it up. Sean.

"You somewhere we're okay to talk?" Sean asked.

"My place."

"Good enough."

It should be. He paid Sean a fortune to keep it and the club free of listening devices.

Cathal willed himself not to get into a pissing contest over not hearing from Sean the night before. Venting that way wouldn't help but he couldn't completely keep the bite out of his voice when he asked, "You have anything you want to share?"

The pause on the other end told him Sean was trying to decide whether to let the barb roll off him or not. He finally answered in a *just the facts, and nothing but the facts* tone.

"I got a tracker on the bike, found out where she lives. She went home and stayed there, alone, lights out until a little after one. I had someone watching, gut instinct, and it's your dime anyway.

"At two fifty-three she leaves on the Harley. Makes a beeline for the Sunset District. Pulls in where two guys are waiting for her in the driveway. She hands something to one of them and he heads into the apartment. She and the other guy follow, but at the door they get into an argument.

"She takes off and goes to a place I'll come back to in a minute. There she knocks on the door and a few minutes later, follows a sedan to an estate close to where your old man and your uncle live. Another guy is waiting for her there. Far as I know she's still there."

Jealousy gripped Cathal and he didn't like the way it felt. "Who?"

"As in *who* is she with? Blond guy. Long hair. Shirtless. That's all the description I got. But the address, now that I can tell you something more definitive about. The house is owned by a corporate entity, a name you'll be familiar with. Aesirs."

Eamon.

"Fuck!" Cathal couldn't hold the curse though it was directed as much at himself as it was at Eamon. He should have called her last night. He should have told her she could call, regardless of the hour. They must have hooked up after she left to meet with her brother and—

Reason overtook anger. Barely.

The timing didn't work for it to be a planned date. Everything about what Sean described seemed off, skewed into weirdness until Cathal connected her handing off something with remembering how he'd wondered if the call from her brother meant a visit with a crime victim.

"Who lives in the Sunset District?"

"Take a guess."

"Her brother."

"Right in one and not easy to confirm. She goes by a different first name than the one she had as a kid, and there are very few pictures of her even from then, but you'll recognize who she is when I give you a last name."

"What is it?"

There was an explosion of breath. Not a good sign. "Chevenier."

Surprise passed through Cathal like an electric charge. He remembered the scandal, only because his father and uncle had talked about it at the dinner table, approving of the fact that a cop who had married into a wealthy and powerful old San Francisco family not only had the balls to acknowledge a bastard child publicly, but take her into his home and raise her.

To be sure, Cathal asked, "As in, daughter of Captain Chevenier?"

"That's right. And sister of Parker Chevenier. Does that name ring any bells?"

Cathal searched his memory but didn't come up with anything. "No."

"How about FBI. The Harlequin Rapist taskforce. And while we're on the subject, is she a psychic, an artist, or a psychic artist?"

Uneasiness exacerbated the edgy frustration Cathal already felt. "You want to get to your point here?"

"I take it you haven't brushed up against the news yet this morning."

A glance at the twisted sheets on his bed had Cathal baring his teeth. "No."

"There's a story circulating about the taskforce calling in a psychic to help them identify the Harlequin Rapist. The source is supposed to be someone at San Francisco General. The claim is that members of the taskforce were seen bringing in a woman who has helped on at least one other case, the one where that kid was traumatized in a home invasion at the beginning of the year. There's also widespread speculation this unknown person is related to a high-level SFPD captain. You want to add anything here?"

"When I called you yesterday she was on her way to meet her brother."

"Then the news that the last victim—now dead—saw something might not be too far off. Since you're paying for my time, I'll give you my opinion. The leak could be for real, or it could be a deliberate attempt to direct this sick bastard at a certain target—Etaín—with her permission, I'd assume, though you know how assumptions go. Look up victim profile and she's a ringer for the women this guy goes for when he grabs a white one. My advice to you, which you might want to pass on to your father and uncle, is to stay away from her until this plays out and the attention of the taskforce and the media aren't on her."

"Fuck!"

"Yeah. Well, I'll keep tabs on her movements with the tracker, but that's all for now."

"Call me when she leaves Pacific Heights."

"Will do."

Cathal hung up. He hesitated for a second, then direct dialed his father.

His father answered immediately. "Your uncle just left. He saw something on the news that upset him."

Cathal rubbed a hand over his chest. He had the feeling everything was spinning out of control. "You calm him down?"

"For now. But Denis can't take much more in the way of bad. He needs something good to keep him holding steady, like you showing up for dinner tonight with that woman you're interested in."

Cathal's gaze once again went to the bed with its tangle of sheets, empty of the woman who'd invaded his dreams and was with another man right now. Determination eradicated any whisper of conscience. He'd have her beneath him by morning.

"Make it a late breakfast tomorrow."

"I'll tell Denis. I'm counting on you, son. Don't let me down."

Cathal's hand tightened on the phone before he set it on the nightstand. He dressed, a plan already forming, so after eating breakfast he went directly to Stylin' Ink.

Her bike wasn't there, but then Sean hadn't called, so he knew it wouldn't be. She was still with Eamon.

The thought made his mood ugly and dangerous, a combination

capable of sending a musician crying from an audition. He shouldn't care where she was or who she was with. On some level he recognized that.

It didn't change anything.

The best he could do to manage the jealousy eating at him was to tell himself she was a challenge. And he wasn't used to losing.

Through the window, the only person he could see was Bryce. Perfect. The conversation during dinner had made it clear to him that Bryce and the other two, Derrick and Jamaal, were more like family to Etaín than coworkers.

He entered the tattoo shop, knowing the advantage was his because Etaín had already given him the leverage he needed.

"She's not here," Bryce said.

It took effort not to snarl. "I know."

Cathal extended a hand and introduced himself. "You're the one I'm here to see. Etaín mentioned Salina and her band. I'd like to get in touch with her as a surprise for Etaín."

Bryce laughed. "Etaín passed on going home with you, huh. You must have spooked her. What happened?"

Cathal fought to keep his lips from pulling back and his fury from rising. "Her brother called."

Bryce's amusement died in a frown. "Asshole."

"She took off afterward. I haven't heard from her since." The inclination toward violence heightened as he imagined her naked, lying beneath Eamon.

Bryce looked at the computer screen, moving and clicking the mouse on the counter. "A couple of hours and she'll be here."

"I'd rather see her at my club later tonight."

"Slick move. So that's where Salina comes in. You give her band a chance to play at Saoirse and Etaín is grateful, meaning maybe you get laid instead of getting the brush-off."

Cathal managed to keep his temper in check. Barely. "I don't need gratitude when it comes to Etaín. I don't need to pay a woman for sex, in favors or in hard cash. Not that what happens between Etaín and me is your business."

"Good thing to know but you're wrong. Coming here and asking for Salina's number makes it my business."

Cathal pulled his phone from his pocket and called up Etaín's number before showing Bryce the screen. "I don't give a fuck about Salina and her band. Any day of the week I've got a dozen musicians trying to crawl up my ass. It suits me to combine business with a surprise for Etaín but I'm flexible when it comes to arranging time with her."

Bryce laughed. "Don't hold back just because Etaín and I are tight. You know, you're not the type she usually goes for. But I'm thinking maybe that's not a bad thing. She needs someone who's not going to let her walk away after a hot night between the sheets."

Cathal's cock throbbed in anticipation of having that hot night. And though his rational mind denied Bryce's assumption that this was about more than a casual fuck, the jealousy clawing through him made it a lie.

He could tell himself he was doing this in order to keep Etaín from ending up on a collision course with his uncle, but there was more to it than that. What had begun as duty, the lesser of two evils, had morphed into something else the moment he'd seen her through the front window of Stylin' Ink.

A couple of clicks with the mouse and Bryce lifted the shop phone, punching in a number. "*Hola, chica.* You interested in playing a gig at Saoirse?"

From across the counter Cathal heard the scream.

Bryce handed off the phone. "All yours."

Cathal didn't bother with setting up an audition. Drinks on the house made even the worst band survivable as far as the club's reputation went.

It took less time to outline his requirements and expectations than it had taken to get Bryce to make the call. Failure to deliver wasn't an option. Not on Salina's part. And not on his when it came to meeting his father and uncle for breakfast and having Etaín accompany him.

"No problem," Salina assured him for the fourth or fifth time. "Etaín won't let me down. She knows how big a deal this is for the band. I'll come by the shop and get her promise in person. When does she work today?"

"You'll have to ask Bryce." Cathal passed the phone back to Bryce and left the shop.

Fierce desire moved downward, settling in his cock at the prospect of Etaín coming to the club. He'd warned her what would happen if she stepped foot in Saoirse.

Tonight he'd make good on the threat. Then follow it up with a long encore at his house.

Nine

Etaín woke to the feel of a warm chest against her back and a hardened cock against her buttocks. She turned to face Eamon, a heated tide of pleasure rolling through her at the sight of him sleeping, the sheet falling erotically across his abdomen.

Last night there hadn't been time to study him, but this morning she took the opportunity to appreciate just how beautiful he truly was.

His features appealed to her as an artist and a woman. Aristocratic nose and chin. Lips that could thin with censure and anger, but, as she had reason to know, could also deliver on the sultry promise of passion.

Need unfurled in her belly. She pressed her thighs together, enjoying the swell and heat of desire. Enjoying the memory of what it had been like with him.

Portraits weren't her natural calling, but looking at him, she thought she could spend hours capturing his image on paper, his moods and expressions, all the subtle nuances of who he was.

Glancing away from him, she took in her surroundings for the first time. The multi-multimillion dollar view of the ocean was breathtaking, but it faded into nothing compared with the paintings hanging on the walls.

Cézanne. Van Gogh. Henri-Edmond Cross. Georges Lemmen. Post-impressionists she'd fallen in love with when she'd taken an art class.

The sight of them made her shiver in an ecstasy there was nothing carnal about. She left the bed, drawn to the artwork though standing a breath away brought uneasiness. *Why had he sought her out?*

Glancing at her palms, she saw the answer there but was unsure of what she would do with it. What he might tell her about her gift and how to gain better control of it would come with a price. And given the masterpieces gracing *Lord* Eamon's walls, she doubted she'd be willing to pay it.

She shrugged the concern away. She'd lived this long without understanding the full truth of what the call to ink meant. She could go a lifetime not knowing.

She was happy most of the time, which was more than most people could say. She loved how she spent her days and valued the friendships that formed as a result of it. And if she wanted to mix things up, she had standing invites to work in Vegas or LA as a guest artist.

Moving from one painting to the next, she studied them with the same intensity she'd studied Eamon, as if she could know everything about them and capture a part of their essence in her own art. She finished with the Lemmen, then turned to find Eamon awake, on his back, watching her, the sheet tented as a result of his erection.

It was a draw of a different kind and one she couldn't resist. She crossed to the bed and straddled him, leaving the sheet between them.

Her hands went to his chest and he immediately imprisoned her wrists.

"Afraid of what I'll see?"

A soft laugh answered her, and a release of her captured wrists. "Do your worst."

"And have you forget me?"

"There's no possibility of that."

"How can you be certain? It's happened before."

He took her hands, holding them so his thumbs brushed over the eyes on her palms. "Spend time with me and I'll give you the answers you need."

It was something she couldn't allow herself when it came to lovers. Something she wasn't sure she'd want even if it were possible, especially if it came with boundaries and conditions. She felt sure involvement with Eamon would bring them.

She glanced down at their joined hands, feeling each of his strokes to the inked eyes as if they were connected directly to a coil of need in her belly. "How do you know what they mean? How do you know about any of it?"

"I've studied magic my entire life."

Her first impulse was to laugh. She stifled it. "Magic?"

"You don't believe in it?"

In the power of belief, definitely. In abilities that slid into the paranormal, sure, she'd have to be an idiot practicing denial not to. But magic . . . She shrugged. "I've never given it much thought."

She tugged her hands from his and leaned forward, placing her palms against his smooth warm chest and changing the angle of her hips so her clit pressed to his sheet-covered erection. A spike of pleasure shot through her, and from the sudden lowering of his eyelids she knew he wasn't unaffected.

"This is the kind of magic that interests me the most," she said, rubbing his nipples with her fingertips and feeling them harden.

His expression went taut, color fanning across his cheeks. He reached up, tangling his fingers in her hair and applying pressure, bringing her lips to his.

She went, but not all the way. Or not fast enough. He lifted to meet her, giving her a hungry moan, his tongue thrusting against hers as he rolled them, putting her beneath him. The sheet disappearing with the movement.

She liked his weight. His strength. The hard press of his body against hers and the inherent danger she sensed in him.

The last should send her running, the same way his obvious wealth should. But the only thing to escape was a whimper when he took his lips from hers.

"Don't stop," she whispered, lifting, engaging him again with the touch of her mouth to his, with the coaxing of her tongue against the seam of his lips and the slow sucking of his when it came out to play.

A hard throb went through Eamon's cock, a wave of heat as he remembered her mouth on him in the shower. With a touch she'd wrested control of the situation away from him, turned him from his mission to convince her that she needed him for more than this.

He ended the kiss for a second time, his mouth going to her ear. Her breath caught when he captured a velvety lobe. He caressed it with his tongue, pulled the lobe deeper. Sucking. Laving.

The breathy sounds she made excited him. The way she ground against his hardened length had him fighting the urge to join his body to hers.

"Now," she said. "I want you now."

In the end it would be *always. I want you always*. But he wasn't so foolish as to voice that claim, or yet so enthralled he wouldn't attempt to use the desire between them to gain an advantage with her.

A thrust and he'd be inside her. And inside her, all that would matter was finding release.

He left the lobe, tongue tracing the edge of her ear, going to the tip that would soon become pointed but was already a pleasure zone. He stroked and sucked, leaving to dip his tongue into her ear canal with an erotic thrust.

She wanted a fuck. He gave her the slow mimic of one, a tormenting seduction as his lower body ruthlessly pinned hers to the mattress.

He would have kept her from orgasming if it were possible. But she was too sensual a creature, too uninhibited in her passion to depend on him for ecstasy.

She writhed, using his cock to deliver what he would have staved off. Pressing and grinding her clit against him.

Her cry of release and relaxed body filled him with satisfaction regardless of his intentions. One day she'd trust him enough to give him total control of her pleasure, allowing herself to be made helpless in tethered restraints.

A shudder went through him at imagining her held open and bound to the bed. It took effort to keep from sheathing himself inside her. He needed her to understand the danger of her situation so she would come to him. *She* needed it. Without him she might not survive the changeling period. And even if she did, there were other dangers equally deadly.

With a final swirl of his tongue in her ear, a last slow suck to the tip, he shifted onto an elbow and rubbed his palm over her nipple, considered how much knowledge to offer. "You use this as an outlet," he guessed, pausing to give the rigid areola a kiss before meeting her eyes. "You use sex to vent the pressure that comes from using your gift."

She laughed. "And maybe I just enjoy it."

He should have expected her amusement, her casual deflection. He wondered if everything would always be a battle with her, and had the question answered when her hand went to his ear, tracing the edges, stroking the tip as if she knew its curve was an illusion.

He shuddered, closing his eyes as intense pleasure cascaded through him, a wave of heated lust that made him vulnerable.

She took advantage of the weakness, tangling her other hand in his hair and pulling him downward as he'd done when she straddled him.

Her mouth went unerringly to his earlobe, her tongue to the earring, not a piece of jewelry but a focus for drawing on elemental power.

He moaned as fiery desire engulfed him. A need easily battering aside any intention other than to have her again.

He entered in a single thrust. Followed it immediately with a second. A third. A relentless, frenzied pounding that didn't end until her channel clamped down savagely on his cock, demanding he yield to her.

He came in a violent release that left the sound of the surf in his head for long moments afterward, a chaotic crashing smoothing into a calm that was only surface deep.

I could get used to having this, Etaín thought, her eyes still closed as she basked in the endorphin afterglow of great sex.

Eamon's harsh breathing slowed and pleasure-inducing lips nuzzled her ear, sending a shiver of reawakened desire through her. "Stay the day with me. We can even spend some of it away from bed."

It was tempting. He was tempting.

She opened her eyes and turned her head to look at him. He was on his side, everything about him calling to her. *Like to like.*

Being with him felt good. Alarmingly good.

"Who are your parents?" he asked, diminishing the warmth with his question.

"Not the man whose name is on my birth certificate. Not the woman he's married to."

"No, they wouldn't be. Not with your gifts. Who is your father, Etaín?"

A burst of pain went through her chest with thoughts of the captain. "I don't know who donated the sperm."

"And your mother, her name?"

A second pang came and went, more distant and less painful than the first. "A new name in every city, and there were a lot of places."

"You don't know her *true name*?"

The words whispered through her like a shared secret, his use of them further proof of the connection between them. Like to like. Etaín was her true name, not one of the many she'd been known by as a child.

"What do you want from me?"

She hadn't intended the question, hadn't consciously been aware of the intention to give it voice, but once out, she didn't attempt to recall it.

His hand cupped her breast, fingers taking possession of a nipple. "The same thing you want. This."

"And that's all?"

"I told you last night I wouldn't always settle for a meaningless physical act. You don't have to settle for it either, though permanence comes at a price, for you and for your lover—or lovers, if you choose to take more than one."

"What's the price?"

"I can only give you a partial answer. The most relevant to you right now is that there is no undoing the choice once it's made. Permanence is just that, permanent."

Her heartbeat accelerated at the thought of it. Did she want the risk that level of intimacy would bring? The pain that would ultimately arrive when love became conditioned on the demand to conform to someone else's expectations? "I think I'll pass on the permanence." *For now*, a traitorous internal voice added.

A muscle spasmed in his cheek. She'd noticed the *tell* before. *Lord* Eamon's aggravation at hearing something he didn't like.

She glanced away. The sight of the Cézanne and Cross on the wall spooked her further. "I need to get to work."

He didn't attempt to stop her as she left the bed. He watched, sprawled like a naked god as she went to where her clothing lay tossed on a chair.

She didn't flee to the bathroom but dressed where she stood. Not a slow show meant to seduce, but not a hurried covering up of flesh, either.

He rewarded her with a husky laugh and rose from the bed, coming to her. "Stay for breakfast?"

It was the press of his will—real or imagined—that had her saying, "No."

This time a tightening around his eyes marked his displeasure. He picked up his discarded pants and pulled them on. "Very well, I'll escort you to your bike."

They made the trip in silence, though unlike the night before, the house wasn't lit only by moonlight and she wasn't preoccupied with getting inside and getting fucked.

The paintings on the walls of the bedroom were only a hint at the magnitude of his wealth, and his desire to surround himself with beautiful things. Everything she saw, furniture included, was exquisite enough to have been created by masters.

She doubted even the family the captain had married into could boast this kind of wealth. Though she'd never been inside their mansion, not when she was believed to be his bastard child, or later, when paternity tests proved she wasn't.

Her existence remained a stain on their name and pride. A blemish he refused to remove by forbidding the truth to spread beyond his family and theirs.

The sight of the Harley was a breeze blowing away thought and hiding pain with the promise of an escape that tasted and smelled of freedom.

Eamon took her arm when they reached the bike, turning her into him before she could put the helmet on as a shield to expression or a barrier to sensual persuasion.

"It's taking considerable restraint on my part to allow you to leave."

Fear slid down her spine at the threat inherent in his words. But it was a fear mixed with eroticism, turned hot by the hard press of his erection against her and the alluring scent of him.

This wasn't the end of it. She read it in his eyes. She read it in herself.

Like to like. She couldn't shake the attraction. Didn't lie to herself by saying she wouldn't be with him again.

"Don't think I'll become one of your possessions," she warned.

His laugh made her ache for the feel of his cock inside her again. "Never that, Etaín. I think it's far more likely I'll be the one possessed."

Foolish or daring, either could describe it. She leaned in, initiating a kiss.

He didn't make her coax or beg. His arms became steel bands around her as he met the kiss, matched it, eliciting a moan from her in the process and making her melt against him and very nearly forget her intention to leave.

As if sensing her weakening resolve, the kiss changed into something soft, a mesmerizing rub of tongue against tongue, the velvet press of lips as his hands pushed under her shirt and settled at the base of her spine, delivering heat and the remembered pleasure of skin touching skin.

She closed her eyes and he became the entirety of her reality. One kiss merged into another, and finally into a trail of them up to her ear. "Join me at Aesirs for lunch and dinner," he murmured, his breath a warm, evocative caress. "And if not that, then at least promise to end your day here."

The sensual fog lifted with another of her mother's lessons relentlessly revisited, drilled in at every opportunity. Never, ever make a promise you aren't willing to pay dearly for if you didn't keep it.

"No promises," she said, relenting before she thought better of it and adding, "but a maybe."

Not a twitch this time, but with his cheek to hers, she felt the tensing of his jaw. "Then I'll settle for maybe."

He brushed a kiss against her ear. "Cathal I'm willing to tolerate, but don't go elsewhere for this."

She shivered. Erotic fear returning, mixing with wariness at her own continued desire to play with fire. "What makes you think I'll get other offers?"

He laughed, a husky masculine sound striking a chord deep inside her. His fingertips traced the sensitive outline of her ear. "Your looks alone draw men and women alike to you. Your inherent magic intensifies the attraction. Combined they're both lure and aphrodisiac."

His mouth returned to hers in a slow, thorough reminder of what he could do for her. And when the kiss ended he said, "If that isn't enough to persuade you to return, Etaín, then think about what it would mean to be the master of your gift rather than its slave. I've got the answers you need not just to control it, but to survive it. If I'm right, you soon won't be able to manage your abilities as you've done up until now."

For a second time in as many days, Eamon watched her ride away from him. She fled, but a part of her hadn't wanted to. She'd found it difficult to leave, reaching for him one last time despite whatever it was that drove her to escape his presence. He would continue building on the start he'd made with her.

He turned toward the house and found Liam, his third, leaning casually in the open doorway, a dark voyeur witnessing Etaín's departure. "So you continue to allow her freedom," he said.

Eamon closed the distance between them without defending his actions. Liam asked, "Did you learn anything of her origins?"

"No."

"I thought as much." Liam gave a slight shake of his head. "I'll say what Rhys was too tactful to. This is a bad course of action. If you won't order us to keep her contained here, then at least let us find out all we can about her."

"I have another task for you. On Saturday she'll be tattooing in a fund-raiser for a homeless shelter. Ask for volunteers among the humans pledged to us. If there aren't enough of them, then choose from among them and make it a requirement. Organize them so they present themselves to her in a steady stream. I don't want her applying ink to anyone on Saturday who isn't one of ours."

"She might have other thoughts on the matter of who she'll tattoo."

"I'll be there to guide her actions."

Liam's eyebrows rose. He spared a quick glance in the direction of the now closed gate to the estate, his lips curving upward just slightly. "That should prove interesting."

"You test my patience."

"A hundred years in your service and neither of us is dead. Forbearance is thy name."

Liam left the doorway. "I'll make the rounds among the humans and those holding first responsibility for them. You might consider though, the risk of what she could learn about us when she touches those we send to her."

"Minimal," Eamon said, frowning as he remembered how the magic in her had weakened between her departure at Aesirs and her arrival at the estate.

"Are you so sure her gift isn't stronger than you've judged it to be?" There was subtext in the question, concern rather than Liam's usual biting amusement.

"Is that your not too subtle way of saying you fear my wards didn't hold and she's done something to me?"

"You are not unaffected by your night with her."

Eamon couldn't deny the charge. His cock hardened at the mere thought of being with her. His body already ached for the feel of her skin touching his and the meld of magic to magic, though only moments had passed since she'd left the estate.

"I'm not unaffected by her. She is my future wife, after all. But I haven't been changed by my involvement with her. Nor will I be."

"My relief at hearing it is incalculable." Liam's smile held just a hint of teeth. "Now I'm off to attend to *your* business, ever hopeful that while I do it, I don't stumble upon a woman tempting enough to make a permanent fixture in *my* life."

Ten

Bryce looked up from the sketchpad on the counter as Etaín entered the shop. "You hear from Derrick after you left here last night?" he asked.

"No."

"Shit. Shit. Shit. Goddamn I'm going to fire his ass. I've already had to deal with one of his pissed-off clients."

She sighed, worry for both Derrick and Bryce dissipating the lingering afterglow of having been with Eamon. "Boyfriend troubles. Terminal stage. You know that, Bryce."

"Easy for you to sound so fucking calm about it. Tell me you've come up with someone to replace his last fucking choice."

The image of Eamon lying naked on his bed caused pleasure to lap over her like warm surf. This was San Francisco. Someone at Aesirs had to be gay and available.

"Working on it."

"Work faster."

She suppressed a smile. Any faster and she'd be a no-show. Then Bryce would be dealing with another really upset client.

Normally she'd tease him about yesterday's blonde and getting laid. But doing it would lead to her admitting where she'd spent the best part of the night and she wasn't ready to share that information or to examine the reasons why.

She retrieved an art file from his office. Opening it, she took a minute to visualize how she'd work the ink into the light brown skin of Tori's upper arm.

The design incorporated musical symbols and a stylus into a blossoming long-stemmed rose. It symbolized Tori's hopes and dreams of making it as both a poet and songwriter.

"Ready?" Etaín asked a few minutes later when Tori walked in.

Tori bounced up and down on the balls of her feet. "More than ready. I barely got any sleep last night."

"Let's get started then."

The prep work went fast. And after the shock of the first few minutes of pain, Tori settled in, sharing some of her poetry while the outline was going in.

Her melodic verse and passionate words were close enough to music lyrics it took Etaín a while to realize Tori's emotions weren't plunging into her bloodstream. She considered it as she set the liner aside, taking a moment to wipe away the excess ink before moving on to the shader.

Eamon had dangled knowledge like a lure. He'd said there were ways to control her gift, but she didn't see anything different about this morning over any other, other than having started it in Eamon's bed.

Probably just the sex, she decided. It *had* been pretty mind-blowing.

She picked up the shader just as the shop door opened. The sight of Salina brought immediate concern. "Hey, everything okay with the tat?"

"Can I come back there?"

"Sure."

Even regulars didn't dare trespass into the work area without an invite. It was one of Bryce's hard and fast rules.

"Sorry," Etaín said to Tori. "This'll just be a minute."

"No problem. I'm cool with you taking time out for Salina."

"You two know each other?"

"Yeah. I love listening to Lady Steel play."

Salina shrieked at that mention of the band, coming around the counter like a Mack truck and slamming right into Etaín, arms going around in a hug that lifted Etaín off her feet.

It was like getting tangled in a live wire. Emotion streaked into her, a high octane whip of excited happiness to match the scream. Followed by an awareness of how their breasts were touching and a surge of desire.

So much for the immunity she'd been experiencing earlier. "You want to put me down now and tell me why you're here? I gather it's not because there's a problem with the art."

Another hug, lust receding under a wave of solid affection, and Salina released her. "You're the best."

Etaín laughed. "Yeah, I am, though Bryce might argue it."

Salina gave a joyous whoop. "This isn't about art, it's about music. You mentioned me to Cathal Dunne. He called me!" She raised both fists and did a victory shimmy. "The band is playing at Saoirse. Tonight!"

Pleasure flooded Etaín, her own this time at seeing how much the gig meant to Salina. It spread through her with thoughts of Cathal and the suspicion this had come about because he wanted to see her again.

"Promise you'll come see the band tonight," Salina said.

"Wouldn't miss it."

Salina grabbed Etaín's hands and despite the purple latex separating skin from skin, a blast of intensity and purpose came with the touch. "Promise, Etaín."

She would have anyway, but the prospect of seeing Cathal sent heat sliding down to pool between her legs. Maybe if she alternated between the two men, she could prolong the time she could be with them before some natural barrier was eaten away by too much intimate contact, and she began erasing who they were by taking their memories.

"I promise."

It elicited another screech, followed by another hug.

Salina released her. "Gotta go. See you tonight. You, too, Bryce. And Tori. I'll square your being there with Cathal."

She left in a rush and Etaín picked up the shader, turning back to Tori. "Ready?"

"Yeah. That was way cool what you did for her. I'm heading to Vegas for my cousin's bachelorette party right after I leave here but I'll be thinking about you guys tonight. You know any musicians you could hook me up with?"

"Get in line," Bryce said. "She's got to find someone for Derrick first."

Tori rolled her eyes. "Not that kind of hook-up. Somebody looking to collaborate with a songwriter now that Etaín knows what my stuff is like."

"I'll think about who might be a fit," Etaín said, stretching Tori's skin and returning to the tattoo, Tori's emotions quiet against her palm as she finished the work, then swapped the shader for a mirror.

"Perfect," Tori said, looking at the tattoo. "Absolutely perfect. I don't want to cover it up."

"It's just for a little while."

He hung back when he saw her putting bandages on a black girl's arm. He knew her routine when it came to this.

Bandages. Give the person a piece of paper. Then walk them to the counter so they could pay.

The thrill he'd felt at seeing the black girl with her grew as he watched them leave the workstation. They weren't touching, but if he squinted really hard, he could see a thin golden string connecting them.

A little shiver of rightness passed through him. If he could make the black girl the choice for next time, it would be more special because they'd known each other. He'd even add a tattoo on his leg for her, too, instead of on his arm like he did for the others that weren't white.

He crossed the street. Slowly, but not too slow. This part always made him the most uncomfortable.

His heart pounded so hard he was afraid it would burst. His palms got sweaty and he felt like he was going to mess his pants.

It was always the worst right before he got close. And then it was over.

He either felt excited because he knew she was going to be his choice. Or he felt disappointed. Though sometimes he felt relieved, too, because it meant he could mark one possibility off and have more time to concentrate on the others.

He opened the door and stepped into the shop as the black girl was paying. The taste of sour milk and Fruit Loops filled his mouth.

He made himself take a few more steps inside.

The black girl moved away from the counter, saying goodbye.

The door opened and closed behind him. Then she looked away from typing something into the computer and he knew there'd be no other choice for him.

She had dark, dark eyes and real blonde hair. She was perfect.

He ducked his head. A giggle slid up his throat at the thought of getting a harlequin tattoo here with her watching. He managed to swallow it down.

"Help you?" a man asked. It was the artist who had lots of tats and body piercings.

"I want to get some work done."

The artist stepped up to the counter. "Name's Bryce. Custom or flash?"

Fear froze him. Stupid, stupid, stupid not to think about having to give a name and fill out forms if he did this.

The urge to leave was strong. But the need to spend time with her now, imagining what it was going to be like when they were finally together, was stronger.

"I'm Kevin," he said, using his brother's name. "It's a custom piece but you can copy what's already there."

Bryce glanced at her and said, "You want to take this one, Etaín?"

His stomach roiled. He took a step backward before he could stop himself.

The door opened behind him and she said, "I'll take Jason unless Derrick shows up by the time I've got him prepped."

She came around the counter, passing close. His mouth went dry and he stuffed his hand into his pocket, unable to keep from touching himself.

"Where's the tat?" Bryce asked.

His face went hot when he thought Bryce might have guessed what he was doing. He pulled his hand from his pocket.

"On my calf."

He started to bend down and roll up his pant leg so he could see her but Bryce said, "You can do that on the table. Let's take care of the paperwork first."

It was hard for him to concentrate on filling out the forms with her talking behind him. Her voice made him think of birds singing. It was beautiful like she was, golden sunshine the same as the glow around her when he squinted.

He put down Kevin's information. They liked a lot of the same things so it was easy to pretend they were the same person.

Kevin was older, but they could almost pass for twins. It was always better to keep things simple rather than having to remember a complicated lie.

She took the man named Jason to her workstation. *Fag.* Like the one she worked with.

He hated that about San Francisco, all the queers. He'd hold his pee all day rather than go into a public bathroom unless Kevin was there to watch his back. He didn't understand how his brother could stand living here.

When the last form was filled out, Bryce took the clipboard and put it out of sight under the counter. "Come on around."

Bryce's workstation was right across from hers. He rolled up his pant leg, then sat down.

A shiver of pleasure went through him. Even though she'd never know he was doing this as a way to remember their time together, he liked it that she was going to see him get this particular tattoo.

"I just want the number thirteen put on the new one," he told Bryce. "The letters will have to wait."

It's a little early in the day to be wearing all that leather," Etaín said as Jason peeled off a vest that laced in the front and on the sides.

He dropped it to the floor next to the massage table and lay down, faceup and chest exposed, the leather of his pants leaving no doubt how well-endowed he was.

Lifting his hips, he said, "Have to give the tourists what they expect to see."

Etaín laughed. "They'll definitely get an eyeful. I'm not sure the cow that skin came from wore it any tighter than you do."

"Some things are better if you have to expend some effort to get at them." He wriggled his hips. "For you, I'll even make an exception to my 'no women allowed' policy."

"So I'd be a one-time deal?"

"No. Packaged like I am, there's no point in pretending humility. Let's just say, when I decide to show someone the goods, the first round is just a warm-up event."

Etaín grinned. "Well, in the spirit of all this honesty, I'll admit to being totally flattered you would peel off that leather for me. I'll also shed the modesty. If I took you up on your offer, being with me would either cure you or ruin you, depending on your perspective. The next morning you'd wake up a straight man."

"No! Not that! Anything but that!" he said, falsetto voiced before cracking up.

"You two are so full of shit," Bryce said.

Etaín glanced over at his workstation. He was smiling but the guy he was working on looked like he was about to bolt for the bathroom to hurl.

Her gaze dropped to his calf and the work there. Crying clowns were embedded in flames, their faces misshapen, oozing downward like they were going to slough off, a number and pair of initials on each of their ruffled collars.

The skin art had a seriously twisted vibe, and the thought of touching him, adding her ink to what was already there was enough to make her skin crawl. Give her Jason any day. He was a work in progress, and one of only a few she would step in and add ink to when she wasn't the original artist.

She turned her attention back to him. The outline was already in place on his chest, and had been for five months. Ultimately it would become part of a full body suit.

The design was Japanese in style and color. Heroes and lotus blossoms with cultural and personal motifs woven in, a tribute to Jason's heritage though he was American born and the only hint of it was a slight tilt at the corners of his eyes.

"You don't seem surprised Derrick's not here," she said.

"Saw him at a club last night. Mascara running and eyes nearly swollen shut. I asked him if I should call and reschedule. He said no and I figured chances were good you'd be around. Whatever time you've got, I'm all yours."

It took a few minutes to clean up from working on Tori, then she pulled Jason's art and studied what was there, checking it against the drawings and making decisions on which area she'd work and what colors she wanted. She set up with new ink and several different shaders, already clean and ready to go. Like most artists, she had a small collection of tattoo machines.

She prepped Jason's chest, getting rid of hair and applying Vaseline. "Speaking of Derrick, you know anyone—"

"I'm the last person you want to ask, babe. Pain is my middle name. I embrace it."

"We'll see about that." She touched the tip of the shader to a lotus petal, believing what Jason said when two flowers later, the leather pants were still outlining an impressive erection.

She was just starting a third flower when Bryce said, "Asshole alert, Etaín."

Jason opened his eyes and turned his head. "They look like Feds."

"That's because they are," Bryce said.

Etaín felt queasy, the breakfast she'd eaten when she went home to shower and change after leaving Eamon threatened to come back up. Parker and Trent being here couldn't mean anything good.

Her stomach cramped at the prospect of touching another one of the Harlequin Rapist's victims. Turning off the machine, she set it on the table. "Sorry, Jason. I need to talk to them." She'd do it outside, because she didn't think she could handle it in the close confines of the shop.

"Hey, if you need help. If you need a lawyer—"

She brushed latex-enclosed fingertips over his shoulder in silent gratitude. "I'm good. The blond is my brother."

*H*e nearly bolted from the chair when he saw the taskforce members. He didn't because he'd have to run right past them and the thought of it froze his muscles in a message he remembered from living with his mother.

Stay still. Stay still. They wouldn't notice him if he stayed still.

His heart pounded so hard that only the sound of her voice made it past the rush of it in his head. The blond is my brother.

A wild giggle surged upward. He clamped down on it, choking it off.

The reporters were telling the truth about an artist being taken to the hospital. The police were lying.

Cops always lied.

She left her station, stirring the air as she passed. The smell of her changed the fear into nervous excitement.

Another giggle bubbled upward. She didn't know who he was. She couldn't.

He looked down at his leg and concentrated on acting normal. The tattoo he was getting for her was almost done.

The door opened and closed. He glanced up as she said something to the two FBI agents and then all three of them walked out of sight.

Bryce said, "The number thirteen? Right?"

He closed his eyes so it'd be easier to imagine having her with him. "Yes."

"What do you want?" Etaín asked, the air crackling between Parker and her as a result of their last encounter.

"Did you hear the news?"

She resisted the urge to fuel his anger by saying she'd been too busy fucking to pay attention to the news. "No. Is there another victim?"

"No one's been reported missing yet."

"Then why are you here?"

"Tyra Nelson died last night," Trent said.

Sadness smothered Etaín's hostility. "Her family?"

"They made it in time. They were with her. We're here because we need you to reach out to other tattoo artists." He glanced at her brother, prompted him by saying, "Parker."

Parker visibly forced himself to relax. He opened a folder she hadn't noticed and extracted a piece of paper, holding it out to her.

Chills swept over her at the image there. She recognized it instantly and panic swept through her as she fought to keep *all* of Tyra's memories from spilling in, as if the sight of the tattoo had opened a crack in the barrier walling off her reality from Tyra's, as if Eamon's warning about not being able to manage as she always had was coming true.

When she was certain of her control she looked again, forcing herself to view the drawing as if it came from a terrible book about someone else's life. They'd cut away everything else but the tattoo, then enlarged it. A band of demonic faces with their mouths open in screams and glee. Clawed and horned, some of them with tails, a seething mass of evil that would unofficially identify the Harlequin Rapist.

"You agree this was done by a professional?" Parker asked.

"Yes."

"Then there's a chance the guy we're looking for has had work done in San Francisco. Other artists will talk to you where they won't give us jack shit. Someone might recognize this and provide a lead on this guy. It's a long shot but you're making the rounds because of the fundraiser, which gives you the perfect opportunity to ask about the tattoo. Just come up with some reason besides the truth. We don't want to accidentally tip this guy off if we end up getting close to him this way."

She looked up at Parker, surprised he knew she was involved in the fund-raiser. Saying no wasn't an option and wouldn't have been even if she hadn't lived those moments of Tyra's terror. She took the drawing and folded it, slipping it into her back pocket. "When's the funeral?"

"What does it matter? You're not going."

"And I gave you permission to boss me around when?"

"Don't be fucking difficult, Etaín. The reporters will have a field day if you show up and they make the connection between the two of us. Somebody talked about your visit to the hospital yesterday, probably the nurse who recognized you."

Trent interceded again, putting a calming hand on her shoulder. "For all we know, this guy thrives on the publicity. We'll have people at the funeral but he might be smart enough to be satisfied with what ends up in the news. Even if you haven't been identified, some asshole cameraman will end up zooming in on you because you fit the profile. This guy is looking for his next victim now, if he hasn't already found her. He'll strike in six to fourteen days unless something's happened and his pattern is changed. Your being at the funeral would be like painting a target on yourself."

Then use me to draw him out.

The thought came in a wave of nausea and was accompanied by a terror that had her mind closing on it. She couldn't make the offer. She couldn't say the words.

"I need to get back inside. As soon as I finish with Jason, I'll visit some shops."

He knew it was her though his back was to the door. He felt her like sun against his skin.

Pulling cash from his wallet he tried to count out what he owed. He had to do it three times, at first because he was listening to see if the other two were with her. And then because she came into view.

He kept getting distracted by her. She was so, so beautiful.

He wished she wasn't wearing a long-sleeved shirt. He wanted to see her bare arms. He wanted to know if she had tattoos there.

His mother had had them, the ugly homemade kind, not skin art like he and Kevin got.

It didn't matter whether she did or not. She was his choice.

He turned away and went to the door. There was a rush of fear as he opened it. A giddy sense of relief when he stepped outside and there were no cops waiting for him.

The thrill of what he'd just done made him laugh out loud. He wouldn't get this close again, not until it was time to take her. But he couldn't stop himself from looking through the window and seeing her one last time before he left.

His pleasure diminished. Not a popped balloon but a leak that filled with anger and made him feel sick inside.

She was talking to the fag again. It made him remember the times his mother had brought strangers home. Once she got high, she always forgot about him and Kevin being there. It didn't matter to her what happened then.

He didn't want to think about that right now so he squinted, blocking out the queer and seeing only her, surrounded by a golden glow. Nothing would change his mind now. She was his choice.

He didn't have to worry about watching the others anymore. He just had to figure out where it would be safe to take her.

Usually the watching and planning made it more exciting. But he didn't think he'd be able to wait once he had the chance to take her.

Already he felt like crying at being apart from her. His heart hurt thinking she'd forget all about him.

Eleven

Etaín gave Jason until well after lunchtime. By then her stomach was growling and her hands were cramping while he was zoned on endorphins and in a place a client into the BDSM scene had likened to subspace.

She wiped off the excess ink and leaned back to assure herself she'd reached a good stopping place for Derrick. "How about we call it a day? I need to visit some other shops. You know about the fund-raiser on Saturday right?"

"Already spreading the word about it." Jason opened his eyes and craned his neck, trying to get a view of the new ink.

She passed the mirror. "There's going to be live music though I don't know who yet."

"I'll let people know." He moved the mirror around. "The work's totally excellent. Thanks for stepping in."

"No problem."

She took the mirror back and bandaged him, giving him the lecture and the handout before ringing him up and saying goodbye. As she cleaned her equipment and station afterward, she made a mental list of the places and artists she'd show the drawing to.

A chill of fear slipped in at how easily Tyra's reality had threatened to overwhelm her own. Looking at her palms she felt sweat trickling down her sides.

What if she was wrong? What if she couldn't keep going like she had been, not understanding the full truth of what the call to ink meant? Only managing it instead of controlling it?

Wiping damp palms on her jeans, she told Bryce, "I'm out of here."

He glanced up from the woman he was working on. "Do me a favor sometime today?"

"What?"

"Derrick's not answering his phone. Can you swing by his apartment? Do what you can to get him put back together? And after you've done that, tell him I've cleared his appointments for tomorrow, but he'd better put on his big girl panties and come to work, or call his clients and reschedule them himself. I'm not his daddy or his mommy. I'm his boss and I've got enough of my own shit to deal with."

"I'll stop by. But I'm going to pretty up your message."

"Pretty it up all you want, just pass it on."

"I'll do it before I go to Saoirse. See you there?"

"Wouldn't miss it." He grinned. "I don't think you're going to get rid of Cathal very easily."

She started to say she hadn't even slept with him, but held the words because Bryce would say, "Yet," and she wouldn't be able to deny it.

"I'm gone."

She was leaving a different shop a couple of hours later when her cell rang. The incoming number was unfamiliar, but she recognized Trent's voice.

"Nothing yet," she said before he asked. "I've shown it to nine artists so far."

"It's a long shot. But we've got to turn over every stone until we find the one this slime-ball crawled out from under."

"I'll call if something pops."

She closed the phone.

It rang before she could pocket it.

"I'm actually calling about something else," Trent said.

Fear jolted her. "Did something happen to Parker?"

"Shit. Sorry. No. He's good."

Her fingers whitened against the black of her phone. She hated that the thought of something happening to Parker still had the power to rip her apart, when he'd written her off unless he needed her help on a case.

"Then why the call?" She cringed at hearing herself sound like a cold-hearted bitch.

The silence on the line lasted long enough she thought maybe Trent had hung up.

He finally answered. "Look, sorry. I'm screwing this up royally. This doesn't have anything to do with the taskforce, and Parker doesn't know I'm calling you. A situation came up that requires a tattoo artist, like yesterday. It's a paying job. Will you help me out?"

A Fed who apologized, that and the fact he'd served as a buffer earlier with Parker tilted the scales in his favor. "When?"

"Now."

"I can be at Stylin' Ink in about thirty."

"No." The quickness and force of it made her pulse jump. "This needs to be kept private. It's cover-up work. The next time this guy is seen in public he's got to be wearing different ink."

"Gang tats?" She was halfway to changing her mind about doing it, paying job or not. She didn't like the dreams that came with that kind of work, not stolen memories but dark reflections of them caught in ink.

"Yeah. But he's one of the good guys. Been on our team from the start."

"Undercover?"

A long pause. "Yeah. Fair enough. You'll find out anyway."

"How big a project is it?"

"Don't know. I haven't seen him since he went under. We grew up together. He's only been in San Francisco a couple of hours."

"Where do you want to do this?"

"I'll pick you up and take you there."

"I've got to be somewhere later tonight, with a stop somewhere else before then." Regardless of the cause she wasn't going to break her promise to Salina.

"You're doing the favor. You say when you have to leave and it'll happen."

"Is he on this side of the bay or Oakland side?"

"This one."

"You know where I live?"

"Yes."

"Pick me up there. I need to get my kit and change clothes, in case there's no time to go back home."

"I'll head that way. Look for a silver mustang. I won't get out."

"Okay. See you in a few."

She made it home fast, an advantage of riding the bike. After putting the Harley in the garage she took the steps to her apartment two at a time, stripping as soon as she closed the door behind her.

A quick shower later and she put on a fuck-me bra and panties before going to the closet. She wasn't much for clothes. Jeans worked for her most of the time. Throw on a long-sleeved shirt and she was ready to go.

Despite being a tattoo artist, she didn't expose the work on her wrists and arms. One of her mother's lessons, maybe too deeply engrained to ignore. Beyond that, she'd never found it mattered what she wore when it came to men. It all came off anyway if she decided to spend the night.

She reached for a light blue shirt, a memory halting her before she tugged the garment from the hanger. Cathal with his dark-as-sin presence and carnal warning about showing up at Saoirse wearing a short skirt.

A hot roar of lust arrowed straight down to her cunt. Her hand followed, sliding beneath the waistband of her panties. She'd see him tonight. She'd be with him tonight.

Her labia grew flushed and swollen, her fingers wet from arousal. A honk in front of the apartment had her pulling her hand back with a soft laugh. Just like a cop to show up and spoil the fun.

She took in her options, going for black, a long-sleeved blouse with buttons up the front and a tight mini-skirt that make her think of Jason's leather. She finished the look with short black boots, not bothering with hose or makeup. She'd never needed either.

A quick transfer of cell phone, billfold, and the picture of the tattoo into a small black purse and she was ready. The kit stayed packed with everything she needed for working away from the shop or the apartment.

On the way out she snagged the black Harley jacket, silently chiding herself for treating it like a security blanket. Trent had pulled up close to the bottom of the steps. She stowed the roll-on suitcase and got into the car.

He gave a low whistle. "Hot date tonight?"

"That's on a need-to-know basis."

He laughed, making his good looks even more pronounced. She wondered how he managed to spend all day working with her brother, Mr. Humorless. Mr. Conform or You're a Low Life, a belief he got from the captain. Then again, Trent was a Fed. So he must fit the mold, too, even if he knew how to lighten up.

"So where are we going?" she asked.

"Quinn's at a hotel in the Castro."

Her eyebrows lifted at that. "A gay FBI agent?"

"No. Castro District was a safe place for him to hole up. That's all."

"Works for me. I've got to stop at a friend's place. His apartment is in Corona Heights." Still, she was curious. "So what gang did this guy infiltrate?"

"Aryan Brotherhood."

Her hands closed in automatic self-defense, fingers covering her palms at the prospect of applying ink to someone who'd managed to successfully pass himself off as an AB member. She focused on something else. "Do you guys have any leads on the Harlequin Rapist, besides the tattoo?"

"The hotline rings constantly, but the tattoo is our best shot. By far." He glanced at her. "After the story broke about the visit to the hospital, Parker and I came clean with the rest of the taskforce—without mentioning your name or admitting your relationship to him. We talked to the profiler.

"Now that we know the escalation of violence is the result of Tyra seeing the tattoo, the profiler thinks it's possible the next victim will be black, kind of a do-over to rebuild his confidence. He's only solidified his signature and started alternating between the different victim types in the last couple months. Before then, almost all of the women were black. The profiler also said that if the news media finds out who you are and starts showing your picture, it might actually make you safer. You'd be high risk for the rapist then. And this guy goes for low."

Uneasiness rippled through her. A need to flee as memories of those years with her mother came unbidden, bringing with them her mother's favorite refrain as they moved from one place to another, to remain uninvolved, invisible to those around them.

Parker and Trent might not have mentioned her by name, but they'd told a bunch of cops skilled at investigation. Her involvement wouldn't remain secret for long, and if—*when*—they caught the Harlequin Rapist and found the tattoo on his arm, she'd be asked to help more often, exposing her gift in an ever-widening circle.

Chill bumps multiplied on her skin. Her heart skipped into a fast beat, then a faster one when the car accelerated and took a corner sharply enough to bang her into the door.

She glanced at Trent and saw his attention alternating between the road ahead and the rearview mirror. "Problem?"

He made another turn. And another. Heading away from the Castro, then back toward it, taking a different route before finally answering, "I picked up a tail. I wasn't positive at first. Young couple. Guy and a girl. Probably wannabe reporters who recognized me as taskforce and now want to get a shot of you. That's the trouble with the fucking Internet. Everybody's after their moment of fame and it doesn't matter if someone else's life goes to shit because of it. Fucking idiots. I brought the Mustang because it's not my usual ride and it'd take digging to trace the plates. Obviously I should have gone for tinted windows."

He glanced over and read her concern. With a visible effort he relaxed. "Don't worry. I lost them. They never got close enough to photograph you."

She knew that. She had a sixth sense when it came to cameras pointed at her. Always had. Her mother was the same way. "Where'd you first see them?"

"Oakland side, near the Bay Bridge. This is just a fluke sighting. I didn't see the car on your street."

Some of the worry left her. "Good."

"You might want to consider staying with friends until interest in you dies down. Your first name is different than the one you grew up with, but it's just a matter of time before someone makes the connection between you and Parker and the captain. Then you're going to have reporters camping out in front of Stylin' Ink and your apartment."

"They won't find the apartment. There's nothing connecting the address to me. If they show up at the shop then I'll head to LA or Vegas. After the fund-raiser."

"Heading out might be a good idea anyway if we don't catch this rapist, in case the profiler is wrong about the likelihood of your being a target. Hotel's up ahead. I was planning on going in with you, but I think it'd be smarter to drop you off. Quinn's in Room 213. I'll call him and let him know you're on your way up. You have cab money? Enough to get you wherever you need to go after Quinn and then back home?"

"I'm good."

He stopped close to the hotel entrance. As she was getting out, he said, "Thanks for doing this. I know you and Parker—"

"Let's not go there. I'll send you my bill if your friend doesn't cover it."

Eamon prowled around his office, moving from one piece of furniture to another, only occasionally glancing down at the human diners on the terrace. Necklaces, rings, hair ornaments, and earrings covered every surface.

The sight of so much glittering wealth would make a Dragon drool but nothing caught his eye. Nothing seemed a suitable gift for Etaín, though all would look more beautiful for being placed on her.

With a sigh he cleared his chair, scooping up the treasure and dumping it on his desk in a careless pile. Amusement found him, saving him from true aggravation.

As a distraction against her absence, this wasn't working. And if he were really so foolish as to present her with a priceless piece of jewelry at this point in their courtship, he'd soon be reduced to ordering Liam and Rhys to capture and bring her to him.

He steepled his hands, touching his fingertips to his mouth. Knowledge was the gift he needed to give her, but as he'd already discovered, being with her distracted him from pursuing any purpose but pleasure. And beyond that, she was more guarded than he'd expected, and much less hungry for information than he'd hoped.

A soft brush of magic announced Rhys's presence, presenting a welcome interruption until he saw the expression on his second's face. "Tell me."

"She slipped away again."

"How?"

"It's the bigger picture that's more important. Two men stopped by the tattoo shop earlier today. She spoke with them outside. Earnestly, I'm told by the humans watching her, and who recognized both men, though it took them a while to determine how they knew the faces.

The men are FBI agents and on the taskforce trying to locate the Harlequin Rapist."

Uneasiness filled Eamon. For the most part he didn't pay attention to human-on-human crime unless it touched someone he was ultimately responsible for, but the topic of this particular predator came up repeatedly among the wealthy and privileged dining at Aesirs. "What did they want of Etaín?"

"They passed her a piece of paper, but after they departed, she went back to work and remained for several hours, finishing up with a client before leaving to visit other shops. Nothing seemed amiss. She returned home and was there for only a few moments before one of the men arrived. She left her apartment, dressed for an evening out and with a suitcase. They followed the car back to San Francisco but either she or the driver became suspicious. The agent purposely lost them."

Eamon kept his fingertips touched to his lips in an effort to affect calm against the emotions battering him. "A date with the intention of being gone several days?"

"Based on what they witnessed outside the shop, neither of those following her thought she was romantically or sexually involved with him. I've stationed humans at all the places where she might reappear."

Rhys's exhale was warning enough that another unpleasant revelation was imminent. "I read up on this rapist before coming to you. There are rumors of an artist, possibly a psychic, visiting the hospital and the latest victim."

"When?"

"Yesterday. She met the taskforce agents there. It took seeing the men a second time for the couple I have watching her to feel certain they should recognize them, and to start actively trying to determine their identities. Knowing what's being said on the news makes me suspect she's been taken to a safe house. There's an additional reason for protective custody. She's a fit for one of the victim types this Harlequin Rapist chooses."

Eamon rose from his chair and began pacing. His emotions running the gamut, cycling from anger to worry to fear with each pass around the office.

If she'd been removed from his territory and was discovered . . .

If something happened to her . . .

Rhys forced the chaos of thought and ceaseless movement to a stop by stepping in front of him then going to one knee with his head bowed. "This failure is mine for not anticipating the skill set necessary in keeping her watched. I will accept the full punishment for her disappearance."

Eamon took a deep, even breath, drawing on the level of control necessary to survive as spell-caster and Elven lord. "I took the risk so I bear the responsibility. Ignorance is rarely rewarded and often punished. Find out everything you can about her life among humans."

"And her current location?"

Eamon looked down at the diners, among them humans whose acquaintance had been cultivated by those in his service. "That would require calling in favors. I think the risk of drawing attention to her by doing so is too great. If you're correct, and she's been placed in protective custody, then I will have to put my faith in the FBI agents to keep her safe for the moment. Regardless of where she is now, I believe she'll return for the fund-raiser."

Twelve

Quinn ushered her into Room 213 without her having to knock. Clothing covered everything but his hands and head. His scalp bristled from hair punching through formerly shaved skin.

He would have looked good bald, she thought. And not many men did.

She guessed he was in his early thirties. He could pass for an ex-con. He had the look, the honed muscles of a prison stint turned into gym sessions.

"Where do you want to set up?" he asked.

"Show me what you've got first."

He grinned. "Now there's an invite. Too bad all the work's above the waist."

He stripped off the shirt, tossing it onto the dresser. Three jagged lightning strikes done in red streaked down the sides of his neck. Swastikas, three leaf clovers, the number 666 and initials AB were the predominant images on his chest and arms. The ink color on some of them a clear indication they'd been done behind bars. It made her wonder if Trent had leveled with her about Quinn being undercover from the start rather than recruited in prison.

She moved around him. There was more work on his back, the same symbols in addition to an eagle, its wingspan spreading from shoulder to shoulder. Not an easy cover job, though in his favor, the work wasn't dense.

The tattoos were more lines than filled-in areas, some of it crude, some done by talented artists. She wouldn't have been able to stand any of it on her skin.

Seeing it, she was glad she'd be with Cathal later. After hours spent inking Quinn, she'd be ready for a different kind of touch.

"Why not laser this shit off?" It'd be painful, much more painful, and a hell of a lot more expensive, but worth it.

"I'm not a good candidate."

"Based on the Kirby-Desai Scale?"

"Yeah. I went in for a consult. It was my first stop after being officially arrested, charged, convicted, and shipped off to prison where I reportedly got shanked by another inmate and bled out.

"The guy I saw said my score put me in the questionable range for successful removal, and it'd take more treatments than I had time for. You think you can do this in one session?"

"I don't know." She walked around him again, seeing the skin as a large canvas marred by ugly spots that needed to be hidden.

On the next pass she cleared her mind, opening it to inspiration. As she continued to circle, an image flowed in. Merging and melding and obliterating what was already there, turning it from something shameful into something empowering.

"Sit," she said. "On the corner of the bed."

"Jesus. Glad to. I was starting to feel dizzy."

Locked on to the image she wanted to capture, she couldn't spare the concentration for a response, or the time it would take to sketch everything out on paper first.

She opened the kit and dug into it, pulling out a box of markers. "Stay as still as possible," she told him, waiting for his nod before touching the tip of a pen to him and transferring the art in her mind to the canvas of his skin.

When it was done she stepped back to give it a critical once-over. "You can look in the mirror."

"I'll hold out and be surprised. Trent says your work is incredible."

She wondered when Trent had seen any of it, then shrugged the question off. He probably based the praise on the drawings from Tyra's memories.

"You should move around a bit while I get set up. Stretch out. Get some water. Go to the bathroom."

Quinn laughed. "Yes, Mom."

She shook her head. "Are you sure you're a Fed?"

He rolled his shoulders, loosening up the muscles. "Who said I was a Fed?"

"Then I'll rephrase, are you sure you're in law enforcement?"

The amusement slid away, replaced by a somber expression. "*Was* in law enforcement. Past tense. Are you going to be able to cover everything up in one session?"

"Depends on how much pain you can stand."

"I can take the pain."

"We'll start with your chest. Probably the easiest way to do this will be with you lying on the bed, then either sitting in a chair or on the floor, so you can brace your hands against something if you need to when it's time for your back."

"You're the boss." He dragged the dresser close to the bed. Then picked up her kit and set it down next to a tattered paperback copy of *Bride of the Fat White Vampire*.

"Great book," Etaín said.

"Yeah. Laugh-your-ass-off funny. You ever read *The Android's Dream*?"

"Sure. I love Scalzi's stuff."

She emptied her kit of the things she needed, arranging them and checking the ink against the colors she saw in her imagination.

"You okay with country music?" Quinn asked.

"Sure."

He found a country station and turned it up loud enough to mask the sound of the tattoo machine.

"Ready?" she asked after getting the ink caps set up.

"Yeah. I'll assume the position." He sprawled on the bed, arms spread.

She made quick work of shaving his chest and coating the first area with a light layer of Vaseline. Stretching his skin she said, "Stay as still as you can. If it gets too much for you, or you need a break, let me know."

"You got it."

She outlined in silence, content to listen to music. Thoughts of Cathal slipped in. And Eamon. Her labia grew flushed and swollen, her nipples taut as she imagined lying in bed between them, hands and mouths roaming, limbs tangled. Both of them inside her at once, or just one, while the other watched.

The explicit fantasies made it difficult to concentrate on what she was doing. She distracted herself from them by asking, "So why the hurry to get these tattoos covered?"

A burst of love and worry poured into her bloodstream, accompanied by the image of an older couple, a white man and black woman.

If not for the steadiness developed over years of using the machine, the force and surprise of having the picture come while she was awake would have made her hand jerk and deviate from the line she inked.

"My dad has been diagnosed with cancer. My stepmom is African American and I have a kid sister who's mixed race. I don't want to show up with AB tats."

"They don't know you've been undercover?"

"They know, but not the details. I'd rather not risk having them walk in unexpectedly and see the tats, then start thinking about what I might have done and said so I could pass for a brotherhood member."

"How long have you been under?"

"Five years. Five long, long years. I haven't seen my sister since she was seven. Haven't seen any of them except for the photo album they keep online."

"They're here in San Francisco?"

"Close by."

She took the hint and didn't press though she didn't need to. Worry and protectiveness flooded into her along with the image of a house, the hills behind it recognizable as East Bay, Livermore or Pleasanton probably.

Her hand trembled slightly, blurring a line. She had no way of knowing if she was stealing his memories or not. The taste of fear filled her mouth at this additional proof Eamon might be right about her losing control of her gift.

She finished the outline and released Quinn's stretched skin, wondering if putting a second glove over the first would make a difference. "You need a break before I start shading?"

"No. I'm good."

She opened and closed her left hand, torn between fear and curiosity. Was her gift changing? Or did the images come because Quinn was somehow projecting them?

She swapped out the liner for the shader, unplugging one from the power source and substituting it for the other. "So what are you going to do now that you're out of law enforcement?"

"Don't know for sure. A buddy of mine is a PI, Sean McAlister of McAlister Investigations, in case you ever need one. He wants me to come onboard. I'm thinking about giving it a try, see if it's a fit."

Etaín put a second glove over the first on her left hand then immediately pulled it off, hating the slippery feel of it. It had taken her a long time to be able to tolerate wearing the latex at all.

The call to ink came with a call to touch skin-to-skin. She'd known from the start that the eyes on her palms were *meant* to see. *What* they were supposed to see was a trickier question, and what she was supposed to do with the knowledge . . .

Familiar discomfort arose, the same she experienced every time

Justine asked her to do one of the special tattoos. Deep-seated denial came with it, at the prospect of any type of monklike existence, be it abstinence from sex or living in some remote location and having people make pilgrimages to her.

She picked up the shader with the resolve not to ask additional questions, or think about her gift. She didn't want it to be changing.

Not even if it meant a future with Cathal and Eamon in it?

She frowned the unwanted question away and placed her hand on Quinn, stretching the skin then touching the shader to it.

Like Jason earlier in the day, Quinn slipped into a kind of subspace, embracing the pain so the endorphins fed a desire that was definitely sexual in nature. It poured into her bloodstream, where earlier in the day the residual effects of being with Eamon had seemed to give her a respite from Tori's and Jason's emotions.

She didn't mind the flow of desire. It helped her work quickly, to go for longer periods without breaking.

Her resolve not to ask questions lasted through the work on his back and chest and upper arms, but broke when she got to the three red lightning bolts on the side of his neck. "I caught a documentary on TV about the Aryan Brotherhood. I thought they said these symbolized kills and—"

Her breath caught with the visceral feel of pushing a knife through flesh and the image of a face in close proximity. She jerked away, breaking the contact reflexively at the same time Quinn came out of subspace.

"Sorry about that. Must have zoned out," he said, his expression tight.

"Hang in there just a little longer. We're almost done." Words for the both of them.

Fighting the urge to rub her gloved palm against her skirt, she forced herself to touch him again.

Relief settled into her. It felt as though a mental barrier had slammed down between them, walling off any leak of emotion or thought.

It made her think what had happened between them was more about him unintentionally projecting and her being a prime candidate to receive, than about her gift changing into something more dangerous than it already was.

The premise seemed validated when she touched the shader to his skin, applying ink but remaining free of his emotion, same as she'd been with Tori and Jason—thanks to the mind-blowing sex with Eamon.

A shiver of need went through her. Her own, coming with thoughts of Eamon, then mingling with those of Cathal as the lightning bolts on Quinn's neck became the final touches of a sinuous water dragon covering a vast area of skin, its wings stretched and curved in flight, enfolding Quinn as though man and beast were one.

She turned off the machine and put it down with a sigh, glad to be finished. "Go ahead and stand up."

He stood, holding his arms away from his side and making a slow rotation. "Satisfied?"

"Very. Ready to see if you are?"

"You bet."

He stepped in front of the mirror, lips parting in a gratifying show of astonishment then curving upward in a genuine smile. "Trent wasn't exaggerating when he said you did amazing work. I'm glad I couldn't get that other shit lasered off."

He turned, looking over his shoulder to check out his back again with a little hitch in his breath, a slight show of pain. Etaín cleaned up and repacked her kit, letting him relax for a few minutes.

Pleasure hummed through her, satisfaction at the way the dragon had turned out and at having managed it in one session. Eamon would probably claim magic was responsible. She thought it was entirely because of Quinn. Not many clients could have handled getting so much ink at one time, but then not very many would have been as highly motivated as he was.

When everything was taken care of but the aftercare, she said,

"Okay gorgeous, enough ogling yourself in the mirror. Let's wrap this up."

He grinned. "Gorgeous, huh?"

She rolled her eyes. "Get over yourself and come sit down."

He glanced at the antibiotic ointment and the small stack of bandages, not nearly enough to cover everything she'd done, but enough to hit the major spots. "No point in wasting the bandages. I'll have them peeled off before you get to the elevator. I'm hitting the Castro tonight. I need it before I show up at my father's place tomorrow."

Despite what Trent had said in the car, Quinn's destination coupled with the sexual need that had poured into her as she worked had her asking, "You're gay?"

He inhaled loudly enough for her to hear it. The exhale was quieter but it came with shoulders going back and a spine straightening. "Yeah. Yeah, I am. Time to stop living a lie. I'm up from undercover and out of the closet at the same time. Dad's cancer changed my perspective."

A smile returned to tilt one corner of his mouth. "That and five years of banging women who shout 'Heil Hitler' when they come."

"Seriously?"

"Yeah. Seriously. And as infrequently as possible. Don't think I could have managed it except for some first class pharmaceuticals and a desperate need to get up and off like your All-American white supremacist so I wouldn't blow my cover."

"A soldier in a different kind of war."

"Yeah."

She started to ask what the prognosis was for his dad but another thought headed off the conversation. Quinn needed a distraction without complications and so did Derrick. Besides that, the last thing Quinn should be doing after taking on so much new ink was hitting the club scene or drinking. "Do you have a car?"

"You need a lift somewhere?"

"Yes. It's not far."

"No problem." He touched a hand to his back pocket, pulling out his keys and his wallet. "We need to settle up for the work, too. Cash okay?"

"Always."

At Derrick's apartment, she went for simple. "You mind coming up with me? My friend is going through a tough spell and I'm not sure what I'm going to find up there."

Eamon stopped in front of a Monet gracing his office wall. Usually he could lose himself in contemplations of it but not today. Since Etaín's disappearance there had been no escape from thoughts of her, not in the beauty he surrounded himself with, nor in the work that came with his duties as Lord.

Noble intentions of allowing her freedom and winning her through courtship warred with possessive desires, the need not only to have her as wife-consort so her gift could be used for the benefit of those he ruled, but to have her ensconced at his estate for his own peace of mind, so he would know at all times she was safe and cared for.

A battle raged inside him, giving him respite from his fear for her by burying it under the assumption she would soon be back and affording him the opportunity to decide what he wanted to do about her. It quieted only when the subtle touch of magic announced Rhys and Liam.

He turned from the painting, relief at seeing their expressions nearly making him stagger. "You've found her."

The sun dangling from Rhys's earlobe swung with the slight shake of his head. "Not found. It would be more accurate to say she returned on her own. She just arrived at a coworker's apartment in the company of an unknown, but recently tattooed man."

Rhys's stiff posture and tone revealed his dismay over erring earlier about her likely whereabouts. His silence beyond the facts showed his hesitance to compound it with further opinion.

Eamon closed the distance and placed a hand on his second's

shoulder. "Your analysis was a sound one, though I'm happy, in this case, it proved incorrect. Of far greater importance is the reasoning behind your initial thoughts on her disappearance. Those facts haven't changed."

"Which is why I'm here," Liam said. "If you're still determined to court Etaín rather than incarcerate her, then dismiss the humans and assign the task of watching her to me."

He'd hoped to avoid the risk of having her brought to the attention of other supernaturals but he saw no choice, nor could he bear another day like today, where worry over her consumed him. "The duty is yours, unless she is with me . . . or with Cathal Dunne, then you are relieved of it."

A hard look fully expressed Liam's opinion about the latter part of the command, but Eamon let it stand.

D errick opened the door with a dramatic fling, sending it crashing against the wall as a cloud of pot smoke spilled out of the apartment. Etaín took in the light blue Victoria's Secret nightgown and said, "The stoned housewife look works for you. I'm sure the guys in prison will love it."

"I'm smoking for medicinal purposes."

"Right."

"Not all of us get the same choice of prime beefcake you do, Etaín."

She resisted the urge to point out that having it didn't make a hell of a lot of difference when it came to anything beyond casual.

"Staying home and high is only going to make the misery last longer, you know that, Derrick. You'll get through this a lot quicker by working. Jason came by today, and a couple of your other clients. They're counting on you. So is Bryce."

Derrick sniffed. "Did *he* send you?"

"Yeah. I would have given you a few more days to wallow before coming over and kicking ass, but Bryce wanted you to know he cleared your schedule for tomorrow. After that, he expects you to handle it."

Steeling herself for a cocktail mix of emotions, she reached out, wanting to offer the comfort of touch. Gripping his bare upper arms, anger and depression and hurt slammed into her in a chaotic torrent. But after the first wave of it, she got a hit of sexual interest that surprised her until he said, "If Etaín's dragged you here to provide a pity fuck, I accept."

She looked to the left and saw Quinn had stepped into view. The way his thumbs were tucked into his front pockets, causing his hands to frame a pretty impressive erection, suggested Derrick's whole tragic-heroine-in-need-of-a-manly-rescuer hit just the right note with Quinn.

Etaín let her hands fall off Derrick's arms and took a step to the side. "Quinn, Derrick. Derrick, Quinn."

Derrick stopped blocking the doorway, silently inviting them in and smoothing nervous hands down the sides of his nightgown.

Etaín hid a smile as Quinn stepped past her and into the apartment. Not wanting to send Derrick into a tailspin by mentioning either Cathal or Salina's playing at Saoirse, she said, "I've got to be somewhere. Is it okay if I stash my kit here?"

Derrick frowned as his eyes traveled from the suitcase she'd hauled with her to Quinn, finally focusing in on how much new art he was wearing. "Someone needs aftercare."

"Yeah." She bit her bottom lip but it didn't help. The words escaped anyway. "Play nurse, take care of him for me?"

"Not funny, Etaín," he said, but the glare accompanying it was shades of Derrick before this current meltdown.

Reaching out he took the handle of the roll-on.

She bolted.

The high of success lasted until the cab she'd hailed drew close to Saoirse. Then an unfamiliar nervousness crept in along with the heat spiraling downward from her belly to her cunt. Usually she felt totally in control when it came to men, and this kind of situation, where sex was a given.

She caught herself rubbing her palms against her short skirt, the same way Derrick had rubbed his against the blue nightie. *Get a grip*, she told herself, blaming the uncharacteristic feelings and uncertainty on Eamon.

His open talk of accepting a ménage arrangement and his hints about permanence being an option had spooked her. That's all. Her gift gave her a very real reason to avoid it, and seeing Derrick cycle through failed relationships was a constant reminder of how much it hurt to lose people you loved and who you thought loved you.

Casual equals comfortable she reminded herself as the cab stopped in front of Saoirse.

Thirteen

Cathal set his empty drink glass down and pushed away from the bar. On stage, Salina and her band were getting ready to play. He didn't need to check his watch to know the time. Every minute of the day had seemed to drag since taking the call from Sean.

He moved through the crowded club, not bothering to lie to himself about his ultimate destination. The front door, so he could step outside and see if she'd arrived yet.

Work had kept him in his office most of the evening and given him an excuse to monitor the entrance via security cameras. He'd seen the line starting to form. It was a good turnout for a Tuesday.

"Etaín promised. She'll be here," Salina had assured him repeatedly since arriving at the club.

He believed that *she* believed it. The question was whether or not Etaín valued the promises she gave.

He prided himself on keeping his word. In that, he and his father and uncle were the same, holding to a code of honor, though there were differences in how they applied it, especially when it came to women.

Both his father and uncle were serial adulterers. They didn't flaunt their mistresses, didn't bring them to Saoirse. But he heard about them all the same, and would have written their behavior off as stereotypical of gangsters, except he knew it was really about power.

Thoughts of Etaín with Eamon had jealousy stabbing and twisting in his gut. He wasn't a man to either turn a blind eye to or accept infidelity. He expected and gave exclusivity when he was seeing a woman on a regular basis, even when the sex came with no promises of it being more than a comfortable and pleasant relationship for both of them.

A hand on his arm stopped him steps away from the door. He followed the bare skin to a generous display of cleavage and above it, an attractive face with a seductive smile.

"Leaving so soon? Just when I'm getting here?"

His cock stirred. He was a man. But he felt no regret at missing the opportunity she presented. "Stepping out to collect my date."

Her hand fell away with a pout. He'd forgotten her with the next step toward the door.

The chill of the night was no match for the heat that moved through him at seeing Etaín. She glittered in comparison to the other women, hardening him with her smile and drawing him forward like a thief to a priceless work of art.

"Never wait in line to come to me," he said, arms going around her waist, pulling her against him.

Her laugh was seduction itself, a tight, hot fist around his dick.

She pressed her lower body to his. "I don't need to ask if you're happy to see me. Thanks for giving Salina's band a chance to play here."

He nuzzled her cheek, inhaling her. Now that she was in his arms he didn't know how he'd managed to get through the day without having her there—or better, underneath him.

The thought should have sent him running as fast as he could away from her. It didn't. And his family wasn't the sole reason.

He was breaking a personal rule about public displays, not for the first time since meeting her. Spearing his fingers through her hair and holding her in place, his lips sought hers.

She welcomed him with a soft sigh and the sensuous slide of tongue against tongue. He wouldn't wait to get her home before he had her. Couldn't. But then that much had been obvious all day.

His hand moved up her side, stopping just short of covering a breast. Possessiveness gripped him. Need.

He forced his mouth away from hers, the hunger to taste her more deeply, more thoroughly, unsatisfied. "A quick tour?" he asked, knowing it would end almost as soon as it began.

She laughed again, lips brushing his. "Show me everything."

Fire raced through his blood, carrying every drop of it downward to his cock. It was all he could manage to escort her into the club, pointing out the VIP section and allowing her to pause long enough to acknowledge Bryce and wave to Salina before getting her into his office and locking the door behind them.

She glanced around. "No gold-plated albums on the walls? No signed pictures of you with famous people?"

He cupped her hips, pulling her lower body against his so she'd feel the hard swell of his erection. "I don't need to overcompensate for failings in one area by turning my office into an ostentatious show of success."

She wound her arms around his neck and smiled against his mouth. "Are you looking for validation of your prowess?"

"I warned you about what would happen if you came to Saoirse."

"I made it more than a few steps inside."

She stirred primal urges to life, enflaming him with her challenge and sexual confidence. He separated from her long enough to take her purse and the biker jacket, tossing them onto a chair. "You won't need either of them while you're in my club."

He was turned on by tight nipples pressed to a thin blouse, by the heady scent of her and the pulse racing in her neck. She backed away when he crowded into her personal space, but he knew she let him force her retreat, allowed him to trap her against the front of the desk.

"You're beautiful," he said, mouth taking hers in a rough kiss as his hand stroked her exposed thigh before grasping the hem of her skirt and jerking upward.

He felt the heat of her through her clothing and couldn't stop himself from cupping her mound to ensure she was wet for him.

Her panties were scraps of material. Easy to push out of his way before impaling her with his fingers.

She clamped down on him with a hungry sound, fierce need mirroring the one raging inside him. A tug of his zipper and he freed himself, desperate to get inside her.

On a moan she broke the kiss. "Condom." Her hands were on his chest, pushing, reinforcing the word.

The shock of having lost control to the point of forgetting about protection should have drenched him in fear. It didn't. Not when it came to what he wanted. *Her.*

He pulled a packet from his back pocket and ripped it open. She took it from him, murmuring against his lips, "Feeling pretty confident? Or do you always carry one?"

Curiosity. Amusement. He bared his teeth, realizing he wanted to hear an edge of jealousy in her voice.

He thought to return to foreplay, so he could wrest a scream of frustration out of her to match what he felt. But she deftly rolled the condom onto his cock and the sight of her doing it, the feel of her hands touching him had a red haze rolling over him, turning aggravation into an aggressive, burning need.

He forced her backward and onto the edge of his desk, his hands returning to arousal-wet panties and pushing them aside. "Now," he said, moaning at finding her slit, his cock entering her in a slow slide to ecstasy.

She wrapped her legs around his hips, her inner muscles squeezing him, clinging to him, making movement imperative.

He acted on the raging lust she incited in him, the tumultuous emotions her presence stirred. Used his arms around her waist and the angle of his body to hold her so each pounding thrust delivered a burst of sensation to her clit.

Her sharp cries and the merciless tightening of her channel heightened his pleasure, building up the need in both of them until he was afraid it would be over for him before it was for her.

Tearing his mouth from hers he kissed his way to her ear. "Give in to it," he said, taking the lobe, sucking hard and deep and firm, as if it were her nipple, her clit.

Her legs became a vise-hold around his hips, making it a fight to thrust, an intense battle that had him grinding, rubbing against her clit.

A gasp, a small cry that was a shout of victory to his ego and she obeyed, her sheath rippling against him, demanding he surrender to pleasure, too.

He came, unable to make himself leave her body afterward. "I wanted you in my bed last night," he said, the truth escaping before he could prevent it. "I kept hoping you'd make it to the club after all."

She rubbed her cheek against his, an affectionate gesture that shouldn't have mattered to him. Shouldn't have had the power to pour warmth into his chest, but did.

"Saoirse was closed by the time I got finished with my brother."

Some perverse part of him made him push, test. "Then we both ended the night alone."

She stilled. He expected her to lie and almost wished she had when she said, "I saw Eamon after I did what I needed to do for my brother."

The admission made the muscles along his arms turn to steel and his hands ball into fists against her back. Jealousy pulsed through him, a possessiveness that would have verged on dangerous obsession if he were a different type of man.

He wrestled it down by reminding himself of what was at stake here. Her life.

Rather than pull away from her in anger, he nuzzled her ear and was rewarded by the fist-tight clamp of her channel on his semi-hard cock. "Why did you go to him when you could have come to me?"

The legs still wrapped around his waist tightened so his cock pushed deeper into her body. "Maybe I like variety. Don't tell me you're not the same."

He let the challenge pass but heard himself warn, "I'm not a man to share when I'm serious about a woman."

She sighed, a soft puff of warmth against his cheek. "Then don't get serious about me."

Protest rippled through him when her legs fell away, no longer holding him against her. Anger and jealousy returned but he pushed them back with forceful denial.

He made himself pull from her hot depths and break the physical contact. What the fuck was wrong with him?

Etaín slid from the desk, smoothing her skirt down over thighs he wanted to touch his lips to. "It's time for a trip to the lady's room," she said, a glance at her jacket and purse an indication she was already thinking about ending her night away from him.

He couldn't allow it, and the promise to his father wasn't the main reason. "You can leave your things in here. The door is locked when I'm not in my office. Drinks and food are on the house."

Her dark, dark eyes were mysterious, impenetrable, unreadable. He had no way of knowing if she felt as out of control as he did, if she burned and needed when she wasn't with him.

It drove him crazy. Challenged him. He didn't like thinking he was interchangeable with another man, with Eamon in particular.

He dealt with the condom, tucking himself in and zipping his pants as she watched, the eroticism of it and the heat that came into her eyes making him touch her again, curl an arm around her waist and pull her to him. "If you keep looking at me that way, we'll never make it out to hear Lady Steel."

She took his bottom lip, sucked it gently. "I guess we should leave then."

But her arms went around his neck. "I want you again."

It soothed some of the raw, chaotic emotion churning inside him, pleased him to hear her say it. "Come home with me tonight?"

His hand drifted down to smooth over a tight, alluring buttock. "It went too fast before. I intended to fuck you with my tongue before my cock."

She smiled against his lips. "Are you saying I rushed you?"

"We can blame it on the skirt."

"That's generous of you."

He gripped her ass, grinding her against an erection that defied the laws of nature with its size and fullness so quickly after the orgasm he'd experienced with her. "If this doesn't tempt you into coming home with me, then I've got a hot tub. I promise to be good."

"What if I want bad?"

His hand moved from her buttock to her breast, covering it, tweaking the nipple through the thin blouse. "I can accommodate you. We can be bad together."

She trailed a fingertip along his jaw, rubbing it against the stubble there. He'd shaved in anticipation of seeing her but he could already use another, complements of his father's genes.

"You make it hard to say no."

"Then don't. Say 'yes, Cathal, I'm dying to spend the night in your bed.'"

Her laugh made him smile. "No confidence issues there. Now it's bed. What happened to the hot tub?"

"Say yes and I'll promise not to fuck you against the wall the moment we get through my front door. I'll wait until we're in the hot tub."

"Yes."

He succumbed to the temptation of her lips, sealing the agreement with the slide of his tongue against hers, a sensuous, heated tangle that was both substitute for sex and prelude to it.

With effort he stopped. With greater effort he escorted her out of the office and to the bathrooms.

"I'll wait for you," he said, suppressing the internal alarm his need to keep her close caused.

Lady Steel was in full swing but he couldn't enjoy the music until Etaín emerged from the lady's room. A fast song morphed into a slow one and he used it as an excuse to guide her to the dance floor and recapture the feel of her pressed to him.

"What do you think of Salina's band?" Etaín asked hours later, once again in his arms, their bodies rubbing and touching as they danced, the low hum she'd felt from the moment he'd pushed his cock inside her now a constant, insistent buzz of desire, an electric heat demanding skin-to-skin contact.

"They've got promise." He nuzzled her ear. "And now I'd like to keep my promise. Ready to leave?"

"Yes."

She gave Salina a thumbs-up before they left. Bryce, in turn, separated himself from a brunette clinging to him long enough to give her one.

Cathal's place was a gorgeous Victorian high enough on a hill to provide privacy, and situated on a large lot in Presidio Heights. He parked in the street rather than the garage, and she smiled, guessing he wanted her to get the full effect of entering his house.

Ten-foot hedges flanked a wrought-iron gate. Steps led up to a red door. He took her hand as she got out of the car and she felt a betraying flutter in the region of her heart.

Hardwood flooring and high ceilings gave off warmth as well as an open feeling. The furniture was made to sprawl on, while a plush rug in front of a fireplace was an invitation to move the lovemaking off the couch and onto the floor.

Her cunt lips grew flushed and swollen imagining herself there with Cathal, seeing the gleam of sweat on his back as his muscles rippled and hips pistoned as a fire blazed in the fireplace.

A shiver of need went through her. A flash of want. Arousal soaked her panties and wet her inner thighs.

Since she'd arrived at his club, he'd maintained near-constant physical contact with her. That she liked it so much should have made her want to bolt.

He turned into her, running his hands down the length of her back. "Like what you see?"

"And if I don't?"

"Then I'll have to convince you otherwise." His smile was wickedly sensuous, dark sin and carnal taunt. His hand bold decadence as it moved from her bare leg, then up, forcing its way between her thighs and underneath her skirt. Finding her wet there. Hot and needy with her clit swollen and firm.

He cupped her mound. Pressed the heel of his hand to her clit, eliciting a soft whimper.

"Deny that I satisfied you earlier. Deny that you want me again. Here. Now. Any way I want to take you."

His voice was husky, revealing just how affected he was at finding her wet and ready for him.

He bit down on the sensitive skin beneath her ear, warning and dare alike when it came to answering with a lie.

This time she was the one to discard her purse and jacket then pull her skirt up, leaving his zipper and the minuscule panties the only barriers to penetration.

"Etaín," he said, moving into her until the wall blocked any further retreat, the raggedness of his voice pleasing her, too.

"What happened to your promise not to fuck me against the wall the moment we got through your front door?"

She knew she was playing a dangerous game with him and with herself. He was like a drug delivered straight to her bloodstream, a growing addiction she couldn't afford, just as Eamon was.

Cathal forced himself to step back though he couldn't break the physical contact. A few seconds longer, enough time to free his cock and rip those panties downward, and it would have been too late.

Fuck, he could come just looking at her standing there with her skirt hiked up, displaying a tanned, flat belly and a cunt covered by his hand and lacy strips of nothing.

"You're right," he said, smoothing his palm over her clit and reveling in the sharp catch of her breath and little mew of pleasure.

Somehow he managed to draw his hand away. A tour was out, not that he'd managed to give her much of one at the club either when she'd first arrived.

"This way," he said, taking a straight path to a garden made private by tall hedges.

The stars and moon were bright, perfect for enjoying the night, but he didn't need any of it with Etaín. At the club, inside his front door, he'd rushed, but outside, steam rising from the water after he removed the hot tub cover, he found the patience to take his time with her, to savor and memorize everything about her.

"Take the blouse off," he ordered, denying himself touch in favor of solidifying his control over himself.

Her smile said she guessed at the reason behind his command. Or maybe it was only an acknowledgment she could play this game, too.

Her fingers went to the top button, slowly freeing it before moving to the next, and the one after that in a strip tease guaranteed to bring him to his knees by the time it was done. Arousal escaped, wetting the tip of his cock as he waited for the first sight of her naked breasts, wondered at the color and size of her nipples.

Her blouse fluttered to the ground and he nearly dropped his hand to his erection in case he needed to use a painful grip to keep from taking her down then and there. The bra matched the panties, revealing almost as much as it concealed.

She was beautifully formed, everything about her pure seduction. She was a siren capable of leading a man to his destruction.

Words caught in his throat but he didn't need to command her to take the bra off. Fingers smoothed over the front clasp, teasing him, tormenting him. Her expression sultry and knowledgeable, promising pleasure and delivering a small measure of it when the scrap of material followed the blouse to the ground.

The sight of her mesmerized him. He couldn't look away. Could barely breathe when she cupped her breasts, brushing her thumbs over dark pink nipples that begged for a man's mouth to capture and suck them.

His cock throbbed. His testicles felt full and heavy with the need to come inside the hot, wet clasp of her channel.

He didn't want to wear a rubber. He didn't want anything separating him from the ecstasy to be found in her body.

She licked her lips. He thought he'd lose all control if he saw her touch either mouth or tongue to her nipples.

He grabbed her wrists. "Now my shirt."

She took her sweet time about it. Peeling his shirt away as slowly as she'd done her blouse.

It fluttered to the ground and she combed her fingers through the hair on his chest. He moaned when she zeroed in on his nipples, rubbing and tweaking until his breathing was little more than shallow, quick inhalations of air.

His hips jerked when she touched her mouth to first one nipple and then the other, wetting them with her tongue as her hands slid downward to his pants.

He didn't stop her from freeing his cock. Only toed off his shoes and socks before kicking away his fallen trousers and Jockeys.

At her sloe-eyed look of appreciation, his cock strained toward her, begging for her attention. She gave it, taking him in hand, filling his head with the roar of lust as the fingers encircling his shaft moved up and down on it.

He nearly begged her to put her mouth on him. Only managed not to because he knew it would be all over the instant her lips and tongue touched him.

He forced her to halt by once again securing a wrist. "The rest of it comes off first."

She reached behind her with her free hand. A tug of the zipper and she stood in short boots and panties.

He couldn't take any more. Patience and the willingness to delay sexual gratification went up in flames. The only thing mattering was touch and taste and getting inside her.

He ripped her panties downward, baring her except for the boots with their thin, fuck-me heels. The image of her standing like that burned into his memory, an erotic centerfold to revisit time and time again.

As he'd done in his office, he crowded her until she was pressed against a wide padded ledge circling the hot tub. She sat as she'd done on the desk, thighs splayed, willing to take him between them.

The sight of her parted folds and glistening slit reinforced a primal imperative, this time he wouldn't settle for less than everything. He grasped her thighs, holding her open as he lowered his mouth to her.

The scent of aroused woman filled his nostrils, the scent of her. A small triangle of rich gold pointed downward but he didn't need the direction. Pink wet flesh and an engorged clit begged for the stroke of his tongue and feel of his lips.

He moaned at the first taste of her, sweet honey and addictive spice. Grew more excited with each lift of her hips as she pushed her clit between his lips, as she forced his tongue deeper into her channel.

She was so uninhibited and responsive, giving him everything. The sounds she made a stroke to his ego, an acknowledgment of the pleasure she found with him.

They were a declaration she didn't care if the neighbors heard and knew how thoroughly he possessed her. Crying out, she came and he was helpless against the roar of lust, the heated demand of his cock to claim her.

He tumbled her backward, pausing to tug the boots off before coming down on top of her. "Tell me you're on the pill," he demanded. "I'm safe. Tell me you are."

The hungry clamping of her channel brought with it the same raw need Etaín had experienced with Eamon. It overrode a lifetime of never letting any lover—even those she'd taken during her drug-ridden teen years—enter her without a barrier between them.

"I've only been with one other man that way. Eamon."

Cathal's expression turned dangerous at hearing the name, at being reminded she'd been with another man the night before. A little thrill went through her at seeing the savage intensity, the smoldering emotion before his mouth took hers in a hard kiss, sharing the carnal taste of her own arousal as he found her opening and pushed inside with nothing between them.

She shivered as waves of ecstasy rippled through her. It felt so good. So right.

Her arms and legs tightened around him. Her tongue met his thrust for thrust, her hips lifting with the desperate need to take him deeper.

She expected a fast hard fuck given the jealous fury radiating from him. She wanted it.

But he gave her slow. Drawing it out. Making her plead with her body and her voice, making her clamp down on him in release before he let go, pounding with a relentlessness that drove her up and over again, the third time opening the floodgates of exhaustion.

Without him lifting and sinking into the hot tub with her settled on his lap, she doubted she would have been able to summon the energy to roll into the water. "This is nice," she said, cuddling against him, her palm resting against his chest, her fingers combing lazily through the thick mat of hair, pausing to circle a small brown nipple.

She was totally sated, tired to the point of being unable to keep her eyes open. She was at her weakest in terms of having any control over her gift.

Usually she avoided touching the men she'd been with when she felt like this. She knew too well the cost of it, had learned that painful lesson when she was a teen, unwittingly stripping a boyfriend of his music the night before he was supposed to play to an audience.

It should be easy to pull her hand away from Cathal, to quit petting him. Fear should have made it an imperative, but the hum of contentment overrode it. It was a continuation of what she'd felt earlier, only muted and mellowed, a low-level buzz of desire creating an electric heat, an internal barrier she was coming to believe would keep him safe from her gift.

Conversation was beyond her. She let herself drift, her reality filtering in through her senses. Hot water and cold air. Cathal and the scent of jasmine. The caress of moonlight and the brush of his lips against her neck, her ear.

"You're falling asleep on me," he murmured, the purr of masculine satisfaction in his voice making her smile.

"And you don't bear any of the responsibility for it?"

He laughed and stood, holding her in his arms as if it were nothing and then setting her on the ledge where he'd stretched her out earlier. "Time for bed. There are towels in the deck box between the lounge chairs."

Her skin pebbled with goose bumps. She slipped off the ledge and went to the cluster of patio furniture, getting towels for both of them as he covered the hot tub.

They dried off, gathering their clothing before going inside. Cathal took her hand, guiding her up a curving staircase and into his bedroom.

Like the rest of what she'd seen of the house, it was high-ceilinged and open. Sconces provided muted light and the moon did the rest, pouring in through bay windows running the length of a sitting area and encompassing all but a six-inch strip at the bottom and top of the wall.

She looked longingly at the bed, a king positioned in a windowed alcove more narrow than wide. "I need to dry my hair."

Cathal pressed kisses along her shoulder. "Sit on the bed. I'll get the hairdryer."

A tug and he took her clothes with him when he left, leaving her standing naked and feeling vulnerable. It brought the urge to bolt for the safety of her apartment.

The intimacy unnerved her, the aftereffects of allowing him inside her without a condom. She was self-aware enough to know that and yet she couldn't look away or stop herself from wanting him again when he returned.

He was naked, masculine perfection. Primal man with his dark mat of chest hair, his cock and testicles on display.

Cathal felt himself hardening as he walked toward her. There was no hiding the power she wielded over him, the fuck-me expression that became a command his body couldn't refuse.

"Get on the bed," he said, fighting the urge to wrap his hand around his cock when she obeyed with a sloe-eyed look, testing his control.

He'd make her wait this time. He'd make *himself* wait. Prove to himself he could, that he didn't have to give in to the craving, the clawing, almost constant desire for her.

"Turn around," he said, kneeling behind her.

He'd intended only to retrieve the hairdryer and a brush for her to use. Now he took care of her hair himself, performing a service he'd never done for another woman.

Intense satisfaction surged through him at the way she enjoyed his tending to her, in how trusting and vulnerable she seemed in the intimacy of it.

Possessiveness gripped him with the thought of her starting the day in Eamon's bed. Fear trickled in. A warning he was getting in too deep and losing sight of his reason for being with her. He suppressed both, rationalizing away his unusual behavior and feelings as normal. She was beautiful and the sex was the best he'd ever had. She was a challenge and he didn't like to lose.

When her hair was dry he stretched her out on his bed, the soft invitation in her eyes an enticement, a reward, her splayed thighs a beckoning he couldn't resist. With a quick thrust he entered her, swallowing her gasp of pleasure, her low moans as he moved in and out, bringing her to climax before giving himself over to the same.

Fourteen

Dreams followed Etaín into a hazy precursor of wakefulness. They blurred the lines between real and imagined, coming with confusion and tumultuous emotions.

Despair and hope. Rage and guilt. Desire bathed in beautiful light, and desire that was dark obsession, making her skin crawl and her heart beat as if it belonged to a trapped, cornered thing.

Flames melted tearful clowns into grotesque mirror-house distortions, turning them into dark puddles that gave birth to demons, a twisting mass of faces with their mouths open, inhaling souls and feeding on terror. A knife slid through flesh while jagged red lightning bolts streaked downward and swastikas spun like martial arts stars, striking shadowy figures to the ground.

She shivered, recognized the images, all of them related to ink and her connection to it.

Heat seeped into her. Comforting. Calming. Like the swipe of a warm, soapy bath sponge across her psyche, cleansing it of toxic debris.

She pressed more tightly to the warm body lying next to her. A fresh image came then. Teresa, the young mother at the shelter. It was followed by the picture of her son, Lothar, with sigils of strengthened resolve concealed in his hair, and others, fortifying resistance to temptation and bad influences in his lips.

Her fingers twitched and moved, capturing the lines in muscle memory. She wasn't aware she sketched out Lothar on the rough texture of a masculine arm until another image followed, one coming with the memory of those first moments after Cathal had entered Stylin' Ink and introduced himself.

Heat pooled in her belly, waking her fully and bringing with it the desire to feel him inside her again. She opened her eyes and looked downward, at Cathal's arm draped across her stomach, her fingers tracing a pattern on his skin, honeysuckle and thorn, stylized, more symbolic sigil than literal interpretation, a tattoo that would pass as tribal art.

The design still wasn't complete but more of it was there and she knew it wasn't something to be inked on with the machine, but done by hand, like those she did at Justine's request and the eyes she'd placed on her own palms.

It wouldn't matter that the dark hair on his arms would grow back, partially obscuring the details. His willingness to accept the ink and her being the one to put it on his inner forearms were the only things bearing any importance.

She sat up, her instinct to reach for the tablet and pencils she kept next to her bed. A precaution. A habit. She wasn't overly worried about forgetting either design.

A scan of Cathal's bedroom revealed there was nothing she could use to write on. "Bad dreams?" he asked, sitting as well, his hand going to her breast while his lips pressed kisses along her neck.

A small shrug. "There are always dreams. One of them was a tattoo for you."

"Not happening."

The certainty in his voice made her smile. "Never say never."

"Some things are an absolute certainty."

His hand moved from her breast, smoothing downward over her belly and pushing between her thighs.

She parted her legs willingly for him and he cupped her mound, burning her with the heat of his palm.

"Like this," he murmured, stroking the underside of her clit and sliding two fingers into her slit. "Wanting you again is a definite yes."

With wakefulness came obligations. Responsibility weighed too heavily on her to stay and play all day though she found she wanted to. *Too much.*

She avoided analysis with thoughts of what she had to do. She needed to collect her kit from Derrick's and change clothes. She needed to show Derrick the demon images she'd stolen from Tyra's memory then stop by the shelter to tattoo Teresa. And after that, visit other artists to see if any of them recognized the art the Harlequin Rapist wore.

"Once more and then I need to leave," she said.

"Once more won't be enough."

"It'll have to be. I've got promises to keep."

So do I, Cathal thought, unwelcome reality crowding in, the firm resolve in her voice tightening his chest with a reminder of the last conversation he'd had with his father. "Make one of your promises that you'll eat breakfast with me this morning."

"Where?"

The lack of an immediate yes was like sandpaper over nerve endings. Since grade school he'd had members of the opposite sex fantasize about playing house with him and being Mrs. Cathal Dunne.

He rubbed a stubble-rough cheek against her neck, finding raw pleasure in the way it abraded her skin, leaving a mark. Not here, he realized. He didn't want his father and uncle seeing her in his home, a place they knew he rarely brought women. He didn't want a new round of law enforcement agencies taking an interest in him.

Not at his father's house, or Denis's, either. That close to Brianna and he couldn't be certain what they'd do.

"We'll go out," he said, wanting Etaín's compliance, needing it for her sake as well as his own. He cupped her breast, taking possession of a nipple as the palm of the other hand glided over her clit, his fingers slowly fucking in and out of her.

"Why go anywhere?"

"Because I can't be in two places at once. My uncle is going through a difficult time and my father is worried. I said I'd meet them for breakfast. I want you to go with me."

She tensed rather than purr with pleasure at the invitation. "What I said last night in your office still holds."

Don't get serious about me.

Aggravation, frustration both bit into him with sharp teeth. In that instant he knew where he'd take her. Aesirs.

"Just breakfast, Etaín." He pressed his fingers deeper, curving them and finding the spot that had her back arching and a moan escaping.

Her hand covered his as if she'd lock him inside her, but she was no match for his strength. He pulled from her channel, eliciting a whimper of protest.

"Give me what I want and I'll give you what you want." She shivered at his taking possession of her clit. "Say yes to breakfast."

"Yes."

He slipped his fingers inside her once again, finding her even wetter.

Capturing her earlobe, he sucked. Loving the way each pull of his lips caused her to clamp down on his fingers.

"Get on your hands and knees for me. Let me see you that way."

She went, thighs open and vulva exposed, nearly making him come with the sight of swollen folds and glistening slit.

He rose behind her, hands cupping her hips as he entered in a single thrust, lodging hard and deep.

His eyes closed at the sensation of wet heat and tight woman. A shudder of ecstasy went through him, silencing any voice other than the one urging him to stay lost in her forever.

He wanted to make it last. Tried to do it with short thrusts. Then longer ones. Pulling out so only his cock head remained inside her before pushing all the way in again in a slow slide.

A sheen of sweat coated his skin. He labored for breath. Fighting himself. Fighting her. Self-denial ending with her cry of release and taking his control with it, leaving only primal emotion and a relentless pistoning to orgasm.

They collapsed onto the mattress with him curled around her, his cock still lodged in the heated paradise of her body. He rubbed his cheek against her neck, her shoulders, following the rough abrasion with the press of lips and caress of tongue.

He loved her taste, her scent, the softness of her skin. Loved how she fit against him as if—

He blocked the thought but a shadow of it remained. Tightening his arms on her he made a promise to himself. If she agreed to help his family, he'd ensure any drawings she did of Brianna's rapists were destroyed. There would be *no* physical evidence linking her to his uncle and father's actions.

Reluctantly he left her body and the bed, padding naked to where their clothes were piled on a chair. He retrieved his phone, calling his father.

"Let's meet at Aesirs in an hour and a half."

"You're bringing her?"

"Yes."

"I'll call Denis."

He put the phone down, lust rippling through him at the sight of Etaín's Mona Lisa smile.

"Eamon won't care I've been with you. If anything, it'll turn him on to see us together and imagine how we spent the night."

Cathal turned away, hiding the reactive snarl that came with a resurgence of anger and possessiveness. "We better hustle if we're going to swing by your place. I assume you don't want to wear what you had on last night."

He heard her rise from the bed. "I need to retrieve my tattoo kit from Derrick's apartment. It's in Corona Heights. I've got a change of clothes there."

Footsteps and he felt her behind him. His buttocks clenched as she touched her lips to his shoulder. He started to harden again as her arms slipped around his waist. "We can shower here before going to Derrick's. I like being in the water with you."

He told himself he should peel her arms away and reject her overture. Put some distance between them until he could get his head straight.

He couldn't make himself do it. Not with her skin touching his, not when all he could think about was the Mona Lisa smile and her mention of Eamon.

E amon prowled the estate, the emotions responsible for his lack of sleep the night before still churning inside him.

Irritation that she hadn't come to him.

Relief that he knew where she was.

Sexual frustration as he imagined what she might be doing with Cathal.

He turned a corner and found Rhys approaching.

"Niall Dunne has called Aesirs to ensure a table for four will be available for breakfast. He and his brother are to be joined on the terrace by Cathal and a guest."

"Etaín?"

"It's a reasonable assumption. She's still with him at his home."

Eamon laughed. Did Cathal think bringing her straight to Aesirs from his bed would change anything? Post an off-limits sign and put a collar around her neck with a leash attached? If so, then Cathal would soon be on the receiving end of a lesson in frustration.

Amusement at the prospect of it lightened Eamon's mood considerably though not enough for him to forget his own recent lesson, thanks to Etaín, on the cost of ignorance. In all the years Niall and Denis Dunne had enjoyed a meal at Aesirs, they'd never sat on the terrace when accompanied by a woman.

"I believe it's time to find out the reason for the Dunnes' sudden interest in my future consort."

Rhys stiffened in outrage on his behalf. "You believe Cathal's motivation for bedding her is solely so she can be used for some purpose?"

Eamon shrugged. "There's attraction between them, perhaps more. For the moment I'm willing to allow it to run its course. If he hurts her emotionally, it will only place her more firmly in my arms. It will make it easier, when she learns of her heritage, for her to put aside her concerns for those humans who aren't part of our world."

"The Dunnes might present a greater danger to her than heartbreak."

"If that proves to be true, then there will be a reckoning as a result of it."

S taying in the car or going with me to Derrick's apartment?" Etaín asked.

"With you," Cathal said, bombarded by the same feeling he'd had at his club, the desire to remain close to her.

He joined her on the sidewalk, his hand going to the base of her spine and remaining there as they made their way to the front door. She tapped lightly, her smile intriguing him, beguiling him to the extent it was all he could do not to touch his mouth to hers so he could taste her amusement, share it.

"Afraid of interrupting something?" he asked as she knocked again, a little harder.

She glanced at him, dark eyes sparkling, her pleasure infectious, pulling an answering smile from him. "I hope so."

The door opened to reveal a bare-chested, barefooted stranger in jeans with an incredible dragon on his skin. "My work," Etaín said, shades of meaning in her voice as her eyes flicked downward at the bulge defined in soft, worn denim.

Jealousy surged through him with the thought she and Derrick might share the same lover. Possessiveness gripped him and he shifted the hand at the base of her spine so it cupped her hip, at the same time fighting to keep the other from balling into a fist.

"Quinn, Cathal, owner of Saoirse. Cathal, Quinn, possibly a PI with McAlister Investigations."

Fuck! The bombshell she casually dropped blew away everything else in an instant of alarm.

His chest went tight and his heartbeat rabbited until he focused on one word—*possibly*. Meaning Quinn wouldn't know about the tracker on the Harley or Sean's brief investigation of Etaín.

He gathered his calm though it was tinged with guilt at ever having set Sean on her to begin with. He told himself knowing who her father and brother were might help keep her safe from his family.

It salved his conscience. And after having been with her, he knew he wasn't sorry for the promise he'd made to his father, not when it had led to Etaín.

He breathed again.

"Derrick in bed?" she asked Quinn.

"Yeah."

"I need to talk to him for a minute and change clothes."

She turned and the feel of her pelvis against his sent a jolt of heat through his cock. "Be right back," she said, giving him a quick kiss.

Etaín slipped into the bedroom, closing the door behind her. Derrick was on his back, sprawled in naked, inked glory, the sheets and blankets spilled onto the floor.

A single eye opened in acknowledgment of her presence.

"I'd say a good time was had by all," she said.

He grunted, then opened the second eye at noticing she was wearing the same outfit he'd seen her in the night before. "Who's the lucky man?"

"Cathal."

Derrick rose onto his elbows. "Was he as delicious as he looked?"

She grinned. "Prime beefcake. And Quinn?"

Derrick's thumb and forefinger went to his mouth in a pinching gesture. "My lips are sealed."

"That'd be a first." She sat down on the bed next to him and opened her purse, removing the drawing and showing him the Harlequin Rapist's tattoo. "Do you recognize the work?"

Derrick gave a dramatic shudder. "No."

She leaned in, touching her mouth briefly to his. "You're happier. I'm glad."

He grabbed her wrist as she stood. "Thanks."

"Call Bryce. Okay?"

"If I must."

"You definitely must."

"Okay. I will. Promise."

She went to the dresser and opened the top drawer, stripping out of her clothes and putting on fresh ones. She transferred the contents of the purse into the pockets of her jeans before dumping last night's outfit into a hamper in the closet and swapping the fuck-me boots for shoes.

"I'm off," she said at the door. "Don't bother behaving yourself."

"Wouldn't think of it."

"Ready?" Cathal asked as soon as she stepped into the living room.

"Just need to grab my kit."

She paused next to Quinn, touching his shoulder. "Prayers for your father. Take care of the artwork."

"Thanks. Will do."

Habit made her pull a sketch pad and pencils from the suitcase when they reached Cathal's car. She drew as they drove to Aesirs, capturing the dream tattoos and putting them on paper by the time they arrived.

"Are you sure you want to do this?" she asked. She hadn't missed the possessive display when Quinn opened the door, though she'd done her best to suppress her own reaction to it.

Cathal's answer was to leave the car, coming around to her side. She let him help her out, desire coiling inside her as they passed through the doorway where bells tinkled and cold blue flames licked along the vines on her arms.

She was underdressed for Aesirs, as she had been the first time she'd walked through its doors with Cathal. The place was full of dealmakers and wealthy sightseers, the men wearing expensive suits and power ties, the women designer dresses and real jewels.

She saw now how much the place was an extension of Eamon. He surrounded himself here with beautiful things, too. Not the least of which were the waiters and maître d', the necessary disguised as total eye candy.

Cathal's hand at the base of her spine burned through the material of her shirt, the electric, barrier hum of need accompanying the heat. She knew he was jealous of Eamon, understood his touching her was as much a possessive, in-your-face gesture meant for Eamon's sake as a desire to extend contact.

It shouldn't turn her on. The underlying danger she felt at being involved with either of them should be enough to have her shunning them completely.

The urge to bolt came, habit more than anything else. She suppressed it because there was no running from herself.

Bells tinkled again as they entered the terraced area, arriving with the muted sound of surf, the inked sensation of flooded streams rushing after a hard rain.

The feel of magic? she wondered, thinking back on the conversation with Eamon.

Looking at the low bridge crossing the shallow waterway, the live plants and decorative brazier burning incense, the word *containment* settled inside of her for a second time. Like a witch's circle, she thought before turning her attention to the diners.

Cathal's uncle and father were unmistakable. Black Irish. Handsome men even with worry lines and hints of gray in their hair.

They rose from their chairs as she and Cathal neared. Greeting him with handshakes extending into a one-armed hug and three slaps on the back in typical male style.

He pulled out her chair for her, making the introductions, "My father Niall. My uncle, Denis. This is Etaín."

Denis took her hand first, trapping it briefly in a hard clasp. She had a fleeting impression of seething emotion barely contained, a boiling cauldron with the lid clamped down hard and tight.

Niall followed, holding her hand between his. Keeping it longer but giving her the same impression as Denis had, only more so, of an intensely private man with his secrets locked behind an iron door of self-control.

"Etaín what?" Niall asked, reclaiming his seat.

"Just Etaín.

He snorted. "One name, like a rock star?"

She laughed but didn't expand on her answer. Taking the menu offered her she studied it as a way to avoid saying more.

There was no point in dredging up old rumors. Everything about Niall and Denis screamed money and plenty of it, not that she would have expected otherwise given the house Cathal called home and the fact they frequented Aesirs.

They probably knew the woman the captain was married to, socially at least. And if not her, then her family. Offering a last name would lead to "are you related to," which would in turn lead to a reminder of the scandal created when the captain was presented with a bastard child.

"You have family in the Bay Area? People you're close to?" Niall asked.

She lowered the menu enough to see his face. He was probably a great poker player. She couldn't tell if he was making polite conversation or trying to get a last name from a different angle.

She limited her answer to, "Yes." Bryce, Derrick, and Jamaal had as much right to wear the label of family as Parker and the captain did.

"That's good," Niall said, glancing at his brother. "Family is important."

Denis nodded. "Family is everything."

Polite conversation, Etaín decided before returning to the breakfast choices. Like the dinner menu, there were no prices.

She handed it off to the hovering waiter and ordered eggs, bacon, and toast, not quite regretting she'd let Cathal's sexual persuasion bring her here, but not wanting to prolong the experience, either.

The men followed suit, ordering before turning their attention back to her.

To her relief the conversation slipped into something easily managed.

What did she do for a living?

How did she and Cathal meet?

Had she been to Saoirse and what did she think of it? Leading to a discussion about the fund-raiser and the shelter, which they seemed genuinely interested in, promising a donation.

She felt relaxed in their company by the time breakfast arrived. And Eamon with it.

Desire intensified inside her, curling like thick, sinuous smoke. He stayed back as plates were set on the table and drinks refilled, then stepped forward, acknowledging Denis and Niall's presence with a small nod before taking up a position to her right, with Cathal at her left.

"I missed seeing you last night," he said, the sexual purr in his voice unmistakable. "But I'm glad to have the chance to say good morning."

He covered her hand with his, lifting it to press a kiss to the eye on her palm before releasing it. "I have every confidence I'll see you tonight."

He met Cathal's gaze fully and for long enough to convey the intended message, his lips curving in a slight smile, challenging and mocking at the same time. "As I promised Etaín yesterday, when the two of you were here, meals at Aesirs are hers for the asking and at no cost. I'll treat her companions as well."

"There's no need," Cathal said, a distinct edge to his voice.

"I insist." Smooth honey and not so sweet amusement.

She realized a part of her had wanted to see Cathal and Eamon together, the murky *why* of it making her uneasy.

Hope for something long-term? To indulge in the fantasy of having them both?

Whatever the truth of her motives, the urge to separate herself from men who were taking up too much of her thoughts returned. She picked up her fork, a hint Eamon took though he leaned down to brush a kiss over her cheek and send a spike of heat to her clit by touching his lips to her ear. "Until later, Etaín."

The silence that descended after he departed was uncomfortable. Cold, cold anger magnified by two and not offset at all by the heated fury in Cathal's eyes as their gazes met.

Not her problem, she told herself, turning her attention to her plate. She made no pretense of taking her time to savor the food or stretch out the necessity of breakfast beyond providing sustenance.

Eat and go. Those were her primary objectives.

Cathal barely tasted the food as he cursed in a long stream of silent invectives. She'd warned him what Eamon's reaction would be. He'd heard her words but hadn't stopped to anticipate what they could mean.

Jealousy pulsed through him, and anger—at himself, at her, at Eamon—but those emotions paled in comparison to the fear making him sweat in the presence of his father and uncle and what he knew they were capable of.

In bringing her to Eamon, he'd cast doubt on his ability to deliver on his promise. He'd increased the risk to her rather than diminished it.

There was ominous weight in the silence, one that ratcheted up his heartbeat. His father and uncle watched. They contemplated. And if he didn't find a way to deter them, they'd act.

Etaín finished eating and stood. "I need to take off. I've got to head to the shelter."

She didn't mouth platitudes, or linger, just said, "See you around."

Maybe. He heard it as surely as his uncle and father did.

It was all he could do to remain at the table long enough for her to get out of hearing range so he could play the only ace he currently held—and that one thanks to Sean. "Chevenier. As in daughter of SFPD Captain Chevenier and sister of Parker, FBI. I'll be in touch."

He left the table, "intense" describing his thoughts and emotions since meeting her. His gut telling him only casual had a chance of working with her now.

He caught her on the bridge, taking her hand and halting her there. "I'm willing to grovel. Or you could remember the great sex and let me off easy by saying 'I told you so.'"

The knot in his chest loosened with her slight smile. "I rarely say those words."

"I'm glad. I hate hearing them." He stepped closer, cupping her cheek, daring to touch his mouth to hers. Reminding her of how good they were together with the trace of his tongue along the seam of her lips. "I have to swing by the shelter to make decisions about the music. Let me give you a lift, Etaín. Your kit is already in my car."

Etaín shoved her free hand into the pocket of her jeans. She should tell him no, she knew she should. Worse, she suspected a part of her had known he'd catch up and make this offer when she'd named her destination.

The urge to separate that had swamped her at the table couldn't hold against the desire resulting from the press of his mouth to hers, or the electric heat originating where her palm touched his skin. She wasn't ready to say goodbye yet. "I'll take the ride."

From above, Eamon watched them on the bridge and contemplated his own actions, his own loss of control. He hadn't intended to do more than make an appearance at the table. But seeing the way her aura permeated Cathal's had stirred his possessiveness, a contradiction given that the thought of sharing her remained arousing.

Close to her he hadn't found it possible to remain sanguine at the prospect Cathal's involvement was motivated by a desire to use her. Next to him Rhys said, "Her mother runs and hides. Are you so certain she won't ultimately follow the same path?"

"I'm certain of it."

If she was a runner, then she would never have entered Aesirs the first time. The wards reacted to her. She felt something though she hadn't asked him about it.

He'd convinced himself knowledge gave him the upper hand and their physical joining would add to her need for him. He'd underestimated the effect of living among humans and outside of Elven culture. She was dangerously independent and unpredictable.

Longevity bred patience into their kind, a belief that there was no need to agonize over a lost opportunity because it was only a matter of time before it presented itself again. When it came to Etaín, that patience was like mist evaporating in the sun. He wouldn't be able to continue this course of action beyond the shelter fund-raiser.

He wanted her with him each day. He wanted her bound to him in the same way the magic seemed to be choosing Cathal.

There were no guarantees a changeling would survive the transition, but given her gift, at some point she would need to anchor herself to a lover or—he strongly suspected—lovers. The details of how such a thing came to pass weren't easily discovered, but what he had ascertained, in those moments he'd been allowed access to a Dragon's hoard, was that sometimes the bond formed spontaneously, while other times it could be created by a willful act.

The few *seidic* born into this world and claimed by the queen, only to be assassinated while ensconced in their luxurious prison, had all inked their chosen mates, low-caste Elves because it was deemed far too dangerous to allow them to claim a spell caster.

It was a risk he believed himself willing to take, though the timing of it was uncertain. She would be his wife-consort, and he, her anchor, if not by spontaneous act, then by willful one.

Below, they left the bridge, passing into the main dining area on their way to the exit. He let them go when an order would have prevented it. She could remain in Cathal's presence for a little while longer. He'd allow them both that much, but no more. Tonight she'd be back in his bed.

Fifteen

Denis watched Cathal leave with Etaín, impatience boiling to the surface. When they'd first stepped through the doorway his hopes had ridden high. A look and it was obvious they were lovers, the sexual chemistry between them enough to heat a room.

He'd been surprised by Cathal's hand on her back and the possessiveness his nephew didn't bother to hide. But he didn't blame Cathal for letting this thing with Etaín turn into something more than carrying out a responsibility to the family.

She was a beautiful woman. Dress her in designer clothes and give her quality jewelry, she could move around in the same circles they did.

His hand tightened on the coffee cup. The searing anger he'd carried since being awakened and told about Brianna was an explosive mass in his chest.

He'd agreed to hold off grabbing Etaín in the hope of Cathal being able to deliver her. But breakfast hadn't given him cause to continue waiting, not when the animals who'd raped his baby girl were still out there.

That guy showing up and making it clear he had a claim on Etaín changed things as far as he was concerned. Her accepting his kiss and not denying the possibility she'd go from Cathal's bed to his was reason to stop waiting.

A wife—or a potential wife—was due respect and protection. But a mistress, a whore, could be taken out as collateral damage. Niall understood that.

"I'm done waiting," he told his brother.

Niall turned his head so their eyes met. "The names attached to hers mean careful planning. No mistakes. There's more at stake here than your need to see justice done for Brianna and Caitlyn, Denis. Cathal's promised to handle this for the family, let *my son* have a chance to take care of it."

Searing rage and burning anguish clawed their way up his throat, but for his brother he forced them back into his chest. "I can give it a little longer."

Unless something else happens to change things.

*I*t felt like a thousand ants were crawling on him. Not the tiny black ones that had streamed across the floors and counters in every place he'd lived with his mother, but the big ugly red ones that bit.

Where was she? Now that he knew she was the one, he wanted to get started.

His hands tightened on the steering wheel until his fingers hurt. He looked at them. They were white against the dark blue vinyl, reminding him of the bandages and Popsicle sticks his mother used once to keep them all straight so they'd heal right.

She'd dragged him up the stairs after catching him outside the apartment. First she'd slammed his hand in the door. Then one-by-one his fingers, so he'd know better than to leave when she'd told him not to.

He'd been so hungry that day, hungry enough he didn't care how she punished him as long as he could find something to eat. Even the cat food left out for strays by the old lady on the first floor made his mouth water after three days of being alone in the apartment.

Reaching over he buried his hand in the mound of candy bars on the passenger seat. She'd taken Kevin with her that time, to sell so she could buy drugs.

He shuddered and looked away from the steering wheel, eyes skimming the tattoos covering the burn marks from where she'd pressed her cigarettes and hot spoons against his arms. Sometimes afterward she was sorry for doing it. She'd make it better with kisses.

The snake between his legs woke up and the stream of ants crawled downward, melting and soaking through his skin so he squirmed at feeling that part of him getting bigger and harder. He reached down and rubbed the new tattoo, pressing the material of his pants into it.

Pain streaked up his leg and the snake stopped swelling until he thought about how he'd gotten the tattoo done while she was there. And how it'd felt when she looked over and saw the one that would always remind him of her.

He touched himself then, through his jeans. It was okay to touch himself now that he knew she was the one, just as it was okay to touch himself when he remembered the others.

Laughter made him jerk his hand away from his lap.

Three teens slowed next to the car, pants hanging off their hips.

"Pervert," one of them said.

"Get a room if you want to jack off."

"Ten bucks and a prostitute will blow you," the third one said and they all laughed again.

He fumbled as he turned the key. Stupid, stupid, stupid to get noticed near the homeless shelter, sitting in a car when usually he shambled along pushing a stolen shopping cart he kept hidden nearby.

The ants re-formed, crawling over his skin and biting him, sending anger rolling through him. She wasn't at her apartment. She wasn't at the tattoo shop. She wasn't here, all places she should have been at this time of the day.

A sports car pulled into a parking place reserved for police and important visitors. He stayed where he was, curious, but also not wanting to pull away from the curb and maybe be noticed by someone else.

The passenger door opened and she got out of the car. His heart started racing in his chest.

The golden glow was there and he ached inside when he saw her smile. She was so, so beautiful. All he needed to do was decide on the best time and place to collect her. Then they'd be together for as long as it took to be sure she wouldn't forget him.

Movement distracted him. The ache turned into anger when he realized her smile was for the man who must have been driving.

It wasn't the blond one he'd seen her with outside the shop. This one was dark-haired.

He met her behind the car, stopping her there with hands on her hips. Making the golden glow turn dirty at the edges.

She didn't fight him off even when his mouth lowered to hers. Her arms went around his neck, her body pressing and rubbing as they kissed.

Whore. He couldn't sit and watch her the way he'd sometimes had to do when his mother brought strangers home.

Ducking his head so he didn't have to see more than a sliver of street above the dashboard, he drove away from the curb, getting a block from the shelter before he realized he hadn't written down the time.

He pulled over. There was only one piece of paper now, with her name on it. He subtracted out a few minutes, then wrote down when and where he'd seen her. Hesitating, he added that she'd been with someone, not because he would forget it, but because being thorough was the key to not getting caught.

He reached down and touched the tattoos. All thirteen of them, not just the one he'd gotten for her.

It wouldn't be much longer, he promised himself. They'd be together soon.

Cathal walked through the shelter alongside the teen Etaín had passed him off to after a quick introduction to Justine. Kitchen. Dining room. Dorm-style sleeping areas. The number of children present dismayed him. They were everywhere and all ages. With one parent or two, often accompanied by someone old enough to be a grandparent.

The crowded conditions made him think of the men and women on Wall Street who'd caused the collapse of the economy with their legalized schemes and paid-for loopholes. They'd swelled the ranks of the homeless and jobless yet they'd never be charged and never see a day of jail time.

He recognized the slippery moral ground, but he couldn't stop himself from comparing them to his father and uncle, and thinking the damage done by those nameless, faceless corporate employees with their golden parachutes and legally untouchable bank accounts was far worse than what could be laid at his family's doorstep.

"Is it like this all day?" he asked.

"Depends on how many kids are here. Unless you're signed up for one of the services that come around, soon as breakfast is over, those who don't need to tend children have to leave and look for work until dinnertime."

They exited through a backdoor. "This is where the tattooing is going to be happening. If you don't need anything else, I got to grab breakfast before the meal is done."

"I'm good."

Cathal pulled his phone from his pocket so he could make notes about providing music for the fund-raiser. His assistants would carry out the tasks.

He wondered what brought Etaín here. What drove her to give her time and talents to this particular . . . *Charity* didn't seem like the right word. Charity was a mind-set, an expectation imposed by society or religion or some outside force.

His mother and the wealthy women she considered her social equals did charity work. Etaín's involvement with the shelter didn't feel like that.

Frustration gnawed at him. He wanted more than just the narrow window into her life sex provided.

Uneasiness crept in at the strength of his interest in her. Every-thing about Etaín complicated his life. Worse, he could no longer distinguish between his desire to keep her safe and his desire to be with her.

Etaín looked up as Teresa slipped into the small storage room, now set up to accommodate the tattooing. A mat was on the floor and the bright light bulbs had been swapped out for a low-wattage glow. Incense burned, a compromise against candles and CDs loaded with nature sounds.

The whole setup made her uncomfortable and close to outright embarrassed. Few of those at the shelter guessed Justine had New-Age leanings hidden beneath the no bullshit exterior, but Etaín had learned in her teens that resistance was futile when it came to this.

Justine thought doing it this way was important, because getting this kind of tattoo was more of a spiritual undertaking than a physical one. There were artists around the country who felt the same way, women who tied their work in with ceremony, some of them even claiming to be practicing witches or pagans.

Etaín tried not to think too much about this aspect of her tie to ink. Gifts came with responsibilities. Of that she was certain though the refrain came from the captain's influence, not her mother's. So she did this, even though the trappings of it nearly spooked her.

Teresa sat down without being prompted, legs crossed and arms resting loosely on them. "This okay?"

"For right now."

Teresa glanced to the side, where a low table held everything needed for the tattoo. Her eyes widened at seeing the hand-needles. Etaín said, "This will hurt a lot more than doing the work with a machine. It'll also take longer."

"Justine said when you've given other people tattoos like this, it made a difference. She said they were able to make a break from their past."

"They still had to work at it. And keep wanting it. But yeah, the changes stuck."

"I want my son back. I want to be a good mother to Lothar."

"Think about that while you're getting the tattoo. Picture the life you want with him." It was as far as Etaín felt comfortable going with the mystical stuff. Any further and she'd freak herself out.

Teresa had dressed in a tank top with spaghetti straps. A few swipes of the razor, followed by a smear of Vaseline, and the small area above her left breast was ready for the tattoo.

"Go ahead and lie down."

Habit made Etaín open the sketch pad to the image of Lothar with its embedded sigils, but the memory of it was in her hands. When she looked at the place where the tattoo would go, she saw it in an inner eye as though it were already inked into Teresa's skin.

Picking up a short hand-needle, she dipped it into a cap of ink. "Ready?"

Teresa didn't ask about the lack of stencil, just said yes, the faith she put in Etaín enough to unnerve her if she let herself think too much about it. She took a deep breath, clearing her mind. Emptying it of everything and giving herself over to the physical act of turning the dream image into a reality.

It took concentration to work the needle in a steady rhythm. It required strength of will as well as physical stamina and control to push the needle through skin by hand and put the ink in at a consistent depth.

Outline first. Then shading. And at the very end, weaving the hidden sigils in.

Until Eamon she'd always thought of the sigils in terms of Jung, as symbols of a collective unconscious giving power to belief and triggered by pain. She'd never seriously considered the existence of some external magic that could be captured and manipulated. And in turn, might manipulate its user.

Fear skittered through her at where changes in her gift might lead. She shivered, pushing worry aside because there was nothing she could do about it.

She made sure the tattoo on Teresa's skin matched the one she'd seen in her dream before saying, "It's done."

Teresa sat and Etaín handed her a small mirror she kept in her kit. With shaky fingers Teresa positioned it so she could see the tattoo. A small intake of breath was followed by the flow of tears.

Her fingertip went unerringly to Lothar's hair and the sigil there. "I'm going to get you back," she whispered.

She touched the ones woven into his mouth. "I'm going to be the best mother in the world for you."

Etaín didn't know whether Teresa was consciously aware of the hidden symbols or not. She didn't think it mattered.

She went over the aftercare instructions, placing a printed copy of them on the mat for Teresa before taking the mirror back and covering the tattoo with ointment and a bandage.

Teresa grabbed Etaín's hand. Gratitude poured into her along with fierce determination. "Thank you. What you've done for me I'll never forget."

She left and Etaín cleaned up, repacking the kit then folding the mat and placing it on a shelf before putting the incense out and doing the same with it. It was a relief to escape the room.

Surprise came at finding Cathal waiting in the hallway for her. Pleasure, but dismay, too. She needed to retrieve her bike and show a few more artists the Harlequin Rapist's distinctive tats.

"I told you I was fine with catching a cab."

"And I stayed because I wanted to give you a ride home. It'll be your choice when we get there whether you grab your bike and bolt or invite me in."

His smile had heat blossoming in her belly and remembered pleasure tightening her nipples. She didn't think she'd be able to let him go without having him inside her one more time. A quickie, she promised herself. Just a quickie.

"Okay then, let's go."

Sixteen

The scent of roses drifted past Denis as he stepped into the back-yard. The need for solace drew him to a pink-streaked flower in an extensive garden of them.

He forgot the name of it though he remembered it had cost him a small fortune to acquire. There were more like it. And others he'd imported for Margo in those last few months when they'd both stopped pretending she was going to beat the cancer.

He reached out, stroking a soft petal. Remembering how he'd compared the flowers to her skin every time they'd come outside together. Remembering when they'd been young and newly married and he still sent her roses any time business took him away from her.

"I need you," he whispered. "Brianna's all that's left of us and I've already failed with her. I didn't keep her safe."

The failure tore at him, striking at the very core of who he was. He touched his lips to the silky petal of the rose. "I don't know how to break through, Margo. I don't know if I can ever bring her back."

He closed his eyes. Hoping for a sense of the wife he'd loved since the moment he first laid eyes on her, for the peace her presence always brought him.

He didn't find the first. But the second came slowly, among the flowers that had always given her pleasure.

He walked on, moving along a pathway through the well-tended bushes, stopping occasionally to bend over and inhale deeply.

His thoughts returned to breakfast at Aesirs and he felt better about holding off, giving Cathal breathing room to step up and do the right thing.

It was important to Niall for his son do this. It was important to him as well.

This was about family. Not business.

The scene around him disappeared as another took its place. The day he'd stood with Niall in the maternity ward, looking through the glass at Cathal, both of them in agreement that it was fine for a son to make his own choice whether or not to follow in his father's footsteps. Then the day Niall had stood with him, looking at Brian.

Pain pulled Denis into the present, a fist gripping his heart with thoughts of his son. He rubbed his chest but the ache wasn't something that could be massaged away.

The rose garden ended, opening up into the pool area. He stepped forward, closing himself off from thoughts of the dead.

The water in the pool sparkled. Chairs and tables were set up steps away from it, an invitation to enjoy the sunshine and fresh air.

Maybe this was what Brianna needed, he thought, taking out his cell phone and calling inside. He spoke with the cook first, telling her that he and Brianna would take lunch at poolside. Then to the nurse, ordering her to bring Brianna out.

Closing his phone, he placed it on a table, a gesture from the old days, when he'd made a show of shutting out the other aspects of his life in order to be fully there with his family. He retrieved cushions for the heavy wrought-iron chairs, finding pleasure in action as he set things up to enjoy lunch with his daughter.

The door opened and she was led outside in a bathrobe, the belt pulled tight, emphasizing her rail-thin body. Pain returned with the sight of her, a savage, raw clawing in his chest. He'd put the animals responsible for this down like the rabid dogs they were.

His hands gripped the back of a chair as she was brought forward, her eyes dulled by sedation. He should have had her dressed in a shirt and shorts.

The nurse guided Brianna into a chair and Denis pushed it forward. "It's too beautiful to be inside," he said. "I thought we'd have lunch out here. The food will be out in a few minutes. You hungry?"

She didn't answer, nor would she eat. Starving herself was another way of trying to die, an attempt he thwarted by forced feedings.

His stomach cramped, his appetite gone though he'd finish what he'd started.

"You can leave us," he told the nurse, not wanting her to witness his painful attempts to communicate with his daughter.

Lunch was brought out and served, the cook fussing over Brianna, pretending everything was normal. When she was gone he picked up his fork, stabbing it into the potato salad.

"I saw Cathal this morning," he said, starting a one-sided conversation with Brianna that lasted through the meal and then petered out in a silence filled by sounds from the past, from better times.

Squeals and splashes.

The spring and bounce of the diving board.

Watch me, Daddy! Watch this!

Brianna tan and healthy and smiling.

Brian doing flips and diving into the water with barely a ripple. Jumping from the side, arms around his knees, a human cannonball showering his parents and sister when he struck water.

Tears came and Denis couldn't stop them. He stood and took several steps away from the table, turning his back on the pool and the past, on the emptiness of his present.

Grant me strength, God, he prayed, even as he did it, knowing he would get through this. The pain would fade, maybe one day to the point he would consider taking another wife and trying for a son with her.

A splash had raw fear gripping him as he spun around. Terror bursting through him at seeing Brianna in the deep end of the pool.

He raced to the edge and dived into the water, frantically kicking, barely able to accept what he saw.

She'd managed to use the belt of her bathrobe to tie herself to the heavy wrought-iron chair. And against all instinct to survive, she'd willfully inhaled water in the seconds it took him to reach her.

There was no struggle in her. No life.

She was facedown, the chair pinning her to the bottom of the pool.

He wrenched it to the side, fumbling with the knots. Ripping at them as his heart thundered in his ears and his lungs burned, his mind screaming.

It took minutes to free them. A living hell of horror and desperation.

Grabbing her, he pushed off the bottom, kicking furiously to the surface and getting her out of the pool. He yelled at the top of his lungs, bellowing for help before administering first aid.

A frantic eternity passed before Brianna vomited water and began breathing. She curled in a ball, silent, defeated, unresponsive to his fury or his pain as he spoke her name over and over again, unable to stop the torrent of it.

His entire body shook. His hands trembled in the aftermath of what had nearly happened.

No one had heard him yelling. No one had come.

He wanted to rail at Brianna. To plead with her.

Emotion howled through him. A wild storm he rode until his hands were steady and he'd gotten himself back under control.

Keeping an eye on her, he retrieved his phone and called the nurse, decision crystallizing in him. As soon as Brianna was seen to and he got to his study, the next call would be to Cathal.

Killing Brianna's rapists might not be therapy for her, but it would be for him. He was done waiting. Cathal would bring Etaín here by the end of the day, or he'd see to it himself.

* * *

"You coming up?" Etaín asked as Cathal pulled into the driveway.

He turned off the engine. "What do you think?

She glanced down at where his cock made a hard, desperate plea against the fabric of his pants, then up at his face, her smile sexual invitation and the promise of carnal sin.

Without a word she got out of the car.

He followed her up the flight of stairs, managing to keep his hands off her until she stopped in front of the door, but then he wrapped his arms around her waist and touched his mouth to the place where her shoulder met her neck.

Satisfaction surged through him at the subtle melting of her body against his. "It feels like it's been hours since we were with each other," he murmured.

"That's because it has been. At least in the way you mean."

The huskiness in her voice had his hands moving up to cover her breasts. "Did you think about this when we were apart?" he asked, rubbing his palms over hardened nipples and reveling in the small sound of need he elicited from her.

"Do you really need to hear me say yes?"

"I'm a man." He bit the soft skin of her neck, following it with a quick suck. "What do you think?"

"That I want you again."

There might as well have been a hot wire from her mouth to his dick. His hips jerked. Fuck. In another minute she'd have him humping against her where they stood.

His hand left her breast and went to the front of her jeans. She didn't protest when he unsnapped them, pushing his way underneath the waistband of her panties to verify the truth of her statement.

His moan echoed hers as he found wet heat and a stiffened clit. "Open the door, Etaín, or I'm going to take you right here."

He barely recognized himself in the threat-rough voice and raw command. In how little he cared about privacy or public decency or the possibility of getting arrested over the lack of it.

"Do it," she dared, her clit a hot throb against his palm.

Make me, came instantly.

He opened his mouth to say the words but they clung to his tongue, held there by some small measure of sanity and self-control. He wasn't sure if she was serious or not, but a shudder went through him with the silent acknowledgment that she had the power to make him. And if he wasn't careful, he'd get to the point where he was happy she did.

His phone rang, the tone indicating it was his uncle. He pulled his hand from her panties, sliding arousal-wet fingers over her belly and growing harder as a result of it.

"I've got to get this," he said, breaking the physical contact and taking a few steps away from Etaín.

"You with your new lady friend?"

Cathal tensed, knowing his uncle hadn't called to check up on his progress. That'd be his father's responsibility. "I'm with her."

"Brianna nearly died today."

The heat of seconds ago disappeared in a cold rush of fear. "How?"

"The pool." A long silence followed, as if his uncle was trying to get himself under control. "I almost didn't get to her in time."

"I'll come by the house and visit her."

"Make it by tonight, Cathal. Those names you mentioned at breakfast aren't going to change how I feel now. The time for words is over. Niall will understand that after I tell him what happened."

The call dropped, the message as clear as if his uncle had spoken it directly, leaving Cathal's heart pounding as if he'd run a mile. He was caught in the middle with no way out.

Pocketing the phone, he turned around and saw Etaín standing in her doorway. His body responded, the heat returning in a rush so all he wanted to do was get naked and lose himself in her for a little while.

"You need to head out?" she asked.

"No." Just the opposite, he needed to stay with her and use the time he had to convince her to help his family.

Etaín didn't know whether to be glad or not. It unnerved her to think about how far they might have taken things if the call hadn't interrupted them. She was comfortable with her sexuality, but making a public show of getting fucked wasn't something she ever intended to do.

He closed the distance between them, bringing the hum of desire with him. His hands settled on her hips as he nuzzled her cheek, her ear, sending a shiver of need through her.

"Where were we?" he asked, touching his mouth to hers.

"Probably on the verge of getting arrested," she said, covering her uneasiness with humor.

He smiled against her lips and she felt it all the way to her toes. "Maybe we should go to bed instead of jail."

"Good idea."

She entered the apartment first, setting the tattoo kit just inside the door. She didn't bring many people home. Jamaal and Derrick and Bryce came by sometimes if they were on this side of the bay, but mostly she went to their places because they lived in San Francisco and that's where she spent most of her time.

For the first time in memory, she saw her apartment through the lens of someone else's eyes. It was comfortable, lived in, the same way Cathal's was, and yet it didn't have the same sense of permanence. It shouldn't have surprised her, but it did when she realized that nothing was irreplaceable. If she had to, she could leave everything behind and disappear, like her mother had always been able to do.

He didn't say anything and she welcomed the silence as they moved in unspoken accord to where the mattress lay on the floor. His hands went to the front of her shirt, slow seduction replacing rough urgency as first one button and then another gave way.

His mouth claimed hers, his tongue sliding between parted lips to rub against hers. She wrapped her arms around his neck, her breasts swelling, anxious for the feel of his hands on them.

A moan came when he rubbed his palms over taut nipples. She pressed her lower body to his, grinding against him until his hands moved to her shoulders, forcing her away long enough to rid her of shirt and bra.

"You're beautiful," he said in between kisses, his fingers tight on her nipples, squeezing, tugging, twisting. Sending pleasure straight to her cunt. "Have you ever posed?"

Her hands dropped to his waistband, undoing his buckle and then the front of his pants. "For a skin mag? So some guy can jerk off looking at me? Or for a lover?"

Cathal bit her bottom lip. A sharp rebuke, maybe, for reminding him there had been other men before him, and would be after, though the thought of not having whatever it was she'd found with him sent an unfamiliar ache through her.

"For other artists," he said. "Or ads."

"No."

She freed his cock, absorbing the smooth heat of him through her palm as she pressed her lips to his, drawing his tongue into her mouth and sucking, ending the conversation for long moments.

"You're a major distraction," he said.

"And you're not?"

"We'll see."

He kissed downward. Pausing to take each nipple into his mouth, every pull of his lips and press of his teeth intensifying the desire and making her grow more wet and swollen.

She tangled her fingers in his hair, unsure whether to hold him to her breasts or push him lower, to her cunt.

He took the decision away from her after tugging her jeans and panties to her ankles, then stripping them off her along with her shoes.

"Get on the bed and spread your legs," he said in the same threat-rough tone he'd used at the front door.

She reacted to it, turned on in the same way she was to the inherent danger Eamon represented. She obeyed, heat rushing to her breasts and swollen folds as she watched Cathal shed his clothing, his eyes riveted to her cunt as he did it.

She lifted her hips when he knelt between her thighs, silently ordering him to deliver on the promise his gaze and parted lips had made.

This time he was the one who did as commanded, putting his mouth on her, pleasuring her with the thrust and swirl of his tongue, with sucks that became a carnal demand she willingly surrendered to.

She came.

Then came again when he used his upper body strength to hold her buttocks and lower back off the sheets while he remained on his knees, the angle allowing him to drive his cock in deep and hard, as if he meant to reach her very core. She tightened on him in climax and was rewarded by the flush of pleasure on his face and the liquid hot release of it in her channel.

He covered her with his body when the last of his semen had jetted through his cock, then rolled so she sprawled across him. She closed her eyes, savoring the lazy caress of his hands on her back and the feel of his fingers combing through her hair.

This is dangerous, she thought, admitting to herself how much she liked their continued physical contact after sex. Worried that even knowing she should roll off and away, putting distance between them, she didn't move.

It's the novelty of it, she rationalized, placing her palm against his side, where smooth, tanned skin was a sensual contrast to the thick mat of hair on his chest. Any other lover—except Eamon possibly—and she'd have to be very, very careful not to allow the tattooed eyes to touch him after this much contact.

Cathal's voice was a rumble in her ear. "Why the shelter? Why are you involved with it?"

"Justine."

"How'd you meet her?"

"She did teen outreach for a while. Still does, though it's unofficial, and she doesn't have much time to dedicate to it."

"You were in trouble? Living on the streets?"

She took refuge in asking a question of her own, her usual dodge. "What makes you think that?"

"You live in a studio apartment and unless you've got pictures in the bathroom or in your closet, I don't see a single one. Not you alone. Not you with friends. And, most importantly, not you with your family though you take your brother's calls and stay out late when he needs your help."

She had a deep-seated aversion to having her image captured. Another of her mother's legacies, and something more, a survival instinct so thoroughly engrained that even as child wanting to please the only father she'd known, she'd battled furiously against being photographed.

"You're very observant," she said, deflecting, turning the conversation. "Maybe you should be cop instead of a club owner."

His chest rose and fell with a laugh that wasn't all mirth, making her wonder if he'd had run-ins with the law at some point in his life. His hands stopped their stroking and his arms went around her, holding her tight. "How come no photographs?"

"Everyone I hang out with draws."

His arms tightened further, his frustration leaching into her as if forced through the electric-hum barrier that still seemed to be protecting him from her gift. "You're a hard woman to get to know."

Her reactive response was *I don't want to be known*. But that wasn't the truth. If it had been, then she wouldn't have ignored the refrain drilled into her by her mother at every opportunity.

*Keep moving. Stay uninvolved in the lives of others. See but don't be
seen.*

He was a complication in her life. A change. A lover who unnerved
her and thrilled her and was rapidly becoming an addiction.

If she continued to evade would it drive him away?

Or draw him closer?

Which of them did she really want?

She didn't know and didn't want to think about it, making answering the easiest course of action. "I went a little wild in my teens.
Drugs. Sex. Violating curfews and rules until it just got easier to stay
out than go back. That's how I met Justine."

"You were living on the streets?"

"For a little while, until the captain had me scooped up and put in
a cell overnight."

She couldn't keep the remembered terror from sliding out of the
mental box she tried to keep it in. It traveled through her in a soul-
deep shudder.

Beneath her Cathal tensed, probably sorry he'd hit a nerve. She
wrestled the fear back inside its cage.

"The captain?"

She sighed. "Chevenier." And because it was easier, a truth still
present in her heart, she added, "My father. You might remember the
scandal my coming to live with him caused."

Cathal rubbed his cheek against her hair, stroking a hand down
her spine in a caress she felt deep inside her. "What I remember is that
a woman showed up and presented your father with a daughter he
accepted right away as his. Speculation followed, about just when the
girl was conceived, before or during the very brief time he was separated from his old-money wife. It wasn't titillating to me as a kid and
I don't give a shit about it as an adult. Your brother's FBI, right?"

"Yes."

"The other day you said you didn't see them often, but you took
your brother's call then rushed off to help him."

"That's true. We're not completely estranged."

"Do they drop by your apartment to check up on you?"

"Parker has been here a couple of times." *To pick up drawings. Not to visit.*

She changed the topic by asking, "Was that your father who called?"

Father or uncle. By Cathal's answer of *I'm with her* it had to be one of them.

He didn't answer for a long time, as if he wrestled with becoming known, too. And she vacillated between pushing closer or backing away until the choice was taken from her.

"It was Denis. He called to tell me my cousin Brianna nearly drowned herself in the pool."

Don't involve yourself.

Etaín ignored the words whispering in her mother's voice. She didn't pretend to misunderstand the way Cathal phrased his answer. "She's tried before?"

"Not the pool, but other ways." His arms tightened, delivering a hint of physical pain along with an emotional one breaching the barrier between them. "She's so heavily sedated, I don't know how she managed to get outside and into the water. She's had a private nurse since coming home from the hospital. She's watched twenty-four, seven."

Like a fogged window clearing to reveal the scene behind it, Etaín saw Cathal in a hospital room with a teenage girl, then that same girl lying glassy-eyed in a bedroom with posters on the wall, movie and rock stars. She remembered seeing it before, along with another one, of Cathal standing near a casket, in the dreams that were a precursor to Tyra's memories.

Don't involve yourself.

Once again she ignored her mother's refrain.

"Someone Brianna was close to died?"

Cathal tensed beneath her. "How do you know that?"

She scrambled for an answer since she couldn't tell him the full truth. "A guess. She wants to die. So either something terrible happened to her, or someone she loved died and she wants to be with them."

Some of the rigidness left Cathal's body. "Both. In the last year her mother died of cancer and her brother Brian in a car accident. A few weeks ago she spent the night with her friend Caitlyn. They went somewhere. We don't know any of the details. Only that they ended up drugged, gang raped, and left to die at Lake Merced. A jogger found them in time for Brianna, but not for Caitlyn."

He didn't hide his pain, his anguish over what had happened to his cousin. "Sixteen. That's how old they are. Were. Until this happened Brianna was coping okay. Denis was there for her. She's also a gifted musician, so it gave her a place to go to deal with losing her mother and Brian."

Etaín remembered the fleeting impression she'd had when she shook hands with Cathal's uncle. Seething emotion barely contained. A boiling cauldron with the lid clamped down hard and tight.

He had good reason for it.

Don't involve yourself.

For a third time she ignored her mother's voice and her mother's lessons. She slid off Cathal to sit next to him, her arms around her legs, her chin resting on her knees. She took her time, finding just the right way to explain without revealing too much.

"Parker needed my help with a rape victim. That's why he called me. It's a gift I have, being able to draw out information from people. If you'd like me try with Brianna . . ."

Cathal's heart became an erratic drumbeat pushing a myriad of different emotions through him. Relief. Fear. Worry. Guilt.

Along with renewed desire.

Naked and in that pose she looked so beautiful, so vulnerable, like some ethereal woodland nymph needing protection. Yet when he met her gaze, he saw a wild spirit in her dark, dark eyes, a sexual fantasy capable of making him hard over and over again.

He sat, drawing his leg up as well, not to hide her effect on him, but to keep himself from tumbling her back to the mattress so neither of them had to cross the line he knew existed for both of them. He'd wanted her to do this willingly, *intended* to ensure she would when he agreed to handle this at his father's request. But now he found he didn't want her made an accessory to murder, even an unwitting one.

If he could get her to leave his uncle's house with the drawings, then arrange, through Sean, for her brother to stop by and *inadvertently* see them while he happened to be there, all of it done in such a way there would be no repercussions . . .

The sweat chilled on his skin. Son or not, betrayal of the family would be a death sentence.

Etaín's arms fell away from her legs. She uncurled her body. Her hand settled on his shoulder and he felt the heat of it all the way down to his cock. She leaned forward, rubbing her cheek against his without caring about the stubble there.

"Let me do what I can for your cousin. My drawing what happened helps some victims. It's almost as if recording the images separates the person from the horror, giving them permission to forget it."

Surprise made him pull back so he could watch her face. "Repressed memory?"

"I'm not a psychiatrist or a psychologist. I've just seen it happen with traumatized victims. They might believe what I've drawn is real because other people tell them it is, but it doesn't *seem* real to them anymore." She shrugged. "Sometimes being able to forget is a blessing. But maybe all your cousin needs is time and medical care and plenty of support."

She stood. "The offer is there, Cathal. You don't need to decide now whether you want to take it. You can let me know anytime, but I need to head out. I've got a list of artists I have to visit today."

A surge of fear for Etaín drove Cathal to his feet when the weight of guilt might have held him down. He pulled her against him, sure she could feel the wild race of his heart.

Her arms went around his waist. "There's something else you've got to know," she said. "The things I draw, they may not be admissible in court. The times I've helped when Parker or the captain asked me to, they haven't been. But providing the pictures told them where to look, and they found the evidence they needed there."

He considered asking her what she thought of vigilante justice, if it would bother her if someone who'd drugged and raped another person was murdered because of it. But no answer she could give would change anything right now, and in the end, ignorance would be her best defense.

"It doesn't matter if they're admissible or not," he said, recognizing the possibility he might fail in his attempt to circumvent his father and uncle, but taking some comfort in knowing they would cover their tracks completely, protecting her as a by-product of it.

Guilt whipped across his conscience as he thought of her shuddering at the memory of being held in a cell when she was a teen. He forced the emotion down, replacing it with protectiveness. This was the only way to keep her safe. Touching his lips to hers, he whispered, "Help Brianna."

"When?"

"Today. As soon as we get dressed."

"Yes. But the drawings won't be ready until tomorrow."

Relief pulsed through him, at not having to find a way to convince her to leave Denis's house without surrendering them. "That's fine."

Her tongue teased the seam of his lips then entered his mouth for a quick rub against his before retreating. Her hands went to his chest, gently separating their bodies.

They dressed. He made a brief call to tell Denis they were on their way.

"I'll take my bike and follow you to your uncle's house," she said when they reached the driveway, the tone of her voice firm enough he knew she wouldn't be persuaded otherwise.

Misgiving tightened his chest but there was no turning back. "I'll try not to lose you."

She laughed. "As if you could manage that while I'm on the Harley."

Seventeen

Etaín stopped the bike next to Cathal's car. His uncle's estate wasn't far from Eamon's.

She took her helmet off and draped it over the Harley's handlebars. Then liberated the drawing tablet and box of pencils to serve as props and mask the truth of her gift.

Uneasiness worked its way into her, at having involved herself in this. At remembering how casually Parker had exposed her ability to Trent and how knowledge of it had expanded to include the rest of the taskforce.

Cathal got out of his car and joined her. His hand settled at the base of her spine and even through the leather of her jacket, the hum she'd come to associate with his presence intensified, not so much desire now, but comfort.

It distracted her from one worry by redirecting her to a new one. What did it mean that his memories seemed safe from her? What did she want it to mean? And would she be willing to pay the price that came with the permanence Eamon had hinted was possible?

The door opened before they reached it, revealing both Cathal's uncle and his father. Denis's eyes met hers, providing enough warning so she was prepared for the tortured anguish and unrelenting fury pouring into her with a handshake.

It was a relief when he released her. And the cold containment of

Cathal's father's emotions when he took her hand was like an icy balm suppressing Denis's scorching rage.

"I'm glad you came here today," Niall said.

"No problem."

"This way," Denis said.

He led them up a spiraled staircase and down a hallway lined with family photographs going all the way back to the 1800s. She caught glimpses of Cathal and found herself smiling, thinking how easy it must have been for him to get his own way growing up. Even as a boy he was handsome, striking with his black hair and blue eyes, his dark good looks.

They entered Brianna's bedroom. The walls were lined with posters just as they'd been in Cathal's memories.

A woman wearing a cheerful, colorful outfit like those Etaín had seen pediatric nurses wearing rose from a chair near the bed. Whatever the woman's thoughts were, her features were schooled into a professional mask.

Etaín moved to the bedside, her attention focused on Brianna. The girl's eyes were closed and her face pale, the bones sharper than they should be, as if the trauma of what she'd undergone had caused sudden weight loss.

"I'll need to be alone with her," she said.

The nurse stiffened, so did Denis. But this was nonnegotiable, though Etaín tried to avoid a confrontation by lightly touching Denis's upper arm, where the fabric of his shirt protected her from his emotion. "Please, I want to help. I can't with anyone else in the room. If you're worried about Brianna, you can wait just outside the door."

A long moment passed before Denis gave a sharp nod. "We'll leave you."

The nurse didn't budge. "What's this about, Mr. Dunne? What's going on here?" A frown in Etaín's direction made it clear she didn't register as any kind of medical professional, even an eccentric one. "What kind of help is this woman offering?"

It was Niall who answered, using the same technique Etaín had used on his brother. He placed a hand on the nurse's arm, though he left it there where she'd retreated. "It's nothing for you to worry about, Clara."

"It is while Brianna's under my care and completely helpless. It'll be hours before enough of the sedation wears off for her to be semi-conscious, much less fully conscious."

"She'll be all right. Etaín's here at Cathal's request. Let's step out into the hallway."

The nurse allowed herself to be guided out of the room, but her reluctance was obvious. Denis followed, with Cathal last.

As soon as the door closed behind them, Etaín's misgiving returned full force. She dropped the tablet and pencil case onto a bedside stand then looked down at her own hands, turning them over to expose the eyes inked into the palms.

Premonition or instinct, she couldn't shake the feeling she was getting in too deep. She couldn't prevent her mother's voice from returning in a whispered refrain not to get involved.

Too late, she acknowledged. She was already involved. With this. With Cathal.

Etaín shifted her focus to the girl on the bed. She should have postponed this when she heard Brianna was sedated to the point of unconsciousness. It hadn't occurred to her, and she knew the reason for it.

Cathal's nearness. His hand on her lower back dulling the sense of self-preservation she'd developed since first answering the call to ink.

Too late to back out now. She took one of Brianna's hands in hers, then picked up the other.

She'd remain long enough to give the impression she'd somehow managed to wake Brianna and engage her in conversation, but afterward she'd leave and stay away from Cathal. He couldn't be there when she lived Brianna's memories in her dreams.

Etaín sat on the edge of the bed, her awareness of her surroundings blurring as sight shifted to the eyes inked onto her palms and pressed to Brianna's skin. "Show me, Brianna," she said, beginning the litany that would continue until the nausea came and overwhelmed her. "Where did you go the last time you spent the night with Caitlyn? Who were you with? Show me, Brianna. What happened to Caitlyn? What happened to you?"

Cathal hated the paranoia that always crept in when he associated with his father and uncle. In the life he'd made for himself, loss of money or opportunity were the worst things to happen if someone overheard a conversation and acted on it.

He pushed away from the hallway wall outside Brianna's bedroom. "I need to talk to you privately," he told Denis.

"Niall, too?"

Cathal glanced at the nurse, heart rate accelerating. What did it say about him that if he had to leave Etaín, he wanted his father to remain at her back?

It's the paranoia.

He shook it off. She was safe. Here. Now. But if things went sideways with Denis, it'd be better if his father was involved in the conversation. "Might as well."

They retreated to Denis's study. Even in his own home he didn't speak freely except in this one room. It was the same in the house Cathal grew up in.

Cathal claimed a seat because doing it projected calm and confidence. His father took the one next to him.

Denis leaned against his desk, picking something up and rubbing it like a worry stone. A trophy, Cathal realized a minute later, a small piano with Brianna's name engraved in it.

"You did well," his uncle said.

"I did what I needed to do."

He understood he was speaking to his own conscience.

"She tell you how this works?" Denis asked. "Her getting what she needs for her pictures?"

"No."

A shrug. "That's okay. As long as we get results. The guy who passed us the name said her being able to draw the faces was freaky."

"Etaín told me this turns out to be therapeutic for some victims, almost as if it gives them permission to forget what happened to them."

"Good. I hope it does that for Brianna."

Cathal did, too. That'd go a long way in keeping Etaín safe if he was able to use her brother to circumvent his father and uncle from delivering their brand of justice. "It'll take her at least a day to turn the pictures around."

The small piano struck the desk with a muted thud. "What does that mean?"

How the hell was he supposed to answer that? "It means she'll be in touch when she's done with the drawings."

His uncle and father exchanged a look. It was Niall who said, "You need to stay with her, son. We have to be sure she doesn't show the pictures to the police. We need to know we got *all* of them."

There was no chance of staying with her. She'd made it clear, though he had no intention of sharing that information with his father and uncle.

He stood abruptly, posturing aggressiveness because he knew they'd understand and respect it. "I'm handling this. As promised. Either you trust me to take care of it or you don't. Etaín's my worry, not yours, so stay out of it. Both of you."

He walked out on them, fear and fury pounding through him with every heartbeat.

Denis waited until the door shut before speaking. "What do you think?"

"The same thing I did when I saw him with her at Aesirs. He feels something for her. Enough to overlook the fact there's another man in her life. I'm concerned."

It was an understatement and Denis knew it. He picked up the small golden trophy Brianna had won when she was eight.

"I don't want you to lose your son over this," he said, looking up to meet his brother's eyes. "If Cathal's not with her and she goes missing later today, people will think the Harlequin Rapist got her. She fits the profile. She's white where the last one was black. If making her disappear permanently becomes the only option . . ."

He shrugged. "The last victim is dead. Even if the police catch this guy and get a confession out of him for everyone but her, most people will still pin it on him."

Niall rose from his chair and paced, a rare show of worry making Denis regret letting himself be talked into involving Cathal in the first place. He didn't speak, just waited his brother out.

"If we step in now, I lose my son anyway," Niall said, halting behind the chair Cathal had been sitting in and placing his hands on the back of it. "He'll suspect we're responsible for her disappearance, but he won't be certain. And we won't know going forward whether we can trust him or not."

Denis nodded in understanding. Strong feelings for a woman could make a man turn his back on his family and betray them, even when betrayal meant death.

Guilt ate at him. He'd been on tilt since Brian's death. Margo's he'd been prepared for, braced for, but not his son's.

Brianna's rape had spun him into a place where he hadn't thought beyond his own needs, hadn't considered what taking care of them might cost his brother. "What do you want to do?"

"We let this play out. For now."

"I'm fine with that."

Denis rubbed his thumb over the place where his daughter's name was on the small gold piano. Tomorrow he'd tell Clara to cut back on the sedation in the hopes Brianna would be one of those to forget after a visit with Etaín.

Eamon glanced up from the paperwork on his desk as Rhys stepped into the room and took a seat across from him. "You've learned something?"

"Yes."

Eamon set his pen down. "What?"

"Rescue workers were called to Lake Merced several weeks ago. Denis Dunne's daughter was found in a car, overdosed, along with a friend. The other girl lingered in a coma but died and was laid to rest on Monday."

The sharp spike of suspicion stabbed Eamon. "The same day Cathal sought Etaín out."

"Yes. Within hours of the funeral service, possibly less."

"And Denis's daughter?"

"Home, against the recommendation of the doctors attending her. She attempted suicide as soon as she regained consciousness and was told of her friend's death."

"She believes herself responsible?"

"She must, though I think there is more to it than that. Both girls were good students with no history of misbehavior or trouble of any kind. One of the emergency workers was willing to share information. He suggested the girls might have been drugged and raped multiple times by a number of different males."

A killing offense as far as Eamon was concerned. "The police are involved?"

"Not actively. There wasn't evidence pointing to anything but bad choices on the girls' parts, and the Dunnes haven't brought any pressure to bear on the authorities to investigate further."

Not surprising if the Dunnes were the type of men he believed them to be. They would see justice done. In that he admired them though it didn't stop anger from settling around him at having confirmation Cathal had been sent to ensnare Etaín.

He could do nothing about Cathal's involvement with his future consort at present, and of greater concern was how the Dunnes had known about her gift. None of the possibilities occurring to him were pleasing to consider.

"Did you discover who directed them to her?"

"Not specifically, no. But the history I've managed to accumulate provides insight enough. Her mother left her in the care of a San Francisco policeman. There's some estrangement between the two of them now, but she has actively used her abilities at his request."

"His name?"

"Captain Chevenier."

It took a moment for Eamon to place the name, to remember the scandal associated with it. He cursed. If only once the captain and his wife had brought Etaín with them when they'd come to Aesirs, then she could have been made to disappear shortly thereafter, and been raised among her own kind.

"There's more to it," Rhys said. "Parker Chevenier is one of the two FBI agents who visited her yesterday."

Eamon's half-formed resolve at breakfast firmed. The shelter fundraiser would mark the end of Etaín's freedom and her ignorance about her future role as consort-wife to an Elven Lord.

"Perhaps it's time she disappeared from the human world," Rhys pressed when the silence stretched into taut moments.

"Not yet." Though Eamon contemplated whether or not to intercede with respect to the Dunnes, and drive a wedge between Etaín and Cathal by revealing the truth of Cathal's motives.

He decided against it in favor of letting Etaín's involvement with the Dunnes proceed to a natural conclusion. If she was made an accessory to murder, then she would have good reason to go into hiding, and he was quite willing to provide it. If she learned Cathal had used her, then the bond forming between them might break naturally.

Better to let it happen that way, and far, far safer. He *respected* the old magic filling her too much to interfere in its course, though as he'd discovered this morning when he saw Etaín and Cathal together, he wasn't averse to having her to himself. Later, should he still desire it, or the magic filling her require it, then he'd prefer sharing her with a lover of *his* choice.

"Where is she now?"

"At Denis's home."

"Notify me when she leaves and settles in a place where I can collect her. I believe it's also time to learn everything that can be learned about Denis and Niall Dunne."

"In case you become responsible for them?"

"A reality I still have some hope of avoiding. It's possible their actions will compel me to send Liam to them. I want to know what ripples their deaths would cause in the human world."

Etaín barely made it to the bathroom down the hall from Brianna's room in time. Nausea rolled through her in waves like a drinking binge ending in bed spins and puke.

She vomited repeatedly and even after her stomach had finally calmed, it took a long time for the clamminess to leave her skin. She sat on the floor, hunched over, shaking, Eamon's words finding her when even standing was beyond her, whispering that he had the answers she needed, not just to control her gift but to *survive* it.

Her head ached and she felt chilled. It didn't help that Cathal was waiting for her, his concern practically chewing through the door.

She felt worse than she'd ever felt after touching a victim. And though her strength came back slowly, her heart continued to beat fast and erratically.

She knew she'd call the clients on the calendar for the evening and reschedule. She couldn't handle ink tonight.

With effort she stood and splashed water on her face, then went through the cabinets and drawers until she found toothpaste and mouthwash. It took longer to feel well enough to leave the bathroom.

She opened the door to find Cathal standing right in front of it. His gaze dropped to the tablet and she caught a glimpse of haunted guilt in his eyes.

Her bout of nausea made the situation worse. But she couldn't set his mind at ease by explaining the reason for it, though she knew it left him to imagine the worst when it came to what had happened to his cousin.

"I need to leave," she said, giving them both an out.

"I'll walk you to your bike."

He took her in his arms when they reached it. She relaxed against him, soaking in his warmth, the comforting hum of desire like soothing background music.

"I'll call you tomorrow morning, after the drawings are done," she said, anticipating he might want another night like the one they'd just shared and heading it off.

He stiffened. Too late she remembered Eamon's appearance at the breakfast table.

She tensed as well, bracing herself for what he might say. Then found she preferred not to get into a discussion with him about Eamon, not now, not when she was without answers herself about what she wanted and what she could have. "I can't draw the pictures of Brianna's rapists if I'm with you," she told him.

His arms tightened around her, the silence around them growing heavy and fraught with warring emotions. "Are you going to be with him tonight?"

"I don't intend to be."

Cathal wanted her to say *no*. He wanted to *know* that if she refused to be with him, then she would spend the night alone.

Frustration, anger, and jealousy churned inside him but once again they were trumped by fear. His father and uncle expected him to remain with her, to ensure no one else saw or knew about the drawings.

He could follow her or have her followed by someone independent of Sean. He could have a record of her phone calls dumped, again by an independent contractor, though the name would come from Sean. Doing those things, and telling his father and uncle about them, would provide a buffer of safety—assuming she didn't have contact with her brother or father.

He wanted to ask her to promise she wouldn't show anyone the drawings, but doing it might lead to her asking questions, and to the very danger he was desperate to keep her from. He settled for saying, "Promise you'll call me when they're done."

"It could be two or three in the morning."

Her quick answer, with its unconscious implication she'd be alone, had the anger and jealousy flowing out of him. Guilt over his own subterfuge replaced them.

He closed his eyes, rubbing his cheek against hers and wondering when he'd lost control of the situation, only to realize it had never been his to begin with. The moment he'd seen her, he'd been lost in a haze of desire that had thickened rather than thinned as he spent time with her.

He touched his mouth to hers, hating their impending separation though he knew he needed it in order to pay Sean a visit. Some things couldn't be risked except in person. Setting a plan in motion to keep Etaín from becoming tainted by his father and uncle's actions was one of them.

"Just call me as soon as the drawings are done, Etaín. Promise you'll do it."

"I promise."

Eighteen

"D on't recognize the work," Juan said, handing the copy of the drawing back to Etaín. It was heavily creased from being folded and unfolded so many times, the white dingy.

Still usable, Etaín thought, putting it in her pocket, though if she carried it on her much longer, she'd have to ask for a new one or open the doorway between her memories and Tyra's to redraw it.

A shiver went through her at the prospect, a wave of cold radiating from her core. She hadn't felt warm since puking her guts out after the session with Brianna.

"You okay?" Juan asked. "You don't look so good."

"Just need to get home and go to bed."

His smile guaranteed he never slept alone. "Another day I'd be hoping that was an invite, *chica*."

"And if I slept with other tattoo artists, I'd be tempted to make the offer."

"Give me one date to change your mind."

She thought of Eamon and Cathal and shook her head. Two men complicating her life was enough. "A date with you and I'd probably have trouble riding the bike."

He laughed and cupped the front of his jeans. "*Es verdad*. But I haven't had any complaints yet."

"I bet." She zipped the Harley jacket, the iciness deep inside her intensifying at the prospect of stepping out into the night. Summer in San Francisco could be as cold as winter when the fog rolled in off a bay full of water that reached up the coastline to Alaska.

"Take care of yourself," Juan said, his frown saying she must really look like shit. "Big day Saturday."

"Definitely a big day. See you there."

"No way I'd miss it. Should be a huge turnout. You managed to get some hot talent. And I'm not meaning just tattoo artists like my magnificent self. I'm talking about the music. People have been texting me about it all day."

"Cool. Justine can use the funds."

She turned to leave. He slowed her by asking, "You want me to ask around about the tat? I could run a copy and show it to some guys I know who work outside the shop scene."

It wasn't the first offer she'd gotten. "Thanks. I'm not ready to go that far yet."

"No problemo. Swing by anytime if you change your mind."

"Will do." She left, mentally checking Juan off the list of artists she could approach casually, without drawing attention to or suspicion about what she was doing. Unless Parker wanted her to branch out into making cold calls or handing out copies of the demon tattoo, there were only two people left, Bryce and Jamaal.

She called Stylin' Ink. Neither was there.

Time to go home. She wasn't up to chasing down Bryce and Jamaal and if she showed up looking terrible, she'd never get out of their places much less avoid the third degree over why she was so rundown.

A glance toward Oakland and she shivered again, hard. It felt as if thin fingers of a cold fog reached out and touched her, sliding through the leather of her jacket and into the tattoos along her forearms.

Usually she found the fog refreshing. Tonight it seemed full of foreboding.

She decided to swing by Stylin' Ink anyway but as she drew closer to the shop, she realized the route she'd chosen would take her past

Aesirs. It made her wonder if her true destination had been Eamon all along.

A red light stopped her.

Go to him? Or don't?

She was undecided as the light changed.

Eamon moved through Aesirs with quick strides, his aggravation matched by his anticipation. He wasn't accustomed to dangling himself in front of a woman like bait on a fisherman's hook. This made twice he'd done it in order to draw Etaín to him when there was the chance she might shy away at the last moment.

The front doors opened as he reached them, the men stationed there clearing the way, though he could have done it using will alone. He stepped outside, the wet chill of the air doing nothing to cool the fire raging inside him.

He heard the bike before he saw her on it. And used the time between to tamp his emotion so it would appear as though he'd come out for fresh air and happened to be there as she passed, when in truth, before Etaín, he'd rarely allowed himself to be seen at Aesirs by humans.

The sound of the engine changed. She slowed and stopped next to the curb, forcing him to come to her as she had when she entered his estate.

He hid a smile. He would always come to her. *For* her. She was his, and he would do what it took to keep her.

She removed her helmet though the bike idled as if she hadn't decided to remain with him. That didn't concern him nearly as much as her paleness and the slight tremors he felt when he cupped her cheek.

"Have you eaten dinner yet?" he asked, brushing his thumb over her bottom lip and feeling a tug at his core, as if she needed some of his magic to sustain her.

She was changeling with a link to the old magic of Elfhome so it was entirely possible she did. Especially if he guessed correctly and she had used her gift earlier in the day when she went to Denis Dunne's home.

He touched his mouth to hers, giving her what she needed, the sensation like fire spreading from him to her, flames of magic and lust merging to become indistinguishable from one another.

Satisfaction replaced his earlier aggravation when she melted into him, her arms going around his waist. Though worry for her safety soon edged out the pleasure that came with her return.

Wards and glamour wouldn't hide his interest in her should there be spies watching. He ended the kiss, reluctant despite the wisdom of it.

In the distance Liam made his presence known, a deadly assassin emerging from darkness just long enough to smile in ripe amusement.

Eamon forced himself from her embrace though he couldn't draw his hand away from its resting place against her cheek.

Her color was better, her eyelids lowered by desire rather than exhaustion or illness. "Let me feed you dinner, Etaín."

A chauffeured limousine chose that moment to stop near them and disgorge its passengers, women in furs and men in five-thousand-dollar suits, among them several state senators. He saw the *no* in her eyes as she took note of the diners bound for Aesirs, felt it begin to take form against the thumb he stroked over her bottom lip.

Before she could utter it he deflected it by once again closing the distance between them, this time touching his mouth to her ear. "Say yes and I'll give you a demonstration of the magic you're not sure you believe in. I have a private suite. No one will bother us."

It was temptation enough for Etaín, given her earlier suspicion that she'd subconsciously intended to seek Eamon out when she came this way instead of going home. The headache and chills that had steadily gotten worse since leaving Denis's house were gone now that she was with Eamon. It had to mean something, and if not, the respite from them was welcome given the dreams she'd soon face, the reality she'd soon live.

"I've got to park the bike."

His laugh was a confident, warm caress against her ear. "I'll have it taken care of."

"Your valets ride?"

She felt the small, teasing smile. "If they don't, I'll replace the Harley with another of your choosing. An upgrade even, so you've got nothing to lose and everything to gain."

"You make it hard to refuse."

"That's my intention."

She racked the kickstand and turned off the engine. He stepped back so she could swing off the bike.

Taking the key from her he passed it off to the maître d' inside along with dinner instructions. A private elevator took them to the top floor.

He'd said "suite" and he'd meant it. Elegant dining and sitting areas. Plants in abundance, their pots beautifully crafted. A large bed visible through an arched doorway. And like his home, the walls held priceless paintings.

A Renoir drew her forward for a closer view. Eamon came up behind her, his arms pulling her against him so she felt the hard ridge of his erection. He pressed kisses along her neck. "Beautiful things please me," he murmured. "Though nothing pleases me as much as having you with me."

It should have come across as a line, total bullshit she could laugh away and enjoy for the play it was. Instead it came across as honest, and worse, unrelated to the message of lust his hard cock gave.

Unease spiraled through her at how her intentions to keep things casual with both men faded quickly when she was with either of them. She couldn't seem to stay away from Eamon any more than she could Cathal, and didn't bother lying to herself. The need for answers hadn't brought her here.

Like to like. It was an attraction that might only be broken if she did as her mother had done. Run and keep running.

It was a mantra often repeated, and yet her mother had left her in San Francisco. At eight years old she'd had no choice but to remain in one place. At eight, she'd been too young to have any defenses against coming to love the man she thought was her father, and the protective boy she thought was her brother.

An idea took shape in her mind, a question she couldn't shake and yet one she would never have an answer to. Was foresight her mother's gift? Is that what the eye on the back of her mother's hand signified?

See, but don't be seen.

Had she chosen San Francisco because she'd seen Eamon there? Had she left Etaín, untrained in the use of her gift, knowing that needing Eamon's help might make her stay with him?

Etaín felt the headache returning and grimaced. This is why she didn't like to think too much about her gift and its uses.

Amusement followed, a by-product of self-knowledge. She pressed backward, against Eamon's hardened cock. "I was promised a demonstration of magic. But if you got me up here to show me sex magic, I'm already a believer."

His laugh made her smile. "Not sex magic despite evidence to the contrary."

He gave a tender bite to her neck then nuzzled her ear. "I can smell his cologne on you."

He made it a dark, erotic discovery and her nipples tightened in response to it. Desire coiled low and deep in her belly. "Is that a problem for you?"

"Quite the contrary. I enjoyed this morning's fun and games. Did Cathal?"

Images of what it had been like with Cathal when they got to her apartment brought the remembered heat of a threat-rough voice and raw demands. Dominance stirred by possessiveness and jealousy.

Her channel clenched repeatedly, violently, with a need that went beyond simple physical joining. "Not at the time, but later . . . Later we both did."

Eamon's husky laugh made her squeeze her thighs together. He pressed another kiss to her ear.

She wanted him, but she was aware of the sweat dried on her skin from the sickness that had vanished in his presence, the griminess left over from retching in the bathroom down the hall from Brianna's room.

"I'd like a shower."

He stroked his hands down her sides. "Perfect. The demonstration I have in mind is best done after you've taken one."

A wave of remembered pleasure went through her, at what it had been like the last time she and Eamon had taken a shower together. "This still sounds like a demonstration of sex magic to me."

"I'm not going to join you. Though fair warning, I'll wait and watch while you do."

"Kinky." And yet it excited her, not just the prospect of being watched, but what she might do, in turn, to the watcher.

He led her to a bathroom easily as large as her apartment. Mirrors took up one wall. Seeing them she asked, "You do this often? Promise a woman a demonstration of magic if she'll come upstairs with you?"

It bothered her that he might. It bothered her more that *she* was bothered by it.

"Jealous?"

A shrug rather than a lie. *This isn't permanent,* she told herself, uneasiness shimmering through her when it didn't feel as completely true as it once would have.

He took the same position he had as they'd stood together in front of the Renoir, his arms encircling her, his mouth close enough to her ear that his words came on an erotic whisper of breath. "You have no cause to be jealous, Etaín. You have my full attention and no competition. I told you, there won't be anyone else now that I've met you."

A shiver went through her at seeing them together in the mirror. They fit. Like to like.

"Watch," he said, hands slowly stripping her of the jacket. The shirt. The bra. The rest of it following, leaving her standing naked while he was fully clothed.

"It pleases me to take care of you," he murmured.

The intimacy of it unnerved her. "So it's not just about getting me out of my clothes so we can do the nasty?" She joked, trying to return to what was familiar, comfortable. Sex without complications.

He ignored the comment, placing a long trail of kisses along her neck, her bare shoulder, his caresses turning her nipples into painful points and making her wet with need before he stepped backward. "Take your shower, Etaín."

She lifted her arms, watching his face tighten with desire in the mirror as she braided, then knotted her hair to keep it from getting wet. "Shower with me, like we did before."

"No."

"Using reverse psychology? So I'll have to work at seducing you now?"

He stepped into her, his hands going to her bare breasts, cupping and molding, sending spikes of pleasure from her nipples to her cunt with each touch to them. "I think maybe I've been too easy a conquest for you."

"There's nothing wrong with that."

"Oh but there is. At the risk of scaring you and making you leave in a rush, I'll repeat myself. I won't always settle for a meaningless physical act."

Reverse psychology, a dare, and yet even recognizing what he was doing, the challenge he presented was too great. She wanted him again, needed him despite being with Cathal earlier in the day.

The possibility Eamon could hold out intrigued her. From the time the dreams of ink started, she'd been fending off advances from men and women of all ages.

She turned in his arms, wrapping her own around his neck as she pressed against him. He didn't bother to keep the desire from his expression. That'd be pointless given the size of his erection, nor did he temper his response when her mouth found his.

Long moments passed. One kiss blending into another, a deep, heated communication of desire as his hands roamed, finally settling on her hips and holding her tightly as he ground his cloth-covered cock against her.

She broke the kiss then, her breathing as fast as his. "Sure you won't shower with me?"

"Yes."

"Your loss."

"We'll see."

She pulled away and walked the short distance to the glass-fronted shower stall, hyperaware of how wet and swollen she was between her thighs. He took a seat and amusement trickled in at having a bathroom large enough to accommodate furniture, though it served a purpose now.

She stepped into the shower stall and turned on the water, lathering her hands and proceeding to apply soap to every inch of her skin. It heightened the sensation, knowing he watched, feeling his eyes on her and his hunger as she touched herself.

Fantasy returned, the same one she'd had when she showered in her apartment after meeting both Cathal and Eamon. The three of them together, though now she knew what it was like to be with them separately.

Release came, enough of one to leave a hum of contentment. She turned the water off and stepped out of shower to find Eamon standing with a towel his hands, his nostrils flared. She smiled. "Do you want me to help you out of your clothes so they won't get wet?"

"Not yet."

She lowered her eyes to the front of his trousers, provocatively running her tongue over her lip. "You're sure?"

"For the moment," he said, the heated need in his voice and the hard outline of his erection assuring her he did have a breaking point, and she would find it before she left him.

He moved closer, refusing to hand her the towel when she reached for it. "I told you before you got into the shower that it pleases me to take care of you."

Their game had gone too far for her to retreat. And then his touch made it impossible.

He wielded cloth like a sensual weapon, applying it to every inch of skin as she'd done with soapy hands. Lingering over breasts and inner thighs and cunt until she was thoroughly aroused again.

"Close your eyes," he ordered.

She complied and felt him step away then return.

"Now open them."

He was holding a hanger. "Dress for me."

Refusal surged into her instantly, the request touching old wounds, the silent message she always heard from the captain and Parker. *Conform to my expectations if you want to be a part of my world.* But if Eamon saw the turmoil he'd caused, he ignored it. Diffused it by saying, "When I bought the dress, I envisioned you accompanying me to Saoirse while wearing it. Now I find I don't want to share the vision of you in it with Cathal."

"I think that might be best." Despite her fantasy and growing need for both of them, she couldn't see Cathal tolerating Eamon's physical presence when he could barely stand knowing she might be with him.

Eamon took the dress from the hanger and handed it to her. It was minimalist in design. Dark blue and backless, with a hemline shorter than the skirt she'd worn to Cathal's club.

The sleeves extended to her wrists, hiding the tattoos on her forearms. The front was equally concealing, elegant, making the show of skin elsewhere seem wickedly erotic.

"There are matching shoes," he said. "Optional for dining in."

"Apparently panties are optional, too."

"Of course."

She tugged the dress on over her head. It clung to her like a second skin.

"Where are the shoes?"

He produced a pair of fuck-me heels. She slipped them on, tormenting him, both of them knowing he had only to free his cock and push the dress upward to have nothing separate them.

Satisfaction purred through her when she saw his hand only just stop before gripping his erection. "Sure you want to keep holding out on me?"

He stepped forward, swamping her with heat and scent, sea blue eyes turbulent with lust. "Until after dinner at least, then we'll see just how persuasive you can be."

A brush of his mouth to hers, a hint of tongue quickly denied. "Now for the demonstration I promised."

With hands on her hips he turned her toward the mirrored wall. But instead of seeing reflections, the entire span was taken up by a mural, a swirling mix of color alive with movement. *Water.* Vast and deep. Calm and raging. Captured in a spectrum of blues and greens and even black, the texture smooth and flowing.

She was drawn forward as she had been to the Renoir, mesmerized by the illusion.

Eamon went with her, hands stroking her arms in a slow caress. "What do you see?"

"Water."

He reached out, touching his fingertips to the wall. "And now?"

Shades of orange and red and yellow, of blue and black. Roaring and flickering, furious and soothing. Warming as well as incinerating, obliterating.

"Fire."

"Yes. Both are the essence of who I am, the elemental magic I'm most strongly linked to. They're revealed here because of a spell woven into the mirror and directed by my will."

She was instantly out of her comfort zone. Yet there was no denying those first impressions. The scent of fire and water, and the sensation of cold blue flames licking along the vines as she passed through the front door of Aesirs. The sound of surf, vines becoming flooded, rushing streams at stepping into the terraced section. Raging fire and stormy seas, the *like calls to like* of Eamon.

Delaying full acceptance of it, she said, "Or I could see both because you've invested in some amazing special effects technology."

He gently bit her earlobe. "I'll never lie to you, Etaín."

His fingertips left the wall, extinguishing the fire and leaving behind a blank canvas and eerie sense of possibility. He captured her hand. "Your turn."

She resisted instinctively, yielding only when he laughed and said, "Afraid? There's no reason to be. Not here. Not now."

The wall felt like a mirror though it came to life with her touch and made her breath catch. Not just fire and water, but earth and air, the sunlight and moonlight she knew in that instant represented the ethereal, spirit.

They were all there, flowing one into the other, coming with sensations so familiar to her that she had to fight not to jerk her hand away. "What do you see?" she asked.

"A dark woods with a fire at its center. Wet sand and rich loam. The day. The night. A wild joy at running through and beneath all of it. Magic's primordial birthplace, Etaín, at least for those like us."

His answer made her heart beat erratically and goose bumps rise on her skin though she wasn't surprised he'd seen the very things she felt whenever she stepped outside after a long period of being indoors.

"Demonstration complete," she said, unable to suppress a shiver.

The wall became a mirror again as soon as her fingertips left it. Eamon turned her in his arms. "Ignorance is deadly, Etaín. Never believe otherwise."

A bell tinkled. Relief surged into her when he said, "Our dinner has arrived," and let the conversation drop as he escorted her to the dining room and seated her next to him.

The food was mouthwatering. Italian served with wine she was fairly certain couldn't be found in a grocery or liquor store.

She was ravenous. Since the visit with Brianna she'd felt too sick to eat.

When the meal was finished he drew her up from her chair and into his arms. She went willingly, ready to return to their challenge and indulge in a different kind of dessert than the one she'd just eaten.

"Stay the night with me," he said against her lips. "Here, if you prefer it to over going to the estate."

She wanted to. She said, "I can't."

He gave a soft sigh. "Guessing at some of your activities today isn't beyond me, Etaín. Tell me, did you visit Brianna Dunne today? Did you touch your palms to her skin? Is that why you seemed ill and weak when you arrived?"

"And if it is?"

"All gifts come at a cost. I told you the truth when I said you wouldn't be able to continue managing yours as you have in the past. The longer you delay in learning how to control the magic that flows into you, the greater the risk to everyone you touch."

His arms tightened around her. "And to you, Etaín. Especially to you if you perceive that your gift is changing."

It was changing. She couldn't deny it.

He'd provided an excuse to stay and his *knowing* meant there was no reason to deny the comfort she'd need later, after the dreams. But habit died hard.

She tried to muster the resolve to leave by thinking about Derrick and what happened each time he allowed himself to fall in love or believe in permanence. Cathal and Eamon might both want her now, but it wouldn't last. Or if it did, it would ultimately lead to an ultimatum to conform to a different set of expectations. Both of them moved about freely in the same elegant world the captain and his wife did.

She tried to pull away but Eamon captured her mouth with his, coaxing desire back into existence with the rub of his tongue against hers, with the slide of his hands up her sides to her breasts. Resistance fled with his touch, with heated need and an emptiness that would only end with the press of skin to skin and the joining of bodies.

"Say you'll stay the night," he whispered, his thumbs grazing over her nipples. "I think it's likely you'll succeed in seducing me."

"I'll stay," she said, allowing him to lead her through the arched doorway and into the bedroom.

The dress fell away easily, becoming a silky pool of dark blue at her feet and leaving her in heels alone. "Dinner was a torment for me," he murmured against her lips. "Sitting, making casual conversation, eating, all the while knowing you wore nothing beneath the dress I'd given you."

"Most would say you brought it on yourself."

Her hands went to the front of his shirt, fingers taking their time over each button as the fabric slowly parted to reveal smooth flesh and small, hardened nipples. She brushed her thumbs over them and was rewarded by the catch of his breath and a flush of need across his cheeks.

"Is this my punishment then?" he asked.

She kissed downward, tongue replacing the pad of her thumb, hands free to undo his belt and pants. "You tell me."

Fire raced through him at the feel of her teeth grasping his nipple, her tongue a lash that whipped through his belly and encircled his cock. His hands met hers at the front of his trousers, anxious to have nothing separate them, to be inside her, bodies joined as intimately as their magic would ultimately be.

A shudder of ecstasy seized him as her hand grasped his cock and her mouth left his nipple, pressing kisses lower and lower as she sank gracefully to her knees, the naked curve of her buttocks not hiding the high-heeled shoes that were the only thing she still wore.

His hands tangled in the golden silk of her hair. He desired her as he would never want another woman. "It's punishment and pleasure alike, Etaín. You'll know the same by morning."

* * *

Cathal made the short leap from pier to boat then followed Sean into a comfortable stateroom. The Giants were playing on a big-screen TV, the sound turned down.

"Want one?" Sean asked, holding up the bottle in his hand.

"Sure."

Cathal claimed a chair and accepted a beer. Sean took the seat next to him, a table between them.

"She's at Aesirs," Sean said. "Might as well get that out of the way first in case it impacts what you want to talk about."

A kick to the stomach would have been easier to take. "How long?"

"Long enough."

"To do what?" Cathal asked, not positive which one of them was fishing for information.

Sean cut him a look. "Fucking the blond whose estate is in Pacific Heights for one. Drawing pictures of the guys you say drugged and raped your cousin and her friend for another. You tell me why she's there. The tracker on her bike had her at your uncle's place earlier today. And now you're here."

Cathal's guts knotted, twisting more with fear for Etaín than with jealousy, though the prospect of his father or uncle ordering a hit on Eamon was darkly tempting.

"Maybe she's doing both," he admitted.

"Nothing you can do about either." Sean picked up the remote control. "Meeting over?"

"No." He didn't have to think about it.

"What's on your mind then?"

"Finding a way to circumvent my father and uncle without sacrificing them to the authorities, or ending up buried in an unmarked grave with Etaín next to me."

Sean laughed and took a swallow of beer. "Something easy. Good."

"I had a rough idea, of sending you to arrange for her brother to swing by her place and see the drawings in a way where there'd be no fault attached to anyone."

"Possibly workable, except her being with the blond has screwed up your chance to be the unsung hero in this story."

"Eamon," Cathal said, washing the name down with some beer. "He owns Aesirs."

Sean whistled. "Smart lady. Since you're paying for my observations and opinions, you're going to get both. Obviously you care about her or you wouldn't put yourself at risk this way, but you need to think outside the box when it comes to this situation."

"As in?"

"She's got something your father and uncle want and, unfortunately for her, they have a long reach and a lot of motivation. Meaning there are definite advantages to sharing her with Eamon. Between the two of you, you might just be able to keep her alive. The real question to look at here is whether you want her badly enough to overcome your social conditioning."

Cathal didn't know whether to laugh or get pissed. "Overcome my social conditioning?"

"Yeah. It's what I would do if I were you. Especially if that's the way she wants it. There are ways to make it work, if the parties involved are committed to it."

"Did I get on the wrong boat? Is this Dr. Phil or McAlister Investigations?"

"Just trying to help you out. You afraid this guy is better than you are?"

"Not even close." Memories of what it had been like with Etaín made it impossible to label himself second in her life. "I just want exclusive."

"More like, if you're in bed alone, you want her to be, too. Misery loves company and all that."

Cathal couldn't argue Sean's assessment so he didn't.

"Eamon know about you?"

"Yes."

"And he's okay with it?"

Cathal remembered Etaín's Mona Lisa smile after he'd set up break-fast at Aesirs and his dick got harder despite the fact that they were talking about Eamon. "He's into the kink. He's willing to share her."

"Hey, don't knock it till you've tried it."

Surprise ripped through him. "You have?"

"Yeah. I have. Not just shared as in *his place*, *my place*, but the three of us living together in *our place*."

Sean lifted his bottle in a silent tribute. "The psychologists have it right. The male of our species is turned on visually and competitive as hell at his core. Thank god. The sex was incredible."

"It didn't last," Cathal said, harsh words mirroring just how ruth-lessly he had to suppress the domination fantasies that accompanied images of walking in and catching Etaín naked with Eamon.

"True, it didn't last, but for reasons that would be TMI, way, way too much information for you to handle given your current puritani-cal frame of mind. Something I find amusing considering how your father and uncle earn their money, and your owning a club where the rich and moral-less come to play."

Sean pushed off his chair and padded over to a small refrigerator, getting himself another beer. "Besides the sex, you want to know what I loved best about sharing a woman with another man?"

Almost unwilling, Cathal found himself asking, "What?"

"When the job consumed me, there was someone there for her. And when I fucked things up with her, she had someone to turn to until I could get my shit together and clean up the mess I'd made out of things."

Sean returned to his chair, plopping down in it with a sigh. "Before we leave the topic, I'll go on record as saying that given the right chemistry all around, I'd rather be part of a threesome instead of a twosome."

His attention diverted to the Giants with three men on base and only one out. Cathal let himself be distracted, too, imagining taking Etaín to PacBell Park and watching from the luxury suite he often used.

Two runs and two outs later, Sean said, "Now back to your problem, which is compounded by not knowing if Eamon is aware of the visit to your uncle's place and the purpose behind it. Any idea whether or not she'd share it with him?"

Something inside Cathal relaxed. Etaín didn't readily share information about herself. She'd only admitted to using her talents to help the police after hearing about Brianna's suicide attempt. Even then, she'd left out that the victim Parker asked her to visit was the Harlequin Rapist's.

He refused to believe Eamon knew her any better than he did. "No. I don't think she'll share the drawings with him. Or tell him she intends to do them."

He thought about her throwing up after visiting Brianna. How ill she'd looked when she emerged from the bathroom. A glimmer of understanding came, at why she might have gone to Eamon. To distance herself from knowledge horrible enough to make her sick, and from what she'd endured because of her involvement with him.

"Time and options are limited," Sean said. "You've got to intercept her after she's finished drawing."

"She's promised to call."

"Good. Your idea about involving her brother is the most expedient. It's high risk but I'm not coming up with anything else even remotely workable. I'll put someone on him so he can be approached in person with a message as soon as you connect with Etaín. How are you going to sell this as an unpreventable accident to your father and uncle?"

"A dump of her cell phone records. Assurances I know where she's been. Her brother showing up and her not knowing anything about the setup. It will play out as believable because of her lack of fear when

I take her with me to see them. They're trusting me to handle this so they'll buy I did my best but it went sideways on me."

"You pretty sure there'll be no repercussions to you?"

"As long as her brother keeps quiet."

"Skirting the edge there, letting an FBI agent get a hook into you even if it's to keep his sister out of trouble. Might be better to put aside your pride and do a face-to-face with Eamon. Guy like that could bring pressure to bear on a lot of different fronts. The two of you joining forces could be unbeatable."

"No."

"Your call. Your woman." Sean took a drink. "Or at least, half your woman."

Cathal bridled at the casual taunt. "Start investigating Eamon."

"Looking for leverage to keep him away from her?" Sean laughed. "Who'd have guessed you'd pay top dollar to consult me, then be so resistant to taking my advice."

"Just do the work I hire you to do."

"Sir. Yes sir." His gaze flicked to the empty beer bottle in Cathal's hand. "You staying for the rest of the game? Or going back to your club?"

Curiosity about Sean's past got the better of him. The certainty that Sean wouldn't be able to resist saying more about the relationship he'd been in made Cathal say, "I'm staying."

"Beer's in the fridge, help yourself. I only serve clients."

Nineteen

There was no prelude to the dream. It filled Etaín's mind, surging into her and becoming her reality as though it were liquid and the force of it, the weight of it easily knocked aside any barrier erected against it.

Caitlyn. The image came with trapped horror and irreconcilable guilt, with drugged haziness and emotional sickness.

A scream welled up inside her, primal and terrified and hopeless. *No!*

She was aware of the heavy breathing above her. The grunting. The pain between her legs that came with having another one of them on top of her. Jordão she thought, by the smell of his hair, doing to her what Adam was doing to Caitlyn.

The bed spun, turning the pictures on the walls into a kaleidoscope. Her vision blurred and when it cleared again, the boy named Mason had taken Adam's place above Caitlyn.

I'm sorry. Sorry. Sorry. Sorry, she screamed silently.

And her scream blended into a boy's, into yelling. Confusion. Panic.

The weight on top of her disappeared but the bed still shook violently. Caitlyn flailing. Thumping. Writhing naked next to her then going completely still, drooling blood and spit so close that if she could make her arm work she could reach out and close Caitlyn's mouth for her.

There was the sound of gagging. The smell of pee and shit.

An arm reached down wearing a Rolex. Jordão. His fingers pressed to Caitlyn's throat.

Alive. Alive. Alive.

The words were underwater. Hazy but she heard them.

Get help. Get help. Get help.

Was that her or one of the boys? She couldn't tell if her mouth moved.

But then she knew it did. Fingers pushed between her lips and she tried to turn her head.

"Come on Brianna, open up."

She sobbed at the sound of Adam's voice. Sobbed again as he forced her jaw open then closed it, holding it shut.

She choked and coughed on something lodged at the back of her throat. Welcomed the darkness when it came, falling into it with the sensation of tears dripping from her eyes.

My fault. My fault. My fault.

There was nothing until she woke in a hospital room.

"Caitlyn!" she screamed, her first thought. "Caitlyn!"

She tried to climb out of bed but a heavy-bodied nurse was there to restrain her. "Caitlyn!"

"Hush, now. Hush, Brianna."

Images pressed in on her, like segments of a terrible, horrible dream. It couldn't have happened. Not Adam. No. None of it was real.

She struggled against the nurse's restraint again. "Let me up!" she screamed, thrashing violently, trying to bite and claw until she noticed the soreness between her thighs.

The first sob felt as though her chest had burst open delivering it. Guilt poured in, panic.

"Where's Caitlyn?" A whimpered question instead of a screamed one.

"Hush. Don't think about your friend now. You're okay. You're okay."

"I want to see Caitlyn! I want to see Caitlyn!"

She screamed it. Bucking. Wild with emotion. Caitlyn's face, blood on a gold comforter, flashing through her mind with every movement.

Above her the nurse yelled for help and suddenly the room was filled with other people. She fought harder as they held her down.

"She's ripped the catheter out," one of them said.

"Let me see Caitlyn. I just want to see Caitlyn."

"Stop, Brianna," her father was there, laying a hand on her forehead. "I'm here. I'm right here with you."

Another sob ripped through her. She couldn't face him.

A scream came from deep inside her. It erupted, piercing the air.

Another welled up as tubing was placed around her arm and a man stepped forward with a syringe. "No!"

He pushed a needle into her arm. "Rest now. Rest is what you need."

"Please. Please. Just tell me where Caitlyn is."

"Let's take care of you now."

The fight went out of her, suppressed by waves of sleepiness. Helplessness.

Hopelessness.

Get help. Get help. Get help.

Are you crazy? Jordão's voice. *They die of an overdose. Too bad. So sad. Shit happens.*

She was conscious of tears rolling down her cheeks. Caitlyn was dead. That's why they wouldn't answer her question. That's why they wouldn't tell me where Caitlyn was.

So sad. So sad. So sad.

Her fault. This was all her fault.

She curled into a ball, hugging her knees to her chest.

She wanted to die. The pain would go away then. It would all go away and she'd be with Mom and Brian and Caitlyn.

Etaín woke shivering, sweating. Her knees pressed to her chest as grief and guilt crushed her into the mattress. Something terrible had happened. Something she was responsible for.

She felt deathly ill, chilled to the core despite the fire at her back. Her thoughts were fuzzy though she recognized she'd experienced this before, a high that had veered into a dangerous, nightmare crash.

Confusion swamped her. Disbelief. Anger. She hadn't touched drugs since the captain had her locked in a cell.

Bands of steel tightened around her chest at the memory of it. She struggled to breathe, struggled to escape until finally the sound of Eamon saying her name penetrated, allowing dissociation, providing the separation from stolen reality and *self* she needed.

She realized she was shaking, her teeth chattering, but still she forced her arms from around her legs, her knees away from her chest. "Let me up."

Panic gathered when he continued to imprison her. Only sheer determination kept her from becoming wild, violent as Brianna had been. "I have to draw."

Eamon bit off a refusal, fighting his worry for her and his anger at Cathal for asking this of her. "Stay in bed. I'll get your things."

He cursed silently. Hating to leave her even to pad across the room to the desk where the tablet and box of colored pencils brought from her bike waited. Hating, too, that he couldn't immediately take her in his arms and warm her as he had when she first arrived at Aesirs, pouring magic tied to fire into her and restoring what had been depleted.

He gathered the supplies and turned, jaw clenching at seeing her sitting, huddled in blankets. The shivering had stopped though she continued to look ill.

A surge of violence welled up inside him. True fear wasn't an emotion he often experienced and yet he'd felt it as she dreamed and seemed to fade away as if she approached death.

If Cathal were here . . .

In that moment it didn't matter that he'd allowed this to play out and seen the advantages of it. He didn't think he could tolerate Etaín seeing Cathal much longer, not unless the relationship was made a permanent one, with all the obligations that would entail for Cathal.

Eamon reached the bed, handing her the drawing supplies. "Don't think you can send me away," he said, taking up a position behind her then lifting her onto his lap.

He needed to understand this, to see how her gift manifested so he could help her control it. Survive it. He needed to offer what comfort he could through the touch of skin to skin.

She didn't resist, only picked out a colored pencil and applied it to the blank white of the paper, unconsciously pulling on his magic as images flowed across each page. Each of her strokes sure, her hand steady, her attention complete.

Nothing existed for her other than her drawing. Not him. Not her surroundings.

Anger toward Cathal disappeared with the disturbing retelling of a terrible story. She was a talented artist, capturing not only the physical details but the sense of violation. Guilt. Anguish and horror.

Elf or human, had what happened to Brianna and Caitlyn been done to someone who called him Lord, he would have used any means at his disposal to find and punish those responsible.

When she finally closed the sketch pad there was no relief in the gesture. Pushing it aside, along with the case of pencils, she pulled her knees to her chest again, wrapping her arms around her legs.

Eamon accommodated the shift in position, his arms settling on top of hers, hugging her to him. His mouth delivering comfort as he kissed her shoulder and neck.

Etaín relaxed into him, grateful for his presence and his touch. Usually she needed a shower to rebuild mental walls. Usually she puked when she first woke.

This was much better.

His heat was like the warm lap of ocean waters onto a beach. Soothing, taking away all evidence of what had passed across the sand in a gentle restoring of her defenses.

"Brianna Dunne's memories?"

"Yes."

A measure of dread returned to mar the peacefulness. Though the barrier against the memories was in place, awareness that they weren't complete remained. She knew she had an ending but no beginning, understood the beginning was of equal importance.

She couldn't suppress the shiver that came with the prospect of returning to Denis's house. She'd never had to touch a victim twice, never felt so physically sick after doing it as she had with Brianna.

"I need to see her again."

She felt the sudden rigidity of his muscles. Heard threads of ice in a smooth-flowing voice when he said, "There's more?"

"Yes."

"I'll come with you." Implacable will set against an impossibility.

Etaín didn't confront him directly. "If you do, Denis will insist on being in the room with us."

She felt the telltale spasm where his cheek touched her neck and it brought a smile despite what they were talking about. *Lord* Eamon's plans thwarted.

"Tell me how you took her memories, Etaín. Tell me if using your gift always affects you this way."

His arms tightened on her painfully for an instant, not threat but conveyed worry. "There was a point when I thought you might slip into death."

"Brianna wants to die."

"Tell me how you took her memories," he repeated.

She hesitated, old caution surfacing before being dismissed. "I took them the same way I always do. I touched the eyes to her skin and asked her to show me what happened."

"But you didn't see it when you were with her." Not a hard thing for him to guess.

"No. I never do. The memories come later, in a dream that seems real. Like it's happening to me."

The muscles in his arms flexed against hers. "And the sickness? The weakness?"

"Usually it doesn't last. I puke my guts out twice, right after I take the memories and right after I live through them, then I'm okay . . ."

She almost didn't add the rest of it, then thought about the mirror demonstration and realized there was probably nothing she could tell him that would seem crazy. "Well, I'm okay after a shower. Usually that's what it takes to lock the memories away. I know they're there, but I don't revisit them because there's always a chance if I do I'll relive them."

She couldn't suppress a tremor at remembering what had happened when the captain scared her straight at sixteen. "Reliving the memories is like being trapped in a looping horror film. I can't alter *anything* in them. Not what happens, not the thoughts or feelings, or even what was said, everything remains exactly the same."

"But something was different this time?" There was only the barest hint of a question in his voice.

She used humor against her fear at where the changes in her gift might ultimately lead. "I didn't throw up this morning for a start. The Italian dinner was great, but I'm happy not to have seen it again in a less palatable form."

He answered with a bite to her shoulder and another painful tightening of his arms. "Did Brianna resist?"

"No. She was unconscious and heavily drugged when I touched her."

"There's a sense of guilt in the pictures you drew."

Etaín glanced at the sketchbook and shivered. But the touch of his skin to hers and his presence at her back gave her the strength to open the door to Brianna's reality just long enough to say, "She blames herself for what happened."

His question made her think of Tyra lying on the hospital bed, the ceaseless rolling of her eyes only stopping when the horror of being taken by the Harlequin Rapist was stripped from her mind.

Maybe Brianna hadn't wanted the peace that came with the loss of her memories. Maybe on some unconscious level she'd fought their removal because she believed she deserved to be punished, and because without the memories she'd lose the will to commit suicide.

"It felt the same as it always does while I was touching her, but it's possible she resisted," Etaín offered tentatively. "That could explain the differences, including why I didn't see everything."

Eamon closed his eyes, savoring the feel of Etaín held safely in his arms. He wondered if this was what it meant to fall in love. To be willing to trade advantage for no gain but to ease the suffering of another. To override personal objections in order to allow another to risk themselves for a purpose they believed in.

Short of imprisoning her, he couldn't prevent her from returning to Denis's home. She'd touch her palms to Brianna's skin and take the memories even knowing how sick she would become afterward. She'd do it despite learning that he'd feared she might die while she dreamed.

"Does Cathal mean so much to you that you'll visit Brianna again regardless of the danger it presents to you?"

"This doesn't have anything to do with Cathal now. I'll finish what I started."

Did her gift compel her? Or her sense of honor?

Both, he thought, fear for her returning at the thought of how many humans might already know of her gift.

What had her mother been thinking to leave Etaín in the home of a policeman?

It was only a matter of time now before Etaín came to the attention of other lords, or far, far worse for all of them, the queen.

His gaze flicked to the sketchbook she'd pushed aside, his mind to the images it contained. Whether the Dunnes ultimately gave their oath and called him Lord or not, he couldn't fault Etaín's choice in seeing this through.

With easy strength he lifted and turned her so she straddled his thighs, facing him. Shackling her wrists, he drew them to his chest, holding her palms to his skin.

There were no humans in Elfhome, or hadn't been in the time of his ancestors' banishment. And those few *seidic* who'd been born into this world and imprisoned in luxury by the ruling family, would never have been called upon to use their abilities on a human.

Etaín's answers only deepened the alarm he'd felt in front of Stylin' Ink. They strengthened his belief that nothing good could come of her using her gifts on humans, and worse, a great deal of harm could come—*to her*.

He pressed against her hands to make her aware of her palms against his chest. "The other morning you hinted that your touch could make me forget you. You said it had happened before. When, Etaín? Under what circumstances?"

She was silent for so long he didn't think she would answer. Frustration built, only to dissipate in a wash of tenderness and satisfaction when she allowed him further into her life.

"Brianna's not the first victim I've worked with. There have been others. Cases Parker or the captain asked for my help on. They call me as a last resort because I *take* the memories. Not just *see* them."

Her words confirmed his suspicions. Without inherent magic of their own, humans had no defense against hers. Even lower-caste Elves might fall to it without conscious intent on her part.

Mind thief. Gift thief. They were epithets applied to the *seidic*.

"It's happened with lovers, too," she whispered. "Though not the same way."

He found he didn't want to hear about the men in her past. Nor did he want to talk about the human in her present, Cathal.

He leaned forward, his lips claiming hers in a series of tender kisses. And though he desperately wanted to join with her physically, demonstrating on a primal level that she was no longer alone, he managed to keep from lifting her onto his cock.

"Magic is a thing of will and belief," he said, glad now for the display of it the night before so this lesson would be easier. "But to make the most of it, to control and wield it, also requires focus."

"The questions I ask," she said, making the intuitive leap. "I speak them. I think them. A part of me concentrates on the eyes, almost as if I can see through them."

"Exactly. All of those serve as a focus."

Pressing her palms harder against his flesh, he brought to mind the images that had come when she touched her fingertip to the mirror. "*See* my memory, Etaín."

She shook her head in denial of the request. Tried to escape his grip but he refused to release her.

"You won't be able to steal from me. Magic flows into the both of us. For the sake of simplicity, believe it is capable of both attracting like and repelling it, depending on the circumstances and the relative strength of those possessing it. Trust me when I say, there is no danger you will steal my memory. Focus, Etaín. See what I'm thinking about."

She closed her eyes, yielding, asking a moment later, "Do you want me to tell you what I saw?"

"I'll tell you. That will prove to you I'm still in possession of the memory," he said before describing the primordial birthplace of Elves without naming their race. "Satisfied?"

"Yes."

He lifted her hands from his chest, kissing each eye in the center of her palm before releasing them in favor of encircling her with his arms and pulling her forward to feel the press of breasts against his chest. "Those without ties to magic have no defenses against you. I suspect one of the reasons you are violently ill when you consciously use your gift is that even as you are taking the memories, you are unconsciously resisting doing it because you understand it's a violation of another's mind."

"Punishing myself?"

"Perhaps, though maybe at war with yourself is more accurate. I also believe the nausea serves as a warning, Etaín. You experience these stolen memories as reality, then lock them away afterward. Gift and magic are inextricably entwined. Where the one takes, the other protects you against what was taken. But there are limits, and when they are reached . . ."

The hard shudder that went through her was acknowledgment she understood his point though it didn't surprise him when she said, "I'm still going to visit Brianna again."

"Here's what advice I can give you. You can't let skin serve as a barrier. Use your gift with razor-sharp intention. When you touch the eyes to her, your will should be like the lens of a movie camera focused on the scenes you wish to capture."

"Is there a way to see without taking?"

"For someone like Brianna Dunne, I don't know. There is knowledge I might be able to access in the future, but there is no guaranteeing the information would be there, and the cost of attempting to find it would be great."

"Is there a way to give back what I've taken?"

"The answer is the same. I could offer suggestions if you are willing to experiment."

The shiver that went through her was answer enough. He rubbed his cheek against hers. "The person who gave you the tattoos you wear should be able to provide answers."

"No chance of that happening."

"You sound certain if it." He let her hear the question in his voice, and choose whether or not to answer it.

"I am. My mother did the wristbands shortly before bringing me to San Francisco. The rest of it was done by friends, over time, but I made the stencils and provided the ink. I dreamed the tattoos."

Her answer sent a ripple of surprise through him. That she'd dreamed them meant something, it had to. Like the inextricable entwining of gift and magic, he believed the inked vines both served and sustained her.

"Some of the symbols on my arms are carved into the door here. They're at your estate, too. You know what they mean."

"Yes. A lesson for another day."

"I should leave anyway. And get this over with. The sooner the better."

He couldn't let her go without joining his body to hers. All it took was the thought of being separated from her and he hardened further, the ache to be inside her intensifying.

He captured her earlobe between his lips and sucked, pleased at the way her breath hitched and her nipples tightened. He caught her hand and carried it to his erection. "Are you in such a rush you're prepared to forfeit the chance to have this?"

Her laugh sent a hot pulse through his aroused cock. "Maybe. Convince me it would be a bad idea to go right now."

It was a challenge he felt confident he could win. He cupped her breast, fingers toying with her nipple while his other hand pushed between them to find her clit, her heated opening.

He kept his movements slow, building the desire between them. Heightening the pleasure with tugs and twists of her nipple as he fucked his fingers into her, rubbing them over her clit.

Her back arched, her breathing became ragged. She moaned in protest when he abandoned her wet folds and swollen knob long enough to capture her hand.

She didn't resist when he guided it so she touched her fingers to her clit, rubbed her palm over it as he forced her fingers into her slit along with his own.

"Will this be enough for you, Etaín? As it was when you showered last night?"

She laughed. "If I say yes, will your ego be able to handle it?"

He bit her neck in punishment though he'd already discovered he loved her provocative self-confidence. Her ignorance of her heritage and the world she would one day be Lady of freed them both from constraint and artifice.

He rose onto his knees, tumbling her to the mattress and positioning her so she lay on her stomach with the pillow beneath her, canting her hips upward.

Covering her body with his, he found her entrance but didn't push into her.

She tried to move, to take what he wasn't yet ready to give her. He tormented her, sliding his cock back and forth over her erect clit, wetting himself with the arousal escaping from her slit.

He relented only when he was ready, and then it was a repeat of what he'd done minutes earlier. A press and retreat as he controlled the depth of penetration. Shallow, slow thrusts.

She grew more swollen, making him fight for each inch in an ecstasy-inducing battle. Coating his skin with sweat before he finally gave in to her pleas to take her harder. Faster.

Even then he didn't allow a rush to completion. Didn't allow himself release until she lay sated beneath him, trembling in the aftermath of the pleasure he'd given her.

He rolled them to their sides, arms holding her tight. He didn't want her to leave at all, but he knew the wisdom of allowing it. For now. And only until after the fund-raiser.

She hadn't said as much, but the extent of her efforts for the event spoke of promises made. And though she hadn't been raised among Elves, he wouldn't have her foresworn by breaking her oath.

"Stay long enough for breakfast?" he asked.

"I'll want a shower first."

He smiled at the prospect of standing beneath the water with her again, of lathering his hands and touching every inch of her skin. Of having her do the same to him until he could no longer prevent himself from lifting and holding her against the wall, their bodies joined again before she left.

"It will delay your departure," he warned, caressing her breast, her belly. Cupping her mound. "This time you won't shower alone."

Cathal lay in bed, vivid memories of what it had been like to wake with Etaín assaulting him, carrying heat and blood downward so the sheets tented with his erection.

He refused to let his hand follow. He wouldn't give her that much power over him.

Pussy whipped. That's what his father and uncle would call him for not being with another woman right now, for wanting Etaín and being willing—more than willing—to keep her with him despite knowing she'd been with another man before coming to him.

He rubbed his chest, his cock throbbing at the remembered sensation of her lying on top of him like a contented cat, a small smile of pleasure on her face as she stroked her fingertips along the length of his side.

Fuck, what was he going do about her?

He closed his eyes, not wanting to see his own defeat even as his hand fisted around his erection.

It was a poor substitute but at least he didn't have to rely on fantasies.

He relived those times she'd been with him. His hand moving up and down on his shaft. His grip tightening, the motion quickening until release came. Hot and wet. A relief quieting the craving for her but not eradicating it.

He rose from the bed, wanting to get the call over with before stepping into the shower, as if somehow he could wash unwanted reality and the images coming with it away.

"Bike's still at Aesirs," Sean said in greeting.

His hand tightened on the phone but he refused to allow himself more of a reaction.

Pussy whipped.

"Anything on Eamon?"

"I'm the best in the business but it's what, not even nine a.m. yet. Cut me some slack here. A *lot* of slack. I do need sleep occasionally though I can tell you Aesirs is a huge, hard-to-penetrate shield. That's bad news in finding out specifics about Eamon but good news in other regards. Anyone who needs to hide like that is going to have some serious stopping power when it comes to applying leverage to your father and uncle. To deaf ears I'll say again, have a face-to-face with Eamon."

Cathal's mood darkened further at hearing Eamon might be able to do what he couldn't be sure of managing, keeping Etaín safe from the consequences of involvement with his family. "Keep digging."

As he once again stood next to Etaín, straddling the Harley and on the cusp of leaving, Eamon was glad he wasn't destined to play out this scene many more times, or be required to endure Liam's mocking smile—though thankfully that was currently from a distance far enough away to preclude hearing any accompanying comments.

He wanted to press her into a promise to return but accepted it would be a losing battle. With Liam watching her, he wasn't concerned for her safety though worry from a different source edged in with thoughts of how drained she'd been when she arrived the previous night.

He didn't know nearly enough about her gift or her magic. It wasn't required to be afraid for her. She was a changeling and that was always a dangerous time in this world, more so for her because she hadn't been raised among her own kind.

Cupping her cheek, touching his mouth to hers, he strengthened her with one last magic-laden kiss before saying, "Be careful, Etaín. I believe it's the nature of your gift to want to see everything, to know everything about whoever you touch. You control your abilities now, either by luck or instinct, but eventually you'll need more than either of those things. You'll need me. And perhaps even Cathal."

"We'll see," she said, and he hid his smile until she'd left him, wary of alerting her to just how much progress he'd made with her.

Twenty

Etaín let herself into Stylin' Ink. The light streaming out of Bryce's office told her the shop wasn't empty despite the locked front door and darkened interior.

She set the bike helmet on the counter as she passed it, anticipating the teasing she would have to endure when Bryce and Derrick got together. Tonight she was sleeping at her own place, or at least planning ahead well enough to have a change of clothes with her instead of having to swap them out somewhere else.

"Hey," she said, stepping into Bryce's office. "Where is everyone?"

He looked up from his sketchpad. "Starting late today, including yours truly. Lot of lunchtime appointments, then some after hours. What are you doing here?"

Not much point in trying to hide the reason, given what she needed was in his office closet. "Changing clothes."

He whistled. "Got laid two nights in a row? Cathal?"

She just smiled and crossed over to the closet, knowing it'd drive him crazy. He cursed while she went through the small stack of choices, picking out what she wanted.

As she closed the closet door he finally ended his rant. "If you're not going to share, then at least tell me the magic words you used on Derrick so I can use them the next time he crashes and burns. He showed up for work yesterday afternoon with a smile on his face and an 'I live to serve' attitude. Burst out and started singing at one point. If I didn't know better, I'd say he's back in love."

"Oh shit," Etaín said, borrowing Bryce's favorite word.

"What was that?"

She crossed to lean against his desk. "I introduced him to someone. Casual. A one-nighter I thought." Though if Quinn was serious about taking a job as a PI . . .

"Who'd you introduce him to?"

"A law-enforcement type."

"Sweet."

"We'll see."

She pulled the copy of the Harlequin Rapist's tat out of a pocket, unfolded it before handing it to Bryce. "You know who might have done this artwork? Or seen anyone wearing it?"

He studied it for a long moment, then refolded it and gave it back to her. "No. Does this have anything to do with your asshole brother stopping by the shop a couple of days ago?"

That was the trouble with Bryce, he was too perceptive, which was one of the reasons she hadn't made more of an effort to show him the drawing before now. "Can't say it does," she answered. Like the importance of keeping a promise, the importance of avoiding a lie was another of her mother's often repeated mantras.

"Cute, Etaín. In other words, 'Yes, Bryce, it does, but I'm not allowed to tell anyone what I'm doing for the Feds.'"

Deflection seemed the best way to deal with him. "So when will Jamaal be in?"

"Won't. Not today. He's spending the day with DaWanda. They're going to a funeral. Scheduled to start at three, at DaWanda's church. It's being held for someone who goes there and was in Narc Anon with DaWanda's sister. Tyra Nelson, ring any bells with you?"

Etaín froze inside, an instinctive reaction against opening the floodgates of memory. "I know who she is. Was."

"Tell me the truth, Etaín. Is your brother using you as bait for the Harlequin Rapist?"

"Not that I know of."

"So it's possible."

Would Parker go that far? Her stomach twisted but the conversations she'd had with Trent about the Harlequin Rapist's likely behavior kept it from knotting. "It's possible, but I don't think he is."

"Be careful."

"You're the second person who's told me that today."

"Cathal the first?"

She smiled and turned away from the desk. A colored pencil bounced off the wall next to the doorway as she stepped through it. "Goddamn tease," Bryce yelled.

She changed in the bathroom and returned to her bike. Straddling it, she thought of her promise to Cathal. Technically she wasn't done, so a call wasn't owed, but she wanted to hear his voice, wanted to feel the warm hum of electric desire she'd come to associate with him. A warding against facing Brianna's memories.

"I'm not finished yet," she told him when he answered.

"When will you be?"

If ice had a voice, it would sound like Cathal's. Her stomach cramped at the curtness of his response and the way it was delivered.

She'd planned on telling him she was heading to his uncle's house for another session with Brianna. Instead she said, "Soon. You'll know when I am," and ended the call, pocketing the phone.

It rang as she was putting her helmet on. She hesitated then started the Harley. She wanted to get this done.

Panic seized Cathal. "Fuck!" He was out of control.

He'd thought he'd come to terms with knowing she was with Eamon. But when she'd said she wasn't finished drawing, he'd imagined her naked, in Eamon's arms, playing instead of following through on her promise to help Brianna.

He'd reacted without thought. Given her cold to offset the heat of the emotions festering inside him because he was trapped in his own subterfuge.

Three more attempts, going straight to voicemail, and he dialed Sean instead.

"Didn't we just talk?" Sean asked. "Fair warning, I'm going to start charging you three times the usual rate. The first bump to keep you out of the pain-in-the-ass category of client, the second for not walking away from this woman if you can't handle the idea of sharing her."

"Where is she?"

"Give me a second, why don't you."

There was a muffled thud, as if Sean had jumped from the dock to the deck of his boat.

Time seemed to crawl. He heard the click of a mouse and keys typed.

"She's on the move. Looks like she just left Stylin' Ink."

He cursed his own lack of control, hand tightening on the phone. He didn't hang up. Neither did Sean.

Long moments passed. Agony ended by Sean saying, "At a guess, I'd say she's heading to Pacific Heights. Your call whether it's to Eamon's estate or your uncle's."

I'm not finished yet.

He felt a jolt of fear. Fierce anger directed at himself.

"She's going to see Brianna again." It was the only thing that made sense to him.

"You're at home?"

"Yes."

"You won't beat her there, but you might make it on her heels."

"I'm gone," he said, shoving the phone into his pocket.

* * *

Denis sat next to the bed, the nurse hovering behind him. "Have you seen any change in her, Clara?"

"No, sir."

He hadn't either and he'd desperately wanted to after Cathal passed on what Etaín had told him. He wanted Brianna to forget, to have what had happened erased from her mind. But maybe he was going to have to settle for erasing the ones responsible.

A knock on the open door had him looking up at one of the men he used for protection work. "There's a woman at the gate, name's Etaín."

"Cathal's not with her?"

"No."

Denis didn't like it. It told him Cathal wasn't in control of the situation. It told him Cathal probably couldn't guarantee she hadn't talked and hadn't shown whatever pictures she came up with to someone. *If* she'd been able to come up with anything at all. And that was a big if in his mind.

Rushing out of the room and puking her guts out in the hallway bathroom could have been an act put on for their benefit—which would make things a whole lot worse for her down the road. Clara didn't believe there was any way Brianna had beat the drugs long enough to talk to Etaín.

"Let her in, Matt," he said, rising from his chair, pausing to lean down and kiss his daughter's forehead. She was lightly sedated but she still whimpered and jerked away from the contact, curling into a ball at his touch.

Even though it had happened before, it felt like a fist plunging into his chest and trying to rip his heart out. He straightened and left the room.

Etaín had better deliver results. He wasn't a man to jerk around.

* * *

Etaín was met in the driveway by a guy who looked like a body-guard instead of a personal assistant. His eyes were emotionless and everything about him screamed *lethal* despite the suit he wore.

She followed him into the house and found Denis waiting in the foyer. He didn't offer either a smile or a handshake.

The first didn't matter to her. The second she was grateful for.

"I want to know what you know," he said after the bodyguard had made himself scarce. Rage and pain simmered in Denis's voice despite the external show of containment.

"I don't have the full story. I need to visit with Brianna again, alone, if I'm going to get the rest of it."

"I want what you do have."

He was a dark lion at the gate. She wouldn't get past him, wouldn't get this finished and behind her if she didn't give him the drawings she'd already done.

She crouched and opened the sketchpad, carefully tearing out pages without looking at what was on them. It made her appreciate how Parker or the captain served as a buffer between her and a victim's family, slipping her in under one pretext or another and always making it clear the success of her work depended on her being left alone to do it.

She'd never had to decide whether family members were better off with the horror they imagined or the reality captured on paper. She wasn't going to decide this time, either. Denis wasn't going to give her the choice.

Standing, she passed the sheaf of papers to him. He rolled them up, expression grim as he escorted her to Brianna's bedroom.

"Clara," he said, and it was enough for the nurse to exit the room.

"I'll see you out when you're ready to leave," Denis said, before closing the door to his daughter's room.

He found Matt. "Wait outside Brianna's room. After Etaín's gone, we sweep for bugs from there to the front gate, and anywhere else she's been."

"Yes, sir." Matt straightened, touching his earpiece. "Cathal's at the gate."

Denis frowned. Etaín hadn't mentioned Cathal following her.

His suspicion Cathal didn't have control of the situation, or Etaín, deepened, though the rolled drawings were proof Cathal was getting results. The jury was still out about what to do with Etaín when this was over.

"Open the gate for him. Tell him where she is. He can wait for her. But she doesn't leave until I say so. Pass that word on to Cathal."

"Yes, sir."

In his office Denis slowly sank into his chair. His heart pounded in his chest like he'd run a four-minute mile. It drowned out the background noise coming from the small TV at the corner of his desk.

He put the rolled-up sketches on his desk. The paper flattened on its own, revealing a picture of Caitlyn with a boy on top of her. Close up, the perspective making it seem as though he was lying on the bed not far away, seeing it through his daughter's eyes.

His guts burned looking at it, sickness joining his fury as he turned the page over, and then the next and the next. Rifling through them as the hair rose on his arms and the back of his neck.

A chill settled deep inside him with the last picture, Brianna returning to consciousness that first time in the hospital. *Creepy.* The guy who'd passed on Etaín's name wasn't kidding.

Denis picked up a burner phone and called the one Niall was carrying, though he still decided to play it safe and cautious when his brother answered.

"Cathal's girlfriend showed up a little while ago wanting to visit with Brianna. I let her in. Brianna's still got me closed out, but she's opening up to her."

"Cathal's not there?"

"He is now. Came in a few minutes behind her."

"I'll stop by later."

Denis glanced down at the small stack of drawings. "That'd be good."

Twenty-one

Etaín stood next to Brianna's bed with a sense of déjà vu. Cathal's cousin was curled into a fetal position, whimpering.

"Brianna," she said, reaching out and lightly touching a shoulder to determine if Brianna slept or was drugged.

Brianna cringed away, but not before leaving an impression of despair so deep there was only one way to escape it. Death.

Etaín opened and closed her hands, the eyes flashing as if they winked. She'd contemplated the morality of using her gift before, and her stomach roiled now despite the lack of physical contact. A warning Eamon had guessed, but to her it seemed a confirmation that the nausea was self-administered punishment, because this was a violation, some would say, a mental rape.

The acknowledgment of it made her cringe, though she didn't allow herself to turn away from Brianna. She silenced moral and ethical questions by picturing some of the children the captain and Parker had taken her to see in the past. It helped.

"Just do it," she whispered. "Get it done." She rubbed slick palms against her jeans before curling her fingers around Brianna's wrists.

Brianna cried out and began struggling, pouring emotion into Etaín, so thick with suffering it choked her. Eradicated her own sense of self, filling her mind with the desire to die, with the determination to get to one of the guns she knew was in the house.

Only the sensation of writhing, thrashing vines along her forearms jerked Etaín clear of Brianna's mind. Fear slammed into her at this new twist to her gift.

She backed away from Brianna, Eamon's words chasing her, an admonition that it was the nature of her gift to want to see everything, to know everything about anyone she touched. *To consume them*, she thought, sweat turning cold on her skin, the vines suddenly seeming like some horror-movie rendition of carnivorous plants.

She forced fear and revulsion away by reminding herself the bands around her wrist had been started by her mother, and the rest had grown from her own dreams. If she lost faith in herself, let panic destroy her confidence or turn her away from the call to ink she wouldn't survive.

Power of suggestion, that's all, she told herself, wondering if the changes that had come since meeting Eamon had come *because* of the things he'd told her.

Ignorance is deadly, Etaín. Never believe otherwise.

"Enough already," she muttered, refusing to think about Eamon or anything else but getting the task that had brought her here done.

She took Brianna's wrists, not releasing them as the girl struggled, and the vines felt like living things that didn't quiet until Brianna lay still, curled once again into a fetal ball as if her mind and body mirrored each other.

Etaín concentrated on where the eyes touched Brianna, making herself ignore the barrier of skin. She focused her will with razor sharp intention.

"Start at the beginning, Brianna, show me what happened the last time you spent the night with Caitlyn."

She repeated it over and over again. Verbally. Mentally. Not a movie camera, not still-life photos, but a melding, the memories becoming a part of her as they always had, a reality she'd relive over and over again if the barrier between her life and Brianna's fell away as it did then.

"Come on, Caitlyn. Just for a little while. We can take your mom's car. We'll be back before your parents get home. It's not like we're going to do anything at the party anyway."

Caitlyn bit her lip in indecision. Her parents were way strict, totally overprotective, the same way Dad was, and he was worse now than when Mom and Brian were alive.

Guilt and sorrow almost made her back away from the idea of going to the party. She forced herself to ignore them. She didn't want to think about the last year, or what would happen if her father found out she went without his permission or one of his watchdogs.

"Please, Caitlyn. I just want Adam to see me there so he'll know I'm not boring."

Maybe then he'd notice her more often. He was so cute and nice. Everyone liked him and his smile . . .

She touched a hand to her chest. Underneath it her heart was doing flip-flops.

"Just for a few minutes, Caitlyn. I promise."

"Okay."

They left Caitlyn's room and went downstairs. A thrill went through her at watching Caitlyn access the security room and turn off the cameras so there would be no record of the car leaving.

Caitlyn was a total brain who happened to play first chair violin. "I wish I could figure out how to do this at my house. My Dad is totally paranoid when it comes to security."

"I'd help you, but it's not like we're ever really alone there. There's always someone around."

"I know. Like I said, Dad's paranoid. So is Uncle Niall. I think it's because they spend time in places where kidnapping for ransom is just another way to make money."

She tried not to talk about Adam the whole time they were driving, but she couldn't help herself. She kept thinking of things, Tweets and stuff on Facebook. He'd friended her though he didn't follow her on Twitter.

He would after tonight. She tingled as she imagined dancing with him.

She'd ask him if he didn't ask her.

Lie.

The thought of him saying no made her stomach sink. She'd never have the nerve to ask him, not with other people around and watching.

The house came into sight and she saw him. It felt like a bird was trapped in her chest with its wings flapping crazily.

"There's Adam," Caitlyn said before she could. "He's getting in the car with Jordão."

"Let's follow them!"

"Okay."

She knew Caitlyn was relieved not to have to go in to the party. She was kind of glad, too.

They followed Jordão's car into the Sunset District. She recognized some of the houses and streets, from times she'd been there with Brian.

Ahead of them Jordão stopped in front of a house. There was no place to turn around, but it was dark and it wasn't like he and Adam knew they were being followed.

She started to hunch over then stopped when Adam's door opened. Just one little peek . . .

"Slow down," she said.

Caitlyn did, probably hoping Adam and Jordão would be going up the walkway when they passed.

Adam got out of the car. Seeing him made her ache inside.

It looked like maybe he was arguing with Jordão. She didn't really like Jordão though he was popular too. A lot of kids she knew had major 'I'm hot shit' issues, but he was the worst, probably because he was a diplomat's son and knew he could do anything, and the only thing bad that might happen to him was being sent back to Brazil by his parents or getting kicked out of the country by the U.S. government.

Jordão turned toward them and waved. Caitlyn gave a little scream and the car sped up.

"Stop! Stop!" she said when Jordão stepped into the street. Her cheeks burned but it would be worse if they raced past and Adam or Jordão ended up telling everyone she and Caitlyn had been following them. How pathetic was that.

Caitlyn stopped the car. Jordão and Adam came over.

"Pretend it's coincidence," she whispered to Caitlyn as they both rolled down their windows.

Her heart was going a mile a minute. She thought she might faint when Adam leaned down so his face was only inches away from hers, close enough she could taste the beer on his breath when he said, "You bailed on the party, too, huh."

She blushed and hoped the darkness in the car hid some of the redness. They must have known all along they were being followed.

"Yeah. We bailed."

"Our lucky day," Jordão said from the other side. "Come in with us?"

She sent a pleading glance in Caitlyn's direction before Caitlyn could say anything. "Please," she mouthed to Caitlyn. Out loud she said, "We can only stay for a few minutes."

"A few minutes would be great," Jordão said. He gave Caitlyn a huge smile. "I've been trying to hack into a site. I could use some advice."

It was the magic thing to say. Caitlyn relaxed totally. She could talk all night about computers.

They parked the car and got out. There was music coming from the house, but it wasn't blaring.

Inside there were only three guys. Adam introduced them as Mason, Owen, and Carter. One of them, Owen, looked vaguely familiar but she wasn't interested in knowing him better.

"Party'll get going soon," Jordão said. "Get you girls a drink?"

"Sure."

"Beer? Rum and Coke?"

She didn't want Adam to be embarrassed hanging out with her. "Beer."

"Just Coke," Caitlyn said.

"One beer, one Coke coming up."

He disappeared along with Adam and the boy named Mason. When they came back, everybody sat on the couch, listening to tunes.

Heaven. It felt like heaven to be sitting next to Adam.

Slow dancing felt even better. She didn't protest when Adam started touching her. Little sparks of fire burned in her breasts and between her legs even though a part of her said she should make him stop, or at least make him take her somewhere private.

She wanted to be with him. She wanted him to be her first. But not like this.

"Finish your beer," he told her in between kisses. His lips were incredibly soft.

She finished it, the bottle falling out of her hand and onto the carpet. She wanted to fall, too.

Another beer was pressed into her hand. She watched it lift, a hand covering her hand and couldn't seem to make herself resist, even when she realized it was Carter's hand instead of Adam's.

Confusion filled her. When had she stopped dancing with Adam?

She opened her mouth to say she didn't want more beer but ended up swallowing it instead. She couldn't help herself.

And then Carter was leading her to a bedroom. A scream welled up inside her at seeing Caitlyn naked on the bed with Jordão on top of her. This was wrong, wrong, wrong.

Carter pushed her down on the bed next to Caitlyn. She tried to pretend it wasn't happening. But it was.

Jordão rolled off Caitlyn and Mason got on top of her. She felt her clothes being removed and tried to protest. She thought she said no, even when she saw it was Adam above her, but she couldn't be sure.

It hurt. Inside and outside.

And when he was done, Carter was there. Then Owen.

She went away in her head and came back—

The scene skipped to the hospital and the abrupt shift was enough to cause Etaín to break the contact.

She swayed. Dizzy. Aware of a ringing in her ears, of her face wet with tears. Nausea building, not guilt but a reaction to what she'd just lived through.

The urge to explode in a fury of violence followed, only calming when she noticed how easily Brianna slept now. Reaching out, she dared to touch her again and found a measure of peace. The guilt was gone, as was the desire to die.

Etaín went to the desk where the sketch pad lay open, the pencils next to it. She hadn't intended to do this here, but with Denis in possession of the ending scenes, there was no reason to do them elsewhere and every reason to get this behind her.

She sat, distancing herself from Brianna's reality by drawing, turning the memories into images on paper. And then, when she was done, by forcing them into a mental prison and walling them away, using *will* to do it. Brianna was better off without them.

She glanced one last time at the girl on the bed before leaving the room. Surprise, longing, caution coming from an instinctive need for emotional survival, all slammed into her at seeing Cathal waiting there.

"I'll get Denis," the man who'd escorted her into the house said.

The nurse slipped into Brianna's bedroom, leaving only the two of them in the hallway.

Need ripped through Cathal with proximity to Etaín. When he was away from her, he caught himself wondering if her impact on him could possibly be real. But when he was with her, his cock made sure there was no room for doubt.

"I guessed you might be heading here," he said, speaking when it became clear she didn't intend to, finding he didn't want to dig himself deeper into the mire of conscience and duty and the acts committed out of protectiveness, with an outright lie.

She shrugged, affecting a casualness at odds with what he'd seen in her face when she'd stepped out of Brianna's bedroom and found him waiting there. He shoved his hands into his pockets to keep from jerking her to him and delivering a kiss that would force a return to the intimacy they'd shared at her apartment.

"I called you back immediately. All I got was voicemail."

She glanced away, one of her rare tells, and he knew she'd been aware of at least one of his calls and chosen not to answer it. A tightness formed in his chest, reverberating in his gut as silence stretched like a taut wire between them.

He wondered if she would lie. She shrugged again and said, "There didn't seem to be any point in talking."

As he had after the ill-advised breakfast at Aesirs, he tried humor. "I can hardly grovel if you don't take my calls."

She met his eyes and he knew she wouldn't let him off the hook this time. "What was going on with you?"

There it was. And whether he intended it or not, the truth spilled out between them. "Did you go to Eamon last night?"

"Not consciously. Not that it matters. Not that you'll believe me even. But yes, I ended up with him. I stayed the night with him."

Why Eamon and not me? The question howled through Cathal but pride kept him from asking it.

"I'll stop seeing him when I decide to stop. Not before then and maybe not for a while. Don't call me if you can't accept that."

There was no defiance in the words, no challenge. Only a sense of defeat that helped him control himself though he couldn't keep the frustration out of his voice when he said, "So that's it? Your way or no way?"

"I can't change how it is."

She started to turn away and panic seized him. He grabbed

her, hands closing around her upper arms. "Make me understand, Etaín."

Before she could answer Denis appeared at the top of the stairway without his soldier. "I'm not going to let this discussion drop," Cathal warned, a different worry consuming him as his uncle neared.

He released Etaín, though his hand settled at the base of her spine, and despite the churn of emotions inside him, he didn't bother lying to himself by claiming he did it only to send a message to his uncle.

"When will I get the rest of the drawings?" Denis asked.

The question was a kick to Cathal's gut. An accusation as he looked from his uncle to Etaín.

"You can have them now," Etaín said.

The dead calmness of Denis's voice after probably having looked at the first set of drawings made her wonder if he intended to take them to the police. *Not my business,* she thought, dismissing the question.

She offered him the tablet but found she couldn't release it without meeting his eyes, without reminding him there could be consequences if he allowed himself to act on the emotions she knew churned inside him. "Brianna needs you to be there for her."

He didn't give a hint of his intentions away, just said, "I am. I will be," before accompanying them to just inside the front door and returning the favor by giving her a warning. "You might want to stay clear of Stylin' Ink for a few days."

Every muscle tensed. "Why?"

"Media is camped out there. News story just broke and they're trying to get a look at the woman they think is helping the Harlequin Rapist taskforce."

"Any pictures of me circulating?"

"No."

"Good. Thanks for letting me know."

Denis placed a hand on Cathal's shoulder. "A moment of your time."

It was the perfect opening for her to leave. "I'll head out now. I've got a funeral to go to." There was no reason to avoid it and if she was careful she wouldn't be noticed.

A quick in and out to show Jamaal the drawing, then she'd figure out what she'd do next. She couldn't bolt until after the fund-raiser. But maybe then she'd head to LA or Vegas and do a stint as a guest artist.

Cathal didn't let her escape that easily. He turned her toward him, taking her mouth in a possessive storming, reaffirming what he'd said moments earlier, that they *would* return to their discussion about Eamon.

She didn't know what she'd tell him. What she could possibly say that would make him okay with her being with Eamon and with him, but she wanted to find those words.

Days ago even the thought of a long-term relationship would have scared her. But with the electric hum of desire coursing through her, it was hard to think of anything beyond getting naked so skin could touch skin.

Cathal ended the kiss and let her go, reluctantly. His uncle waited for the sound of the Harley's engine before saying. "You need to stay away from her now."

"I could say the same to you. She's my concern, not yours."

Something moved through Denis's eyes. There and gone too quickly for him to read it.

"Think, Cathal, with your head instead of your dick. Consider what might happen if some news reporter snaps off a picture of her with you. You want to give them a face to go with the name they've already got? You want her family to see who she's associating with and reel her in? Ask questions? She doesn't need the danger being identified with you would bring her."

Denis's voice was smooth glass delivering a truth Cathal wanted to ignore. He was often photographed, especially when he took a woman somewhere other than Saoirse.

And beneath the truth was a message it would be foolish to ever forget. If Etaín talked, implicating his father and uncle in any way after they'd delivered their brand of justice, they'd have her killed.

He didn't think he'd be able to turn Denis away from his chosen course, but for Etaín, he had to risk trying. He glanced down at the sketchpad. "There's her father to consider. Her brother. They would be willing to take action."

"It's too late for that."

"I'm going to see her again. I'm not going to let anything happen to her."

"Then be careful. And make sure she is. Everybody knows this Harlequin Rapist is going to take another woman."

A chill swept through Cathal. Fear for Etaín, that his uncle might already be thinking of a way to cover her disappearance. Meanings within meanings or just the usual paranoia, he couldn't be certain what was behind Denis's warning.

Sean's assertion that sharing Etaín with Eamon might be necessary to keep her safe sliced through Cathal's chest like talons and dug into his heart. "If that's all, I need to get to Saoirse."

Denis clapped his nephew on the back. "Go. Your father's proud of what you've accomplished. So am I."

He turned from the door after Cathal's departure, mind seizing with the sight of Matt coming to an abrupt halt at the top of the staircase. "Clara said come quick."

He took the steps at a run. His heart pounding the way it had when he'd raced to the pool.

The hallway telescoped into a kaleidoscope of images from the past. Of the dead.

He braced himself. Prepared for the worst, his throat clogging as he stepped into Brianna's room, then clogging further at discovering her awake, her eyes clear and comprehending, seeming huge in a face that was still gaunt and pale from her attempts to starve herself.

"Dad? I want to get out of bed but she says I can't. What's going on? Why do I have catheters in my arms and this thing my stomach?"

Tears streamed down his cheeks then, and he didn't care they were witnessed. He rushed to her side, sitting on the edge of the bed and gathering her into a hug, trying to be gentle in spite of the fierce, wild emotions boiling inside him.

"You're crushing me," she said, the laughter in her voice and the way she hugged him making the tears fall harder.

"Some privacy, Clara."

The nurse left them.

"Dad, what's going on?"

Fear now in her voice. Worry. And it was intolerable to him.

"What do you remember?" he asked, aware of the sketchpad he'd dropped on the floor in his haste to get to Brianna, the hair on his arms and neck rising again because of Etaín.

"I . . . I went to Caitlyn's house." It ended in a whisper. "What happened, Dad? Please tell me what happened."

Nothing. Nothing. Everything inside him wanted to shield her from the truth. How could he tell his baby girl that she'd been raped, violated?

He closed his eyes, willing the tears to stop and praying for answers. He couldn't go through what he'd just gone through. He couldn't lose her again.

Her arms tightened on him. "Did Caitlyn and I go somewhere?"

Her question helped him find his way, like a man in an abyss following a faint, faint light out of it. "Yes, but I don't know where." Not the full truth but enough for now. "You were found in her mother's car, overdosed. Caitlyn died without regaining consciousness."

Sobs wracked Brianna, so violent he opened his mouth, ready to call for Clara only to shut it when he imagined the nurse drawing a syringe. He couldn't stand the thought of having Brianna sedated again.

Her cries ripped through him, but as bad as they made him feel, this was better than before. She was clinging to him, her tears wetting his neck and soaking his shirt.

"You're going to be okay," he told her, over and over again, rubbing her back, rocking her until exhaustion left her limp and her sobs became tiny gasps of sound.

He leaned forward, settling her onto the mattress and pulling the covers up to her chin. There was bruising beneath her eyes and he cupped her cheek, rubbing his thumb over the dark stain of undeserved suffering. "Sleep, Brianna. Clara will come back and sit with you."

She grabbed his hand before he could stand. "We wouldn't have taken drugs on purpose."

"I know, sweetheart. I know."

"I don't remember any of it, Daddy."

"It's better that way. You've been . . . lost in your own mind. Now all that matters is what happens from this day forward."

He reached down, picking up the sketch pad before pressing a kiss to her forehead. "Sleep now. I've got some business I need to attend to."

Twenty-two

Etaín blended easily into the streams of people heading toward the church DaWanda attended. She'd been there a couple of times before, for a client's wedding and then to listen to one of Jamaal's cousins sing.

It sat on the corner, a building originating as a church rather than a converted storefront as several others on the block had. The people making their way toward it were a mix of races, some dressed up and some dressed down.

The media waited in force. Policemen were visible, too, officers in uniforms and a few others she recognized in plain clothes.

She'd braided her hair and tucked it under a ball cap blocks away where she'd left the Harley. Still, as she neared the front doors, she ducked her head and hunched her shoulders, attaching herself to a cluster of people to pass unnoticed into the church.

It was already standing room only inside.

The sight of the casket at the front made her shiver. In the pockets of her jacket, she curled her hands into fists, the vines along her arms seeming to whisper as she fought to keep Tyra's reality from overwhelming her.

Looking away from the dark box, she pushed further into the packed church, searching for Jamaal. Sweat clinging to her skin from the growing heat of so many people crammed into one room.

Finally she spotted him, seated near the front next to DaWanda and impossible to get to. She maneuvered to a place where she thought she'd be able to intercept him at the end of the service.

He felt her stare and turned his head. Their eyes met. *Are you fucking insane?* he mouthed.

She used hand signals to indicate she needed to talk to him. He held up his phone but she shook her head.

The music grew louder, blanketing the hushed murmur of hundreds of conversations before ebbing into silence.

The service began.

A homegoing, they called it.

It became harder and harder to hold back Tyra's stolen reality as they talked about her life. Her struggles with addiction and victory over it. Her hopes and dreams and her faith.

Etaín dug her fingernails into her palms as if she would blind the eyes there. Tears flowed down her cheeks as around her she saw the same on other faces.

The urge to escape built. Only sheer determination kept her standing until the final hymn and the dismissal.

The pressure lessened as the church began emptying.

It disappeared completely when Jamaal and DaWanda reached her.

"Hey girl," DaWanda said, embracing her in a bone crushing hug. "They're talking some crazy stuff about you on the radio."

"I know. Mind if I talk to Jamaal privately for a few minutes?"

"He'll take you through the church so you can leave out the kitchen door."

Another hug and DaWanda joined the flow of people exiting the building.

Etaín followed Jamaal into a hallway crowded by robed choir members. As soon as they got clear of them he pulled her into a room that looked like it was used for Sunday school.

Jamaal's smooth features turned fierce. "Bryce said your brother and another Fed came around the other day. Tell me you're not letting Parker put a big fucking bull's-eye on your back."

"I'm not."

"Then what's all this shit the news people are talking? Why are you here?"

"Later, okay? Right now I need you to look at a tat and tell me if you know whose work it is or if you remember seeing it on anyone."

Pulling the picture from her pocket she held it out to him. He crossed his arms, his face hardening into a mask of refusal. "This involve the Harlequin Rapist?"

Nobody did *impasse* better than Jamaal. "Yes."

"Your brother put you up to this? Doing the job for the PO-lice now? When he knows this twisted motherfucker might go for you?"

"All the more reason to catch him, don't you think?"

Jamaal cursed and unfolded his arms. He took the paper and opened it.

She saw the answer on his face. "You recognize it."

"Looks like Deon Gold's work. Pass that name on to your brother, then leave town for a while. Take Ladell up on his invite to do work on the rich and stoned down in LA."

"You know where they can find Deon?"

"Jail or dead. Dropped off the face of the earth a while back. Did some bad shit and got the FBI wanting him. Easy enough for your brother to get the details."

There was more, something in his voice alerted her to it. He started to turn and the hand she had on his suit-jacketed arm slid downward, toward bare skin.

Insidious temptation crept into her. The touch of the eye to his hand and she could know what he was hiding.

She tightened her fingers, to stop herself instead of him, horror rolling through her at having evidence that if she wasn't careful, her gift might control her, might take where she would ask.

"Please, Jamaal. You know more than you're saying. Tell me. For Tyra, if you won't do it because I'm asking."

Against her palm she felt him deflate, the air going out on a long-suffering sigh. "Friends don't let friends do crazy shit by themselves. But if I skip out on DaWanda now to go with you—because I know you're not going to wait—there'll be trouble at home until I get back on her good side."

Etaín smothered a smile. For all his talk he didn't cheat on DaWanda.

"True enough. You and Mr. Hand could end up on real friendly terms."

That got her a sour look. "You remember Anton Charles? Rides with the Curs and had it bad for you a while back. Kept coming around for new art?"

"I remember him."

"He's back in town. Saw him the other day. If anyone knows where Deon is and is inclined to talk *to you* about him, it'd be Anton. Don't bother passing his name on to Parker. Anton won't give him shit. He's not going to give you something for free, either."

"Wouldn't expect him to."

"You'll take someone with you?"

They both knew she wouldn't.

"I'll be safe enough. He rides with some guys who wear my ink from back when I was just getting started."

In the early days, when she was running wild with the arrival of her gift.

Jamaal handed the drawing to her. "I'll let you out through the kitchen. You should be able to get away from here without being noticed, as long as you're smart about it."

"I'll be smart."

He snorted and turned away. "I'm beginning to think you don't know the meaning of that word."

She laughed. "Insulting my intelligence now? Just remember payback's a bitch."

"Yeah, but the bitch has got to stay alive if she's going to do the paying back."

A sharp rap on the office door announced Niall's arrival. Denis looked up from his work as his brother stepped into the room, closing the door with barely a glance at the guns and rifles lying openly on every piece of furniture.

The drawings were spread across the desk, surreal and terrible, dripping with emotion. Boys on Caitlyn. Faces above Brianna's.

Niall stopped next to him and looked down at them. "This everything?"

"Yes."

"We could have it taken care of. Distance ourselves from it."

Denis tilted his head toward the rifle leaning against the desk at his right. "That distance is good enough. Pop. Pop. Pop. Pop. Pop. Five shots and it's done. This business is behind us."

"Cathal's with her?"

"I don't think so. Not if she's at a funeral. Her name's in the news but not her face. I told him to stay away from her." Denis smiled. "Your son has balls. He said I should do the same."

"How'd you leave it?"

"He knows the score. These are dangerous times."

Niall gave a slight nod, acknowledging the truth of it. "I recognize a couple of the boys from Brianna's school." He touched a fingertip to a face. "This one looks familiar, too."

Denis fought to tamp down the rage that started to build. Justice was best served cold.

"His brother used to come around here with Brian. Low-level drug dealer."

Denis tapped his finger on a name written on one of the pages. Jordão. "This one's a diplomat's son. Brazilian. There's a possibility his family may be connected to a cartel. I decided against floating any questions. Whether they are or not, this could bring a lot of heat down on us."

"You planning on getting careless?"

He laughed. "You know me better than that."

"Then this shouldn't lead back to us. And if it does then the motive will surface, too. There'll be noise, but in the end, it'll be, 'Don't ask. Don't tell.'"

Denis was counting on it, but it didn't really matter. If he had to, he'd pack up and leave. There was plenty of money in off-shore accounts, and plenty of business he could tend without living in the United States.

"When are you going to do this thing?" Niall asked.

"Today." He set the gun he'd rubbed clean on a picture of a boy with a line of little hearts drawn to him. "Starting with this one. He's going to band practice like nothing happened. Like he didn't rape my daughter and leave her to die."

Niall's hand came down on Denis's shoulder in a familiar show of solidarity. They'd had each other's backs since they were kids. "You want my help with this?"

"No. I need to do this myself."

"And Etaín?"

I don't remember any of it, Daddy.

"I told Clara to cut back on the drugs. Brianna woke up a few minutes after Etaín left. She looked right at me. She let me hug her while she cried on my shoulder." His voice broke. "She doesn't remember what happened to her."

Niall's grip tightened on his shoulder. "Then we play wait and see for now?"

Denis picked up another gun. He wouldn't know until he got into position which one he would use. Caution and preparation had always served him.

His thoughts went to that instant when Etaín's eyes had met his before she released the sketchpad. Not, *what are you going to do with them*, but worry for his daughter, *Brianna needs you to be there for her.*

"We wait," he said. "And if she becomes a problem Cathal can't get under control, we have the situation taken care of in a way that won't tear apart the family."

Etaín recognized Anton's Harley by the custom paint job and abundance of chrome. She parked next to it and entered the bar, the noise lessening enough so "This hot piece is mine," carried through the room.

She ignored the guy directing the comment at her. His jacket revealed he was a club hanger-on and not a member or a prospect. When she would have walked past him, he grabbed her arm. "Now hold on, mama. Why you ignoring me? What you being so unfriendly for?"

"'Cause she's not interested in your sorry ass," came a rough voice from Etaín's left.

"Hey, hey, don't want no trouble with you, Anton."

He released her arm, backing away as she turned toward Anton and took in the bulked-up muscle and the new ink compliments of a stay in the US prison system.

Anton opened his arms in greeting but she knew better than to step into them. She'd start as she meant to go on. "In your dreams."

He gave a belly laugh. "You got that right, Etaín. And you've starred in some mighty fine ones."

She took his hand when he offered it, going through the series of complicated moves while imagining there was a wall and her gift was locked behind it.

"I know you're not stopping in 'cause you were in the neighborhood. Who you coming here to see?"

"You. Jamaal said you were the one I should talk to. I need a favor."

He smiled big. "Maybe those dreams going to turn real after all. Wash this talk down with a beer?"

"Sure."

"My treat. You get the next round."

"Fine by me."

They stopped by the bar then claimed a booth in the back. A few steps away, men were gathered around pool tables. The clack of ball on ball relaxed her, the joking and swearing and the sound of rap music blocking off the world outside of this one.

Twenty-three

The fog swirled around Denis the same as it had the day Caitlyn was put in the ground. It wet his face like tears. Hugged him. Concealed him as he waited.

Kids today . . . He shook his head. With their Tweets and their Facebook and their YouTube they made it easy to know things about them. To *find* them. They lived like nothing they said or did would ever lead to repercussions.

He wasn't a man who liked to shit in his own backyard, but this business had to be taken care of personally. It would be smarter to wait, to kill them one at a time, spread out over months or years like random acts of violence.

He knew it. But knew, too, he wouldn't hold off. The prospect of letting them live another day was intolerable.

If he was a man to lie to himself, he'd claim he was doing a public service, preventing another girl from being victimized. He knew himself better than that. Accepted who he was though he had no problem with doing a good deed for society.

This was about honor and retribution and seeing justice done on behalf of his family. It was about burying his failure in a grave so he could move past it.

A fire-red Porsche entered the parking lot, music blaring, the driver oblivious to his impending fate. A burn started in Denis's gut. Brianna thought she loved this boy, Adam. She'd trusted him and he'd betrayed her in the worst possible way.

Denis pulled a gloved hand from a deep pocket in his coat, the gun in it a familiar weight, the silencer a long black cylinder already screwed in place. As he moved toward the car, he shut himself off from feeling. He emptied his mind of everything except cold determination, a steadiness that came from complete concentration and the objectification of a target.

The car door swung open, illuminating the boy. He got a foot on the ground before realizing he wasn't alone.

Denis lifted the gun and fired.

A hole appeared dead center in the boy's forehead.

He put a second one in the chest. Insurance. Not rage.

Eamon gave up the pointless study of financial statements, pushing them into a pile at one corner of his desk and acknowledging the impossibility of concentrating on them. He lifted the flier for the shelter fund-raiser and crushed it into a ball in his frustration. Time crawled in a way it hadn't in hundreds of years of existence, all because of her.

Though he knew he would have to endure Liam's amused tone, he called his third to ask, "Where is she?"

The question elicited a laugh. "At a bar catering to what the police would label outlaw bikers."

More of Eamon's patience fled at having additional evidence of just how dangerously independent she was. "You didn't think to report this?"

"As if I might need reinforcements? Hardly. Am I to intuit that you now wish to curtail her freedom? Give the order and I will happily extract her."

"Give me the location," Eamon said. "I will deal with my intended."

* * *

Etaín took a pull on the beer, content to wait for Anton to bring up the purpose of her visit, her thoughts drifting to Cathal. *Coward,* she called herself, for being relieved Denis's arrival had interrupted their discussion outside Brianna's room and given her a chance to leave without continuing it.

It wasn't like her not to take things head-on. Then again, it wasn't like her to think in terms of lovers and relationships.

Somehow he'd gotten to her. Hot sex, but something more.

Her gift responding to him maybe? The irresistible draw of being able to touch someone and know it wouldn't destroy them?

That'd do it, weakening her resistance to allowing intimacy. Making it seem as though the feelings that came along with it didn't seem so risky.

And Eamon?

Warmth stole into her. This morning, fresh from Brianna's memories and knowing there were more of them to take, she might have met whatever price he named to better control her gift, but he hadn't demanded anything of her.

He would. The certainty of it crept in cold against the heat, making her think of magic and mirrors, water and fire. He'd made it clear from the start he wasn't thinking short-term. What would she do when he pressed her for more? Run from him the same way she'd done from Cathal?

Not run. Get some breathing room. That's all.

Irritation flickered through her. At herself for thinking about Cathal and Eamon at all except in terms of physical pleasure. Derrick and Bryce and Jamaal were as complicated as she wanted when it came to relationships. And if she really wanted to fuck with her own head, then she could think about the captain and Parker.

"What you want with me?" Anton finally asked.

She pulled the drawing from her pocket, unfolding it and putting it down on the table between them. He might care what the Harlequin Rapist was doing, he might not. Same was true of Deon, but the mention of a high-profile case would spook them both, even if the idea of helping the police didn't kill their willingness to share information from the start.

"I'm looking for the guy wearing this ink. I need a name. An address would be even better. Jamaal says he recognizes the work. It's Deon Gold's."

Anton laughed. "You don't ask for nothing small, do you girl?"

"Might as well live large if you're going to live at all."

"Got that right. Saying I could put this picture in front of Deon, what's in it for me?"

"Not a fuck. I've got boyfriend problems enough without adding to them."

She hadn't intended to mention the men in her life. Finding how easily the label of boyfriend settled on them had her nerves jangling.

Anton held up his hand and pointed, cocking his thumb. "Bang. Bang. A little drive-by action and no more boyfriend problems. Might even do that favor for nothing."

Something savage moved through her with the implied threat to Cathal and Eamon. Insidious temptation followed, much, much stronger than when she'd been standing in the church with Jamaal.

She could reach over and lay her palm against Anton's hand. She could take what she wanted and if it led to the Harlequin Rapist being stopped, then the end would justify the means. It wasn't any worse than what she'd done when she visited Brianna.

Ice slid down her spine at how quickly the thought had come. How easily it would be to give in to impulse and follow through with the use of her gift.

She wanted to deny the change in herself. Questioned in that instant if this was the reason her mother ran, because getting involved

made it too easy to step on a dark path. To be consumed by the gift—
the magic—rather than remain in control of it.

"Let me worry about the men in my life," she said, pressing her
palms against the wet chill of the beer bottle. "Are you willing to connect me with Deon for some fresh ink?"

Her conscience whispered, *say yes, say yes, say yes*. Because she didn't
think she could accept *no*.

"Most I'm going to do is pass this picture on and say what you
want. Tell Deon you an artist too and real tight with Jamaal."

She pulled a pencil from a pocket and wrote her cell number on
one corner of the paper. "Long as you let me know one way or another,
we'd be good."

He picked up the drawing and folded it. "Be better if the two of us
play some pool. Then dance a song so nobody thinks I don't know
what to do with a beautiful woman before she leaves."

"I'm good with that."

He slipped the drawing into his pocket, then left the booth. She
polished off the beer and followed.

A table cleared as soon as Anton stopped next to it, one of the men
at it saying, "Go ahead, all yours."

Etaín selected a cue and chalked the tip. "Nine-ball? Eight? Or
straight?"

Anton picked up a couple of cues before deciding on one. "Nine.
First one to seven wins the round."

Another man stepped forward, racking the balls without a word
from Anton. "I'm impressed," she said. "Always been like this? Or just
since you rode back into town?"

"Always been a real popular brother. Ladies first."

She fouled out after sinking the first three balls but came back to
win when he missed a shot and she pocketed the nine ball.

"Not bad for a white girl, only now I'm done fooling around."

Anton was up five games to Etaín's four when a tingling sensation

raced along the vines on her forearms. She made her shot, watching as
the cue ball kissed the low five, knocking it into the nine and dropping it into a pocket for another win.

She looked up and around because instead of going away, the sensation grew strong. *Magic.* She had a name for the phenomenon even
if she didn't have a full understanding of what it meant with respect
to her.

As soon as she saw the man leaning casually against the wall a few
pool cues length away, she had a source for the sensation crawling
along her arms—and a suspicion as to why he was there. Neither his
skin color nor the hair worn in a multitude of long braids set him
apart from the other black men in the bar, but his sheer beauty did.
And though she hadn't seen him at Aesirs, she knew he easily belonged there. Even dressed in the jeans and ribbed tank he had on,
if he walked through the restaurant, the diners would view him as a
visual treat served up for their enjoyment.

She met his eyes and found nothing in them. They were flat and
dark, empty of recognition or acknowledgment.

A shiver of fear slid through her at the possibility she was wrong
about Eamon being responsible for this man's presence here. When it
came to her gift and the world of magic her mother must have been a
part of, slowly, she was beginning to realize how running might be
easier and safer than staying in place.

She forced her attention back to Anton and watched as the cue ball
touched the three before hitting the low two, creating a foul. "I'm
done fooling around now," she joked, tossing his words back at him
though she was serious about finishing her business and putting distance between herself and the deadly stranger with vibes of magic.

"Fine with me if you win the round." Anton held his arms wide.
"'Cause I'm in the mood for a little dancing, a nice slow song with a
sweet, willing woman."

She let him play for his audience without denying his claim, calcu-
lating her shots, lining them up in her mind first.

One.

Two.

Three.

The nine-ball dropped with a soft thud. "Let's dance," she said, putting the cue back in the rack and feeling an icy burn along the forearms when doing it took her closer to the stranger.

A fast rap song moved into a slow, dirty bump-and-grind beat almost as soon as they stepped onto the dance floor. Anton's hands settled on her hips. "Your doing?" she asked.

"Think I was gonna miss this opportunity to show you what you've been turning down?"

She put her hands on his chest, as much to keep some distance between them as to keep her palms from touching bare skin. "Like I can't see that massive piece of hardware you're toting around at the front of your pants?"

He laughed hard, eyes shining with amusement. "That's right, girl. Stroke my ego if you ain't gonna stroke nothing else. You're lucky I got too much pride to take an unwilling woman else you'd be at the top of the list."

She shuddered, her thoughts returning to Tyra in the hospital. Then to Brianna curled in a fetal ball, heavily sedated to keep her from insanity and suicide.

Anton's forehead touched hers. "You scared of somebody? Or remembering something bad was done to you? Give me a name. I'll take care of it."

This close and touching, she was hyperaware of the ink she'd put on him. It made her wonder if his offer came as much from that connection as a desire to get in her pants.

Use it, a voice whispered. And she wasn't sure whether it was the magic talking, or her desire to see the Harlequin Rapist stopped.

"Just show Deon the picture. Press him to tell you what he knows about the guy wearing his art. If he can be found, there are other people lined up to take care of him."

Whatever Anton might have answered, it was aborted when fingers encircled her upper arm, burning her with familiar flame and abruptly ending the dance with a sharp jerk away from Anton.

"I think I warned you I'd accept Cathal, but no one else, Etaín."

If Cathal's voice had been ice earlier in the day then Eamon's was fire, a raging storm of it looking for an excuse to obliterate. One he got when Anton said, "Who the fuck you think you are?" and followed the question with his fists.

Eamon moved like smooth liquid, pushing Etaín away from him and using Anton's momentum against him. Flipping and sending him flying into patch-wearing bikers who'd stopped dancing at the prospect of trouble.

Anton got to his feet. He charged and was sent flying again.

"Liam, take her outside while I finish this," Eamon said, and the stranger was instantly there, taking her arm.

"Fuck that," said the guy who'd tried to claim her when she entered the bar, jumping into the fight, his action pulling others into it with him.

It should have been a beat down ending in homicide. It would have been except for the magic.

Trapped between Eamon's back and Liam's, their fighting looked like martial arts training but Etaín knew there was more to it. She felt them draw on something outside themselves. Magic rushed over the ink on her skin, accompanying the sound of flesh hitting flesh and bodies striking chairs and tables and walls.

Glass shattered. Bottles falling to the floor and broken against edges to become weapons.

More men joined the fight while women cheered them on.

Knives came out.

Etaín's adrenaline surged.

A shot was fired and suddenly it seemed as though every hand held a gun.

"Enough!" a voice bellowed.

Etaín found the man responsible and saw the family resemblance to Anton. He pointed the gun at Eamon and Liam. "You two mother-fuckers. Get the fuck out of here. Anton, you want her to stay?"

Her eyes met Anton's. He touched a hand to the pocket holding the drawing and winked. "We gonna hook up later. She go willingly, I'm fine as long as they pay for the damage done to your place."

Eamon paid, pulling her against him roughly once they left the bar and slamming his mouth down on hers. Fury and lust poured into her with the hot, raw sweep of his tongue. Naked aggression and primitive possession that she answered in kind in the aftermath of violence coupled with magic.

Her cunt clenched and unclenched. Desire rode her, a need to be filled by him. It eradicated logical thought, blurred everything that had happened since leaving Aesirs that morning.

The kiss ended with both of them breathing raggedly, their bodies pressed tight, his cock hard and ready between them. She started to suggest they go to her apartment since it was closer, opened her mouth to say it, but he spoke first.

"I've been patient, Etaín, foolish even, in allowing you the amount of freedom I have. Another wouldn't tolerate your doing as you please and involving yourself in unwise, dangerous activities. I've done so because I thought you needed time. No more."

She jerked out of his arms, fury engulfing her as his arrogant tone and arrogant words touched the very place where pain over her es-trangement with the captain and rocky relationship with Parker lived. "Allow? Tolerate? Who the fuck do you think you are in my life?"

A muscle spasmed in his cheek. His eyes were molten with anger. "You will learn the full truth of that soon enough, though I had thought this morning's lessons would have demonstrated how much you need me if you're to survive your gift and the magic it's tied to."

She clamped her jaws against responding to his claim in the heat of anger, some tiny, rational instinct for self-preservation advising against it, even as the urge to escape welled up inside her and her mother's voice whispered *run*. "You've had me followed."

"Of course."

Her fury went white-hot, a nova exploding into silence in her head. "I'm going home."

He reached for her and instinctively she put her hand up to ward him off, only it felt as though an electric current pulsed through the vines on her arm, turning the eye on her palm into a lethal weapon, a tool to drain reality away with a touch.

She saw by his expression he felt the charge of magic. And also that it pleased him rather than frightened him. Stepping sideways, to her bike, she straddled it.

"This isn't finished, Etaín," he said, promise in his voice.

She said nothing. Putting on the helmet and riding away.

Clapping marked Etaín's departure and Eamon sent a censorious glare in his third's direction. It had no effect. As Etaín's ignorance of her heritage freed them both from constraint and artifice, his deep friendship with Liam and Rhys allowed for a level of familiarity and oftentimes brutal honesty that others would never dare.

"Well done," Liam said, "if your intention was to further develop her gift."

Not his intention, but he'd found a measure of calm in knowing she could protect herself—at least against humans and lower-born Elves. "Follow her."

The command was met with a mocking bow. "Of course, Lord. I live to serve you as well you know. But might I make an observation before I rush after your future wife?"

"There's no stopping you from it."

"True." Liam's smile widened. "If what I just witnessed is a demonstration of how you intend to *guide her actions* at the fund-raiser, then I'd advise you to send Rhys in your stead."

Twenty-four

*H*e drove by her apartment. It was still dark.

Slut. Filthy whore. He'd seen her with two different men but there was no way to know which one of them she was with now.

She was like his mother. Disappearing. Coming back smelling like men's cologne and sweat. Disappearing again. Sometimes bringing strangers to the house. Men who touched him and Kevin after she'd passed out, forgetting them. She was always forgetting them.

He wouldn't let that happen to him again. He refused to be forgotten ever again.

He looked at her apartment in the side-view mirror before turning the corner. He couldn't wait for things to be perfect anymore, the way he'd had to since coming to San Francisco.

A little thrill swept into him with the decision. The same way it had when he decided to go into the tattoo shop.

He liked *choosing* which one would be next, and then waiting inside for her to come home. He liked laying out the things he would need so they'd be ready when she got there.

He liked touching her things, holding her clothes against his face. He liked eating the food she'd bought and cooked.

Before coming to San Francisco that's the way he'd always been with them. He'd never taken any of them away from where they lived. He'd wanted them to remember him there.

He licked his lips, thinking about the darkened apartment and the news reports. *It would be too risky to stay in her apartment for long. But after he gagged her, there would be time to have her once, just once, before taking her to their special place.*

Imagining it excited him. His heart sped up, leaving him feeling jittery, scared but happy, too. This would be like combining the old way with the new way.

He'd take her tonight. No one would be expecting it.

They didn't think the Harlequin Rapist would strike before next Monday. Kevin had even told him about a news reporter saying the next woman might be black instead of white.

He smiled, thinking about the black girl she'd been tattooing, and how when he squinted, he could see a golden thread touching both of them, connecting them so she had to be a choice, too.

Tonight, he told himself again. He didn't want to wait any longer.

Queasiness rippled through his stomach with the decision. He dropped what was left of the red licorice vine he'd been sucking onto a pile of candy in the passenger seat.

He still didn't believe in psychics, but what if the news reporters were working with the police? What if the story was all made up, so he'd know about her, and want her? What if this was a trap?

He pulled over so he could think. It felt like the wind was howling inside his chest.

If he went back to Kevin's apartment, the fear of getting caught might take hold. He might be forced to make another choice.

He couldn't give her up. All day long, she was all he thought about. He even dreamed about her, something he'd never done with the others until after he'd been with them.

The snake between his legs started to wake up as he remembered all the times he'd gotten close to her without her noticing him, when he'd passed her on the street as she visited tattoo shops. He wouldn't give her up. He couldn't.

If there were policemen watching her apartment or her, he would have seen them by now. Besides, all the others had been taken close to where they worked and no one expected him to take her yet.

The wind howling inside him went quiet. He licked his lips and reached for the red vine, seeing the black sleeve of his jacket and thinking about the mask and gloves he'd bought today to replace the ones that got bloody last time.

They were still in their separate bags underneath his seat. They were right next to the Taser he shouldn't have in the car, but did.

It was a sign. He was meant to take her tonight. He would go inside and wait for her there like he did in New York.

The queasiness returned as he thought about her bringing one of the men home with her. Angry pounding started in his chest, raging until an idea came.

He'd be ready, just in case. He'd do what he hadn't been able to do when he was younger.

If she brought someone home with her, he'd make them both sorry. He'd make her watch as he cut off the thing between the other man's legs.

A giggle escaped. He almost hoped she did bring one of the two men home.

Pulling away from the curb he started cruising, looking for a car exactly like his. He'd figured this out for himself after choosing the very first one in New York. Most people didn't know what their license plate numbers were, or didn't notice the difference as long as the plates looked normal.

If he'd known ahead of time that tonight was the night he would take her, he would have planned a little better. But he didn't dare drive on her street another time or park close to her apartment without changing out the plates again.

It took him a while to find them. He checked the list he kept so he could be sure he wasn't stealing plates he'd already used. When he saw they were different, he swapped them out, his mouth going dry and his heart beating fast as he got back in the car and headed toward her apartment.

D enis pressed his eye to the scope and the world narrowed to the front window of a house in the Sunset District. A teenage girl passed through his sight. A heavyset woman. Another teen, this one a boy but not the right one.

In the darkness of the car, Denis shifted the barrel of the assault rifle silenced for sniper work to focus on the front door. He didn't want any innocent victims here. So far there hadn't been any.

Only with the first, Adam, had he taken care of things up close. The diplomat's son he'd hit at the beach, using a long-range weapon, and the boy, Carter, with a shot through a bedroom window.

The door opened and the target stepped outside, ball glove in hand, uniform crisp white. The woman joined him there, giving him a hug then remaining there, watching as the boy headed toward a car parked on the street.

Through the scope Denis followed him, giving the woman a chance to get back inside. Sparing her from witnessing the boy's death, self-preservation and altruism both factoring into his reason for waiting.

He hadn't remembered it at first, but later, after he started gathering information, it came back to him. Brian saying his friend's tag-along brother played baseball and football. Telling him the kid was good enough at both to have scouts already sniffing around after him.

Owen, that was the boy's name. He was almost to his car before the woman stepped into the house and closed the door. It was a clear shot. An easy one.

Denis took it. Watching the boy drop, the back of his head gone, leaving no possibility of survival.

Four dead. One to go.

Etaín rounded the corner, slow and cautious. Ready to spin the Harley around in case she was wrong about reporters being able to find her apartment.

The street was quiet and clear. Tension left her in a rush, a testament that emotions suppressed didn't mean turmoil gone.

She pulled into the driveway and parked the bike in the garage, then took the steps two at a time to her apartment. At the doorway she remembered the last time she'd been home, when Cathal had been with her, angry because of Eamon, a jealousy leading to amazing sex and intense feelings of intimacy.

Inside the apartment she purposely avoided looking at the mattress on the floor. The day had definitely turned into a bust when it came to men.

She checked her phone, realizing it was still off. She'd powered it down as she made her way to the church and never turned it on again.

A check of messages showed Cathal had called more than once since she'd left him with his uncle. *Distance is better,* she told herself, even if this time her gift wasn't the reason for it. Hadn't she seen the mess love made out of people's lives?

Draping her jacket over the back of a chair, she sat at her desk, opening a tablet and selecting a pencil in the hopes of losing herself in her art.

The only image to come was the design she'd worked on before, honeysuckle and thorn laid onto Cathal's skin. Coming with a little more detail, as if the full truth of it was being rationed out in ink.

She set the pencil down and closed her eyes. Elbows on the desk, she pressed her eyes to those on her palms, willing the tattoos to go away. She didn't want to think about men or magic.

Leave, her mother's voice whispered through her. A new city, a new name. Run and keep running. Hide and keep hiding.

A part of her was tempted by the ease of it, more than she'd ever been before. But it wasn't a soul-deep longing. She knew she would never outdistance herself or her gift. Or a truth that would have seemed unfathomable days ago. Eamon and Cathal had become important to her, necessary enough she had to see whatever this was with them through to the end, even if anger dominated her feelings when it came to one of them, and frustration when it came to the other.

*T*he closer he got to her street, the more excited he became. He touched himself through his pants. It didn't matter now that the snake was wide awake and swollen to its full size. It was okay, because it was her and they'd be together soon.

Excitement and nervousness twisted inside him. All along he must have known he was going to do this. That's why he'd broken so many of the rules.

Kevin would be so, so mad if he found out that he'd come here when he knew no one was home, sticking Kevin's painting signs on the van and pretending to be a painter who was showing up for work. He'd wanted to look at her door lock and make sure he could open it.

He could.

Imagining Kevin's expression, he started giggling. But that was choked off when he turned the corner and saw the light in her window.

Frustration swelled up inside him. He felt like a balloon that was ready to pop until the air came out of him in a howl. "No! No! No!"

He slammed his foot down on the gas pedal. Lifted it, almost doing the same to the brake but stopping himself in time.

Stupid. Stupid. Stupid.

He gently touched the brake pedal, slowing the car down. He passed her apartment and pulled over so he could use the binoculars and see if she was alone.

A police car turned the corner and came toward him. He froze, not even daring to breathe until it had passed.

In the rearview mirror he saw another police car, coming from the opposite direction. It stopped in front of her apartment, blocking the garage where she must have parked her bike.

A dark sedan stopped along the curb and the other police car stopped, too. Men got out and moved toward the house, hands on their guns.

One policeman went toward the door of the people who owned the house. The others concentrated on her apartment.

His bladder felt full. He realized he was whimpering.

He wanted to stay, but now he knew this was a trap after all and they thought he was inside with her. He needed to leave. He'd be in trouble if they started looking for him nearby when they didn't find him with her.

He was glad he hadn't turned the engine off. They weren't paying any attention to the street.

He pulled away. It would be okay. Nothing had really changed. She was still his choice and there were other places he could take her from.

E taín lifted her head on a sigh. The image wouldn't be banished no matter how hard she tried to concentrate on creating something else.

She opened her eyes and took up the pencil again, only to still at the sound of footsteps climbing the stairs. Her heart gave a betraying lurch as she wondered which one of them it was, Cathal or Eamon.

The involuntary, welcoming anticipation at the prospect of seeing one of them made her curse and slam the pencil onto the desk. She gathered her anger like a shield but that emotion fled with the pounding on the door and a man's voice yelling, "Police! Open up!"

Caution had her looking out the window first. The sight of the cars, their lights flashing, sent fear racing through her, tripping her heartbeat into a furious throb and her mind into a nightmare from her own past.

"Open the door! Police!"

She opened it and a man in a suit immediately grabbed and turned her, sending her to her knees and then onto her stomach in a practiced move of suppressed violence. He jerked her arms behind her back, handcuffing her, his anger and grief slamming into her so forcefully that instinct took over and she began struggling, fighting to get away from the skin-on-skin contact despite knowing better.

He wrenched her to her feet, pulling her up by her forearms, the leverage sending pain screaming from her shoulders downward. "Get her out of here," he said, thrusting her roughly at a uniformed officer.

Her mind cleared with the loss of contact though adrenaline raced through her so the vines on her arms felt alive, the eyes on her palms turned into deadly weapons once again.

"What's this about?" she asked.

The uniformed cop jerked her from the apartment, not answering.

She saw a second suited man standing at her desk, leafing through a sketchbook before she was propelled down the stairways so quickly it took all her concentration to keep from tumbling to the bottom of them.

Her heart pounded in her chest and ears as she was marched toward the police car blocking the garage door. She staved off panic by looking around. Desperate, hoping to see Liam, when earlier she'd been infuriated by the revelation he'd been following her at Eamon's command.

Seeing no sight of him, she asked again, "What's this about?" And was ignored.

She dug in her heels only to be pulled off her feet to stumble the last few steps.

The uniformed officer opened the back door of the patrol car, shoving her in.

She struggled to a sitting position, aware of her ragged breathing.

Calm down. Calm down.

Calm down. Calm down.

She matched the words to her heartbeats.

It helped. She hadn't been read her rights. They hadn't patted her down. She knew to lawyer up when it seemed smart to say those magic words.

This was all about intimidation. Not a stretch given the fury and anguish that had poured into her when the suited cop put her on the ground.

Why? The answer came in the solitary confinement of the car, with the image of the cop standing over her desk and the open tablet, looking at what she'd drawn.

Denis Dunne. Her mouth went dry and her mind seized, freezing on that instant when she'd wondered if he intended to give the drawings to the police.

Not my business, she'd thought then.

Not my business, she told herself now, thoughts spiraling, jumbling as she wondered why they'd come to her at all, remembering those moments just inside the door, when she'd given Denis the sketch pad as Cathal stood next to them both.

Pain stabbed into her as it occurred to her Cathal had been aware of what his uncle intended. Suspicion sharpened and twisted the blade. Had he known all along about her gift? Had he sought her out because of it?

The suited cops left her apartment, descending the stairs empty-handed. Other men emerged from the shadows, going to cars and getting in them. Engines started. The patrol car she was in backed up, joining a caravan to San Francisco and the Hall of Justice, a building she hadn't been in since the day the captain had her taken off the street and locked in a cell overnight.

Panic flared. Intense, nearly paralyzing.

She forced breath into her lungs. Reminding herself she hadn't been read her rights. She wasn't under arrest. She hadn't done anything wrong.

She'd be questioned and released. And if she wasn't—

The sweat clinging to her skin turned cold. She fought to suppress the fear though the vines on her forearms pulsed with it.

She blocked her mind against memories of that day her father had her put in a cell. *It won't come to that.* Eamon wouldn't *allow* it to happen, she told herself, finding comfort from the very argument that had made her so furious with him.

Twenty-five

～～～

Cathal rubbed his thumb along the edge of his phone. How many calls would have to go directly to her voicemail before he finally broke down and contacted Sean to find out where she was?

He wanted to see her. *Needed* to. And not just to continue the discussion about Eamon.

His hand tightened around the phone as his eyes settled on a small TV at the corner of his desk. The sound was turned down, the music coming from the band onstage drowning out any talking on the screen. But unless the view shifted to a new murder scene, he no longer needed to listen to the reporters speculate on motive and the likelihood the four killings were related.

He felt the same sense of icy foreboding he had after standing with his father and uncle at Caitlyn's graveside. He'd known what they intended, but not like *this*. When he allowed himself to think about it at all, he'd imagined them taking care of it elsewhere, and further out into the future so it wouldn't raise suspicions. Doing it when the likelihood of Etaín making the connection between her drawings and the killings would be minimal.

Was this justice? He didn't have an answer, only knew that there'd been a small window of opportunity to take this in another direction but he'd slammed it shut with his jealousy this morning. And now none of it could be undone, and he bore some of the guilt, the responsibility.

He called Sean. "Where is she?"

"Bike's at her apartment. But you remember I don't have eyes on her, right?"

Meaning she might not be alone. She might not even be there if she was with Eamon.

"I remember," he said, ending the call, his eyes going to the television screen as he accepted the possibility of sharing her if that was the only way to keep her safe.

He needed to attend to some club business that couldn't be put off any longer. But afterward he'd find her. He'd confess what she had to have guessed at hearing the news. He'd come clean about his involvement and his motives.

Fury engulfed Eamon at hearing Liam's report. He had guessed at the Dunnes' intentions even if Etaín hadn't. He had known she might be questioned by the police, but he had not anticipated she would be cuffed and treated like a criminal.

Imagining her scared intensified the desire to strike out at those who'd dared threaten her. Magic howled inside him, begging to be unleashed as it hadn't since he was a changeling.

He forced himself to calm. She was safe enough for the moment. She had grown up in the home of a policeman and interacted with them since. She would know how to handle the situation until he could intervene.

"You did well not to kill them when they came for her," he told Liam. Doing so would have been easy for his third in those moments of threat to her.

Even now, Eamon didn't fault the Dunnes for the justice they had served. But the high-profile nature of it concerned him greatly.

It brought with it the fear she might be taken from his territory, and he was not conversant enough with the intricacies of the human legal system to know best how to prevent it. Those he ruled avoided coming to the attention of the authorities. For them *his* word was the only law that mattered.

To Rhys he said, "I believe it's time to begin calling in favors from the humans whose acquaintances have been cultivated. I want her released, quickly and unharmed." And when his gaze shifted to Liam, he saw no amusement glittering in his third's eyes over this courtship dance with Etaín, there was only deadly promise.

The handcuffs remained locked around Etaín's wrists as she was escorted to a small, windowless interrogation room. Then the second of the suited men removed them, both cops leaving in the same silence they'd maintained since taking custody of her from the uniformed officer.

She knew the door was locked, but she tried it anyway, her chest tightening at the confinement, her breathing growing ragged again.

She knew, too, that they were watching her. Listening. Recording. Waiting. Letting time and silence and unanswered questions ratchet up her anxiety and fear.

The knife blade of suspicion returned, cutting her again as she wondered if Parker and the captain were somehow involved in this. If they'd told the suited detectives the best way to gain her cooperation was like this, with an implied threat of incarceration. By locking her in a small enclosed space.

She tried to distract herself by worrying at the question of why she'd been brought in. If they had the unsigned drawings, then they also had Denis.

Time became distorted. She couldn't tell how much of it had passed since they put her in the room.

A blurred disorientation was the only forewarning she got before the wall separating Brianna's stolen reality from her own cracked, flooding her consciousness with memory. A scream welled up inside her, primal and terrified and hopeless. *No!*

She was aware of the heavy breathing above her. The grunting. The pain between her legs that came with having another one of them on top of her. Jordão she thought, by the smell of his hair, doing to her what Adam was doing to Caitlyn.

The bed spun, turning the pictures on the walls into a kaleidoscope. Her vision blurred and when it cleared again, the boy named Mason had taken Adam's place above Caitlyn.

I'm sorry. Sorry. Sorry. Sorry, she screamed silently.

And her scream blended into a boy's, into yelling. Confusion. Panic.

The weight on top of her disappeared but the bed still shook violently. Caitlyn flailing. Thumping. Writhing naked next to her then going completely still, drooling blood and spit so close that if she could make her arm work she could reach out and close Caitlyn's mouth for her.

A different reality snapped into place with the sound of her own whimpering in the sterile white room, the feel of tears against her cheeks and the stink of fear rising off her skin. She was on her back on the floor though she didn't remember falling.

Panic threatened at how quickly the barriers had broken. It had taken almost twenty-four hours before, when the captain tried incarceration as a way of scaring her straight, and the friend monitoring her grew afraid she'd experienced a psychotic break.

A hard tremor passed through her. She'd only just come into her gift then. She hadn't had years of touching the victims of crime, of applying ink and unconsciously getting something back in the exchange.

She got to her feet, clenching her fists to keep from pounding on the walls and doors. From screaming that she wanted a lawyer.

Show more weakness now and she'd only be here longer. She just had to hold out a little longer, at least long enough to find out *exactly* why she'd been brought in.

Still trembling, she took a seat, trying to keep Brianna's escaped reality distant, like pages from a book. Desperate not to relive them, or worse, an expanded version of them.

All doubt, all ability to hide in denial about the necessity of finding answers when it came to her abilities, had been stripped away by this latest demonstration of change. She believed Eamon's warning when it came to it, needed also to believe he was arranging for a lawyer right now, or was somewhere in the building, applying pressure in order to get to her side.

She put her head down on the table, blocking out the room and hiding her face in her arms. The action brought someone to the door within minutes. It opened and she looked up to see the two suited cops from her apartment enter the room.

They took seats across from her, not bothering to give their names. The one who could have driven her to the floor with his emotions alone dealt a stack of pictures onto the desk, spreading them like a deck of horror cards.

There was no looking away from them. Four boys lay in various poses, their eyes vacant in death, their clothing bloodstained.

Etaín couldn't feel sorry for them. Brianna's memories were too close to the surface for that. These were executions, death a consequence of the choices they'd made, the acts they'd participated in.

She looked away from the pictures, stomach roiling and sweat making her clothing cling to her skin at being trapped in this small room where the walls separating her reality from so many others felt thinned and fragile. If she'd known that's what Denis intended—

But she hadn't, and there was no undoing what had been done. He'd meted out justice to the boys—or paid to have it done.

The knife blade of suspicion twisted more deeply into her heart. Given the circles the Dunnes moved in, it wasn't a stretch to imagine Denis had somehow found out about her gift.

The quickness of his actions made her wonder if he'd guessed at their identities, adding weight to the possibility Cathal had sought her out in order to seduce her into providing the proof his uncle wanted before acting.

A traitorous ache spread through her chest. Her throat tightened on the belief it had all been a subterfuge by Cathal, but despite that, she didn't want to see him imprisoned. And for Brianna's sake, she didn't want it for Denis, either.

A fist slammed down on the table, making her jump and look at the detectives across from her. "You see this kid?" the one radiating fury and grief asked, shoving the photograph so it slammed into her arm. "Murdered in front of his home, with his family inside. They came out to find him dead."

She felt a clutch of sorrow before a second picture was shoved against her arm. "And this one, he's the son of a diplomat."

He lifted two pictures, holding them inches away from her face before slamming them down on the table, panting with his own emotions. "You know what connects all four of these boys? All four of these murders?"

She avoiding both truth and lie by saying, "What?"

Her response infuriated him, reddening his face. "Don't play blonde and dumb. Cooperate now. Otherwise, it won't matter who your father and brother are. It won't matter that you've helped out before, you'll end up doing time as an accessory to murder."

A chill swept over her at the threat, with the acknowledgment they knew about her relationship with Parker and the captain but hadn't questioned her at home or asked her to come in like they would have someone else in the same position, as they *should have* with her. They'd gone for expedience, for invading her apartment and bringing her to a place she associated with terror, though they couldn't know that unless they'd been told.

She crossed her arms over her chest as if holding in her courage. "I haven't been read my rights or arrested, so unless you've got a reason to keep me here, I want to leave."

"Let's calm down here," the second detective said, speaking for the first time. "Emotions are running high and that's understandable. My partner is too close to this, he knew one of the boys. Coached him when he was in Little League, so you can see why he's not on his best behavior."

It didn't change anything. For all she knew, it might be a lie.

"Etaín, can I call you that?" He didn't wait for an answer but continued on. "I'm Detective Lee. My partner is Detective Corwin. Why don't we try to start over? Take this from the top?"

He pulled a photograph from a folder on the table in front of him, turning it and placing it so she could see it. Not one of the dead, or even a picture taken at a crime scene, but her on the Harley, taken as she followed Cathal through the gate of his uncle's estate.

Lee used a red marker to circle the sketch pad bungeed in place on the saddle. He pulled a second photo from the folder. It was date and time stamped on the bottom right, same as on the first one, only taken this morning instead of yesterday.

He circled the pad and she knew what came next. A departure shot, and this time a red circle with only the bike showing because the box of pencils was in the saddlebag.

Seeing the date and time-stamped photographs deepened the pain, spreading the ache of suspicion to encompass Parker, and the possibility he'd made her bait for the Harlequin Rapist. "Why do you have these pictures? Where did you get them?"

"I'm not at liberty to say. That's not important." Lee's expression radiated compassion and concern. He tapped the circle empty of the sketchpad. "Save yourself from being charged as an accessory to murder, Etaín. However you got dragged into this, I believe you went in thinking you were doing a good thing. Now do the right thing. Tell us about the drawings you did for the Dunnes."

Corwin leaned forward, hot breath in her face as he said, "And before you waste your time and ours by coming up with a load of bullshit, I'll tell you that we already know. This is vigilante justice for what was done to Brianna Dunne and Caitlyn Llewellyn."

The outburst gained him a frown from Lee. But nothing of what either detective said changed her intentions. Ignorance was deadly, and she now knew enough. "I'd like to go home."

"Not going to happen," Corwin said, angry satisfaction in his voice.

She forced her arms away from her chest, rubbed damp palms against her jeans before balling her hands into fists beneath the table. Why hadn't Eamon intervened by now?

The sense of betrayal she felt expanded beyond Cathal and Parker and the captain to include Eamon as she remembered what he'd said outside the bar, and thought he held off, teaching her a lesson, demonstrating how much she needed him if she was going to survive her gift and the magic it was tied to.

She spoke to Lee because he was the more reasonable, or at least playing the good cop role. "If I'm not free to leave then I want a lawyer."

His eyes filled with what looked like genuine regret. "I'm sorry to hear that. It tells me you're guilty and you know you're going to go down for accessory to murder. But if that's the way you want to play this . . ."

She didn't fall for the ploy. If something good still remained of the years she'd lived in the captain's house, believing he was her father, it came from the times she and Parker had avidly listened to stories of arrests he'd made and confessions he'd gained.

Cops didn't have to tell the truth. They could lie to get a confession, even use manufactured evidence as a prop. And beyond that, no DA would risk the public black eye that would come from filing charges against her when there was nothing to substantiate them.

"If I'm not free to leave then I want a lawyer," she repeated.

Corwin and Lee left without speaking again or gathering the photographs, the door closed and locked behind them.

Twenty-six

Strains of an Irish dirge filled the room. Somber and desolate, like a banshee's wail in the fog. A soulful lament about love and loss.

Brianna grieved.

For her friend. For herself maybe.

Denis didn't know what she'd remembered since those moments in her bedroom. He didn't ask. Hopefully those memories were wiped clean, the same way four of the five boys were now erased, though missing the last one, Mason, left a bad taste in his mouth.

He lifted the glass in his hand and took a swallow, washing the temporary failure away with whiskey.

The fifth one could wait, at least for a little while. None of Etaín's pictures showed him touching Brianna.

Denis took another swallow, thoughts lingering on Etaín and bringing with them a feeling of gratitude. What she'd done for his daughter was a miracle. A spooky, creepy one he didn't intend to dwell on, but a miracle all the same.

Deep down he hadn't thought he'd ever get Brianna back. He'd wondered if one day her torment would demand a different act.

His faith told him suicide was a sin. He didn't know if he believed that, but when it came to Brianna, he'd hedge the bet in her favor.

He wasn't a man who'd lock his daughter away in a crazy bin, no matter how exclusive, and leave her to the mercy of others.

He had blood on his hands. It'd been there since he was Brianna's age. One more death, this one done with compassion and love—

Denis shook off the dark thoughts. No need to go there now, thanks to Etaín.

He closed his eyes, letting the music wash into him like a cold tide along a desolate stretch of shore.

Brianna had done this after Margo's death.

She'd done this after Brian's.

Playing the piano for hours on end, drawing him from the isolation of his own grief so they shared it.

He'd sat with her, both of them finding solace in the music.

This was how Brianna dealt with her pain.

Better that she let it go this way.

Eventually happier songs would work their way in. When that happened, he'd know it was okay to let her go back to her everyday routine. Until then he'd keep her protected, cocooned and safe from anything that might set her back.

Like the boy's death. The one she believed herself in love with.

The thought of her crying over him made Denis's hand tighten on the glass. The news of the murders would die down quickly. It always did. But tomorrow he'd start making arrangements for a vacation. No cell phone. No computer. He'd get Brianna out of the country for a while, occupy her with the things she loved.

The notes faded but rather than sliding immediately into a new song, Brianna said, "Hi, Uncle Niall."

Denis opened his eyes to see his brother lean down and give Brianna a hug. "Beautiful as always, Brianna. Can I take your dad away for a few minutes?"

"Yes."

He gave the top of her head a kiss before they retreated to the office.

"The police have Etaín," Niall said, pouring himself a glass of whiskey from the bottle on the desk. "I just got word they took her from her apartment."

"Where is she now?"

"The Hall of Justice."

"One of the boys wasn't where he was supposed to be. He must have spooked and gone to the police figuring jail time was better than grave time."

"What he says will get them looking, but without the pictures there's nothing solid. It's her testimony they'll build their case on. It'd be golden considering who her father and brother are, and the work she's done for them."

Denis shrugged. "If she cooperates, she's dead."

"There's more," Niall said. "The guy who called said he thinks ATF and FBI agents are in the queue to talk to her."

"Looking into whether or not she's got enough of a connection with Cathal to plant her in exchange for immunity and protection?"

"That'd be my take on it." Niall took a sip from his glass. "Cathal will have heard about the boys by now. It's all over the news. He'll know he needs to be careful about what he says in front of her in case she's got ears on her."

"Assuming he's not thinking with his dick when he's with her." Denis poured more whiskey into the glass. "I shouldn't have rushed this. I should have spread it out."

"I don't blame you for handling it like you did."

They drank in silence, each of them contemplating options. Each of them knowing with a call it could all be made to go away.

"What do you want to do about this?" Niall finally asked.

Denis tried, but he couldn't shake the gratitude he felt toward Etaín. She deserved the benefit of the doubt for what she'd done for Brianna.

"I say let it ride for now. I wouldn't mind having Etaín in the family if it turns out Cathal wants her enough to marry her. Let's see what she does, where her loyalties lie and if she can be trusted not to betray us. Worst case, Homeland Security gains more leverage and wants us to branch out to accommodate their interests. We serve their purposes. They clean up this mess for us, including Etaín if it needs doing."

"Fair enough. What Homeland Security wants will trump what all the others want."

The walls continued closing in on Etaín, the room shrinking so it was difficult for her to breathe. Chills swept over her skin, the only warning she got before the mental barrier ruptured and her reality drowned under Brianna's again.

"Beer? Rum and Coke?"

She didn't want Adam to be embarrassed hanging out with her. "Beer."

"Just Coke," Caitlyn said.

"One beer, one Coke coming up."

He disappeared along with Adam and the boy named Mason. When they came back, everybody sat on the couch, listening to tunes.

Heaven. It felt like heaven to be sitting next to Adam.

Slow dancing felt even better. She didn't protest when Adam started touching her. Little sparks of fire burned in her breasts and between her legs even though a part of her said she should make him stop, or at least make him take her somewhere private.

She wanted to be with him. She wanted him to be her first. But not like this.

"Finish your beer," he told her in between kisses. His lips were incredibly soft.

She finished it, the bottle falling out of her hand and onto the carpet. She wanted to fall, too.

Another beer was pressed into her hand. She watched it lift, a hand covering her hand and couldn't seem to make herself resist, even when she realized it was Carter's hand instead of Adam's.

Confusion filled her. When had she stopped dancing with Adam?

She opened her mouth to say she didn't want more beer but ended up swallowing it instead. She couldn't help herself.

And then Carter was leading her to a bedroom. A scream welled up inside her at seeing Caitlyn naked on the bed with Jordão on top of her. This was wrong, wrong, wrong.

Carter pushed her down on the bed next to Caitlyn. She tried to pretend it wasn't happening. But it was.

Jordão rolled off Caitlyn and Mason got on top of her. She felt her clothes being removed and tried to protest. She thought she said no, even when she saw it was Adam above her, but she couldn't be sure.

It hurt. Inside and outside.

And when he was done, Carter was there. Then Owen.

She went away in her head and came back—

Rough hands shook her, then jerked her into a sitting position. Etaín's eyes snapped open.

It took long moments for the drugged haze of Brianna's memory to recede. It took all the mental strength she possessed to flatten that separate reality into imaginary words in a book about someone else's life.

Two strangers were in the room with her. A man and a woman. Feds this time. She recognized the stamp on them.

They took the seats vacated by Lee and Corwin, the woman turning the photographs facedown, the man saying, "I'm Zimmerman, she's Rachlin. FBI and ATF respectively. We can make this problem go away for you, guaranteed immunity. We know you're not a killer. You have a record of helping put the bad guys away. All we want is your cooperation in sending the Dunnes where they belong, to prison. They're organized crime. Parasites living off the pain and suffering of others."

He tapped the back of one of the photographs. "They screwed up here. Understandable given what happened to Brianna Dunne and her friend. There was a fifth boy involved, but then you know that already. His parents couldn't get him here fast enough when he spilled his guts after finding out his buddies were dead."

Zimmerman sighed and glanced at Rachlin. "I give him less than a fifty percent chance of surviving, even if he's segregated from the regular prison population. The Dunnes will get to him. I give her zero percent. You agree with those odds?"

The ATF agent nodded. "Sounds about right to me. She helped them, but she's still a loose end they're going to need to take care of."

"Unless they think she's going to be joining the family," Zimmerman said. "That might get her a stay of execution."

Rachlin frowned, pretending to study her. "She'd have to be a damn good actress to keep sleeping with Cathal now that she knows what he is."

"Yeah, but if she wants to work that angle in exchange for immunity. . . ."

Etaín saw where this was going. She shivered, aware of how her shirt clung to her, wet with sweat and stinking of fear. "What I want is to go home. Now. And if that's not going to happen then I want a phone call and a lawyer."

"Bad choice," Zimmerman said, standing. "Last time I checked, the phones were all in use and this room needed to be vacated. I'm sure there's a cell free somewhere in the building. We can stash you there to wait for a chance at the phones."

A hard tremor went through her. There was no preventing it. But anger came to her defense, that Parker or the captain had told them how she'd once been reduced to begging and crying, to pounding on the walls and, finally, curling into a fetal ball beneath the bed.

"Sure you don't want to talk to us?" Zimmerman asked.

"Positive." She let them hear the angry determination she felt.

They moved to the door. Zimmerman opened it and left.

Rachlin paused and turned, false sympathy on her face. "We're the best chance you have of surviving this. Cathal used you. Here's your chance to pay him back for it. The Dunnes are cold-blooded killers. Don't wait too long to reach out for our help."

The ATF agent left, closing the door behind her, the lock clicking firmly into place.

Etaín stood and paced the square of the room, using movement and anger to keep the mental barriers in place. Counting each step as a way to block any other thought.

When the door opened next, Parker was there. "Let's go," he said.

Fear dumped into her, overwhelming the pain and anger. "Where?"

"Your place. Mine. I'll give you a lift wherever you want to go."

Relief made her shaky. It suppressed all other emotion until they were driving away from the building. Then the anger returned, washing into her with the pain.

His appearance wasn't a coincidence. He was probably meant to gain her confidence.

Fists slammed on the steering wheel, making her jump. "Christ, Etaín! Why the fuck did you get involved with the Dunnes?"

She fought back instinctively. "What's it to you? Afraid they'll kill me before you're finished using me as bait for the Harlequin Rapist?"

The car jerked to the right and came to a jolting stop along the curb. "Is that what you think I'm doing?"

His fury engulfed her, beating back some of her own, though not all of it. "They had pictures of me going through the gate at Denis's house."

"Duh. That's because the fucking Dunnes have been under investigation for years. Christ, Etaín. If you let them pull you into their world—"

His jaw clamped on whatever he intended to say. He reached into his pocket and tossed her cell phone into her lap.

She stilled, knowing it had been in the jacket she'd slung over a chair when she'd first entered her apartment. Had he been there all along? Tucked away in a dark sedan as they manhandled her into the back of the police cruiser?

Had he been watching a video feed of her in the small interrogation room? Advising them when to approach her. Finally suggesting they cut her loose for a little while and let him work a different angle.

She didn't ask him. Ignorance might be deadly but it could also be less painful, and the evidence she held was already enough to convict him.

He scrubbed his hands over his face then attacked. "Goddamn it, Etaín. Why can't you just fucking toe the line like the rest of us do?"

The familiarity of the words didn't lessen their impact. The refrain with its message of denied acceptance only caused the ache in her chest to grow so it equaled the anger.

"Maybe because I'm not a Chevenier. Not even a pretend one."

"That's bullshit and you know it. You're my sister despite some fuck-all paternity test." Parker slammed his hands on the steering wheel again. "This stunt is going to get you killed if you don't cooperate. Tell me what happened with the Dunnes."

His outburst should have made her heart sing. Instead his pressing her to confide right after claiming she was family only deepened her suspicions.

But if he wanted to know what had happened with the Dunnes, she wanted it more, for a different reason. She'd let Cathal get too close and now she needed the truth, so she could put him behind her.

"Just drop me off at Saoirse."

"Goddamn, Etaín. If you go to the Dunnes now I'll—"

"What? Stop calling me? Oh, that's right, we only see each other when a case warrants it."

Exposing the vulnerability, that it bothered her to be called only when he needed her to touch a victim, pissed her off. She reached for the door handle. "You know what, Parker, forget the ride. I'll call a cab."

She was out of the car before he could stop her. And then he was out, standing next to the driver's side. "You can't fucking run away this time, Etaín."

Watch me, she said, hearing the hollowness in that internal voice.

Twenty-seven

Etaín pushed through the crowded club, using her shoulder and the force of her anger to cut a path toward Cathal's office. They must have told him she'd arrived, or he'd seen it on a security camera because steps away from his door, he opened it to allow her inside.

Wild emotion surged through her with the sight of him. A tumultuous mix stripping away personal rules and leaving her as defenseless as she'd been in the shrinking confines of the interrogation room. The urge to get this over with dominated, her magic and gift shattering what little control she had left, taking over with ruthless purpose when he reached for her.

She captured his hands. The eyes on her palms pressed to his skin, her will poised to cut directly to the answer. "Why me? Why did you come to Stylin' Ink and ask me out?"

Pain sliced into her with an unfolding scene, Cathal sitting in the backseat of a car with his father. Niall saying, "Show her a little love so she'll *want* to help out here, and be willing to keep quiet about it afterwards. If you set your mind to it, you can get it done."

Cathal jerked out of her grasp before more of it played out, but she'd seen enough, though she understood that where it'd always been an excising before, with him it was a shared viewing.

She didn't care.

"Now we both know where things stand," she said, voice tight with a refusal to cry. "The cops came to my apartment tonight. They took me to the floor and handcuffed me, then hauled me in for sweating because they saw me visiting your uncle's place. They told me the Dunnes are cold-blooded killers. For the record, I'll tell you what I think about rapists. A quick death is too good for them, but I have no objection to it. I've *seen* what their victims saw. And because I've seen it, I've *lived* it."

She whirled away from Cathal and bolted from the office, determined to put distance between them, Parker's words chasing her again. *You can't fucking run away this time, Etaín.* Only she knew she could. She would. Not the run and hide of her mother's life, but a return to the way she'd been before meeting Cathal and . . .

Eamon.

He waited for her outside the club, and despite thinking he might have viewed her time in custody as the opportunity to teach her a lesson, she couldn't handle a fight with him. Not after the loss of control in Cathal's office and the reliving of Brianna's rape at the Hall of Justice. She felt too raw, too on edge.

"I won't ask how you knew I was here." She willed herself to believe that exhaustion, the lingering aftereffects of trauma and terror, the freefall of surviving on adrenaline accounted for the tears sliding down her cheeks.

He closed the distance between them as if approaching a wild, trapped animal. "Let me help you," he murmured, and the gentleness of his voice, the depth of caring in his eyes affected her, stripping away her resistance to him so she allowed him to take her into his arms.

He touched his mouth to hers. Not a kiss, but a gift she finally understood enough to recognize.

Magic. He'd done it before, in front of Aesirs, when she'd been ill and weak after visiting Brianna the first time. He'd said her gift and magic were inextricably entwined, that where the one took the other protected her against what was taken, and now he demonstrated the truth of it. Magic flowed into her like a cool stream, turning Brianna's escaped memories into leaves that were carried out of sight and once again sealed behind mental barriers.

Her arms wrapped around him, the heat from his body warming her. He rubbed his cheek against hers, brushed his lips over her earlobe. "Liam came to me as soon as you were taken. I did what I could to send you aid, but some tasks take time to accomplish, even for me, Etaín. Despite what you might think, I'm not *known* to the people who come to Aesirs. I've made it a point not to be, though that will change so I can take better care of you."

Learning he'd been working to get her released loosened the tight knot her heart had become. He'd said he would never lie to her and she believed him. Like to like, if he was a part of the world her mother ran from, then he knew the value of both promises and truths.

"Come home with me," he said, stroking her back.

The intensity of her desire to say *yes* scared her into saying, "No." After Cathal, she couldn't handle the increased vulnerability that would come with spending the night with Eamon.

"No," she repeated, pulling back, away from the comfort he offered.

Eamon easily guessed what lay at the root of her denial, and though a part of him wanted Cathal excluded from her life, seeing her lost and hurting, her spirit subdued, eradicated any satisfaction he might feel at Cathal's letting her go.

"Cathal's a fool," he said, cupping her cheek.

He felt her tears against his palm. Preferred her fury to this.

She didn't resist when he claimed her lips, silently promising them both that soon all separation would end. Another day, and then the fund-raiser. After that she would learn what her future held. She would become part of the world she was meant for.

His tongue slid into the wet heat of her mouth. Twined gently with hers, delivering pleasure and comfort even as the flames of lust flickered into existence, burning hot between them as the kiss extended from one moment into another, and then yet another.

"Let me drive you home," he said against her mouth.

"No. I'll take a cab." Her smile was a shadow of what it once would have been as she pulled away again. "I won't be able to stop myself from inviting you in."

He didn't press against her defenses but let her go, giving her the space she needed, Liam emerging from unlit night as she got into a taxi.

"The same exit though a different vehicle," Liam said, though there was less mockery in his voice and far more concern for the woman he would one day kneel before and call Lady.

"Consider yourself freed of your task until morning. I'll watch over Etaín tonight."

Cathal didn't look away from the security monitor until Eamon got into a sedan. She hadn't arrived with him, and by the expression on her face, hadn't expected to find him waiting outside the club.

Coward, he called himself for not joining them. He'd wanted a confrontation with Etaín over Eamon but in those moments after she'd—

Even now his mind skittered away from acknowledging it, conscious, rational thought and instinctive fear battling against the radical shifting of reality. He forced himself to confront what had happened, though the shock and disbelief of it had glued him in place as she whirled and left his office.

She'd *seen* his memory. His pulse throbbed wildly in his throat with the admission. He made himself face it again, more fully. *She saw my memory.*

He understood then, how she'd been able to draw Brianna's rapists. And what it had cost her to volunteer to help his family. She'd seen it. She'd *lived* it.

Guilt threatened to savage him as pain rippled through him. He closed his eyes as if doing it would block out the tears he'd seen on her face as she stood outside with Eamon.

He wanted to hate Eamon for being there, wanted to hate her for finding comfort in Eamon's arms. Instead the conversation with Sean returned like a chisel opening his mind further to something he wouldn't have considered days ago, that sharing a woman gave her someone to turn to, someone who might even hold the door of reconciliation open for a return to the relationship.

Cathal replayed the scene he'd witnessed in his mind, the melding of her body to Eamon's, the kiss full of tenderness and passion. He began hardening as a result of it, his cock becoming fully engorged as he remembered the last time she'd been in his office. When he'd pressed into her personal space and she'd allowed him to maneuver her backward, everything about her daring him to make good on his threat to fuck her if she showed up at Saoirse.

I'm not a man to share when I'm serious about a woman.

Then don't get serious about me.

He had outs. She'd given them to him.

Eamon.

The freakiness of what had just happened.

The way she'd come here, carefully revealing what had happened and where she'd been without implicating either herself or Denis, then assuring him she had no problem with the justice meted out by his family.

Now we both know where things stand.

She wouldn't come back. She wouldn't contact him.

He knew it with certainty.

It should relieve him. Instead the prospect of it twisted his gut and made him curse.

His arm swept across the desk, sending papers flying. "Fuck!" he said, and his cock throbbed in agreement.

He wanted her, on more levels than the physical. He couldn't let her walk away or end things between them. Somehow, he had to convince her that the reason for their meeting in the first place didn't matter.

He turned away from the desk and the papers scattered on the floor. As he did it, he heard a reporter's voice on the small television mention the Harlequin Rapist.

His stomach knotted at remembering his uncle's warning with its multiple meanings. A chill swept into him at now having evidence she could be a real threat to the rapist, a target for more reasons than her appearance.

If she disappeared, he would never know the truth of who took her. He might never know what had happened to her.

By now his father and uncle would have heard she'd been taken in for questioning. They'd know she was no longer in custody.

He went to his childhood home, brushing a kiss against his mother's cheek before following his father into the office. The layout was similar to the one in Denis's home and, like his uncle's, the only place considered safe to talk freely.

"Drink?" his father asked.

"No. This is a quick stop for me."

"About?"

"Etaín."

His father directed him to a grouping of furniture positioned next to a fireplace with kindling laid beneath an empty grate. They sat, a small table between them.

"Go on," his father said.

"You know she was taken in for questioning."

"Yes. You've seen her since they cut her loose?"

"She came by the club."

"And?"

"She didn't tell the authorities about the drawings."

"You're sure?"

"She has no sympathy for rapists. She has no problem with what you and Denis did."

"She said that?"

"Carefully and in a way the authorities can't use."

"Good. I'm glad to hear it. You believe her?"

"Yes." He met his father's eyes. "I'd stake my life on it."

The barest nod indicated the message had been received. "Are you equally certain she didn't cut a deal to make nice with you for a long game?"

Cathal laughed at that. "If I let her, she'd be done with me after today."

"So she means something to you."

"Yes." Cathal leaned forward. "I want a promise of safety for her. From you and Uncle Denis both. No hits ordered. No accidents. No disappearances."

"And if we won't give it?"

It was an effort not to bare his teeth. "If anything happens to her because of her involvement with us, then I'll do everything I can, put every resource I have into getting justice for her."

His father swirled the liquid in his glass then took a sip. "I'm glad you understand about the need for justice. You haven't asked about your cousin."

"How is she?"

"On the mend. Like Etaín told you might happen, she doesn't remember any of it."

He chilled with an icy reminder of what had happened in his office. *Better get used to it if you intend to stay in her life.*

He turned his attention to the second of his reasons for approaching his father. "Where are the drawings?"

"Here."

His father set the drink down long enough to retrieve a sheaf of papers from a wall safe. Returning, he spilled them across the table like still frames in a movie, giving reality to what had happened to Brianna and Caitlyn.

A surge of protectiveness rolled through Cathal along with anger and regret and guilt. "These need to be destroyed." He was surprised they hadn't been.

"I wanted you to see them first. So you'd know in your heart that what you did for the family was the right thing."

His father reached into a decorative Wedgewood bowl at the center of the table and removed a box of matches, offering it to Cathal.

Cathal took it. "This is all of them?"

"Unless you're wrong about your girlfriend."

Fear came with the realization that Etaín living Brianna's memories meant she could reproduce the pictures. His heart beat against his chest in an unneeded warning of danger. "I'm sure about her," he said, lighting the stack of kindling in the fireplace.

He placed the drawings on the grate one by one, forcing himself to look, to endure, to face a question he had no answer for even after the last of them had burned and he'd left his father's home. What would he have done if he'd seen them first and had a choice between turning them over to his uncle or involving Parker?

He slowed instinctively when he spotted the sedan parked a short distance from Etaín's apartment. Though he couldn't read the license plate number, the odds told him it was the same one Eamon had gotten into outside Saoirse.

Seeing it here, imagining them inside together making love was like slamming into a brick wall. *Truth time.* Stop or continue on?

His fingers tightened on the steering wheel, wisps of jealousy returning though they were drowned out by a greater need. He wanted her, almost to the point of obsession.

He couldn't explain it, other than she felt *right* on so many levels. With her, he didn't have to worry she was with him because of his club, or his money, or his family.

There was a moral core to her, as evidenced by her involvement with the shelter and her willingness to help Brianna and other victims, despite the cost to her. And yet that moral core was threaded through with the kind of loyalty it would take to keep her alive and safe from his father and uncle.

His heart beat like he was about to step into a fight ring. But he

knew he had no choice other than to climb into it or she'd be gone
from his life.

If he was going to do this thing, accept another man in her life, he
needed to confront it up close and personal. He slowed the car further,
but only so he could make the turn into the driveway.

Not a fool after all, Eamon thought as he watched Cathal park in
front of the garage housing Etaín's bike as the Hummer following it pulled to a stop along the curb.

Cathal emerged from his car, but the driver of the other didn't get
out. Protection, Eamon guessed, pleased by Cathal's actions despite
having mixed emotions about Cathal being part of Etaín's life.

Not my choice, but the magic's, he reminded himself, and nothing
had changed in that regard. He wouldn't challenge the primordial
elements of Elfhome. Nor would he do anything to risk Etaín as she
neared the point when she would successfully transition from changeling to Elf, or would die as a result of it.

Twenty-eight

Etaín startled in reaction to the knock on the door, dropping the hairbrush as her heart rabbited in her chest with an instantaneous urge to bolt and run.

No, she told herself. *No.* She refused to live like this. She left the bathroom, hair still slightly damp from her shower.

Tugging on shorts and a sweatshirt over naked skin, she crossed to the window and peeked out to see Cathal standing there. An ache blossomed in her chest at the sight of him, slowing the fast beat of her heart into a painful throb.

She tried to cloak herself in anger as a way of protecting against the insidious emotions and needs his presence brought, but it didn't come. The fury sustaining her earlier had burned itself out, leaving something far more frightening in its place, a craving for comfort and connection, for the intimacy that came not just from shared pleasure but shared, inextricably entwined lives.

He knocked again, lightly, as if he sensed her on the other side of the door. "Etaín. Please."

His voice was husky and low, raw with echoes of the pain she felt. She closed her eyes and rested her forehead against the back of the door.

It wasn't supposed to be this way. She'd never had trouble avoiding relationships before.

But then she'd known in the instant when she'd seen him through the window of the shop that he wasn't like the men she usually chose. Instinct had warned her away from him and she'd ignored it, just as she'd chosen to ignore the warning against offering to help Brianna. Just as, apparently, she couldn't let her stop by Saoirse be the end of things with Cathal.

She sent a skittering glance sideways, to the sketchpad on the desk and the drawing of the tattoo she'd been compelled to embellish when she first got home, despite what she'd learned when she touched him at Saoirse. She opened the door.

His eyes met hers. Determined. Pleading. "Talk with me?"

"Yes."

She stepped backward to let him in but rather than enter he said, "In my car, unless it's okay if I have your place swept for listening devices. I'm sorry, Etaín. This is part of the baggage that comes with the Dunne name. I arranged for someone to take care of it, if you're willing."

She shivered at the thought of having her privacy violated. It hadn't occurred to her that listening devices might have been left behind. "I'm willing."

Cathal turned and motioned with his hand. A man emerged from a black Hummer parked along the curb in front of her apartment.

Surprise lightened her mood. Given the choice of vehicle, she expected a military haircut and clothes sharp enough to be a uniform. Instead he wore a Harley jacket and black jeans.

His hair was pulled back in a ponytail and he sported a thin mustache and goatee, shades of Johnny Depp, and she was a fan. She'd have looked at him twice if she'd encountered him on the street.

"Sean McAlister," Cathal said by way of introduction.

"Quinn's friend."

Sean smiled. "The very same."

She stepped aside and he entered the apartment, opening a briefcase and quickly assembling a piece of equipment. No one spoke as he made a methodical sweep through her living space. Finally saying, "Clean," and repacking the scanner.

"The cell phones?" Cathal asked.

"No warrants issued so far." He glanced at Etaín. "They can be turned into mobile listening devices. You're probably in the clear but I'd recommend you pop the battery or put your phone somewhere that's too far away to pick up a conversation if you're talking about anything sensitive."

She acknowledged the advice with a nod, a chill coming with the implicit reminder she was under suspicion. He left and Cathal stepped forward as if he'd pull her against him.

She stepped back, crossing her arms over her chest as a defense against being swayed by the feel of his body against hers. "You wanted to talk. Then talk, Cathal. Or leave."

He shrugged out of his jacket, throwing it to the floor then unbuttoning his shirt, letting it hang open rather than removing it. Heat stole through her at the sight of his chest. Her nipples tightened as sensory memories bombarded her and she dug her fingers into her arms to keep from touching him.

"I went to see my father, that's why I wasn't here sooner," he told her, cautiously reaching out, encircling her wrists and gently tugging, pulling her arms away from her body, the hum of connection and electric desire flaming into existence with the contact. "I wanted to make sure he understood how important you are to me, and what I'd do if anything happened to you."

There was no fear in his eyes when he carried her hands to his bare chest, stopping just beyond the dark hair she loved to comb her fingers through and feel against her bare skin. His thumbs stroked over the eyes on her palms, as if he'd guessed at their importance, though all he said was, "When you came by the club, you only saw part of the truth, a very, very small part of it. I want you to see all of it. I want you to know everything."

He pressed her palms to his chest and held them there. Beneath them, his heart slid into a racing beat, primal fear mastered by desire and strength of purpose.

"I can't promise you're safe from my father and uncle. I believe you are. They have a code they live by. There are parts of it I respect, but I'm not involved in their business. Never have been and never will be."

"Organized crime?"

"Yes. Don't ask me for details. I don't know them. I don't want to know them."

He leaned in, touching his forehead to hers, his hands tightening on hers. "Look at my memories, Etaín. Don't just take my word for it."

"Show me the truth," she said, and it was as easy and safe for Cathal as it had been with Eamon, only it was different too. Seeing Cathal's memories was like stepping into a darkened movie theater, except instead of being alone, phantom arms wrapped around her.

An imagined chest served as a pillar of strength for her to lean on as they both watched fast moving images on a mental screen. Glimpses of reality focused on his seeking her out and his desire to keep her safe, ending with his burning the drawings and protecting her further by not revealing she could easily re-create them.

She couldn't fault him, not when she knew his motives and saw how he was caught in a situation beyond his control. She couldn't separate herself from him in anger, not after the visits with Brianna.

"Forgive me?" he asked, voice soft and uncertain, hopeful.

"Yes."

She didn't protest when his hands went to her hips, pulling her against him as his mouth sought hers. It felt good, right. Inevitable.

If ignorance was deadly, then knowledge was empowering, freeing. Her lips parted with the first touch of his tongue to them. Desire burned through her, desperate need demanding a deeper revelation of truth, a joining of bodies.

Cathal hardly dared to believe she was back in his arms, the small sounds she made going straight to his heart, urging him to greater intimacy so he pushed her shorts downward.

They dropped to the floor and his hands cupped bare buttocks, his mouth sealed to hers as his tongue thrust, retreated, hungrily revealing the depth of his need to be inside her.

Stroking his hands upward he found only skin beneath the sweat-shirt she wore. Desire deepened to see, to touch, to taste every inch of her in a carnal possession.

He drew back, stripping the sweatshirt off so she stood completely naked, nipples hardened and lips swollen, eyes dark, sultry, beckoning with the power of a born seductress.

A hard throb went through his cock. She was beautiful, more than beautiful. He'd had beautiful women before but none of them had affected him the way she did.

In days she'd made it impossible for him to want anyone else, to imagine being with anyone else. He pulled her against him, pleasure rippling through him at the feel of her breasts pressed to his chest. He tangled his fingers in silky hair, holding her as he plundered her mouth until they were both panting, their lower bodies rubbing and grinding.

Her hands went to his belt and his joined them there, making fast work of unbuckling, unzipping. He moaned when she captured his cock, her thumb teasing over the head, wetting it with escaped desire.

"Bed," he said against her lips, buttocks clenching as her fist moved up and down on his shaft.

"I think you need help getting undressed first."

She knelt, electric heat surging through his cock at its proximity to her mouth. If not for her grip on it, it would have pulled away from his body to go to her.

She laughed, knowing her effect on him, the sound of her amusement a sensual caress, a taunt that had him burrowing his fingers through the wheat-gold strands of her hair again, his clothes no longer mattering.

"Do it," he ordered.

And she did.

Slowly. In her own time.

Delivering ecstasy with the touch of her tongue to his cock head, with wet swirls and flicked exploration.

Delivering punishment with the barest incarceration of it between her lips, with tormenting hints of suction.

Fire burned in his testicles as she cupped them, her touch a craving that had already lodged itself in his soul.

A light sheen of sweat coated his skin as he worked desperately against the restraint of her fist. Trying to drive himself into her mouth and the nearly unbearable pleasure to be found there.

She gave. An inch at a time. White heat filling his head with each one of them. Each pull of her mouth delivering a lesson. His body didn't belong to him. It belonged to her.

"Finish it," he said, fingers sliding through her hair, trying to urge her to take all of him. But she refused to hurry and give him the release he thought he'd die without.

E amon stopped in front of the apartment door. He'd given Cathal long enough to make his case with Etaín, and Etaín long enough to decide whether or not she wanted Cathal in her life. Time now to put Cathal to a different test, and to remind Etaín that another had a claim to her.

He traced a glyph into the wooden door, delivering a magical announcement of his presence, pausing for a moment to allow her to feel the whisper of a tropical-scented breeze where there could be none, before he knocked.

Through the barrier separating them he heard Cathal's voice, a ragged curse of pleasure interrupted, followed by a command to ignore the summons. Eamon smiled, but his amusement lasted only until she opened the door.

The sight of her swollen lips and another man's shirt covering her body shredded organized thought and left only the incendiary combination of magic and sex in its place. He wanted her. Here. Now. Always. Everything about her called to him, making it easy to forget the myriad dangers she presented, the change to Elf she had yet to survive.

He stepped forward, tearing his eyes away from her just long enough to meet Cathal's gaze in challenge and acknowledgment. *Leave or join me in this.*

His fingers went to the buttons of his own shirt, freeing them before he shrugged it off, leaving him standing bare-chested as Cathal was. He felt the heat and fast currents of his magic combine with the wild, primordial aspects of hers, saw an awareness of it in the black, deep ocean depths of eyes he could get lost in.

"Perfect timing," Etaín said, molten lust flooding into her bloodstream, a fever heralding desire beyond reasoning. Leaving her nipples aching and arousal wetting her inner thighs as fantasy and reality merged at having both men with her at the same time.

Eamon reached for her, undoing the buttons of the shirt and stripping it away. She moaned, wanting them both.

She expected him to pull her into his arms and take possession of her mouth in a demonstration of ownership. Instead he moved behind her, turning her so they both faced Cathal.

He cupped her breasts as if in an offer to share, his touch and the eroticism of their positioning making her channel clench. A whimper escaped when his thumbs brushed over her nipples and she saw Cathal's eyes fix on them, darkening not with jealousy but with passion.

He closed the distance, his cock rigid against the front of his hastily fastened pants. She wondered if it was still wet from her mouth, licked her lips thinking about it, and knew by the hitch in his breathing he was remembering her mouth being on him.

She lifted her arms, hands spearing through Eamon's hair, the stretch of her body, the offering of it, making her feel like a sexual priestess, a follower of some ancient goddess dedicated to pleasure.

She widened her stance and the movement drew Cathal's gaze downward to swollen folds and a clit standing erect, flushed, the hood pulled back to reveal a tiny darkened head.

Color fanned across stubbled cheeks taut with lust, exciting her further. He was raw to Eamon's refined. Dark, dangerous masculinity to Eamon's golden beauty. Together they were everything she would ever need or want in a lover.

A shiver went through her when Cathal stopped inches away. The vines on her arms didn't react to him the same way they did to Eamon, the call of like to like, magic to magic, but deep inside her, something resonated, hungered for him, reached out in reaction to his scent and his nearness as if it would anchor itself in his very existence.

The intensity of the feeling sent a spike of fear through her, but before it could lodge itself and spread, Eamon's fingers clamped onto her nipples and his mouth captured her earlobe, need forcing a plea from her. "Please, Cathal. I want you, too."

Cathal took the final step so their bodies touched, lust soaking through his skin like a drug despite an awareness of Eamon's hands on her breasts. Desire suppressed all resistance and separated him from any objection to sharing her. He couldn't think, couldn't remember why he'd fought against the very idea of it, not when it turned him on to see them together, to see her skin flush with pleasure, her eyes bottomless pools of promised ecstasy.

He wanted to lose himself in her. To pull the same sounds from her that she gave Eamon as he sucked her lobe, leaving it to fuck into her ear canal so her hips jerked.

Cathal panted as her cunt ground into a cock craving the wet heat of either her mouth or slit. He captured her lips, thrust his tongue against hers and was rewarded by whimpers and the urgent press of her clit to his erection.

He couldn't stand the separation, didn't wait for her to reach down and free him as she had before Eamon's arrival. A moan escaped as his pants dropped away and hot skin touched hot skin.

He cupped her hips, need pulsing between them as he rubbed against her clit, constrained from lifting her and sheathing himself in heated ecstasy by Eamon's presence behind her.

Greedily he kissed downward, ready to rip Eamon's fingers from her nipple if necessary, but instead of finding confrontation, he found cooperation, the dark eroticism of a breast offered, held for him by another man.

Cathal latched on to the nipple, greeting it first with the swirl of his tongue. Lapping over it, biting then sucking, loving the way she cried out.

His hand went to her mound, covering it possessively, fingers going to her opening and thrusting inside. She was wet, dripping with the need for a man's cock.

He fucked her with his fingers and she writhed between them, powerless. And that powerlessness excited him after being so desperately in her thrall since he'd met her.

The urge to dominate rose, bringing with it images of her on elbows and knees, the remembered rush of mounting her. It came with heightened anticipation, the promise of a more intense experience at having Eamon there to witness the claiming, to cover her afterward.

He gripped his cock to keep from coming. He was primed, ready, and had been from the instant she'd put her mouth on him after their reconciliation.

Remembering the torment she'd delivered, the lesson in ownership, he left her breast, intent on delivering the same to her. Kissing downward, pausing to explore her navel, the flat perfection of her abdomen, nuzzling into the dark honey of a small triangle of pubic hair.

Her plea for him to put his mouth on her filled him with carnal satisfaction. Her clit was engorged, an erogenous zone he had no intention of ignoring. He knew what she liked, intended to make her scream with pleasure as he had after stretching her out on the padded rim of the hot tub beneath a night sky.

She bucked when he took the swollen knob between his lips, her hands leaving Eamon's hair to tangle in his so she could hold him to her.

He tightened his grip on his cock, knowing he couldn't hold out much longer. Fierce competitiveness and masculine pride refused to let him come as he had when he'd been alone, splashing his stomach and chest with semen while fantasizing about her.

Intentions of making her scream fell to the greater need to be inside her. He forced himself to abandon her clit, but couldn't leave without the intimate press of his lips to her lower ones and the thrust of his tongue into her channel, hard and fast and deep as she clenched on it, ground against his face.

Her movements grew more urgent, a frantic reaching for a release he wanted when she was impaled on his cock. He stood. Her "No!" music to his ears, though the sight of Eamon turned his smile at hearing it into little more than a baring of teeth.

"Take her," Eamon said, and Cathal did, lifting Etaín and carrying her the short distance to the bed, lust making him deaf to any command in Eamon's voice.

Eamon watched, held in place by the enthrallment of magic and the sheer eroticism of seeing Cathal tumble Etaín onto her hands and knees before entering her in a single hard thrust. With their bodies joined, her aura totally eclipsed Cathal's, sending a call Eamon couldn't refuse.

He removed the remainder of his clothing and joined them, lying on his back and positioning himself so he could cup her head and draw her mouth to his. Always before the magic had flowed from him into her, a gift to replenish and strengthen, but with Cathal's presence came the opposite, a rich pour of Elfhome and Earth magic, as if sex with Etaín widened some ethereal crack between worlds, and Cathal served as a conduit for this world's magic where he couldn't serve as a vessel for it as the Elven did.

It was an intoxicating rush, elemental power mixed with lust and insatiable desire. Eamon drank hungrily from her lips, cock swelling further until its urgent demand dominated, and her swallowed cry of release, followed by Cathal's, freed him from one type of enchantment only to ensnare him in another.

There was an instant to note purple spikes through the gold of her aura, but the splintered effect disappeared as he moved, shifting position and pulling her down and beneath him, in the process making Cathal's cock slide from her channel.

She welcomed him readily, legs parting, eyes wickedly inviting. He was aware of Cathal watching as he joined his body to Etaín's, twined his fingers with hers and held them to the mattress, palms touching, safe from her still because of his power as a spell caster.

In the presence of Elven pheromones and magic, he knew Cathal would harden again as a human rarely could so quickly after spending himself. He was content to let Cathal benefit from the effect.

Eamon sealed his lips to hers once again, a sharing of magic this time. A twining as their tongues rubbed and her legs encircled his hips, holding him against her even as the position allowed him to thrust deeper.

As he'd done when it was Cathal who'd pleasured her, he swallowed her sharp cries, her husky moans, and finally her cry of release. The tight clenching of her channel milking him of seed in a white-hot rush of raw magic that left his body humming even after he'd rolled to his side, facing Cathal with Etaín's feminine perfection between them.

Etaín felt like purring and suspected the smile on her face made her look like a well-satisfied cat. She suppressed a laugh. *Or a cat very much in heat.*

"That was better than the fantasy," she said, touching a hand to the smooth heat of Eamon's chest as she combed through the dark hair on Cathal's before zeroing in on a nipple. "Much better."

Cathal's eyes heated, whether at mention of the fantasy or from the stroke of her fingertips over his nipple, she didn't know, only thrilled at the hungry expression on his face. A glance at Eamon and she saw the same, though from the very first he'd made it clear he found the thought of sharing her arousing.

Her fingers zeroed in on his nipple, its color lighter than Cathal's though it was equally hard, as were the cocks pressed to her thighs. The effects of magic she guessed but the thought was still accompanied by a small thrill of feminine power.

Her knowledge of their bodies gave her the advantage. "I want you both again," she said, fingers tightening on male nipples in a command to pleasure.

Cathal moaned and lowered his head, claiming her lips as Eamon's mouth went to her breast, the combined assault sending a scorching wave of lust to her cunt.

A sound of need escaped, and then a second as their hands settled between her thighs.

Her hips jerked upward with the rub and press, the strokes of masculine fingertips along the underside of her clit and over its head. With firm grips and a pumping that wrested any illusion of control away from her.

Desire pulsed through her. Overwhelming her so she trembled, begged.

Eamon drew back and she welcomed Cathal, wrapping arms and legs around him as his cock found her opening and pushed inside. His claiming a hard rush to an exquisite release for both of them.

His eyes held satisfaction and it made her heart sing. She felt his cock begin to firm though his eyes held sleepy contentment. His mouth lowered, but before it touched hers, the vines along her arms flared to life and Cathal went lax.

Eamon tugged her from beneath Cathal and covered her with his own body. "You knocked him out," Etaín accused, affronted on Cathal's behalf.

"I believe we've given Cathal plenty to think about for one night. He'll have enough to consider in the morning without including a discussion of magic and it's enhancement of male performance."

The comment made her laugh despite her aggravation at Eamon's high-handedness. He capitalized on it by brushing his lips over the top of her ear, sending a spike of heat downward.

"Beyond that, Etaín, I wanted time alone with you before I leave."

Conversation ended with the touch of his mouth to hers. She resisted at first, until punishing him became a punishment for herself, and then she yielded, the joining of their bodies becoming pleasure drawn out so she was left slumberous, relaxed, and sated afterward.

"You're really leaving?" she murmured.

He didn't want to, but for all of their sakes he thought it best if Cathal didn't have to confront the reality of his choice upon waking. "Yes," he said, though long moments passed before he could force himself away from her, and even then he couldn't resist cupping her cheek and brushing his thumb across her lip. "I'll give Cathal until the fund-raiser to have you to himself. After that, things will change, Etaín."

Lord Eamon's edict stirred resistance in her. She wasn't sure whether she reacted to the idea of change or his underlying attitude, one he'd already infuriated her with by using worlds like allow and tolerate. But rather than mar the enjoyment that had come before it, she let it go as a battle for another day.

With a final kiss he rose and dressed. In the doorway the moonlight caressed his features as he sent a heated glance and silent promise her way. There was no going back, only forward.

Etaín sighed and snuggled against Cathal, smiling when he immediately draped an arm and a leg over her, possessive even in his sleep.

It seemed as though she'd only just closed her eyes when her cell phone chimed. The darkness outside confirmed it was too early for a call to be anything but bad news. Dread gripped her as she left the bed and answered.

"You owe me, girl," Anton said, and in a heartbeat excitement replaced everything else.

"You talked to Deon."

"I told you, I've always been a real popular brother."

"Did he give you a name?"

"Better than that, gave me an address, too. Not an apartment number, but he thinks third floor. Should be easy enough to find. Guy's a painter. Has a van he's got signs for, got a phone number on the signs."

She crossed to the table and turned on a small lamp. The sketchpad with the Cathal-inspired tattoo was open but she flipped a different tablet to a clean page and picked up a pencil. "I'm ready."

"Say the word, I'll take care of this guy then you and me can celebrate afterward."

"I promised him to someone else."

Anton grunted. "Too bad. Name's Kevin Wheat."

She wrote it down, along with the address that followed, then read it back to Anton.

"You got it. Be seeing you soon, girl."

Parker's number she knew by heart. Trent's she had because he'd asked for her help on Quinn's behalf.

She hit send and Trent answered immediately, sounding alert, as if the Harlequin Rapist case left no time for sleep. "I found the artist."

"Who?"

"Not someone you can reach out to. But I did, through someone else. He just called and gave me a name and an address to go with the tattoo."

"Give it to me." His voice held the same excitement she felt.

She relayed everything she'd learned from Anton. Trent said, "I assume you didn't call Parker with this."

"That would be a correct assumption. Good hunting."

Twenty-nine

~

*H*e stank as badly as the winos sitting on either side of him. Even the smell of the food couldn't mask it.

The feel of stiff, dirty clothes against his skin made him itch. Eating was a chore. But he applied himself to it, hunching over the plate of eggs and toast.

Men and women and children were still shuffling though the line, claiming seats in the shelter dining room as soon as they emptied. He'd already been here longer than the people he'd come in with.

No one noticed. They were used to him now.

He stayed because he wanted to see her. He ached to see her.

Before he chose her, he could go without seeing her for days and it didn't bother him. Now he couldn't.

He didn't dare go near her apartment again. Or the tattoo shop. The police might be there, hiding, watching. He didn't want to be noticed.

They'd be here tomorrow, too, for the fund-raiser, but he wasn't worried. They'd never catch him, and after tomorrow, he wouldn't come back here. He wouldn't need to.

He'd be with her in their special place. He didn't think he'd want to leave it for a long time.

He finished breakfast and stood, shuffling over to the place where the trays and dirty dishes went. He didn't want to leave without seeing her, but he had to.

Kevin didn't like how much time he was spending away from the apartment. Even though they'd only argue when he got back, he needed to go. His skin itched.

It was hard to keep from clawing at the filthy clothing to get it away from his body. One more time, he told himself. He'd put them on one more time, then he could throw them away.

He left the shelter, a howl rising inside him at not having seen her. He kept it from escaping by thinking about the supplies already loaded in the van.

Duct tape and Taser. A syringe with a sedative that should make her sleep until he got her to their special place and it was time to begin. And best off all, most clever of all, the hollowed-out speaker strapped to a dolly.

He giggled. Having live musicians at the fund-raiser had made it easy to come up with the perfect plan. Even if someone noticed him with the speaker, they'd just think a musician had paid him to haul it to where they were parked. No one would guess she was inside it and he was taking her away.

She'd thought she'd sleep until noon but she woke early, not dreaming but restless all the same when she should have been content to lie with Cathal. She opened and closed her fist, making the eye on her palm blink and her thoughts drift to the ones her mother wore on the backs of her hands.

She wondered again if her mother had a different gift of sight, and if she'd foreseen this. Eamon and Cathal.

Heat moved through Etaín with thoughts of the night. She closed her eyes to incorporate it into a fantasy spinning out into the future. But the restlessness returned, intensifying, making it impossible to lose herself in sexual imagery or remain in bed.

Careful not to wake Cathal, she got up, glad she'd taken a shower after the call to Trent. She hoped they'd found probable cause to take

Kevin Wheat into custody and search his apartment. Her tip alone wasn't enough. It would only point them in the right direction.

A chill swept through her, like a small fissure in the wall separating Tyra Nelson's reality from her own. She crossed her arms, wishing Eamon were there to shore up her defenses.

Dressing, she had the vague intention of getting a bowl of cereal. It disappeared when she saw the open sketchpad.

The reason for the restlessness crystallized with the sight of Cathal's tattoo. She glanced at him, eyes going to his exposed forearms and seeing the ink there in more detail than what was on the paper.

She didn't fight the compulsion to draw. There was no point in it though it had never been like this before.

A thought piggy-backed on to the one she'd had earlier. If her mother had the gift of sight, did she have a small measure of it, too? Was that the reason she returned again and again to a tattoo Cathal told her he would never wear? Because he needed it?

With a sigh of frustration she picked up a pencil and began working in the additional detail, finishing it only moments before Cathal got up. He came to her, bending down to rub his cheek against hers.

"There's cereal in the cabinet," she said. "Or better still, we could hit McDonald's."

He nibbled along her neck. "What if I rummage around and make us something decent to eat."

"Good luck with that."

"You doubt my ability to cook?" His tone one of mock affront.

She smiled at his playfulness. "More like I question the contents of my fridge and cabinets."

"A challenge then." He kissed the place where her neck met her shoulder, sucked, the pull of his mouth reaching her nipples, and lower. "I can rise to any challenge."

"Can you? Prove it by letting me tattoo your forearms," she said, the ink—the magic—using her mouth to deliver a dare she hadn't intended.

It sent fear skittering through her. But if she lost her faith in this and recalled the words, where would she be? Where would he be? If he needed whatever the design stood for?

"Leaving your mark on me?" Cathal asked, unable to explain the primitive satisfaction coursing through him at the idea of it.

Days ago he would have said no without hesitation. But then days ago, he wouldn't have shared her with Eamon, though at the moment he didn't want to either talk about it or look any closer than accepting Sean's theory about men being turned on visually and competitive as hell at their core.

"I've never tattooed anyone I've been with, either before or after. But every time I look at your arms, I see these on them."

He reached around her, taking her hands and turning them so the palms faced upward. Last night all he'd cared about was bridging the distance between them, and afterward, rational thought had been beyond him.

He wasn't sure if he wanted to be exposed to any more of the freaky stuff. He handled it now the same way he intended to handle the reality of Eamon, at least for today, by *not* thinking about it. But as he stroked his thumbs over the eyes inked into her skin he felt compelled to ask, "Does your seeing the tattoos have something to do with these?"

"Yes."

Not the answer he wanted though he expected it. The skin of his forearms tingled, and he remembered waking with her in his bed, her fingers tracing the design captured on paper in front of him. "This is important to you?"

"Yes."

She'd sacrificed for him, taking Brianna's memories and reliving them. It seemed fair to take Etaín's ink in turn. Pain for pain, even if a traitorous part of him found true pleasure in the idea of it.

"Okay," he said, nuzzling her. "But you don't get to demonstrate your artistic ability until after I've shown off my culinary talents."

* * *

*T*he sight of the police cars barricading the street made him slam on the brakes. Tires squealed, the van belonging to Kevin and the car following it.

The driver behind him gave a long blast on the horn. And then another. And another.

His heart lurched as the cops standing near a squad car turned to look. Automatically his hands went to the seatbelt release and door handle but the policemen turned back toward the apartment before he bolted from the van.

Beyond their car he could see men in SWAT uniforms and more cops. Two of the taskforce members climbed out of a car and he whimpered, grabbing one of the candy bars on the seat next to him at the same time he grabbed the phone so he could call Kevin.

POP. POP. POP.

He jerked at the sound of gunfire.

POP. POP. POP. POP. POP. POP.

He sobbed, the candy bar and phone biting into his lip as he held them against his mouth.

Kevin. Kevin was in the apartment waiting for him to come home so they could argue again about her, and why she wasn't a good choice right now. He wanted them to go to New York. He said they could come back to San Francisco for her in a couple of months because he was afraid they'd be caught if she really had visited the hospital and learned something. Kevin believed in psychics.

They fought over her. And now tears streamed down his face because he knew they wouldn't fight again.

He lurched over, vomiting the breakfast he'd eaten at the shelter onto the passenger seat floor. Sweat broke out on his skin, reviving the stink left over from the clothes he'd changed out of after reaching the van.

When he sat up again the cops were moving, no longer hiding behind their parked cars. They were talking into radios and putting away their guns. He saw the FBI agents, including the one who was her brother, go inside.

They'd find the pictures. Kevin had started getting tattoos to remember the women by, but he liked looking at pictures best.

The candy bar and phone dropped to his lap. He had to leave before someone saw how much he looked like Kevin. Or before a neighbor told them there might be someone staying with Kevin. Or they noticed the van and decided to check to see if it was Kevin's.

The man behind him had gotten out of his car so he could watch. That meant using the sidewalk, turning and going forward, backing up and turning.

He was careful to keep his head ducked and go slow. Not to act like someone trying to run away.

It took all his concentration. It helped him forget for a few minutes.

He turned the radio on when he got out of sight of the apartment. The song stopped and a voice cut in. "We've got breaking news. Sources at the scene of a shootout between SWAT members and an unidentified individual say the man who has been killed by police is believed to be the same one who has been terrorizing the Bay Area for months as the Harlequin Rapist."

A howl erupted from inside him. He pounded on the steering wheel and screamed. "No! No! No!

"No! No! No!"

He screamed until he was hoarse, until the front of his shirt was wet from spit and bile. Until the word became sobs and finally hiccups.

"Kevin," he whispered. "I'm sorry. I should have . . ."

He couldn't say it.

It would be a lie.

He looked in the rearview mirror and saw the dead speaker. Inside it were the Taser and duct tape and syringe, ready for tomorrow. He couldn't give her up.

They could have argued a hundred times. It wouldn't have mattered. He hadn't even told Kevin his plan because he knew Kevin wouldn't *go along with it, wouldn't have anything to do with her until after she was at their special place.*

"I'm sorry, Kevin. I'm sorry," he whispered. "I'll make it up to you. I didn't mean for this to happen."

No! This wasn't his fault. He didn't know how the police had found the apartment, but it wasn't his fault.

If anything, it was her fault. She was the reason he and Kevin weren't on their way to New York right now.

He shivered at the truth of it. It was just like their mother all over again. Everything bad that had ever happened to Kevin and him had been because of her.

A shuddering breath left him. His nostrils were clogged with snot.

Resolve filled him as he breathed through his mouth. He'd wanted her to remember him after their time together, like all the others before the last one had. But she had to pay for what had happened to Kevin.

His stomach quivered and threatened to flip over as he remembered the way it felt and sounded when a skull started to cave in. But some of the familiar excitement came back, too, when he realized it would make taking her from the fund-raiser easier. If she wasn't going to remember their time together, then it didn't matter if she saw his face.

Etaín stepped back, studying the tattoos on Cathal's forearms. They were mirror images of each other. Perfect. They were more, though she didn't know what, only that she felt a fierce satisfaction at seeing them on his skin, at his acceptance of them.

It had taken most of the day, with lengthy breaks, not because it had to but because neither of them wanted to leave the apartment. She was grateful for the respite, for the chance to talk, more about music than anything else, and Eamon not at all—something she let slide because she needed a timeout from turmoil before the organized chaos that would define the fund-raiser tomorrow.

"What do you think?" she asked, setting the hand-needle next to the ink she'd made herself and taking his hands, warmth flowing into her, a mellow tide rather than an electric buzz of desire.

"Worried I'm going to lie?" he asked, fingers tightening on hers so she couldn't break the contact, ensuring she understood he was making a joke.

"Wouldn't be much point in it."

He laughed, attention shifting to his extended arms. "You do beautiful work, Etaín. Seeing them there is going to take some getting used to. But . . . no regrets. Definitely no regrets."

"I'm glad." She pulled her hands from his. She'd already gone over aftercare instructions, even though she'd be around to take care of the artwork. It took only a few minutes to cover the fresh tattoos with ointment and bandages. When it was done she wrapped her arms around his waist and kissed him, a long thorough reunion of lips and tongues.

"I'm going to need more of those to make it all better," he said, voice husky when she lifted her mouth from his.

"I'll keep that in mind. And I'll go easy on you tonight."

His eyes flicked to the bed. "What about going easy on me now?"

"And I thought I was a sex addict."

He smiled against her mouth. "Like to like."

She couldn't bring herself to ruin the moment by telling him that's how it was with Eamon. She would. The subject couldn't be avoided much longer.

"Shelter next," she said. "I've got to make sure everything's set for tomorrow. Then I can crawl in bed and stay there until morning."

"Stay at my place tonight?"

It made sense. "Yes."

Her phone rang before they were ready to leave. Relief hit her when she saw Trent's number in the display.

"Tell me you're calling to say you got him," she said instead of hello.

"I take it you don't watch TV or listen to the radio much."

"I don't. Bad habit." Left over from those years with her mother, when it seemed nothing going on in the world around them mattered.

"He's dead," Trent said. "Tried his best to take the SWAT team with him but no one else was hurt. Sick pervert had pictures in his bedroom, enough evidence to have put him on death row even if we never find the place where he took his victims."

She heard Parker's voice in the background and stiffened. "Be right there," Trent said, obviously talking to her brother.

"Gotta go," he said to her. "Press conference is about to start. Get to a TV or turn on the radio. This is important, Etaín."

She put the phone in her jacket pocket. "That was one of the task-force members. Turn on the TV. The Harlequin Rapist is dead."

They settled on her couch and watched as the taskforce members filed into a room filled with reporters. She steeled herself against feeling anything at seeing Parker, but couldn't suppress the ache that came when the captain joined the others.

The press conference went as she expected, with the spokesman claiming a tip had led them to the suspect. He gave minimal details of what they'd found in Kevin Wheat's apartment, but enough of them so women in the Bay Area could feel safe—at least when it came to this particular predator—and interest in the story would die down as far as the media went.

She tried to stop herself from repeatedly glancing at the captain. It'd been months since they'd talked, and that had ended in a familiar argument about her wasting her talent using skin as a canvas instead of producing work to be sold in galleries.

He didn't like that she worked in Bryce's shop. Didn't like that word got back to him she was often out with musicians. He thought at any minute she was going to spiral downward on drugs because of her choice of friends and profession.

She forced her attention back to the spokesman but he was stepping aside and the captain was taking his place behind the podium. "I've been asked to participate in order to clear up the rumor concerning my daughter's involvement with the taskforce," he said, and her heart gave a lurch, knowing her anonymity was about to be stripped away.

"Though Etaín is an artist, and has on occasion worked with the authorities, she was asked to visit Tyra Nelson in the hospital, and the subsequent rumors about it circulated in an effort to draw the Harlequin Rapist out. She fit the profile of the type of woman the taskforce believed he would choose as his next victim. That was the extent of her involvement. It was a long shot, and at no time was she ever in danger, nor did he make an attempt to take her. In the end, it was solid police work and a tip from a citizen that led to his being identified and stopped."

The captain stepped away from the podium and the spokesman opened the conference to questions. Cathal captured her hand, lacing his fingers with hers. "What's the truth? Did they make you a target? Or are they trying to kill any media interest in you?"

She wanted to believe the captain's presence and his speech were about deflecting attention, and given the fund-raiser tomorrow, she appreciated it. But . . .

"I don't know what the truth is," she said, her thoughts going to Liam's showing up at the bar, and the fight that ensued when Eamon followed. "Except that I've been kept safe."

A reporter's question intruded, cutting through the air with a sharp-voiced, "Has a taskforce been formed to deal with last night's murder of a diplomat's son and three other boys?"

"I can't comment on that."

Another question about Brianna's rapists came after that one. Cathal rose from the couch and turned off the TV. His back still to her, he asked, "Did you know they'd been killed before the police showed up here?"

"No."

She went to him, arms going around his waist, cheek rubbing against the solid muscles of his back. "It can't be undone."

"I know. I'm not sure I wish it could be even though I've been fighting against being like my father and uncle since I was thirteen."

The same age she'd been when the call to ink had come. "A turning point?"

He laughed but there was no humor in it. "You could call it that."

"What happened?"

"I fell in love with poker. I played it online some but for the wins to be satisfying, I had to pit myself against people who were *real* to me, not names on a screen. My parents' house is a couple of blocks away from Uncle Denis's. The kids in my social network had money, the same as I did. Even at the start, these weren't low-stakes games, and I had a talent for cards.

"At thirteen, I had a couple hundred grand in winnings. Cash, just sitting around my room. And for a cut, one of the guys my father kept around for protection had fifty or sixty K in jewelry he was converting into cash for me."

"Your father and uncle knew what you were doing?"

"At the time, I didn't think so. Looking back, they knew. They just didn't say anything because letting things play out is how they operate. They wanted to see where I'd go with it. If it would bother me kids might be stealing to cover their losses. And what I'd do when someone gambled big and couldn't pay up."

"And that happened?"

"Yes."

Cathal forced himself to face the memory, knowing if she chose to, she could see it. "There was this one boy who was a degenerate gambler at seventeen. He also played football. He was twice my size. Popular. I extended him credit, a huge line of it. He used it up then told me he wasn't going to pay and I couldn't make him."

Cathal tensed, bracing himself to have her pull away. "He was wrong. I did make him."

She tightened her arms rather than reject him. "How?"

"Access to guns wasn't a problem. I can't remember the first time my father put one in my hand and let me fire it, that's how young I must have been. He drew the line at letting me keep one in my room, but it was easy enough to take one of his.

"I waited in the backseat of the kid's car. He got in and as soon as he started driving, I sat up and put the barrel against his head, then proceeded to convince him he could either pay his debt or live in fear of an injury that might leave him unable to play football if he survived at all. The car smelled like piss and shit by the time I was done talking, that's how effective I was."

"Would you have gone through with your threat if he hadn't paid?"

He took a deep breath and exhaled it slowly, facing the ugliness. "When I made it, it was real. After I got out of the car and he drove away, I puked."

"You scared yourself straight."

"I thought so."

She bit his shoulder before he could express the doubts he'd experienced as he looked at the drawings, feeding them to the fire one-by-one. "Given no good options," she said, "you chose the best one and I'm here with you as a result of it. You tried to change the course of something you knew you couldn't stop, but you weren't able to. The only innocent victims are Brianna and Caitlyn."

Turning in her arms he rubbed his nose against hers. "Let's go away after the fund-raiser. You name the place. Hawaii. Europe. The Caribbean. My treat. We'll go for a week at least. Stay longer if we decide we want to."

She was tempted. Beyond tempted.

It wouldn't be a working vacation. The only skin she'd touch was his and he was safe from her gift. Her *changing* gift.

She sighed, finally confronting what she hadn't been willing to for most of the day. She closed her hands, a sign she had no intention of reading him. "What about Eamon?"

Cathal stiffened in answer, but when she would have pulled out of his arms, he stopped her with the tightening of them. "You can invite him. Just promise to pick a place and let me take you there after the fund-raiser."

"I'll need to wrap things up and reschedule some appointments."

"Same here." He nuzzled her ear, took the lobe between his lips and gave a sweet suck. "Promise, Etaín."

"I promise."

Thirty

E amon took a final sip of coffee and set the mug down on the elegant table. "Shall we leave, gentlemen?"

Liam exchanged a glance with Rhys. "And here I was beginning
to think having a woman in his life definitely *didn't* improve his per-
sonality."

Rhys gave a small tilt of his head. "I had the same fear, especially
given yesterday's testiness."

Eamon could afford to be amused by them. Today marked the end
of his allowing Etaín the unfettered freedom to do as she pleased.
Adjustments would be required due to her involvement with Cathal.
And he found himself willing to grant her more leeway than he once
would have thought possible, but certain risky behaviors would cease.

Involving herself with the police was one of them. Tattooing anyone other than those he gave approval to was another. Despite what
he felt for her, he would be Lord, and she the Lady who answered
to him.

"The humans are organized?" he asked Liam.

"They should be arriving at the shelter now. Twenty to begin with
and another twenty to come later if necessary. They'll pay, sign waiv-
ers, and get their artist tickets so they can be in Etaín's line as soon she
settles at a workstation."

"Excellent." Eamon rose from his seat. "I believe it's now time to check on my intended."

He sat near a grocery cart full of junk, whimpering when he saw her, then shoving his knuckles into his mouth to keep from doing it again. Whore. Slut.

She was with the dark-haired man, but in spite of it, in spite of what she'd done to Kevin, he still wanted to be with her. She was so, so beautiful. Golden like the sun, warming the snake between his legs so it started waking.

He hunched his back. Drawing his knees against his chest so he could hide the growing bulge at the front of his pants.

Just a little while longer. He just had to wait a little while longer and they'd be together.

Kevin wouldn't be there and that made him sad. But a part of him, a small guilty part was glad he didn't have to share her.

He could keep her as long as he wanted that way. Kevin wouldn't say when to let her go like he had with the others. And when he was done . . .

He shied away from thinking about ruining her face and caving in her skull. He'd keep the promise he made to Kevin, but not right away.

The artists had started tattooing, and on a short stage a couple of musicians were warming up. He watched her as she moved around, talking to lots of different people. He wished he could get closer but he didn't dare.

He hoped the black girl would come. When he saw her at the tattoo shop he hadn't paid attention to what car she got into, or if she rode the bus.

He didn't like the black ones as much. In New York he only chose ones that looked like her. But maybe he'd stay in San Francisco long enough for one more, for Kevin, and because of the golden thread that went from her to the black girl.

He saw the blond-haired man from the fancy restaurant heading to-

ward her. And when he reached her, she went willingly into his arms, kissing him back while the dark-haired one watched.

Whore! Slut! She was just like his mother.

He squeezed his eyes shut and bit down on his knuckles to keep from making another sound. She wouldn't act like this anymore. He'd punish her and love her at the same time. And then he'd make sure she never did it again.

She'd live in his memory then. Only there.

He just had to wait now. For the right time to take her.

Eamon reluctantly allowed Etaín to escape his embrace. He wouldn't have been able to tolerate any of this if he didn't know it was his people she would touch, and at the end of this day, her true education would begin.

He extended his hand to Cathal, memories of the night before stirring anticipation for the future. Cathal's handshake was firm, his gaze steady, though a hint of color appeared beneath the dark stubble on his cheeks.

Eamon managed to suppress his amusement, but only barely. Her magic clung to Cathal like a rich, heady perfume and he could well imagine Cathal's reaction to learning of it.

If he was a man to desire other men, he'd find Cathal irresistible. As it was, he found Cathal . . . a problem with only one apparent solution. Acceptance.

Cathal released Eamon's hand and took Etaín's, pulling her into a hug. Seeing her return Eamon's kiss was all it had taken for fantasies to spiral out of control, expanding on the reality of the night before and bringing with them a hard dick and a whirl of conflicting thoughts. Not regret, the sex had been too incredible for that, but he wasn't convinced sharing her for the long term was really possible, not when he wanted her with him at his club, and afterward in his home each night. "You'll be tattooing soon?"

"In just a few minutes. Justine and the other volunteers have everything under control. Most of the artists are already here, plus a few I didn't think would show up until later. So we're in good shape."

She smiled and he felt it in his heart. "Thanks for the music," she said, initiating a kiss that said other things as well. "It's the reason why we've got so many people showing up this early."

"My pleasure." He heard the huskiness in his own voice, the private bubble they were in expanding so he became aware of Eamon again, close enough that a step would have Etaín trapped between them.

It wasn't a comfortable intimacy. *Yet.*

He escaped it by saying, "I'm going over to the stage area. Be thinking of where you want to go after this. Anywhere in the world. You've promised me a week."

A nearby chuckle made him look to the right, at a black man with braids reaching to his shoulders and eyes laughing openly at Eamon who said, "Leave. Find Rhys. Let him endure your company for a while."

Etaín watched Liam go, then Cathal after a final kiss. "Probably time for me to start putting on some ink."

Eamon stopped her before she could take a step, shackling her wrist. "You're going away with Cathal?"

The twitch in his cheek would have given him away even if the tone of his voice failed to deliver the message. *Lord* Eamon was not happy about it.

"You're invited."

She expected him to relax and smile, to see this as a positive step. If anything his expression became more intense.

"Did you promise to make this trip?"

"Yes, and I won't break it." She tugged at her captured wrist. When he didn't release it, she said, "Let go, Eamon. I can get off on dominance games in the right situations, but this is not one of them."

"We'll talk about acceptable destinations later."

Her temper flared at his choice of wording. She suppressed it, giving him the benefit of the doubt, because even though sharing her turned him on, working out the details of it would no doubt come with some aggravating moments.

A lot of them, she was beginning to think, glad to have the fundraiser to concentrate on for the remainder of the day.

She gave another tug and said, "Why don't you go bond with Cathal over some tunes."

It coaxed a startled laugh out of Eamon, followed by a smile. And just like that, the tension between them was gone. "Somehow I don't think he's quite ready to spend time in my company."

He gave her a brief kiss then released her. "Do what you need to do. I'll stay close, but out of your way."

Jamaal's arrival drew her away from Eamon.

"You did good, girl," Jamaal said, nearly crushing her in a hug. "Even if the place Anton's brother owns got trashed thanks to you being there. That the guy who came after you?"

"Eamon. He owns Aesirs."

A laugh erupted. "Damn, you're something else when you decide you're tired of doing without. Where do you want me to set up?"

"Your choice." She pointed to a station at the far end. "That's where I'm going to be."

"I'll grab the one next to it. Bryce and Derrick are going to be here early, soon as they finish the clients they've got with them right now at the shop."

Etaín looked at the rapidly swelling crowd. A lot of them were there just for the music, but they'd end up buying hotdogs, hamburgers, and soft drinks—a last minute add because of the live bands.

"Should have put a cover charge in place," Jamaal said as they headed toward the workstations.

"Next year."

A line had already formed by the time she looked up from laying out her supplies. Surprise hit her first, then consternation at having at least twenty people—none of them former clients, none of them with a reason to pick her—waiting when there were other artists available.

"You're famous now," Jamaal joked.

She laughed, relaxing. Better this than a crowd of reporters. She gave a come-on wave to the man at the front of the line.

He practically bounced forward in his enthusiasm, putting his ticket on her table and claiming the empty seat.

"Which design?" she asked. All the shared ones were on display where the money was being collected and the release forms signed. And while some of the artists had stencils exclusive to them or their shop on their table, she didn't.

The man bit his bottom lip, enthusiasm sliding into nervousness as he leaned forward, expression earnest. Unnervingly so. "Please. You choose."

Her answer was immediate. "No."

His skin, his choice. She had no trouble with artists who went with the flow of a client's request, but from the very start she'd never put randomly chosen art on anyone.

She picked up the ticket and handed it back to him. He looked stricken.

"I can't," she said, trying to gentle her refusal. "Not in good conscience. You can write the cost off as a donation if you don't go through with this today. But if you choose to go to another artist, I would seriously suggest you go back and look at the designs, and decide if you want to be wearing one of them for the rest of your life. Lasering it off later will be expensive and very painful."

There was the slightest tremble in his voice when he said thank you and left. Another man immediately took his place. He was sweating, but when she asked him for a design, he answered promptly. "Number seven."

She pulled a stencil from a box containing numbered folders and showed it to him. "This one?"

"Yes." He pushed his sleeve out of the way and touched the place where his upper arm met his shoulder. "Right here."

"That'll work."

She set the stencil aside and pulled on latex gloves before opening an antiseptic wipe. But the moment her hand curled around his arm to steady it, her gift woke.

An overwhelming sense of *wrongness* came with it. The tattoo he'd selected didn't belong on his skin. None of the ones offered here today did though she could catch the barest glimpse of one that might be right. And knew with a certainty she couldn't explain except with one word—magic—that to fully see the image would require her to open the eyes on her palms and fully see *him*.

"I'm sorry," she said, wondering how she could possibly explain the refusal. "Do you mind if another artist does this?"

The ease in which he left, and the fact he *didn't* go to another workstation should have made her suspicious. But it took a few more aborted starts, and finally a woman leaning forward, whispering, "Please, Lady, don't send me away like the others," before she understood what was going on, and understood too, in a small way, why her gift had reacted to all of them.

"Eamon's responsible for your being here," she said, and the fear spiking into her from where her hand rested on the woman's forearm was answer enough. She didn't need the accompanying glance to the place Eamon now stood with Liam and Rhys to confirm it.

Anger pulsed into her to match the woman's fear. This felt like shades of the argument outside the bar, with Eamon using words like *tolerate* and *allow*, as if he were Lord to her as apparently he was to those standing in line.

She left the station. Liam and Rhys scattered as she approached.

"Why?" she asked, not bothering to interpret Eamon's actions as a way of supporting the shelter. He had money enough to make a donation.

"Your gift is changing, you've admitted as much. My people have some small measure of protection against it."

His answer mollified her somewhat but only because it showed concern for others. "First, you should have discussed this with me before ordering them to show up. If you had, then I would have told you I can handle doing this. And second, send them home. They're all going to be a no. If you doubt it, then I'll go down the entire line and touch each one of them."

She turned away and he grabbed her wrist as he had earlier. "If not them, then no one, Etaín. Don't waste your gift here."

His tone and his words were too close to the argument she'd remembered with the captain's appearance at the news conference, too much like the fight she'd had with Parker. She couldn't contain either the fury or the hurt though she managed to keep her voice low to avoid creating a scene.

"I'm done with you for now. Maybe permanently unless you back the hell off and experience a major attitude adjustment. This is what I do. This is who I am. Accept it or get out of my life. I can find the answers I need about my gift later on my own. For now I'm going to go into the shelter on a little timeout. When I come back, I am going to resume work, and the only ones standing in my line had better be people who don't have anything to do with you."

She jerked her arm and he let her go. She hadn't been sure he would, though when she turned around she saw Jamaal standing, correctly reading her body language and ready to come to her aid.

"I'm good," she said as she passed him, "just going to take a little break."

Another time he would have snorted and pointed out she hadn't even lifted the tattoo machine yet. He would have joked about how fast she went through men. This time he gave a small nod and directed a scowl in Eamon's direction.

Rhys and Liam drifted to Eamon's side like a pair of bad omens as Etaín stalked away. "Do you wish me to follow her?" Liam asked, wisely holding his amusement and muzzling the urge to say *I advised you against being here.*

Eamon sighed. "No." She was safe here and he didn't fear she'd run. There was no point in compounding problems brought about by a temper and patience more frayed than he'd realized.

The depth of her fury and the promise he heard in her voice when it came to cutting him out of her life surprised him, concerned him, *scared him*, though he would never let it come to that. Getting better acquainted with Cathal seemed like a far safer activity than remaining in Etaín's sight.

"Release them from their duty," he told Liam before finding Cathal near the stage.

The cautious need to forge a workable relationship with him became a more urgent one at seeing the *seidic* tattoos lying dormant along Cathal's forearms. When he'd decided to leave her apartment and allow them the previous day and night together, he'd suspected she might put her ink on Cathal.

Seeing the tattoos, he wasn't sure whether to be pleased or not. He doubted Etaín understood what she'd done, or what it meant for Cathal. An infusion of magic and a permanent bond would form between them, a connection that would extend Cathal's life beyond the short span of a human's—or in all likelihood, kill him if she died.

"One of your bands?" he asked, turning his attention to the task of becoming better acquainted with the man the magic had chosen.

The argument with the blond-haired man changed everything. He'd planned on taking her at the end of day. It would be longer before anyone noticed she was missing then. But right now was the perfect time.

Almost everyone was outside helping while she was going toward the door leading into the shelter. He thought she'd go to the bathroom. Maybe to cry or wash her face. Women always did that when they were upset.

There was a line of Porta-Potties outside. He'd noticed even the volunteers were using them because it was quicker and they wanted to stay close to the music and everything else going on.

She should be alone in the bathroom. No one would see him take her then, and the closet where he'd hidden the speaker was right across from it.

He was good with locks. He'd always been good with them. Better even than Kevin. No one would look in the closet because everyone knew it was locked.

He ducked his head and shuffled forward, heart beating so fast he could barely breathe. There was a chance someone would notice him going in after her, then coming out with the speaker, but he couldn't do anything about it.

Fear worked its way up his throat. He stuffed a candy bar into his mouth to keep quiet, then touched his jacket pocket, feeling the syringe and the smaller roll of duct tape he'd use over her mouth, just in case.

The Taser was in his waistband. Pointing down while the snake pointed up.

The thought made him giggle. Just a little sound before he could stop it.

He hunched his shoulders, going through the door she'd gone through without anyone stopping him. The music followed him in and stayed even after he closed the door.

Sweat rolled down his sides. It always did, he reminded himself. This was always a scary part. Then afterward, he liked remembering.

He unzipped the sticky, garbage-stained army jacket so he could get the Taser out when he needed it. He hurried forward, stopping outside the bathroom door.

The music made it impossible to hear if she was inside. He touched the handle on the closet to make sure. Still unlocked, just the way he'd left it. Licking his lips and tasting chocolate, he reached out and slowly pushed the bathroom door open, just a crack, squinting because if she was there, he'd see the golden glow.

His heart leapt in his chest at seeing it. He pushed all the way in, pulling the Taser out of his pants. She turned, but it was already too late. The barb was in her and she was falling, twitching like a stunned fish on the line, her eyes watching him, shining with fear.

He went to her, hearing himself panting, mumbling. There were only three stalls in the bathroom and all of them were empty.

The duct tape over her mouth came first, then he pushed her shirtsleeve up, shivering in pleasure at the sight of the tattoos on her skin.

He clamped his hand around her arm, raising a vein and stabbing the needle into it like he'd seen his mother do a thousand times. He pressed his thumb down, but not all the way.

He didn't give her the full dose, just enough so her eyes closed and she went limp, so she'd sleep for only a little while. He didn't want to wait until tonight to be with her.

Hurry! His heartbeat screamed in his head. Hurry!

He checked the hallway before carrying her into the closet. He used a flashlight instead of turning on the light overhead even though he didn't think anyone could see beneath the door.

The speaker was already open. He wrapped duct tape around her wrists and ankles before putting her in it. With her knees against her chest, the box was the perfect size for her.

He was so anxious to leave he almost forgot to check her pockets before he left the closet. He had to unscrew the front of the speaker after remembering she carried a phone.

Sweat rolled down his chest and back. He was afraid someone would hear him breathing hard.

He found the phone and turned it off, hiding it behind a box of toilet paper on the bottom shelf before screwing the black part of the speaker back in place.

He left the closet. Excited. Scared. His heart feeling like it was going to burst as he got out of the building without being stopped. And then away from the fund-raiser and finally into the van with its swapped out license plates so no one would know it belonged to Kevin.

He touched the hardness between his legs as he drove away. Everything they needed was already at their special place. They could stay there for weeks. She wouldn't leave him. And he wouldn't leave her until the very end.

Thirty-one

Eamon hoped enough time had passed for Etaín's temper to have cooled. If not, then surely Cathal's presence at his side would help.

Her empty workstation surprised him. Relieved him. Maybe whatever had caused her to reject the humans Liam had organized also made it impossible for her to tattoo anyone else today.

"Where's Etaín," Cathal asked Jamaal, wondering what had happened when Etaín's coworker glared at Eamon and said, "Don't know. Haven't seen her since she went inside."

"To get something?"

"To cool off more like."

"How long ago?"

Jamaal's eyebrows drew together. "Thirty minutes? An hour maybe? I got busy and wasn't paying much attention. Something must have come up. Etaín's not one to stay pissed for long."

It sounded reasonable but Cathal couldn't shake the sense of uneasiness he felt at not having seen her anywhere in the crowd as he passed through it. He called her and got voicemail.

"She didn't answer. I'm going to look for her inside."

"I'll take the outside," Eamon said.

Cathal's uneasiness increased as he made his way through the shelter, checking each of the open rooms, and after finding Justine, the locked ones. A nameless fear slid into him at returning to her workstation and seeing Eamon standing there without her.

"She's not inside."

"There's no sign of her out here either. No one's seen her."

"What did you fight with her about?"

A muscle jerked in Eamon's cheek. "Nothing to make her break her promise to be here."

Bryce arrived then, directing the same question they had at Jamaal. "Where's Etaín?"

"Fuck if any of us know. She can't be found inside or out. My calls keep going directly to voicemail. She's got no reason to dodge me even if she wants to dodge her men."

"Shit! Shit! Shit!" Bryce ripped his phone from its holder, his hands and voice shaking as he made a call. "She's gone. Missing, you asshole. He's got her! He's fucking got her! All you're going to find when you get here is her phone."

Cathal's chest constricted, every muscle suddenly tight. "Who has her?"

Bryce's face was taut, the piercings standing out painfully. "The Harlequin Rapist."

Cathal shook his head in denial, though it didn't shake the deepening sense of dread. "He's dead."

"One of them is. The other came to the shop the other day. Freak had me tattoo him while Etaín was there. I recognized the name and address from the forms when they took him down yesterday. They just started showing a picture of the guy the police killed on the news. As soon as I saw it I knew it wasn't the same one I put ink on. Close, but not the same. The fucking taskforce didn't have a clue he was out there."

"That was Parker on the phone?" Jamaal asked.

"Yeah. Asshole made her a target and then gave this guy more reasons to go after her. If he can't find her—"

Bryce turned away, inhaling loudly. "I called her old man first.

Then Parker. Then I started calling her but it went to voicemail, same as Derrick's calls did. He took off to check her apartment, thinking maybe she forgot her phone. I came here."

"Did her brother tell you anything that would help find her?" Cathal asked, willing to involve his father and uncle.

"Nothing," Bryce said, the word a choked sound.

"Stop imaging the worst," Jamaal said, throwing an arm around Bryce's shoulder. "Keep your mind busy on something else, like making sure this fund-raiser goes off the way she wants it to. That's what I intend to do until we know something."

Cathal felt Eamon's hand on his shoulder. "Come," Eamon murmured.

He went, accompanied by Liam and Rhys.

Eamon halted them next to the sedan. He hadn't intended to tie Etaín to him in this manner, but only a fool would pass up the opportunity and he couldn't afford to be one, even for love.

"There's a way we can find her," he said, knowing what Cathal could not, that a vow made by him would be binding on Etaín.

"How?"

"You already know something about how her gift works. You already understand it is beyond what can readily be explained."

"Yes."

"I've made it a point to study such things. There's more to her abilities than even she understands. The tattoos she put on you can be used to find her, but before I show you how, promise on her behalf that she'll put ink on me with the same meaning should I ask it of her."

"I promise," Cathal said, his expression revealing his suspicion and doubt.

Satisfaction surged through Eamon at gaining the pledge. He grasped Cathal's wrists and traced sigils onto his skin, sharing the essence of who and what he was as he had before with Etaín, the magic he'd been created to serve as a vessel for.

Cathal gasped as fire poured into the deep tracks made by Etaín's needles. It roared up his forearms, incendiary, wild and hungry. Breathtakingly painful before it was doused by frigid water, a stinging flow of it that warmed like a tropical sea when hot merged with cold.

In its wake the tattoos changed, holding not only solid black ink, but shades of red and blue and gold locked in healed skin. His rational mind wanted to deny the evidence. His heart refused to allow it.

"Concentrate on Etaín," Eamon said. "Find her. The tattoos are a direct link to her."

Etaín, he thought, turning her name into the embodiment of everything he felt for her. *Believing* without reservation that he could find her when his emotions flowed away from him, reshaping in his mind's eye so they became an extension of the designs on his arms, reaching as if they'd tangle themselves in the vines inked into Etaín's skin.

The instant they did he was filled with terrible urgency and the hard, fast throbbing of a heart thundering *hurry, hurry.* "I've got her. Let's go!"

Consciousness returned in a wave of confusion followed by the rush of nausea. Etaín rolled to her knees, barely aware of her nakedness or the fetid, stained mattress she'd been lying on until she'd vomited the contents of her stomach onto splintered wooden flooring.

Then terror came, memory overlapping memory with the metal walls surrounding her, all illuminated by a lit candle. For long moments she was herself and Tyra Nelson. Their realities flickering back and forth like a flame hungrily eating wax and wick.

I can survive this. I WILL survive this.

Tyra's thoughts. Her thoughts.

She didn't try to separate Tyra's memories from her own. She couldn't afford to, not when she needed to guard against the walls falling, allowing all the ones that had come before Tyra's to tumble in.

Insanity would come then. Death would be a welcome release from it. She'd learned that lesson at sixteen, when the captain's method of scaring her straight had nearly destroyed her.

She staggered to her feet. The vines on her forearms writhing, turning the eyes into a weapon.

A touch of her hands to her attacker's skin and she could erase who he was, willfully take all his memories and stop him, praying all the while Eamon could teach her how to forever seal them away. It was her only chance of surviving. She'd seen his face, and knew because of it, that he didn't intend for her to live beyond the rape and torture he planned for her.

She remembered him coming to the shop. Remembered the dream afterward, not stolen memory but a message she hadn't recognized and interpreted, that there were two rapists, not one.

Flames melting tearful clowns into grotesque mirror-house distortions, turning them into dark puddles that gave birth to demons, a twisting mass of faces with their mouths open.

The knowledge was there in Tyra's memories, too. A black van and the whisper of a door opening, but the trunk of a blue car becoming a dark prison.

On shaky legs Etaín moved toward the front of the metal shipping container. The walls had already begun closing in, but adrenaline, the desperate need to survive, would keep the memories of all the other victims behind mental walls, at least for a little while.

Sweat coated her skin. Each breath brought the fetid stink of urine and bowls, the harsh smell of terror that had a scream building inside her, one choked off because she knew it would bring only one person.

He came anyway. Drawn by the sound of her vomiting or by a guess the drug he'd injected would have worn off by now.

The metal latch lifted and, remembering the Taser, she pulled the mattress over puke and stood it on its side, turning it into a shield and battering ram in the instant before the door began opening.

Everything inside her demanded she escape the metal container as external light entered in a narrow wedge. She waited, nearly panting, ears straining to hear his movements.

He widened the opening, finally, cautiously showing himself. Part of a face. A chest, an arm extended, the Taser visible.

She attacked, slamming the mattress into the door. Driving him back but out of view. Leaving no other option except to continue forward.

She'd hoped he would fire the Taser reflexively and have to reload. He didn't.

He kicked at the mattress. Wrestled against it, trying to get a shot rather than simply tackling her.

She'd welcome the tackle if it gave her the opportunity she needed. The vines on her arms were on fire. Magic gathered, but she knew only one way to use it, her only goal to get close enough to touch the eyes to his skin, until she saw the pistol.

It lay on a table. A foot away from a homemade S&M bench, the legs and arms already spread, restraints open in preparation for binding her to it.

She backed toward it, slowed by her crouched position and the need to keep the mattress in place. Hope and desperation feeding her strength.

He screamed in angry frustration. "No!"

Charged, using fists and feet in a fury. Grabbing the mattress and jerking it down.

Firing. The barb sinking in just beneath her collarbone.

She dropped.

Helpless.

And he vented. Kicking her side repeatedly, until she knew by the pain and the sound of cracking bone that he'd damaged her ribs.

Tears leaked out of her eyes. Terror gripped her, knowing the injury was only the first she would sustain. Remembering the hospital room and Tyra.

He sobbed. "Stupid bitch. Stupid bitch. Look what you made me do."

Then he picked her up gently, tenderly, the anger draining out of his face as he carried her to the bench.

She tried to struggle. But she was a mind without a body.

A whimper escaped. *I can survive this. I WILL survive this.*

All she needed was a single opportunity.

He laid her down, fingers encircling her wrist and carrying it upward, only to go completely still, an animal alert to danger. Primitive instinct kicked in so instead of tethering her he jerked her off the table, shielding himself with her as he dropped the Taser and grabbed the pistol, pressing it against her forehead.

Her legs and feet tingled, control returning, but her arms and hands were useless.

The door exploded inward and her heart sang at the sight of Eamon and Cathal. She drank them in, accepting in a heartbeat that she would fight to keep both of them, and her life would change because of it.

They entered flanked by Rhys and Liam, the four of them spreading out. Weaponless, seemingly harmless. Engendering a confidence that pulled the gun from her temple to take aim at them.

Magic flashed, a jet of blue fire from Eamon's fingertips, engulfing hand and gun. Filling the room with a scream and the smell of burning flesh as she was set free.

Time slowed for Cathal even as both he and Eamon rushed forward. Eamon reached Etaín first, stripping off his shirt and covering her with it, leaving Cathal's arms empty. His hands empty. His mind empty of everything except for the desire to kill the man who'd taken her.

He didn't allow himself to think of her nakedness and what had been done to her before they got to her. All that mattered was putting an end to the pain howling through him. The agony of knowing that despite his wealth and power, he hadn't been able to keep her safe.

He picked up the gun. Feeling the places where flesh was burned onto the metal, the only physical evidence of a fire whose damage had disappeared when it did.

Liam and Rhys had the rapist held between them and Cathal preferred the solid reality of it to the inexplicable things he had witnessed and experienced since Eamon drew him away from the fund-raiser.

He approached, facing the truth about himself. One shielded earlier by the desire to protect Etaín. For Caitlyn and Brianna, he would have accepted a different version of justice for a rapist. For Etaín, he would be like his father and uncle.

He aimed the gun, knowing that no one in this room would dispute whatever story he told authorities. But before he could pull the trigger, Etaín's hand was there, covering his, pushing it lower. "No, Cathal. No. Not like this."

He let her force his hand downward until the gun pointed at the floor, accepting her choice and with it the reminder it had once been his too, though now he knew with certainty what he'd do without remorse when it came to her.

She put her arms around him. Hugging him tightly, the scent of her mingling with the smell of Eamon's cologne on the shirt she wore.

"You got here in time," she said. "You got here in time. Let the taskforce have him. Let the other victims have the satisfaction of seeing him tried."

He returned the hug, feeling her stiffen, hearing the catch of her breath and the whimper she couldn't contain.

"You're hurt," he said, renewed anguish rushing through him.

"I'll be fine after a stop at the hospital."

Eamon joined them, compassion ruling as Cathal yielded sole possession so Etaín could be held safe between both of them. He could allow Cathal his peace of mind, his choice to be other than his father and uncle. He could wait out the tedious wheels of human justice as Etaín desired. But he would never allow any threat to her to remain alive.

It was a hardly a challenge for an Elven assassin, much less a warm-up for what was to come when Etaín's existence became *known*. Yet the anger burning in Liam's eyes when Eamon met them relayed the message he expected to find there.

It will be your task, Eamon mouthed before touching his lips to the silk of Etaín's hair and saying, "You'll see a healer. One of my people and then we'll go home. My home."

Cathal tensed, breath caught in his chest as he waited for what she would say. She met his eyes. "I want to be with you both tonight."

He couldn't deny her. Couldn't deny himself, not when he craved the feel of her skin against his, the press of her body, its heat coming with the knowledge she was safe.

"Anywhere, Etaín. His place. Mine. Yours. It doesn't matter."

"His then, for tonight anyway. Let's call the police now. So we can get this over with. This is where they brought Tyra. It's probably where they brought all of their victims."

Parker was the first to arrive, the squeal of tires preceding his running entrance. He didn't acknowledge any of the men present, only glanced briefly at the rapist who lay hog-tied with duct tape before pulling Etaín into his arms and sending physical pain screaming through her even as it soothed the open wound in her heart.

"Jesus, Etaín. Jesus." He trembled against her and for the first time in a long time, there was no doubt that he loved her as he had when they were children.

Touch him. Know the full truth, an insidious voice whispered in her mind, bringing panic with it.

Etaín clutched Parker's FBI emblazed jacket in her hands in denial of it. But the voice grew louder, more demanding, frightening her with its intensity and the slide of her palms downward.

Her heart pounded as if attempting to escape. The helplessness she felt was worse than what had come with being Tasered, more terrifying because it was her gift turning her into a mind with no control over her body.

She tried to step out of the embrace but couldn't, heard herself whimpering and felt Parker drawing back, the movement speeding the descent of her hands and bringing them closer to his.

"Eamon," she managed to whisper before her throat was closed off, an entreaty he answered with the brush of fingertips at the nape of her neck, spell sigils that flowed like fire and water down the vines of her forearms and into wristbands her mother had put on her at eight, turning them into shackles that freed her from the demands of the magic.

"Etaín suffered injuries before we arrived," Eamon said, easing her away from Parker whose anguished face made Etaín nearly risk hugging him again.

"Just to my ribs, Parker. That's all, but I'd like to leave now."

Already there were more police on the scene. There'd be questions, difficult ones about how she'd been located. The answer to which Parker had been willing to let go at the word *psychic* because he'd witnessed the things she could do that couldn't be explained, and because she was safe.

She didn't want to be trapped into making a statement, doubted the others did, either. Crossing her arms over her chest and drawing attention to the fact she wore only Eamon's shirt, she asked, "Can we go, Parker?"

For the first time he acknowledged the men, his expression hardening at recognizing Cathal, censure returning when his eyes met hers. She wanted to say, *Be happy for me*, but didn't. And Eamon filled the weighted silence by introducing himself as the owner of Aesirs, by giving Parker his address and telling him that's where she could be found.

It was enough to gain a nod, permission to leave. Revulsion gripped her as she turned and saw the rapist being escorted out by Trent and a couple of uniformed officers. Her skin crawled at imagining him removing her clothing, touching her while she'd been unconscious.

A shudder went through her with memories of lying on the fetid mattress. Tyra's memories were sealed behind mental barriers again thanks to Eamon, but a permanent chill now lived in the center of her chest at how thin the wall separating her reality from all of the other victims she'd touched was.

"I want a shower," she said, and after stopping at a modest home long enough for her ribs to be healed, found herself with both men in front of the shower where Eamon had been the first lover ever to enter her with nothing between them.

She removed the shirt and it fluttered to the ground. "Join me?" she asked, not waiting for an answer.

The hot blast of water washed away everything but pleasure and anticipation. It heightened the need for physical intimacy, one that intensified when Cathal entered the shower, his dark looks filling her with a primal craving.

She ate him hungrily with her eyes as her gaze traveled downward, lingering on the tattoos. She was still amazed by the change in them and how they'd led to her being found.

She'd thought in those moments before she'd dared Cathal to take the ink that *he* needed the tattoos, but in fact, *she* had. Foresight. She wondered again as she had then, if that was her mother's gift and she'd inherited some of it.

And then she knew something more as rivulets of water streamed down his arms, the movement of it curling the design and turning it into a circle in her mind's eye, washing away a blindness she hadn't been aware of. Her mother wore this same design around her wrists, hidden by the entwining of other sigils.

"Like what you see?" Cathal asked, the husky sound of his voice making it easy to set aside unanswered questions and speculation about any type of magic other than what existed between them.

"Definitely," she said, taking the single step necessary to reach him, her arms going around his neck.

Cathal hugged her to him, loving the feel of her body against his.

So profoundly grateful she was unharmed that the emotion still threatened to overwhelm him.

He touched his lips to hers, breached the seam of them with his tongue and reveled in the welcome he got, the hum of pleasure she made as her hands tangled in his hair.

He was aware of Eamon naked on the other side of the glass, watching before joining them in the shower. A part of him was aroused by it. But there remained a part that wanted to carry Etaín back to his place and tell Eamon to stay the fuck away from her.

It wasn't going to happen. Today had demonstrated a truth he couldn't deny. It had taken both of them to find her in time. It might require the same to keep her safe given his family and the work she did for the authorities.

He tightened his arms on her. Deepened the kiss as if he could hold her to him forever.

Eamon opened the shower door and stepped into his element. Water cascaded over him, its voice a harmonious melody sung to notes of his creation. His eyes flicked briefly to the tattoos Cathal wore and he found satisfaction in knowing the bond with Etaín was his whenever he was willing to accept it.

There was risk involved in taking her ink, great at the best of times, which was why no *seidic* born into this world had ever been allowed to claim a spell caster. A danger magnified by Etaín's being on the cusp of change, though tomorrow was soon enough to reveal the truth of her heritage.

The gold of her aura had deepened almost to that of a pure Elf. The events of the day leading to a tipping point clearly demonstrated by how close she'd come to harming the man she called her brother.

Eamon brushed the wet strands of her hair aside. Hands settling on her hips, the backs of his fingers touched to Cathal's skin, he pressed kisses along her shoulder and felt the hot seductive twine of her magic with his, the call to join his body to hers, his life to hers.

She was everything he wanted, the Lady his people needed. But there were no guarantees she would survive the transition despite the inked-bond with Cathal and what he himself might do in an effort to help her through it. There were no certainties save one. If she failed to gain control of the magic and her gift, then his duty as Lord would require him to kill her.

ABOUT THE AUTHOR

Jory Strong has been writing since childhood and has never outgrown being a daydreamer. When she's not hunched over her computer, lost in the muse and conjuring up new heroes and heroines, she can usually be found reading, riding horses, or walking dogs.

She has won numerous awards for her writing. She lives in California with her husband and a menagerie of pets. Visit her website at www.jorystrong.com.